Praise for the science fiction novels of Stephen Leigh

"Leigh puts an inventive spin on a familiar trope in this provocative tale of first contact set in the far future. Long before the novel's start, a devastating meteor strike cut Earth off from other colonized worlds, forcing the now isolated colonists to biologically adapt to their adopted outposts. Now Earth starship *Odysseus* visits one such outpost, the planet Canis Lupus, for the first time. . . . Exploring big ideas about interplanetary travel, this finely crafted sci-fi saga is full of both surprises and charm."   —*Publishers Weekly*

"Leigh builds a vivid, thrilling, and exciting new world that will captivate and hold the imagination."   —*RT Reviews*

"I enjoyed my time with *Amid the Crowd of Stars* . . . a powerful thought experiment."   —The Quill to Live

"*Amid the Crowd of Stars* is a very different tale of science fiction by a great voice in the genre."   —Midwest Book Review

"Action, adventure, character, humor and a strong philosophical base: Stephen Leigh does it all!"
     —Janet Morris, author of *The Sacred Band*

"Intriguing, deeply layered . . . [and] highly recommended."
     — Garth Nix, *New York Times*-bestselling author
     of the Old Kingdom series

AMID THE CROWD OF STARS

STEPHEN LEIGH

DAW BOOKS, INC.

DONALD A. WOLLHEIM, FOUNDER

1745 Broadway, New York, NY 10019

ELIZABETH R. WOLLHEIM

SHEILA E. GILBERT

PUBLISHERS

www.dawbooks.com

First Paperback Printing, February 2022
1st Printing

DAW TRADEMARK REGISTERED
U.S. PAT. AND TM. OFF. AND FOREIGN COUNTRIES
—MARCA REGISTRADA
HECHO EN U.S.A.

PRINTED IN THE U.S.A.

*This book is dedicated to my parents, Walter and Betty Leigh,
who introduced me to Ireland. They're both gone now, though
they remain in memories where I hear their voices, see their faces,
and where I can imagine I'm talking to them once more.*

*And, as always and ever, to Denise, whose support and love make all
of my books possible.*

Table of Contents

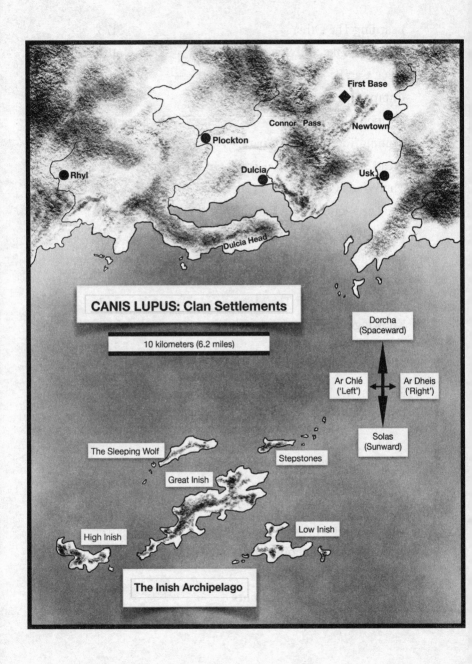

CANIS LUPUS: Clan Settlements

10 kilometers (6.2 miles)

First Base

Newtown

Connor Pass

Plockton

Rhyl

Dulcia

Usk

Dulcia Head

Dorcha
(Spaceward)

Ar Chlé
('Left')

Ar Dheis
('Right')

Solas
(Sunward)

The Sleeping Wolf

Stepstones

Great Inish

High Inish

Low Inish

The Inish Archipelago

Faeries, come take me out of this dull world,
For I would ride with you upon the wind,
Run on the top of the disheveled tide,
And dance upon the mountains like a flame.

—William Butler Yeats

Is buaine port ná glór na n-éan
Is buaine focal ná toice an tsael
A tune is more lasting than the song of the birds,
And a word more lasting than the wealth of the world.

—Irish Proverb

No one can live without relationships. You may withdraw into the mountains, become a monk, a sannyasi, wander off into the desert by yourself, but you are related. You cannot escape from that absolute fact. You cannot exist in isolation.

—Jiddu Krishnamurti

An Arrival In Clamor And Fury

THE RIDE DOWNWORLD from orbit on *Odysseus'* shuttle was far rougher than Ichiko expected, despite what she'd been told beforehand. Shivering rivulets of pale pink rain like diluted blood streaked the monitor above her seat, relaying the view from the craft's nose camera. The rain was tinted by the red dwarf star around which Canis Lupus orbited. The shuttle descended between coiled, airy ramparts of towering thunderheads stretching to the horizon as the craft shook like a toy in an angry child's hand, buffeted by strong winds that Ichiko imagined she could hear screaming outside. She felt her stomach lurch as the shuttle suddenly dropped several meters and swayed before settling momentarily. The seats and flooring chattered metallically, making Ichiko grateful for the invisible grip of the field-harness holding her in her seat, though Ichiko still found herself clutching the armrests with whitened fingers.

The two other passengers in the shuttle—she'd been introduced to them before they left *Odysseus* but had forgotten their names—were a pair of uniformed ensigns assigned planet-side for duty rotation at First Base. They both seemed entirely untroubled, relaxed in their seats across the aisle, eyes closed; the male had his mouth open as he snored. Ichiko could only shake her head, unable to envision sleeping through this ordeal.

Ichiko pressed her thumb against the contact embedded in the pad of her left hand's ring finger; a blue glow emanated from between where finger and thumb touched, indicating that the direct thought-connection to the Autonomous Mnemonic Interface implanted in each member of the *Odysseus* crew—her AMI—was active. <*Is this normal?*> she asked. <*Please tell me we're not going to crash.*> Ichiko lifted her thumb, and the contact went back to its nearly invisible skin color again.

<*This is entirely normal for shuttle craft to the surface,*> the implant's voice answered in her head. When the AMI chip had been placed at the base of her skull back on Earth, she'd had them program it to speak to her in Japanese, providing the engineers with a sample of her mother's voice as well as the parameters of her personality. That was a choice Ichiko now doubly regretted, though she'd yet to actually edit the programming. She loved her mother, but there were times when hearing the voice that had both soothed and scolded her in her childhood felt distinctly wrong. <*The probability of crashing is very low,*> AMI concluded with the false sincerity of a mother soothing her child.

The shuttle shuddered like a fish caught on a line, and Ichiko stifled an alarmed shout as she again touched thumb to ring finger. <*That's so comforting.*>

<*I'm glad you feel that way,*> AMI replied. <*Your comfort is what I live for.*>

With AMI's statement, in her mother's soft voice, Ichiko pressed her lips together. <*Sarcasm? That's what you're giving me? Really?*>

<*I do understand sarcasm, you know,*> AMI replied. <*You employ that modality yourself, when you think it useful.*> The voice in her head changed to Ichiko's own, playing back Ichiko's own thoughts in her own voice. <*That's so comforting . . .* >

Ichiko lifted her thumb from AMI's contact as a memory swept over her: being on the beach near her parents' vacation villa in southern France—while her mother was Japanese, her father was

French—and picking up a jellyfish stranded at the tidal line. The gelatinous strands underneath the animal stung her badly and she ran wailing to her mother, who looked at Ichiko's swelling hands and shook her head. "How many times have I warned you that you shouldn't pick up jellyfish?" her mother intoned in her heavily accented and poor French—she always believed in speaking the local language if possible. Her mother sighed and grabbed Ichiko by a sand-sprinkled wrist. "Well, it's done now. Come along; we need to get you to the clinic . . ."

When I get back to Odysseus, *I'm definitely going to wipe this AMI.* Ichiko sighed, feeling a momentary stab of guilt. Then she toggled the connection on once more. *<Sorry,>* she thought to her AMI. No, the AMI wasn't her mother, but apologizing felt right, even to an artificial intelligence.

<Not to worry. I take no offense at anything you say. Ever. You needn't apologize, but I hope I did briefly take your mind away from your flight. You should find things smoother now—look at your monitor; you're below the cloud deck and the rough air.>

A glance showed Ichiko that her AMI was right. The monitor's view was still streaked with the bloody rain, but through the watery distortion the world had gone dark with gray-black clouds sliding past and massed overhead. Below was a curve of shadowed, vegetation-clad shoreline, outlined by an erratic line of pale white where waves crashed against a shore. The shoreline was interrupted by the mouth of an inlet leading to a narrow bay with a cluster of buildings set on the landward side; Ichiko wondered if that was the town called Dulcia. Beyond the land, an expanse of empty gray-green ocean eventually blended into rain and cloud. Ichiko tried to peer through the mist for a glimpse of Great Inish or the other islands in the archipelago off the main coast, but they were either too far away or lost in the storm.

She could feel the pull of the planet's gravity now. Canis Lupus had a radius 1.5 times that of Earth and the rotation of *Odysseus'* living quarters had been set to mimic its higher than Earth-normal gravity. Still, experiencing the reality seemed somehow different and uncomfortable. Ichiko felt too heavy for comfort.

<*Arrival at First Base in five minutes.*> The announcement, in a bland and somehow genderless voice entirely unlike her AMI's, sounded in Ichiko's head and in the heads of the two ensigns as well; they both opened their eyes and sat up, looking around sleepily with a nod in her direction. The shuttle banked sharply, Ichiko's ears clogging with the quick change in air pressure; she yawned, and her ears popped. A green-and-purple-clad slope was sliding by the monitor, while ahead was an unassuming, squat gray building set halfway up its flank with a fast-flowing stream foaming white among the stones alongside it: First Base, Ichiko presumed.

The ship banked again and settled; she heard the landing jets scream as the shuttle came to a shivering halt in midair, now descending slowly toward the roof of the base as rain dripped from the wings and fuselage. As they touched down, Ichiko saw two halves of a dome rising to enclose them. Harsh lights clicked on inside the dome as the shuttle's voice spoke again: <*Decontamination underway.*> An orange spray enveloped the shuttle, hissing hard against the outside of the craft and blurring the lights until a fierce wind from the fans ripped the fluid away, leaving the shuttle dry. They began to descend into the base itself, into what Ichiko assumed was the shuttle's bay. The descent ended with a jerk. Outside the window, Ichiko saw the squared end of an air lock extend toward them and latch onto the shuttle's hull. A few moments later, there came the audible *pop* of a pressure change and the shuttle's hatch opened, letting in a waft of air that smelled of antiseptic. A woman's head appeared in the opening, arranged somewhere between smile and frown. Ichiko could see the lieutenant's insignia on her uniform work shirt, and the brass nameplate that gave her surname as *BISHARA*.

"Welcome to First Base," she said. "Grab your gear, people." She nodded to the ensigns. "You two report to Chief McDermott on Level Two. You know the way." They saluted her, pulled their duffels from the overhead compartment, and were off through the air lock. Bishara's pale, almost colorless eyes found Ichiko. "Dr. Aguilar, you can come with me."

Ichiko grabbed the handles of her own duffel and swung it down, then followed Lieutenant Bishara through the air lock tube and into a room inside the base; the tube slowly accordioning in behind them as they walked. She somehow felt heavier here than on *Odysseus*. <*It's just in your head,*> AMI commented, and Ichiko glanced quickly at her ring finger and saw the contact glowing blue—probably she'd accidentally double-tapped it, leaving AMI open to her thoughts.

<*Maybe, but that's not where I feel it,*> she answered, then immediately touched her finger to the contact again to sever the open connection. The lieutenant closed the hatch to the shuttle bay end of the flexible corridor before moving to open the other, allowing them to descend a small set of stairs. The astringent smell was stronger here, and Ichiko wished she already had on the bio-shield she'd need when she ventured outside. Bishara waved to two men behind a glass-walled compartment, giving them a thumbs-up, then led Ichiko to a door and into the base proper. Ichiko couldn't help but think that First Base was hardly hospitable. It was like walking into a construction zone.

<*They could certainly use a decent interior decorator,*> AMI commented. Ichiko started at the unexpected comment in her head. She glanced at her fingertip—it was still glowing a soft blue. She tried severing the connection again, but the fingertip continued to glow. <*AMI?*> she thought.

<*I was just agreeing with you,*> came the answer. <*The place looks a total wreck.*>

Ichiko pressed the contact again, harder this time; finally, the azure glow underneath her skin faded. She shook her head. *I need to get this checked the next time I'm up on* Odysseus. *I don't want or need AMI accidentally listening to everything I'm thinking.*

Since *Odysseus'* arrival, First Base had been under reconstruction after being largely abandoned for almost three centuries. That restoration work was still ongoing. There were people in military work fatigues all around them, intent on their tasks. The walls were open to conduits and electrical relays; large wires snaked over the floor, requiring Ichiko to watch where she was stepping. The building's interior smelled of paint, grease, and arcing connections; the lighting panels were mostly working, but there were occasional shadowed spots, and several of the holo arrays intended to make up for the lack of windows on the outside wall remained stubbornly black.

Still, after surviving the shuttle descent, it felt good to have something solid under her feet again.

Ichiko had studied the records from Canis Lupus on *Odysseus'* five-year–long journey here. She could only imagine what it had been like for the original inhabitants of First Base during the Interregnum—the time after the meteor strike on Earth that devastated the homeworld and left abandoned the half dozen new worlds that had just begun to be explored by humankind. Ichiko knew that the first years on Canis Lupus had been especially hard, as those stranded here realized from the initial erratic communications from Earth that they were now effectively marooned and on their own. Bereft of factories, spare parts, resources, and skilled personnel, those on Canis Lupus couldn't repair their machinery and technology as things inevitably broke down.

The bio barriers put up around First Base (as well as Second Base, on the southern continent) failed in the first few decades; the colonists had no choice but to expose themselves to the local viruses and bacteria. New and untreatable diseases stalked them, with infant and senior mortality rates especially high. Their technological level quickly dropped back to nearly preindustrial times. The colonists had to learn what native crops they could grow and eat, what native animals they could eat or use as work and farm animals. Everything boiled down to answering the question, "Will doing this or not doing this help us or will it kill us?" They had no research labs to search for cures for the new diseases that stalked them, no hospitals able to treat serious injuries. Out of contact with Earth, for all they knew they might be the last humans anywhere in the universe. Reproduction became an imperative; monogamy had been the first social casualty. For several decades, it wasn't certain *any* of them would survive at all. That prognosis had become a somber fact for those on the southern continent: *Odysseus'* surveys had shown that they'd all died within a few years of Second Base being open to Canis Lupus.

But for those here on the northern continent, things had been marginally better. There were now small towns outside First Base, with everyone several generations removed from the original humans who had come here. The population was now over 300,000 and rising. Ichiko's assignment was to learn all she could of these people, undoubtedly changed from their long exposure to their world.

She wondered if these descendants were now more Homo lupus than Homo sapiens—and, if they were, whether those of the United Congress of Earth would or even could ever permit them to return to their original homeworld.

"I've sent word to Commander Mercado that you've arrived safely," Lieutenant Bishara said to Ichiko over her shoulder as they walked through the construction and into a section that looked somewhat more finished. Ichiko had the feeling that Bishara wasn't entirely pleased with her role as escort. "He said to give you his best wishes and to let you know that he'd try to contact you around 1600 ship-time, if you're available." The appraising glance Lieutenant Bishara gave her told Ichiko that the lieutenant was also aware of the relationship between Ichiko and the commander, though that was hardly surprising; it was difficult to keep secrets aboard the ship. Bishara looked like she was eager to be about her normal duties and no longer having to nursemaid Ichiko.

Still, Ichiko felt a stab of irritation, knowing that Bishara was undoubtedly judging her. *If she is, it's your own damn fault. You made the choice. You continue to sleep with Luciano, after all.* The internal accusation burned in her head, as it often did of late.

Her AMI stayed silent. That, at least, was a small blessing. She could unfortunately imagine what her mother-analogue might have said.

"Thank you, Lieutenant," Ichiko told her; it seemed the safest reply. "Is my transport to Dulcia ready? I'd like to see the town so I can start to familiarize myself with it. Satellite photos and data reproductions . . . well, they're just not the same."

Bishara smiled briefly at that—probably because it meant that Ichiko would be quickly out from underfoot. "Understood. And having been to Dulcia once myself, I'd agree. I think you're going to be surprised by what you find there."

"Pleasantly so?" Ichiko asked, and Bishara laughed.

"It depends on what you're expecting and what you're looking for," she answered. "But yes, your flitter's waiting outside, and you can leave as soon as we've gone over protocol and you've been shown how to use your bio-shield. Your AMI can provide guidance to the town; it's about twenty minutes away, ship-time; you may have seen it from your shuttle as you came in."

An ensign came up to Bishara holding two thick and wide belts studded with circuitry—Bishara must have summoned him through her own AMI. He saluted and handed Bishara the belts, glancing once at Ichiko with strange intensity. *Does he know about Luciano, too?*

"Thank you, Ensign," Bishara told him; he saluted again and left them as Bishara handed the belts to Ichiko. Their weight surprised Ichiko; she nearly dropped them. Bishara raised her eyebrows but said nothing.

"Those are your bio-shields," Bishara told her. "Each one is good for roughly 48 hours, ship-time, before you need to recharge it; that way you have a cushion if you get stuck out there somewhere since the flitter itself can't keep out the local environment. The shield will turn on automatically once you fasten it; if you need it, your AMI can interface with the other controls and give you status updates and charge levels. The bio-shield will keep you in a safe, filtered bubble: no local bugs or pathogens can get through—though you also can't eat or drink the local fare or even actually touch someone—and of course you need to wear the special pants that go with it so you can relieve yourself if you need to." Bishara grinned at that.

"I know," Ichiko said, grimacing. "They made us wear them during training. Didn't like the experience then, and I'm sure I still won't."

Bishara shrugged. "Make sure your shield is activated before you step outside the base and make sure it stays on until you're safely back inside. Otherwise . . ."

Bishara gave a double-shouldered shrug. Ichiko knew what she wasn't saying: *otherwise, you could be stuck here for the rest of your life*. The warnings in the sheaf of liability waiver forms Ichiko had needed to sign before she'd been permitted to go downworld had been extremely explicit about that possibility. "Any other questions for me or my AMI?" Bishara asked.

Ichiko shook her head. "I'm sure my AMI can answer them if any arise." She wondered what Bishara's AMI sounded like. Would the lieutenant be someone who just stuck with the generic, standard voices? Would her AMI be male or female or gender-neutral? Would it speak to her in Standard English or in some other language?

"Fine. When you get back, I can show you the dormitory here. At Commander Mercado's request, I've made arrangements for you to have a private room while you're on-planet. Just leave your duffel with me unless you have equipment in it you need to take with you to Dulcia; I'll have someone put it in your room. The room's small, but . . ."

"I'm sure it will be fine." Ichiko put down her duffel and unzipped it, taking out the small armpack with her recording equipment and zipping it again. "I really appreciate your putting up with me here. I know I'm just one more duty you have to deal with."

Another shrug accompanied by a tentative smile slightly more genuine than her previous efforts. "I'll radio Minister Hugh Plunkett and tell him you'll be on your way," the lieutenant said.

"Minister Plunkett's in charge of Dulcia, and he's a decent enough sort for a Canine. I'll expect to see you back here in six hours or so. That should give you enough time for your first foray onto Canis Lupus. As you undoubtedly experienced on the way down, this world's not always the kindest host. If you'll follow me again, I'll take you down to the flitters."

A World Full Of
Magic Things

ICHIKO DECIDED THAT "not always the kindest host" was an understatement.

A trio of flitters were parked in a bay on the ground level of First Base, set off from First Base by an air lock since once the bay doors opened, the vehicles were bathed in Canis Lupus' atmosphere. Bishara had left Ichiko at the door to the air lock with another ensign. Glancing through the air lock windows, she could see the flitters snared in blinding spotlights with the bay doors yawning wide to expose the local landscape. Outside, curtains of the wind-driven rain that Ichiko had managed to nearly forget hammered the ground and splashed up to pool on the concrete floor.

"Put your bio-shield on now," the ensign instructed her, "and I'll open the inside air lock door. Once you're in, the outside door will open as soon as the pressure's equalized. Your flitter's the one in the middle; I've already made sure that the flitter can see your AMI and pair with it. All you have to do is instruct your AMI to take the flitter to Dulcia."

Ichiko nodded that she understood. She put on the belt of the bio-shield; a mild tingling surrounded her momentarily as it activated. The ensign touched the contact on his own hand to communicate with his own AMI; a moment later, the base-side air lock door opened with a hiss. Ichiko stepped inside the air lock chamber, and the door swung shut behind her. She looked back and saw the ensign waving encouragingly. A few breaths later, the outside door to the flitter bay opened and she stepped outside—for the first time surrounded by Canis Lupus' atmosphere. She felt herself unconsciously holding her breath. *It's okay. You're safe.* She inhaled deliberately; the bio-shield's air tasted coppery and metallic.

She wondered how the air of this world actually tasted, what it smelled like, or how the wind or the humidity might actually feel. *You'll never know that. You can't ever know such things if you want to go home again.*

She stepped into the flitter, the control panel illuminating as soon as she sat down. The bio-shield was like a gelatinous membrane extending a millimeter or two from her skin and clothing, a bulky, invisible suit between her and anything she tried to sit on or touch. Her boot soles didn't quite contact the floor plates. The belt of the bio-shield felt warm around her waist, and she could swear it made a low hum that lurked irritatingly just below the range of her hearing. She touched thumb to ring finger, pressing a little harder this time. *<AMI,>* she thought, *<take me to Dulcia.>*

She heard fans engaging as the flitter lifted, settled, then moved forward and away from the base. She looked back to see the bay doors closing.

The ride down from First Base, set on a high plateau, to Dulcia nestled in its harbor, was nearly as bad as the shuttle descent.

The rain and wind remained a constant presence, smearing water across the windshield of the vehicle that blurred the violet-tinged landscape outside. The flitter rocked from side to side in the gusts as it hovered over the terrain. At least, she didn't have to actually drive the damn thing. Her AMI did that for her though there were manual controls that would extend from the dashboard to use if she wished. She didn't.

And the light . . . Canis Lupus was tidally locked to its star,

Wolf 1061, with one hemisphere always facing Wolf 1061 and the other always facing starward: one side eternally hellish, the other eternally glacial. The planet's habitable zone was a 1,000-kilometer-wide swath along the terminator strip between the two sides, where water was liquid and the temperature moderate. That also meant the sun never quite fully rose or fully set. The inhabitants lived in a perpetual, reddish twilight—when they could see the sun at all through the cloud cover. Even though the *Odysseus* kept shipboard lighting at similar levels and coloration, this world never seemed quite bright enough to Ichiko.

<How long?> she asked AMI, double touching her contact this time so that she'd have continual access for the trip. <Oh, and *what's the weather like down there?*>

<We should arrive by 1053, ship-time. And it's raining, though it's *not as windy as it is at First Base up in the mountains.*>

<Lovely.>

<If you like rain, it might be. At least you can't get wet.>

The flitter banked left over a ridge of the mountain, and there, suddenly, was Dulcia laid out before her, stretched along the interior edge of a narrow inlet of the aptly named Storm Sea and protected by a headland on the other side of the harbor. Closer to the flitter, there were cleared farm fields planted with rows of purple, pink, and orange-leafed crops that Ichiko didn't recognize and couldn't eat even if she did. A few of the fields were occupied by the six-legged, round-bodied, and extraordinarily hairy ruminants that the locals had dubbed "sheepers"—a portmanteau word combining "sheep" and "spider"—raised both for meat and for their pale, woollike hair.

The flitter passed over the farms cut into the lowering slopes of the mountains before finally descending into the town proper where, through the rain, Ichiko saw a strange amalgam of stone buildings, some with thatched roofs, others with roofs of slatelike stone, but all of them small and none that looked to be more than two stories tall. A quay stretched the length of the town's center at the water's edge. Ichiko glimpsed fishing boats moored here and there, rocking gently with the gray-green swells.

There were people in the streets, staring at the flitter as it passed above them. Ichiko noted what she already knew from the records on *Odysseus*: the people here were far more homogenous than the crew of their starship, whose crew was deliberately multinational and multiracial. That had not been the case for those who had crewed the original exploratory ships before the Interregnum. The crew for those first starships had been chosen because they all spoke the same language and shared the same general culture: British Isles, North American, Chinese, Arabic, Portuguese, Spanish, Japanese, German, and so on.

<*There appears to be a greeting party near the quay. Minister Plunkett is among the group,*> AMI said.

<*I see them. Set us down there.*>

The flitter shivered as if cold. The sound of the wing fans grew louder as the flitter slowly settled to the ground near the gathering, wafting down as gently as an autumn leaf—though there were no deciduous trees on this world where the climate remained largely uniform throughout the year. The hatch opened as Ichiko unbuckled her seat harness and a short set of stairs extruded from the hull. A burly man in a woven flat cap beaded with the rain stepped forward, a fringe of unruly white hair curling out from underneath the cap and several days' growth of beard on his chin. He walked with a limp as if his hips or knees pained him. His hands were thick and obviously used to manual labor: broken fingernails with dirt caked underneath. He was missing an upper incisor; the gap showed as he smiled. "Dr. Aguilar?" he said, nodding to Ichiko as she stepped from the flitter. He extended his hand toward her, then pulled it back before she could respond as if he understood that she couldn't actually shake hands. "I'm Minister Plunkett, but please call me Hugh. Welcome to Dulcia."

In the case of Canis Lupus, the original crew had been drawn almost entirely from the British Isles—their common language had been British English. From the recordings Ichiko had heard, their accent sounded like an odd blend of Irish and Scottish with a touch of Midlands and Welsh thrown in, and their idioms and even vocabulary sometimes drew on the older languages of the region: Irish, Scottish Gaelic, Welsh, Breton.

"Thank you, Min . . ." Ichiko stopped and smiled. "Hugh," she finished. "And please call me Ichiko." She looked around the harbor. What looked to be a translucent, huge slug was passing along the street, though she could see the half dozen stubby legs on which the creature moved. On its head was what looked like the folded starnose of a tardigrade, set below two huge eyes that moved independently, one looking at Ichiko and the other trained on the group of humans. The beast—called a *capall*, Ichiko knew from the database—was hitched to a cart filled with bricks of local peat and driven by a young woman, prodding the creature with a long stick.

Ichiko could feel the small crowd behind Hugh staring at her. Waiting. They were all heavier and thicker than nearly any of the *Odysseus* crew: an artifact of the heavier gravity producing increased muscle mass. She made a mental note to look for other bodily changes wrought by the environment. Nagasi Tinubu, the head of Ichiko's sociological/archeological/biological team on *Odysseus* and the person to whom Ichiko reported, had blood and skin samples; by now they'd have run DNA tests. She'd have to ask AMI to send her those later.

"Dulcia is so . . ." Ichiko began, then stopped. <*Charming,*> she heard AMI suggest. ". . . charming. It reminds me a little of a village I once knew in France, on the Atlantic." *Except that there were horses there, not capall, and the sky was such an incredible blue, and the light from the sun was so strong I had to wear sunglasses against the glare . . .*

"It's not so much, compared with what you have on Earth, I'm certain." Hugh shrugged, as if he'd guessed what Ichiko was thinking as he watched the capall and cart lurch past. "But it suits us. We're comfortable enough here, and better than when all of our ancestors were crowded into your First Base." Ichiko decided she loved the accent, with the subtle rolling of his "r"s, the sibilance, and the shortening of words (*'Tis not s'much, compared wit wat yeh have on Eart . . .*), though the speed of his speech required her to listen carefully. She'd also have to look into how much their language and idioms had changed over the centuries of isolation. "What is it yeh be wanting here, Ichiko?"

"I'm an archeologist, sociologist, and an exobiologist. That should give you an idea of my interests."

"That's a bleedin' lot of schooling yeh must have, then." Hugh cocked his head appraisingly. "Yeh don't look old enough to have studied so many subjects."

Ichiko laughed. "I'm older than I look, and there's only so much room on a starship, even one like *Odysseus*. Almost everyone has more than one area of expertise. I'm here to try to understand the society you've put together—without any judgment or prejudice. Your survival here is . . . well, it's nothing short of remarkable. We've learned that too many of the other bases and settlements left behind on other worlds didn't survive at all— they died just like your people on the southern continent. But you've managed to live and thrive. I want to understand why."

"And will the answer to that help those of us who might be thinkin' of returning to Earth? Meself, I'd love to see County Clare in Ireland one day; that's where me own ancestors came from."

<*Ah, there it is. The question they'll all have for you.*>

Ichiko could only shrug at AMI's comment. "I'm afraid that decision's not in my hands," she told Hugh, "and nothing that I'm doing here is likely to affect it. I'm just a researcher exploring and recording the culture and society you've put together here." The lines of the man's face tightened, and his cheeks grew more flushed. "I know that's not the answer you wanted," Ichiko hurried to say.

"It's the one I expected yeh to give me. Can't have any of those wicked alien bugs in our bodies making it back to Earth. Not until yeh know if yeh can kill 'em. It's why yer wearing what yer wearing, after all." Hugh sighed before she could make a rejoinder, moving away from the gathered crowd, which was growing larger and noisier. "Why don't I give yeh a little tour of Dulcia from yer flitter first, and afterward yeh can walk around as yeh wish."

"I have to say, it was lashing out there while I was waiting for yeh," Hugh said once he was inside the flitter. "At least it's dry in here."

"Glad you like it."

"I hope yeh don't mind my taking yeh off private-like, but some of the others were getting restless," Hugh said as the flitter lifted from the ground. He pointed to the west, and AMI obediently headed the flitter that way, moving slowly along the quay toward a cluster of buildings at the end of the town. "Truth is, we're all a little suspicious of yeh Terrans and I didn't want any of 'em bothering yeh and asking questions yeh couldn't or can't answer. Given that Earth abandoned us once, I suppose yeh can understand. I thought it better if we could talk here alone for a bit."

"Is this where you warn me to watch what I say or do?" Ichiko asked. "Or are you suggesting I should bring a few marines with me next time?"

Hugh chuckled. "Nothing's quite so dire that yeh need armed guards, I'm thinkin'. But aye, yeh should watch what yeh say. Everyone's going to be trying to decipher the subtext."

"And if there's no subtext at all?"

"Then it's even worse since everyone will just make up their own. 'Tis the way it is with people here."

Ichiko nodded. "Point taken, and I have a question for you, Minister. Were any in the crowd back there Inish?"

Plunkett's thick eyebrows climbed his head under his cap. "Inish? Neh. There was no one from the archipelago. Why would yeh be askin' that?"

"As a sociologist, I'm curious about the island folk and the way they live. I want to learn about them as well as your townspeople."

Hugh gave a scoffing laugh. "Good luck with that. The Inish ain't the friendliest folk in the world, and if yeh think Dulcia is backward compared to what yer used to, just wait until yeh see their compounds on Great Inish. Even so, being a fair man, I made certain that yer people took a couple Inish up to yer ship with the other volunteer clanfolk so yer people could see if they can get rid of the local bugs and diseases and let us go back to Earth if we want. Of course, Clan Plunkett sent the most volunteers to yer ship because . . . well, because I made certain of that. But the Inish . . ."

"What about them?"

Plunkett shrugged. "Inishers like things the way they always were. They even claim yer technologies won't work out on the islands. And I don't think they give a damn about Earth. If you ask me, they're all as mad as a box of pishmires."

<*A local insect pest,*> AMI answered before Ichiko could ask. "Is that true?" Ichiko said to Plunkett.

"Truth is a slippery thing with the Inish," he answered. "Worse of all, they like those nasty arracht."

"The what?" AMI sent Ichiko a mental image, evidently a painting by a local artist, of a sea creature with a hooded hard shell over its head, six limbs ending in a tangle of muscular tentacles, and the end of the body ending in a large horizontal fin.

"The arracht. Generations ago, all the clans used to hunt them for food and for their fat, which we could boil down to a useful oil. Dangerous work, that, but worth it. Or it was until the Inish stopped it, back in the mid-1800s. The arracht killed quite a lot of the fisherfolk from the other clans during that time. It's old history, but the clans remember all too well." He pointed ahead. "Yeh can slow down a bit. That's Market Street just ahead. That big building right at the end of the quay is Fitzpatrick's, the fishmongers. The butchers are there as well, and you can see the stalls for the farmers market; it's open every 18 cycles—once a year."

"Is that a pub at the end of the street, next to the bakery?"

" 'Tis. Clan Murphy runs that one; there are four taverns in Dulcia," Hugh answered. "Two more up on High Street, and another down at the far end of the harbor, which me own clan owns. One thing yeh can say for this place, our grains and water do produce some damn fine whiskey and beers. Dulcia has the best of any of the towns, and Clan Plunkett brews the finest liquor of all. My own tenth great-grandfather Robert Plunkett was the very first person to distill a batch of local grain poitín here on Canis Lupus. Too bad yeh can't sample any . . ."

In the next several ship-hours, Ichiko would learn far more about the genealogy and history of the Twenty-Eight Clans, as the matriarchal family lines were called, and especially about Clan Plunkett as they cruised slowly above the town's lanes—the majority simply unpaved paths, though Plunkett said nothing more about the Inish. By the time Plunkett had finished his guided tour of Dulcia, Ichiko was already exhausted. She decided to make her first day on-planet a short one and dropped off the minister back at the harbor.

"Thank you for the fascinating tour," she told him. "I appreciate your being so helpful and open with me, and I promise I'll be back soon."

"If I can give yeh any assistance, just call at me office," he answered. "Yeh know where it is now, so yeh can skedaddle aff if yeh wish."

"I must, I'm afraid." *Or at least AMI will remember for me*, she thought. "Give my best to your clan," she told him, then closed the door of the flitter. She leaned back on her seat, closing her eyes.

<*Let's get back to First Base,*> she said to AMI. <*As they'd say here, I'm positively knackered.*>

<*Commander Mercado is calling,*> AMI said, waking Ichiko from a nap she hadn't intended to take. <*Should I connect you?*>

Ichiko sat up in her bed, suddenly glad that Lieutenant Bishara had given her a private room. "Lights," she said. "Mirror." The room illuminated, and a patch of the opposite wall turned reflective.

Ichiko scowled at the image, ruffling her hair. Sighing, she touched thumb to ring finger. <*Okay, AMI,*> she sighed. <*I'm not going to look any better. Go ahead.*>

A low reverberant chime, like a bronze bowl struck by a wooden mallet, sounded in Ichiko's head and an oval portal appeared at the foot of the bed, with a man seated behind an office desk in the middle of the apparent opening. He wore his naval uniform, though the collar was open and unbuttoned, and his chin displayed gray-speckled stubble, as did his close-cropped hair. *That man's too old for you.* Ichiko imagined that's what her mother would have said if she knew she was sleeping with him. She was fairly certain that some of *Odysseus'* crew felt the same— or, worse, thought she was simply trying to sleep her way into influence.

In reflective moments, she, too, questioned exactly why she'd allowed herself to become the commander's lover. In the past, back on Earth, she'd been rather omnivorous about those she'd allowed in her bed: men, women, whomever she found interesting and attractive. Most of those affairs had been purely physical in nature and also quickly over, but she'd been with Luciano for over two ship-years now. And (in those reflective moments) she wondered if that was because she actually loved him or if she stayed with him because of the possible complications if she ever ended things. Even with the new Fold Drive *Odysseus* had been fitted with, theirs was at minimum an eleven-year mission: five years out and five years back, with a planned Earth year or so in orbit around Canis Lupus. It could be a long and uncomfortable return trip if a split between them turned ugly, especially if Ichiko were the one to instigate the breakup. *It would be easier just to pretend and get along as best as I can until we get back.*

Luciano's eyes—a pale blue that Ichiko found both foreign and attractive, and not unlike many of the locals' eyes in color and shape—found her, and he smiled. "Hey," he said, his voice a low growl. "Already in bed, I see. Wish I was there."

In those same reflective moments, she also wondered why he

had pursued *her*—was she just an attempt to reclaim his lost youth or was there something more? Why *her*? Was it because she wasn't military herself and that just made it easier? Regulations stated that an officer wasn't allowed to become involved with someone of lower rank without the express permission of the captain, and it was absolutely forbidden to have a relationship with a direct report at all, military or not. But Ichiko was—like several on the research staff aboard *Odysseus*—civilian. She had no rank at all, and she didn't report to Luciano. In that sense, there was nothing in the regs forbidding their being lovers. Still . . .

We're not equals aboard ship. Not even close. And am I really in love with him, or is he just convenient and comfortable?

Those were questions to which she didn't have an answer.

"It's after 2300 hours, ship-time," she said. "Why aren't *you* in bed?"

"The captain kept me on bridge duty for a few extra hours, so she could attend to her weekly report. My relief arrived just twenty minutes ago."

"Then we've both had busy days."

"Did the Canines treat you well?" Luciano asked, and Ichiko's eyes widened as Luciano chuckled; she remembered Lieutenant Bishara using the same term. "I know, I know—that's not what we're supposed to call them since they seem to find the term insulting, but we're the only ones listening. My AMI says we have a secure, unrecorded channel."

"You'd better hope so, or you might lose a pip or two from your collar if word gets back to the captain." She shook her head at him. "I enjoyed finally talking to the Lupusians," she said, deliberately using the term the locals used themselves. "And Minister Plunkett was just fine, if rather on the loquacious and narcissistic side. Would you like me to recite the genealogy of the minister's family line? I can take you all the way back to Mary Anne Plunkett, who came from County Clare in Ireland back on Earth."

Lucian grinned. "Y'know, that sounds utterly fascinating, but I think I'll pass at the moment. I'm sure it's already in your AMI's report; I'll be certain to read it if I have trouble falling asleep tonight."

"Very funny. Actually, I did find it interesting. They don't trace ancestry at all in the way we tend to do on Earth, and frankly I think their way makes sense given their circumstances. As Hugh said to me, 'Here, the only thing you can be certain about is who your mother is.' The family lines are matrilineal, and they're evidently fairly casual about sexual relations in general. Within the clans, all the adult men are simply referred to as 'Uncle' and a woman who isn't your mother or grandmother is 'Aunt.'"

Luciano gave an amused sniff at that. "And did you come across any of those people from the archipelago you're so interested in?"

"Not yet, though I did get the distinct impression that the Mainlanders and the Inish don't always get along, at least for Plunkett and his people. There's some mutual antipathy there that I don't yet entirely understand. Only two of the Twenty-Eight Clans live out in the archipelago; they don't mix with the mainland clans much—that's probably got a lot to do with it." Ichiko yawned involuntarily, covering her mouth. "Sorry," she said. "I was actually asleep when you called."

"Then I won't keep you up any longer. Are you coming back soon?"

"I figure I'll be here at least a local year—which is what? Only a little more than eighteen ship-days? If they do have seasons here, then I'll get to see them all and celebrate every holiday. According to Minister Plunkett, humans have been living on Canis Lupus for close to seven thousand local years. Mind you, he also claims to be over a thousand years old himself."

"I spoke with the man when we first arrived. Remarkably well-preserved for a millennarium, don't you think? Birthday cakes must be a real fire hazard down there."

Ichiko laughed with him at that. "Good night, Luciano. Now I'll be dreaming about cakes and enormous numbers of candles."

"Not me?"

"And you," she added. *Maybe.* "Satisfied?"

"Not for at least another local year."

"Good night, Commander," she told him firmly. She touched thumb to ring finger. Nothing happened, so she pressed harder, and blue finally tinted her skin there. "AMI, disconnect."

The portal at the foot of her bed collapsed and vanished.

Neither one of them had said anything about love. But then, they never did.

The Gesture Of
A Pale Woman

THROUGH THE MISTY RAIN that speckled her glasses, Saoirse could see the Pale Woman at the end of Dulcia Head, pointing toward the opening of Dulcia Bay. The Pale Woman was a tall standing stone, painted a stark and unadorned white. A single arm jutted out from it to indicate the narrow opening to the bay, which was otherwise hidden behind Dulcia Head and difficult for boats returning from the Storm Sea to find. The sail fluttered, losing the wind as they passed Dulcia Head; Saoirse's Uncle Angus and her brother Liam pulled hard on the oars of their currach, the canoe-like boats the Inish used for fishing and transportation.

Once past the headland, the water smoothed and the boat moved easily toward the quay at Dulcia's harbor, at the sea-dampened terminus of the long slope on which the town had been built. At Saoirse's feet, the bottom of the boat was filled with bluefins they'd found shoaling just off Great Inish; they'd fetch a decent batch of supplies in the town. Angus looked back at Saoirse handling the sail and nodded; she let the halyard drop and moved forward to furl the sail. That done, she pulled the wire arms of the spectacles from around her ears and cleaned the glasses on the hem of her shirt.

Saoirse found herself smiling at the prospect of reaching

Dulcia soon; Liam, glancing back at her, grinned in response. "Look at her, Uncle," he said. "She's already wondering which one of those Mainlander boys might scratch her itch."

Saoirse put her glasses in the pockets of her oilcloth jacket, then picked up one of the bluefins by its rear tentacle and hurled it at her brother. The fish slapped against the arm he lifted up as a shield, leaving a gelatinous trail on the sleeve of his own oil-cloth Jacket. "At least my itch might get scratched," she told her brother. "An' it probably won't be with a boy, as yeh already know. But with the way yeh reek, big brother, yeh don't stand a chance either way."

Both men laughed.

It was true that she was eager to reach Dulcia, though not for the reasons that her uncle and brother might surmise. The gossip had reached the Inish archipelago that one of the Terrans was regularly in the town, and Saoirse desperately wanted to see this woman. Like many on Canis Lupus, she'd been fascinated by the arrival of the Terrans, and the thought of being able to go back and actually see Earth—a near-mythological place—was like dangling a fat tartberry in front of a ravenous bumblewort.

I want to go there. I want that far more than following the same boring life me mam and aunts and uncles have here.

As the currach nosed into the quay near Fitzpatrick's Fish-mongers, Saoirse jumped out into the boards to wrap the bowline around the hawser there. Johnny Fitzpatrick—one of Clan Fitzpatrick's many offspring—came lumbering up to them with a two-wheeled cart. He nodded to Saoirse, smiled at her a bit too much, then leaned over to look into the boat.

"Ah, that's a fine lot of bluefins yeh have there, Rí Mullin," he said to Angus—he held the titular title of "Rí" as the person who directed the fishing efforts for the island and who also served as the postmaster for the archipelago. It was Saoirse's and Liam's mother Iona Mullin who held the title of "Banríon," the head of Clan Mullin.

"Then yer mam Doireann will be giving us a fine price for them, I hope," Angus said.

"That'll be between yeh and Mam," Johnny answered. He leaned closer. "I shouldn't tell yeh this, but she *was* just saying that she wished the bluefins were shoaling," he added in a stage whisper. "We're out of 'em an' people have been asking."

"Then bring yer cart over so we can get them to her before she changes her mind," Angus said. "Liam, Saoirse, look lively now . . ."

Saoirse sighed audibly, and Angus gave her a sour look. Angus and Liam began tossing bluefins onto the dock. Saoirse could see greenish purple blotches on both their muscular arms; the skin fungi called "plotch" that infected many of the Inishers. Saoirse also had the blotches, though hers were mostly on her legs and abdomen, usually hidden from the Mainlanders by her clothing. Saoirse and Johnny loaded the catch into the cart. "I understand there's a Terran been coming to Dulcia," Saoirse said to Johnny as they worked. "Have yeh met the woman?"

"Ain't met her proper-like, but I've seen her about," Johnny told her. "Wears one of those belts they have, so she don't breathe our air and none of us can touch her and she can't accidentally touch us. Can't eat or drink nothing either that didn't come from their ship. Seems nice enough otherwise, but yeh never know with them people."

"She here now?"

"Dunno. I ain't seen her this cycle, but Mam's kept me working inside." He picked up another bluefin and tossed it on the cart, then stopped and looked down the length of the harbor. "That's one of their flitters near Plunkett's Pub. So I'd say aye, she's here somewhere. No telling where, though."

Saoirse squinted as she looked down the quay and saw a white blur there that she assumed was this flitter. "What's the Terran look like?"

The misty rain had stopped for the moment, though darker thunderheads still massed behind Dulcia Headland, promising a later downpour. Johnny pulled his cap from his head, smearing a track of bluefin slime over his forehead and the bill of his cap. Saoirse decided not to mention that; Johnny was never one of the young men she'd consider for "itch scratching" even though she suspected he found her interesting enough. For that matter, she had to admit that he and most of the Fitzpatricks were among the Mainlanders who didn't harbor much bias against the Inish, most likely because Clan Fitzpatrick, here in Dulcia, depended on Inish fishing skills for much of the product they sold to the other clans. Johnny settled the cap back on his head. "She don't look or dress like any of us, that's for certain. Awfully damned thin, like she'd blow away in a good gale. Yeh'll know when you see her, believe me. And her skin color . . . . well, she's just *different*—like a lot of the Terrans supposedly are."

Saoirse nodded. She tossed the last of the bluefins into the cart as Angus and Liam stepped from their boat onto the quay, with her uncle also picking up the leather mail sack from Great Inish. They followed behind Johnny as he swung the cart around and headed for his mother's store.

The haggling over how much Doireann Fitzpatrick would pay for the bluefins was quick enough. The Mainlanders and the Inish might have their long-standing clan quarrels, but Doireann was always polite even in bargaining and as fair in her pricing as any person could be who also had to make a profit. They eventually settled on 10p for each bluefin; Doireann counted out the brass coins into a small purse that she handed to Angus, though making quiet mutterings about paying too much even as she nodded to Angus and smiled at her son's well-loaded cart.

Outside, Angus gave Liam and Saoirse each a pound coin for their own use and handed five additional one-pound coins to Saoirse. "Me and Liam will go to the post office and take care of business there, then we're off to the ironworks for nails and hooks and to pick up a few other necessities," he told Saoirse. "Yeh can check with the butchers about the meat the Banríon ordered, as well as to whether the weavers have ever made those bolts of heavy cloth she wanted—did yer mam tell yeh how much the cloth would be?"

So I'm to do most of the work again, as usual. Until recently, it had been Saoirse's mam who'd handled negotiations with the Mainlanders, coming across from the archipelago with Angus and Liam. But of late, she'd been sending Saoirse in her stead. *"It's time you started learning some of what a Banríon must do,"* she'd said when Saoirse had objected. *"And I'm getting too old for being out on the sea in the weather."*

"Mam said that they'd settled on two pounds for the wool and the bolts should have been ready two cycles ago," Saoirse told Angus, and he nodded.

"Everything's well tidy, then. Five pounds should cover all, if not more. Otherwise, enjoy yerself and be back before twelfth bell and cycle's end."

"And if I don't see the two of yeh then, I'll suppose I should be looking for yeh at Murphy's Alehouse behind a stack of pints," Saoirse said, then added, "Unless one or both of yeh get lucky and decides we need to stay another cycle. Because of the weather."

Angus and Liam grinned at that. They headed off up the street; Saoirse looked at the butcher's establishment, Hearns' Fine Meats, next door to Fitzpatrick's, then shrugged. "That can feckin' wait a bit," she muttered to herself and set off down the quay toward the Terran's flitter.

There was no sign of any Terran anywhere around the flitter; an elderly man from Clan Stuart she encountered near the vehicle simply looked at her blandly and shrugged when she asked. "Aye, I saw the woman when she arrived, but I don't know where she is now," he said before turning away entirely, obviously not willing to talk more.

The Terran wasn't in Plunkett's either, not that Saoirse stayed that long to check all the alcoves with several blurry-faced Mainlanders staring at her over their pints. Outside, she gave a sigh, then decided she might as well walk up Cairn Hill Lane to High Street, where the weavers of Clan Bancroft had their shop.

The Bancroft Woolery had a fine view of the harbor, with Dulcia Head and the Pale Woman sitting just beyond. The town, with its few streets and lanes wandering the hillside, was laid out before her. Putting her glasses on again, Saoirse could see the Terran's flitter as well as her Uncle Angus' currach moored at the quay. Some of the town's fishing vessels were just now heading out, their sides draped with nets, though they rarely fished around the archipelago or on the open sea beyond the islands—which meant that their nets were rarely full. They preferred to stay close to the mainland's coast where they could duck into a cove or river mouth or behind a headland if the weather deteriorated, as it often did. Ever since the Great Fishing War, mainland boats stayed well away from the archipelago, as if the thought of encountering an arracht terrified them.

Saoirse shook her head at their cowardice and stupidity. " *'Twas the sheepers taught the Mainlanders everything they know about fishing"* was a well-known saying within the archipelago, usually followed by *"an' no sheeper ain't ever caught a feckin' fish"* and laughter.

The bell over the door chimed as Saoirse entered the workshop's small customer area, hung with samples of Clan Bancroft's handiwork. She inhaled the scent of drying sheeper wool and heard the percussive clacking of the big floor looms working in the room beyond. A young woman about Saoirse's age emerged from the curtained doorway to the production facility. The smile she wore vanished as she saw Saoirse in her bluefin-stained clothing. "What is it yeh want?" she asked. Her nose wrinkled as if the lingering bluefin odor bothered her.

"Clan Mullin has an order with yeh. I'm here to pick up."

"Clan Mullin, eh? Let me check." As the woman slid the curtain aside, Saoirse heard her call into the darkness beyond—"Auntie Aoife, there's some stinking Inisher here . . ."—before the curtain closed behind her and the voices became too muffled to understand. Minutes passed, then finally an older woman came out, the front of her dress dotted with scraps of clinging wool and carrying three thick bolts of off-white cloth in her arms. She set the cloth on the counter, folded her arms in front of her, and looked Saoirse up and down without a smile.

"That'll be three pounds," she said.

"The Banríon said yeh'd agreed on two pounds."

"Yeh wouldn't be calling me a liar now, girl, would yeh?" The woman's eyebrows lifted high on her forehead. "The Banríon was obviously mistaken when she told you that."

So yer saying that me mam was the liar? Saoirse bit her lip against the rebuttal, saying nothing in response; she'd been with her mother, watching her during her own haggling sessions with the Mainlanders. *"The thing none of them can stand is silence,"* her mam had told her often enough. *"Just stare at them and wait."*

She did that now. The woman—Auntie Aoife, she assumed—was shaking her head, shifting her weight from foot to foot as if waiting for Saoirse's objection and counteroffer. When the silence dragged on, the woman finally huffed in exasperation. "Two pounds and fifty," Aoife said finally. "Since the Banríon seems to have forgotten what we agreed on."

"Two pounds," Saoirse responded, "since the Banríon's memory is quite excellent, as I know very well." Saoirse took out two one-pound coins from the purse tied to her belt and placed them on the counter next to the bolts. "Or you can keep your cloth and hope you can sell it to someone else. I hear that Clan Rhydderch over in Plocton has lovely woolen cloth from their sheepers this year, and cheaper."

Aoife gave another huff; Saoirse just looked at her for several breaths, then reached out toward the coins on the counter. *"Yeh always have to be willing to walk away"* was another piece of advice her mam had given her. Just as she was about to take back the coins, Aoife scowled and put her own hand over the money. "Two pounds, then, and be glad that I'm willing to take a loss. Tell the Banríon that next time we negotiate a price, she'll need to open her purse a little wider, and we'll put the price in writing, so we don't have to worry about memory loss."

Saoirse suppressed the grin that threatened and bowed her

head toward the woman. "I'll be certain to let her know, and I'll tell her of yer generosity."

Yeh taught me well, Mam, she thought as she walked out with the cloth.

The bolts of cloth heavy in her arms, Saoirse strode back down to the quay, hoping to reach the boat so that she could wrap the bolts in oilcloth before the rain returned. As she passed the flitter—which she realized now was a flying vehicle of some sort—still parked by Plunkett's, she saw a strangely dressed woman emerge from the pub and approach her. The woman wore a form-fitted uniform of some material Saoirse had never seen, with a wide, thick belt around her waist and the insignia of a stylized starship above her heart. The woman's hair was glossy black and cropped short, her skin an odd color a few shades lighter than most of the clans but touched with a hue that Saoirse couldn't quite identify, and her eyes were of a shape that Saoirse had never glimpsed in any children of the Twenty-Eight. She was also impossibly skinny, as if she would break in half if struck hard in the stomach—Saoirse wondered if all Terrans were like her. The woman's feet, she noticed, never quite made contact with the stones of the quay, as if there was a sliver of solidified air always between the soles of her boots and the surface. The light didn't seem to touch her in the same way that it touched everything and everyone else. Saoirse guessed her to be 450 to 550 years old, though she wasn't sure how reliable that guess might be.

But the woman had to be the Terran. For all Saoirse knew, she could be over a thousand.

Saoirse stopped, her arms still clutching the bolts of cloth to her chest. The Terran had halted as well. Saoirse thought she saw the woman touch her thumb to a finger of the same hand; a blue light gleamed between them briefly.

"Excuse me," the woman said aloud. "You're Inish, aren't you?"

Her voice was also strange, higher pitched than Saoirse expected, and with an odd lilting, heavy, and unrecognizable accent. A hand waved toward her, palm up, as if in invitation.

"Aye, I'm Inish and yer Terran," Saoirse answered.

"Yes. My name's Dr. Ichiko Aguilar—but please, just call me Ichiko." Saoirse could see the Terran waiting for her to respond with her own name. She said nothing, just hugged the bolts of cloth tighter. "I'd love to sit down and talk with you for a bit if you have the time," the Terran finally continued. "I've heard so much about the Inish and the archipelago, and I want to know more."

"Yeh've heard most of it from Mainlanders, did yeh?" A nod. "I doubt many of them who talked to yeh ever came out to Great Inish or really know us a'tall," Saoirse continued. "So what yeh heard was likely gossip, speculation, and lies. No more'n that."

"Then I'd love for you to tell me some of the truth. If you're willing."

Now it was the Terran who waited, silently, as Saoirse pondered the offer. Saoirse shrugged, adjusting the bolts in her arms.

"Aye. Yeh can walk with me and talk, if yeh like," she said to Ichiko.

The Fragrance Of Garlands And The Smoke Of Incense

"**M**AY I ASK YOUR NAME?" Ichiko said to the Inish woman as she followed her along the quay. She tapped her thumb against her ring finger. <Record this,> she told her AMI.

The Inisher glanced back. Ichiko found it difficult to assess her age: mid-to late 20s in ship-time, perhaps? Like most of the locals, she was stocky and short, her physique shaped by Canis Lupus' higher gravity. The hair that peeked from underneath her woolen hat was straw-colored, and her eyes—though hidden behind two round circles of glass in a wire frame—were the same startling pale blue as Luciano's, she realized. No one aboard ship wore glasses; myopia and other eyesight issues could all be fixed with a quick automated surgery, but that was an option no Lupusian had.

"My name's Saoirse, of Clan Mullin."

<That makes her the daughter of the Banríon Iona Mullin,> AMI commented. Ichiko started at the unexpected commentary. She glanced down at her ring finger, where a faint sapphire hue emanated from under the flesh—so AMI hadn't disconnected as it should have. *Ignore it for now; have it fixed later.*

"Saoirse. That's a lovely-sounding name," Ichiko answered, hoping her slight pause had gone unnoticed.

"Thanks, I guess."

<Check the database. Does she have children?> Ichiko thought to AMI as they continued to walk.

<None recorded in our database, which is slightly unusual for her age. Banríon Iona Mullin has had five children: her youngest, a daughter, died of a bloodworm infection two years ago ship-time; her second child, a boy, was washed out of a fishing boat during a storm and presumably drowned. Saoirse is the middle child of the survivors. She has an older brother Liam and a younger sister Gráinne.>

Saoirse stopped at a small boat tied up on the quay. Ichiko stared at the vessel, shivering at the thought of being out on the sea in such a small and fragile-looking craft with the weather and high waves she'd witnessed here. "You came all the way from the archipelago in *this*?" she asked.

Saoirse laughed as she easily stepped down into the boat and opened a compartment built into the stern. "Well, I could hardly have walked, could I?" Saoirse pulled out a folded oilskin from the rear compartment, wrapped the bolts of woolen cloth she was carrying in it, then placed the bundle inside, closing the compartment door again. <No locks,> Ichiko noted to AMI. <They must not worry about theft here.>

Saoirse pulled herself back up on the quay, removing her glasses and cleaning them before putting them back on. "Yeh've never been in a boat?"

"Not for a long time, back on Earth," Ichiko answered. "When I was a child, we lived for a time in a little village on the coast of Japan, and my father would take us out around the bay sometimes. Back then, we owned a boat easily the size of my flitter with a big, powerful inboard engine."

"Engines fail when arms don't," Saoirse said vaguely. "Yeh *knew* who your father was? He helped to raise yeh?"

"Things are different here than they are on Earth," Ichiko answered. "On Earth, yes, people generally know who their father is; if for some reason they don't, a simple DNA test can identify them. And we don't have the large extended family settlements you have with everyone cooperating to raise the children. My mother and father are married—do you know that custom?" Saoirse nodded. "Mom is Japanese, Dad is French. They're *still* married, as far as I know," Ichiko continued, smiling at Saoirse. "But your way of doing things makes more sense here than ours would, I'd think."

"Mebbe. Is it true that yer here to look at allowing people to go back to Earth if they want?"

Ichiko could hear the eagerness in Saoirse's voice. *<Careful,>* AMI warned. *<Remember the protocols.>* Ichiko nodded, though she was annoyed at the unnecessary warning delivered in her mother's voice. "I'm not doing that myself, but yes, that's part of why we're here, studying whether or not that's feasible. There are already several volunteers from the clans up on *Odysseus* in isolation in the medical ward, including, I understand, one or two from the archipelago."

"Aye, there *were* a few Inish who went up," Saoirse answered. "Aulie from Clan Craig and Elspeth from Clan Mullin, who's me Aunt Lileas' daughter. But they were both returned to Dulcia ten cycles ago for some reason without any explanation. And right now yeh Terrans won't even breathe our air," Saoirse said, looking significantly at the belt around Ichiko's waist.

<Funny how Minister Plunkett never mentioned that the Inish volunteers had been sent back.> "While I'm planet-side, you're correct. My bio-shield keeps me isolated from your environment and everything in it. That's the way it has to be until we know more about Canis Lupus."

" 'Tis a shame." Saoirse inhaled deeply, letting her breath out again with a sigh. "I can smell the brine of the sea, the odor of the bluefins we brought in with us, some lovely bread that's baking over near the market that's making me stomach growl with wanting it, and in the wind there's a hint of the storm that's coming in. What do yeh smell, Ichiko? The inside of a sealed can?"

"I smell mostly nothing," Ichiko admitted.

"What does Earth smell like?"

Ichiko had to laugh at the question. "Earth's a huge place. I can't give you a quick or simple answer to that. Every place is different."

"Then what does Japan smell like?"

Ichiko had to smile at the memories that brought back to her; she saw Saoirse smile tentatively in response. "Japan's a pretty big place, too. But the village where I grew up was on a bay looking out at the Pacific Ocean. I can remember the smell of the sea there, and I imagine it's probably much the same here: briny but somehow clean and pleasant. I don't remember anyone baking bread, but rice steaming can still make my own stomach tell me that it wants some. And there was the smell of *dashi*—that's a soup stock for miso and other dishes—wafting from the houses. My mother would often have dashi simmering on the stove, and its fragrance was delightful. There was a soy sauce brewery in the town, and often you could smell and almost taste the soy. And incense sticks burning for the lost loved ones in the house shrines . . ." Ichiko smiled again. "You miss so much if you can't smell. I'm sure I'm missing a lot here as a result."

"Japan sounds wonderful. I'd like to go there someday."

<Careful . . .> AMI whispered. "Let me repeat," Ichiko told Saoirse, "that I'm not part of the team looking into whether the people here can be allowed to return, so I really can't and won't speak to that. My job here is to learn about the society you've created and how you've integrated with this world. It's wonderful that you'd like to come to Earth, but for myself I'd love to come out to the archipelago." Ichiko glanced again at the Inish boat. "Though maybe not in that," she added.

Saoirse laughed again, and Ichiko found herself chuckling with her. It was beginning to rain once more, and Saoirse took off her glasses and put them in a pocket. A bell began ringing from across the harbor, up on the spine of Dulcia Head where the Pale Woman stood. Both Ichiko and Saoirse stood there counting the peals. "Low Tenth," Saoirse said when the last one had sounded. "I still have an errand or two to get to before we leave." Her head tilted as she looked at Ichiko. "If yeh want to come along, we might talk some more—and yeh might see how things are done here."

As they walked further down the quay toward Market Street, Ichiko watched one of the local Dulcia fishing boats draped with nets heading out to sea, its primitive motor chugging asthmatically and puffs of dark gray smoke emerging from the chimney stack near the forward cabin. "The locals—" she began, but Saoirse interrupted.

"Yeh mean the Mainlanders. I'm also 'local' to this world."

"The Mainlanders, then—they use motors in their boats, and I've seen some mechanized vehicles on the farms outside town as well, mixed in with the work animals you have like the capall. I understand that you don't do the same out in the archipelago."

"What works here doesn't necessarily work there," the woman answered. "That's all."

"Why not?"

Saoirse simply shrugged. "It's just not done." She pointed to a sign: *Hearns' Fine Meats.* "I have to go there."

Ichiko wanted to follow up on that comment, but she walked behind Saoirse into the shop, gawking at the carcasses split open and dangling from iron hooks behind the counter, with trays of various filets, cuts, and sausages on display under glass, all unidentifiable to her. An insect whined past Ichiko's ear; she noticed many of its relatives snared on coils of sticky paper hung around the shop. *Are those pishmires?*

<*Yes,*> came the unasked-for reply from her AMI. Ichiko could only imagine what the shop must smell like, and decided she was grateful for the bio-suit here, at least. Compared to meat shops at home, this looked decidedly unsanitary.

An elderly, nearly bald man came through the open, curtained door at the back of the shopfront, beyond which Ichiko could hear other people talking as well as the sounds of heavy cutlery striking wood. The apron the man wore was smeared with blood and other stains that Ichiko was glad she couldn't recognize. He wiped his hands on the filthy cloth as he entered. Neither one was improved by the effort.

"Ah, yeh must be that Dr. Aguilar from First Base," he said to Ichiko, ignoring Saoirse standing at the counter. "Good to actually meet yeh. I'm Arthur Hearns, the proprietor here." He started to extend his hand to her, then drew it back ruefully. "I forgot; yeh can't actually touch us. I'm afraid Minister Plunkett didn't tell me to expect yeh. Have yer ship's cooks decided they need fresh meat? We have the absolute best there is."

Ichiko shook her head and managed a smile. "I'm afraid not," she said. "I was just chatting with Saoirse Mullin on the quay. She's your customer, not me."

"Ah. Saoirse, good to see you again." His words were friendly enough, but there wasn't much enthusiasm in them. "Yer here for that order, then."

"I am," Saoirse told him.

"I'm sorry, but t'ain't ready just yet," the man answered. <*He's lying,*> AMI commented. <*The facial expression, his breathing, the way he won't look at her directly.*> "I didn't expect anyone coming in from Great Inish this cycle."

"Then can yer clanmates get started on it now?" Saoirse asked. "Rí Angus is leaving at Low Twelfth, and we may not be back for another three or four cycles since the bluefins are running lately."

The man's lips twisted in what might have been an attempt at a smile. He wiped his hands on the apron again. Ichiko could see that he wanted to protest. He glanced over to Ichiko, and she smiled back at him. He ran a thick hand over his bald scalp; it did nothing to improve things. "Two pounds now for the rush, and t'other two when yeh come back at Low Twelfth," he told Saoirse.

"It'll be a pound now, and the other two when we come back," Saoirse told him.

Again, the butcher glanced at Ichiko. "Fine, then. I'll have it for yeh at Low Twelfth." Ichiko was certain that last sentence was directed to her rather than Saoirse.

Saoirse took a pound coin from her purse and placed it on the counter, nodded to the man, and headed for the door. Ichiko smiled again at the butcher and followed her out.

"*Musha,* what an old stook!" Ichiko heard Saoirse exclaim as the door closed behind them. "Look, thanks for chumming with me back there. Yeh made it easy for me."

"He was lying to you."

Saoirse laughed once more. "Aye, I knew that. I'm sure he has the package already made up and ready in his icehouse. He just wanted to see how fast and hard I'd dance for it, but yeh sucked all the fun out of it for him. I appreciate that. Yeh said yeh wanted to see how our society works? Well, now yeh've seen how it can be between Mainlander and Inish."

"Why is that?"

Saoirse only shook her head. "That's a long story, and Spiorad Mór knows I don't understand all the details."

<Spiorad Mór is Great Spirit in Irish,> AMI said in Ichiko's head. <An Inish affectation, perhaps? The Mainlanders mostly still believe in some form of the Christian religion.>

"I'd still like to hear it."

Saoirse shrugged. "Well, close to five millennia ago," <A little less than two and a half centuries,> AMI translated, "Clan Mullin and Clan Craig had a severe falling out with several of the other clans and left the mainland to live out on the archipelago. I doubt anyone remembers exactly what that falling out was over—fishing rights, probably, and likely both sides had fine arguments for why they felt the way they felt. Memories of grievances can be long here. But the Mullins and Craigs have been on the islands ever since. We don't *hate* Mainlanders precisely, and they don't precisely hate us. In fact, some of them are quite civil overall, and there's been some intermingling if yeh take my meaning. It's just . . . we live differently than they do here, so . . ." Saoirse shrugged. "Look, why don't we go over to Murphy's Alehouse if yeh still want to talk? That's where I'm supposed to meet my uncle and my brother. I can have some of their stout, and yeh . . . well, yeh can have whatever yeh can."

Once in the pub, Ichiko watched as Saoirse slipped on her wire-rimmed spectacles again, making her eyes seem larger behind the lenses. "I have weak eyes," she told Ichiko. "Out in the rain, sometimes glasses are more trouble than they're worth, and on the boat there's mostly lots of close work where I don't need 'em," she explained as she put them on.

Ichiko asked her about the clans, about how they raised the children since most of the time there wasn't a parenting couple. "*Everyone* raises the bairns," Saoirse told her. "A child's mam does the bulk at first, of course, since her milk's generally in, but everyone in the compound helps some. Babies around the age of fifty or sixty will usually stay in the compound's creche with the other children until they're old enough to have their own rooms— usually by the time they're 200 or a little later. Uncles and aunts who enjoy working with children are in charge of the creche on a rotating basis: teaching the children, changing their nappies, and so on. The kitchens in the clan compounds are communal, so once the children are eating solid food, they can eat with their mothers and siblings or with any of the uncles or aunts or cousins if they want."

"Minister Plunkett told me that a young Lupusian woman might start having children around . . ."

<385 or so,> AMI supplied.

". . . 385 or so. You're older than that. Do you have children?"

<You already know the answer to that,> AMI said. Ichiko ignored the voice.

There were two empty pints sitting in front of Saoirse, with a third one that was half-full. Saoirse took a long swallow from it as Ichiko asked the question. The woman shook her head as she set the pint down again on the rough wooden table. Her gaze seemed somehow defiant as she looked at Ichiko.

"Neh," she said flatly. "I don't."

<*I wouldn't push her,*> AMI said. <*That question obviously made her uncomfortable.*>

"It doesn't matter; I was just curious. After all, I'm . . ." She paused. <*568,*> came the answer from AMI. ". . . 568 in your years, and I don't have children either." Saoirse's eyes were still narrowed, and Ichiko decided it would be best to change the subject. "So does this 'Sleeping Wolf' island in the archipelago actually look like a wolf resting on the water from the mainland?" Ichiko asked. "I haven't had a chance to see it yet, though I've heard about it."

The pub had become more crowded since the two of them had entered. "Can't say," she told Ichiko, "since I've never seen a wolf, only heard about them in old stories. I guess it might to yeh, though from Great Inish, it just looks like an island. But everyone's called it the Sleeping Wolf, from the time the First came here, so I suppose it must."

"The Mainlanders say that you treat the island like it's a holy place."

"Holy?" Saoirse scoffed. "There's nothing religious about—" She stopped and waved her hand at someone behind Ichiko. "Uncle Angus! Liam! Over here!"

Ichiko looked over her shoulder to see two Inishers—one an older man with gray hair, the other nearly the same age as Saoirse, both with the same coloring. They already had pints of stout in their hands. They made their way through the tables to where Ichiko and Saoirse were talking in an alcove to the rear of the establishment, grabbing chairs from an adjacent table and sitting to either side of Ichiko. She could feel them staring at her, looking her over closely. She looked at them also. Both men had large blotches on the skin of their forearms. <*Some kind of birthmark?*> she asked AMI.

<*That's plotch. A common fungal infection of the skin among the Inish,*> AMI responded. <*Not something you have to worry about, at least. It might stop the Inish from being allowed to travel to Earth, however, if it's contagious. According to the ship's medical records, both the*>

Inishers Minister Plunkett sent up to Odysseus *were heavily infected with it, and that's why they were sent back.>*

"Uncle Angus, Liam, this is Dr. Ichiko Aguilar from the *Odysseus*," Saoirse was saying. "She's here studying our society, and she's interested in the archipelago."

"Dr. Aguilar, eh? So yer the one the Mainlanders are all flapping their gobs about, the one who's asking everyone questions and not answering any o' theirs," Angus said. His voice was graveled, though slower paced than Minister Plunkett and most of the other townfolk. Still, the accent was more pronounced, so Ichiko had to pay close attention to understand what he was saying.

"That would be me," Ichiko answered, "though I'd prefer if you'd just call me Ichiko. And yes, I'm interested in the archipelago, as Saoirse said."

"Yeh mean they haven't warned yeh about us primitive Inishers?" Liam interjected. "They've told yeh that we eat our dead, certainly. It's a sign of deep respect out on the islands."

<That's a lie,> AMI said, and Ichiko shook her head in mute response

"Liam!" Saoirse said, slapping him on the arm. "Stop talking such blather, or she might start believing yeh. Ichiko, forgive my brother; his head's completely stuffed with mince."

Liam laughed—his laugh reminded Ichiko of Saoirse's.

"Don't worry, Saoirse. I can sniff out a tall tale when I hear one. But Saoirse's right," she continued, looking more at Angus than Liam. "I'd love to come out to the archipelago. When you leave, I could follow you in my flitter—"

"Neh." The single word from Angus interrupted her with the same finality as Saoirse's answer regarding children. He took a long swallow from his pint, his eyes watching her over the rim of the glass. He set it down hard on the table. "Yeh can't. Look around yeh, woman," he said, waving a gnarled, thick-knuckled hand to encompass those in the room, some of whom were watching their table intently. "The Mainlanders are like clams: those here in Dulcia and those in all their towns. They've erected safe little shells around themselves that they're afraid to leave.

They think we're all ignorant and wrong-headed out in the archipelago, but they don't see it's the other way around. Even though they breathe the air here, they're still blind and deaf to much of what this world offers. We're not. And yeh Terrans . . ."

He gave a scoffing laugh and took a long drink from his pint, swallowing before continuing. "Yer hiding away in even tighter and thicker shells than the feckin' Mainlanders. No offense, missy, but I can see all that fancy equipment yer wearing, just to keep out what yer type are all afraid of. Surely the people here have told yeh that, out in the archipelago, things like yer fancy suit tend not to work. That's why even the Mainlanders stay well away with their noisy, stinking motorboats. They don't fish near the islands because the islands don't like 'em and too many of 'em have lost their lives out there. What if yer shield fails while you're asking yer questions on Great Inish? So neh. Yeh can't follow us because I don't want to be responsible for yeh becoming stuck here just like us."

"You may not be stuck here," Ichiko began, but Angus was already shaking his head.

"Oh, I know yeh Terrans have sweet tongues that give us all the optimistic words we want to hear, about how mebbe some of us can go back to Earth once we can prove we're not going to infect your planet with bloodworms or the Gray Threads or the Wasting. Or mebbe we can establish trade between our worlds since now yeh promise never to abandon us again. That's all well and good, but I won't believe it until I actually see it happen, and neither will anyone out in the archipelago. Tell me, Dr. Aguilar, can yeh guarantee me that Saoirse here can visit Earth if she wants to go—because I *know* that's what she thinks she wants more than anything: to leave the islands and travel to Earth."

Saoirse's eyes had widened behind her glasses, angrily staring at her uncle. From outside, they heard the first peals of Low Twelfth from the Pale Woman. <*Protocol. You can't make promises.*> "Rí Mullin, I wish I could tell both you and Saoirse exactly that, but we all know I can't. The decision isn't in my hands at all."

"Uncle Angus, yer being rude to my guest, and I don't like it,"

Saoirse interjected. "And I don't like yeh telling her what yeh think I want. It ain't yer feckin' place to do that."

Angus' eyebrows lifted slightly. "I'm only talking the truth here," Angus replied.

"Neh, yer talking yer own prejudices," Saoirse answered, "and I want yeh to apologize to my friend Ichiko."

Ichiko saw Angus glare at Saoirse while Liam covered a smirk by drinking from his pint. Then the man's expression softened. He looked at Ichiko and audibly exhaled. "My niece is right, and I'm sorry. I've been rude, and I hope yeh'll forgive me for that." He paused, a forefinger sliding along the edge of his pint glass. "But I still won't have yeh coming out to the archipelago," he continued. "I don't want the responsibility."

"No one would hold you responsible," Ichiko told him. "I'm willing to assume whatever risk there might be."

"Which is fine for yeh, but . . ." Angus answered.

"Uncle . . ." Saoirse said, and Angus heaved another put-upon sigh.

"Let me talk to yer mam," he said to Saoirse, then turned again to Ichiko. "Yeh know we have to do that first. The Banríon can decide. If she says aye, then . . . Does that satisfy yeh both?"

Ichiko and Saoirse nodded simultaneously. "Then that's where we'll leave it for now," Angus said. "Saoirse, did yeh get the cloth and talk to Hearns?"

"I did," she answered. "I have the cloth and Hearns should have the meat ready for us by now. We can pick it up on the way to the quay."

Angus nodded. "Then let's finish our drinks and be off. I can smell a new storm coming in, and we should get back before we lose the good wind." Angus lifted his pint and drained it, as did Saoirse and Liam. They all stood.

Ichiko followed them out.

There Is Another World, But It Is In This One

ICHIKO STOOD AT THE quay's edge as the trio readied their currach for the journey back, packing the supplies they'd bought and the Rí's full mailbag. The clouds were low over Dulcia Head and still drizzling rain; Ichiko watched Saoirse remove her spectacles, wipe them carefully, and put them away again under her oilcoth jacket. *<Yes, one of the doctors aboard* Odysseus *could correct her vision easily,>* Ichiko heard AMI comment, as if the AI could guess at her thoughts. *<But protocol . . . >*

Thumb touched finger, but it remained stubbornly lit. *<I know all this,>* Ichiko thought to her AMI. *<You don't need to tell me.>*

Liam and Angus put their oars in the water and Saoirse unwrapped the bowline from the quay's hawser. She tossed the coiled rope into the bow and stepped in after it. Ichiko watched her easy, natural movements. The trio pushed away from the quay as Liam and Angus began to pull in earnest at their oars. Saoirse waved to Ichiko; she waved back.

<AMI, have one of the satellite feeds track them; I want to make certain they get back safely.>

<Done. So you're really not going to follow them?>

<They made their feelings clear enough. I'll wait until I know more about why they don't want me there.>

Ichiko watched them until they reached the mouth of the harbor and Saoirse raised the sail, which billowed out as it caught the wind. The currach began to cut more of a wake in the harbor's relatively quiet water, then started to bounce as it reached the harbor's mouth and the choppier open water there. The rain began in earnest, large drops bouncing from the repellant surface of the bio-shield. Ichiko went to her flitter.

<Take me over to the Pale Woman,> she thought to AMI; in response, the craft shuddered and lifted on its rotors. They crossed the harbor, flying only a few meters above the water, then rising as they approached Dulcia Head, ascending higher until Ichiko could see over the summit, with the painted, one-armed standing stone of the Pale Woman below and to her right.

Out over the open water, she could see Saoirse's boat far below, still in the harbor's mouth. Well out near where the horizon of the sea blended into the gray curtains of rain, two faint, darker shapes lurked, perhaps 15 to 20 kilometers out. <AMI, adjust the window filters so I can see more clearly.>

The windshield of the flitter shimmered once, then the contrast deepened. Yes, Ichiko realized, that one to the right had to be the Sleeping Wolf. She could see how it had received its name. That rising headland was the muzzle, with a "paw" stretched out alongside. Two sheer peaks were the ears of the beast. The back of the head fell to the spine, before lifting again into what imagination could see as a resting haunch, with a low tail stretching out behind to the right.

Ichiko stared at it, as well as the faint shapes of the Stepstones to the left of the Sleeping Wolf, and the vague bulk of Great Inish further off in the distance between the two. A speck in the gray expanse, Saoirse's boat was now just past the tip of Dulcia Head.

It was tempting to simply disobey Rí Mullin and go out to where the archipelago waited. Half an hour, ship-time, maybe a little more, and she could be there—far faster than Saoirse with her uncle and brother could make the trip. Almost, she gave the command.

Almost.

Instead, she shook her head, looking again out to the Sleeping Wolf.

<AMI, take me back to First Base.>

Saoirse could see the flitter hovering above the Pale Woman, a fuzzy, indistinct shape in Saoirse's vision. Uncle Angus and Liam saw it, too, undoubtedly better than she did. "Is that feckin' Terran going to follow us anyway after I told her she couldn't?" Angus asked, looking at Saoirse, who could only shrug.

"How am I supposed to know what she's going to do?" she answered. She was holding the boom line for the sail. The currach was running before a strong following wind; that and the outflow current from the harbor had them making good headway. Her uncle and Liam were using the oars mostly to keep the bow pointed toward the harbor opening; Angus had lowered the centerboard to give them extra stability in the rolling waves.

"Yer the one who spent time in the pub with the Terran instead of looking for one of the Mainlander men," Liam said. He grinned. "Mam will be disappointed in yeh. Yet again."

"Just shut yer gob, Liam," Saoirse snapped at him. She squinted toward the flitter. "Look," she said, "she's moving away now. I think she just wanted to find out if she could see the Sleeping Wolf. She said she'd heard about it but hadn't yet seen it." The flitter had turned and banked sharply, heading back toward Dulcia and the mountains behind. "Are yeh happy now, Uncle?"

"I'll be happier when we're back home," Angus answered. He peered sharply at the sky and the sea ahead of them—Angus had always had excellent vision, though he complained that cataracts were beginning to blur and darken things for him. "But we should make it back just before the storm front reaches us. We're making good time with this following wind. With any luck a'tall, we'll be back on Great Inish before High Third."

The luck stayed with them. There were just starting to pass the first of the Stepstones when they heard High Second ring out from the bell tower on Great Inish. The wind had stayed strong and with them the entire time. As they moved along the line of low islands that were the Stepstones, Saoirse could see a rippling disturbance on the surface of the waves around them caused by a school of wrigglers feeding on purple algae. A nearby flock of bright red flapjacks from the Stepstones had seen the wrigglers as well. They circled overheard, the undulating edges of their flying surfaces tightening and contracting as they repeatedly dove into the waves, breaking the surface a moment later with a wriggler or two snagged in the seine-like teeth of their mouths. The flock gave off the high-pitched keening wail of satisfaction as they gulped down the wrigglers, circling high before diving again.

Their boat was suddenly surrounded by a hard rain of plummeting flapjacks, white splashes rising all around them.

"Should we try to net a few of the flapjacks for breakfast tomorrow, Uncle Angus?" Liam asked.

"Yeh know we can't do that," the Rí answered.

"No one would miss a few flapjacks from this crowd," Liam groused. "Just because the arracht have put them off-limits lately doesn't mean they won't taste as good as they always have."

"Neh," Angus said. "And that's the end of it."

Liam sighed. A flapjack rose from the water immediately alongside him, showering him with salty drops. As it started to rise, it regurgitated a pale stream of wriggler guts which landed heavily across Liam's shoulders and flat cap. Liam flailed wildly at himself as Angus laughed and Saoirse smiled despite her irritation.

"Ah, they *were* listening to yeh," Saoirse said. "And they didn't like what they heard any more than the arracht would."

"Very funny." Liam ducked as another flapjack hit the water behind him. He slapped his flat cap on the gunwale, scowled at the resulting smear, and put it back on his head. "Let's get home," he said. "I need to take a bath."

This time, she was the one calling Luciano, though the commander was in a meeting with Captain Keshmiri and other officers and wasn't available. She talked instead to his AMI, who promised that he'd be notified that she'd called as soon as he was out of the meeting. Luciano's AMI was decidedly feminine with a smoky voice and what sounded to Ichiko like an overdone Italian accent; she'd sometimes wondered if the AMI was modeled on someone Luciano had once known, a lover perhaps, but she'd never asked.

Still energized by her encounter with Saoirse and the Inish, she left her room and walked around First Base, enjoying the sensation of being out of the bio-shield, breathing air that didn't smell and taste of being "canned," able to touch anything she wished. As she walked, Ichiko pressed her thumb to her finger with all the pressure she could muster and was pleased to finally see the light go off. <AMI?> she thought. There was no answer. Ichiko smiled.

"Doctor Aguilar, having a problem?" The question came from behind her. Ichiko turned to see Lieutenant Bishara looking at her, not quite smiling.

"Ah, Lieutenant Bishara. Just a little issue with my AMI contact." She held up her hand. "I'll need to have someone look at it when I'm back up on *Odysseus*."

Bishara nodded. "My AMI's been acting up a bit, too—I'm thinking it's the lag between here and *Odysseus*. Have you been enjoying your time out in Dulcia, Doctor?"

"So far, it's been interesting," Ichiko answered. "And please just call me Ichiko. There's no need to be so formal."

"Ichiko," the lieutenant said, as if she were tasting the word. "Then you should call me Chava—at least when we're not in front of the people working under me."

"I'll remember that."

"Have you eaten yet since you've been back?"

Ichiko shook her head, suddenly aware that the only thing she'd had in hours was the thick, bland paste sucked from the bio-shield's food compartment. Her stomach growled at the thought of actual food. "No, I haven't."

"I'm just off duty and was heading to my office for dinner. I can have Cook send up an extra plate: vegetables from the hydropon-ics bay on the ship and tofu masquerading as chicken, I think. Though I'm trying to convince them that irradiated and cooked sheeper or bluefin would be safe—and hopefully better tasting. The Canines seem to like eating them, anyway."

Ichiko narrowed her eyes a bit at the use of the term but said nothing—no need to alienate the person in charge of her current residence. "I'll remember to ask Commander Mercado to add me to your petition. But veggies and tofu sound delightful for now."

Ichiko saw a flash of azure light as Chava passed the request to her AMI, then she said, "Follow me . . ."

Chava's quarters were spartan: plain, unpainted metal walls enclosing a paper-littered desk, a bed, a furled holoscreen on the wall opposite the bed, a small kitchenette area, and a small table with four chairs set around it. On the desk was a frame display-ing a looped shortvid of a family, with Chava in uniform smiling between two children, a girl who looked to be about ten and a much younger boy. A man stood behind the three of them, his hands on Chava's shoulders as the loop started. "Your family?" Ichiko asked.

"Yes," Chava said, smiling as she looked at the vid. "That's me with Geoff, and our kids Aria and Owen. That was taken not long before *Odysseus* left."

"That must be hard, being away from your family for a decade or more."

"It is. I won't really know them or recognize them when I get back—Aria will be at least 21 by then, and I'll have been absent for half of her life. It'll be worse with Owen; at best, all I'll be to him is a few pictures and vids and some vague memories. But . . ." She took in a long breath, looking away from the images. "Geoff and I divorced when I accepted this mission. He has the kids and is already remarried. Last I heard, wife number two was pregnant. So they're all part of a new family now. They've moved on—and I'll do the same."

"I'm sorry, Chava." Ichiko put her hand on the woman's arm, pressing lightly. Chava smiled, tight-lipped, at the gesture. Her eyes were glistening in the room's lights.

"Don't be," she said. "It was my choice and it's better this way, for all of us. Our marriage was always on the rocky side, and my accepting the *Odysseus* mission was just the final blow." There was a knock on the door. Chava went to the door and opened it; an ensign entered, pushing a cart. He put the covered plates on the table, saluted Chava, and left again with the cart.

"We should eat while it's still hot—believe me, it tastes best that way. Wine, tea, coffee, or water?" Chava asked.

"Whatever you're having."

"Water and coffee. Go ahead and take a seat." While Chava prepared the drinks, she spoke over her shoulder to Ichiko. "Are you enjoying being out and about on this world?"

"I'm not sure 'enjoying' is the right word."

"Let me guess. The bio-shield?"

"You got it. The worst part of the job is having to move around in a little bubble of fake Earth while all around me there's this new alien world, with people like us walking around entirely unencumbered. I can't smell the sea or feel the wind or touch anyone or eat or drink anything. It's . . . well, it's frustrating. It's not much better than just sending out a camera-bot and watching on a screen."

"But it's necessary," Chava said. "And you know that probably better than I do." She came to the table and set a mug of steaming coffee and a tumbler of ice water in front of Ichiko, then did the same for herself. She lifted the covering from the plate and sniffed. "Ah, the lovely fragrance of ship food. Not being able to smell *that* might be a blessing."

Ichiko chuckled at that. She lifted her own plate covering— the odor was familiar, much like every meal she'd eaten over the last five years of the voyage here. She remembered telling Saoirse about the smell of dashi back in Japan; this smelled nowhere near as appetizing. "You may be right."

"Just wait until you taste it and you'll know I am," Chava added. "I understand you met one of the Inish today."

<Evidently, like radio, gossip moves at the speed of light,> AMI commented in Ichiko's head. <Or perhaps even uses a Fold Drive.>

"Chikushō," Ichiko muttered.

"Excuse me?"

Ichiko lifted up her hand, showing Chava the glowing tip of her ring finger. "My AMI keeps activating itself on its own. It's really annoying." She pressed the finger hard with her thumb; the light went off. "Sorry. How did you know I met an Inish?"

"Minister Plunkett called me earlier," Chava answered. "He wanted to know why you were spending so much time with 'that feckin' nasty Inish girl.'" Chava's imitation of Plunkett's accent made Ichiko grin. "Those were the actual words he used, so he obviously wasn't happy about your choice of companion. Nothing we do goes unnoticed here, if you didn't already realize that." She lifted a fork laden with unidentifiable green-and-white chunks and put it in her mouth. "Hmm . . . . Needs more soy—would you pass it to me?"

Ichiko handed the bottle to Chava. "Why would Minister Plunkett care that I was talking to one of the Inish?"

"Oh, I think he's just afraid we're going to give them more attention than the Mainlander clans. He was really pleased when the medical staff up on the ship sent back the two Inish because they had that terrible fungus in their skin." Chava closed her eyes momentarily and again did a recognizable imitation of Plunkett's voice. "'If yeh were wantin' t'give our world an enema, that's where yeh'd be stickin' in the feckin' tube.'" Chava grinned. "Who knows, he might even be right. Did you know we've lost three drones out in the archipelago?" She sprinkled brown sauce over her plate before glancing at Ichiko's face. "You didn't? Then maybe I shouldn't have told you. Tell your commander you heard a rumor about that, then see what he says. Makes you wonder if the Mainlanders don't have it right about the archipelago being a strange and dangerous place." Chava pointed with her fork at Ichiko's plate. "You really should eat that while it's still hot. You don't want to try it lukewarm; I think that's even worse than cold."

Ichiko took a bite, mostly to think about what she wanted to ask. It tasted like ship food, but it did start to take the edge off her hunger. She took another bite and swallowed it before she spoke.

"Are you saying that the Inish took out the drones? I know they're suspicious of us, and they don't seem to like people prying into their lives. Still—" Ichiko would have said more, but Chava was shaking her head.

"It wasn't the Inish that did it, from what I heard," she said. "Something else. Something stranger."

<Before you ask me, no, I don't have access to the drone footage,> AMI whispered. *<Your clearance level isn't high enough.>*

"What 'something else'?" Ichiko asked Chava.

"That's for the commander to tell you—or not. Officially, I don't know any more than what I've already told you, and I probably shouldn't have told you this much. So fill me in about these Inishers you met," Chava said. "I'm curious—and I'm sure your commander will be, too, so you can practice what you want to tell him on me . . ."

They'd left behind the last and largest of the Stepstones and turned toward Great Inish, passing the long beach at the foot of Great Inish called the White Strand and sailing into the narrow, sheltered cleft that led to Great Inish's only quay. Despite the lateness of the cycle, Saoirse could see people gathered at the cliff face above them and at the top of the steep path up to the village. Already several of the younger ones were running down to meet them at the quay. "Mail's here!" they shouted as they ran. "The Rí's back. Candy!"

"Are yeh sure yeh'd really want to leave this?" Saoirse heard her uncle ask as she loosed the halyard line and dropped the sail, letting Liam row the currach to the stone jetty that waited for them. There were several other currachs already tied up there, the Inishers knowing that a storm was coming in. "It's a sad thing already, the way Inish young men and even women are moving to the mainland and taking up residence with other clans. Now, if the Terrans let us go back to Earth, the drain on the clans is only going to get worse." Angus spit over the side of the boat. "Would yeh really want to go back there with the Terrans, Saoirse? Is spending yer life here that awful?"

Aye, 'tis. "No, Uncle, it's not awful. It's just . . ." She shook her head. He wouldn't understand; he didn't *want* to understand. She'd tried to explain her feelings a hundred times already and failed: with Angus, with her mam, with others on the island.

Angus sighed. Reaching down, he heaved the coiled bowline onto the jetty, where one of the youngsters caught it and pulled them in as Liam shipped the oars.

"Ah, my dear niece, yeh don't have to answer," Angus said. "I know. I know." Saoirse sniffed. *But yeh don't know. Yer just saying that.* As the bowline was tied around one of the rocks, Angus continued. "I worry about our future here. There are already too many temptations for the young ones, and the Terrans are adding the largest one yet. I may end up being the last Rí and yer mam the last Banríon of the archipelago. That would be a true shame. And who'd look after the arracht?"

"The arracht can look after themselves," Saoirse retorted. "The way they always did before we came here."

Shaking his head, Angus stepped out of the boat and onto the quay with his mailbag draped over one shoulder; now that they were out of the salt spray, Saoirse slipped on her glasses to see better. Everyone crowded around the Rí, with calls of "Mail for me?" from the adults and "Candy?" from the youngest—the Rí always brought candies as well as mail back from the mainland.

"Back up an' give me a chance, now," he said to the hands plucking at him and those calling his name and asking if there was a letter or candy for them. "When we get to the top, I'll hand out the mail. And aye, I have candy as well. There's stuff enough to carry up and distribute before the storm gets here—Liam, open up the locker and hand out what's there . . ."

The chattering, noisy throng set out—aunts and uncles, cousins, and siblings from both Clan Mullin and Clan Craig, among them Saoirse's younger sister Gráinne (the right side of her face liberally marked with plotch). They walked up the rutted dirt path to the top of the hill where the village and the clan compounds were set, overlooking the white-capped expanse of sea between Great Inish and the mainland. On the grassy sward at the top, the Rí finally stopped, sitting on a mossy boulder. He set the mailbag between his knees, first pulling out small paper bags of hard candy and tossing them out as the children squealed and started running after the packets, while Angus started distributing letters and other missives, calling out the name of the person to whom each was addressed.

Saoirse had carried up the cloth her mam had asked for. She called Gráinne over (a packet of candy clutched in one hand), handed her one of the bolts, and together they left the Rí and Liam in the middle of the crowd, moving past them up the lane toward the Clan Mullin compound.

The compound was a cluster of a few dozen buildings gathered like thatch-capped mushrooms on a large, rocky knoll with narrow lanes winding between them. A drystone wall as high as a person had been erected around the base of the knoll, though over the long years stones had fallen from the wall in several places and never been replaced. The iron gate set in the wall was, as always, wide open, the hinges so rusted that Saoirse doubted it even *could* close—Clan Mullin and Clan Craig had no quarrels with each other, unlike some of the clans, and it was unlikely that any of the mainland clans would ever care to attack the compounds. That time was, thankfully, long past.

The Banríon's house was near the summit of the knoll, one of the largest of the buildings; Saoirse and Gráinne made the long trek along the main lane winding up the rocky hill. Six-legged milch-goats looked up from chewing contentedly on the sparse grass of the hill to watch them pass. Saoirse still lived with her mother Iona, Liam, and a smattering of uncles, aunts, and those aunts' children in the Banríon's house, which also served as Banríon Iona's unofficial "office." The top half of the main door, as usual, was open. Gráinne had run ahead, calling for their mam as she pushed open the bottom half of the door. Saoirse could hear her still calling as she vanished into the cool darkness beyond. Saoirse followed her. "We're back from Dulcia, Mam," she shouted. "I have yer cloth from the weavers."

An older woman, plump and gray-haired, appeared from the twilight at the back of the room where a peat fire sputtered blue flames in the hearth. The left side of Iona's face was marked with a large, irregular splash of plotch, much like that of her daughter Gráinne. She smiled at Saoirse as Gráinne ran up to her, stooping down to take the bolt of cloth from her. She tousled Gráinne's hair. "Glad you're back. It's goin' to storm soon, and I was afraid yeh all might get caught out in it." She paused as she stood again, cocking her head. "Though I was hoping that perhaps yeh might be staying a bit longer."

"Mam . . ." Saoirse sighed. "That's not why I went to Dulcia." *I wanted to meet the Terran, and I did. I really want to go to Earth, Mam. I want that so much more than giving yeh grandchildren.* But she hid those thoughts behind a scowl.

"Perhaps it should be. Yer not getting any younger, and I'd love to see a grand or three before it's Gráinne's time." She unrolled a bit of the cloth and rubbed it between her fingers. "This feels very nice; it'll make some fine clothes. Gráinne, why don't yeh take the rest of the cloth from your sister and put it in the big chest in the sewing room." As Gráinne took the folded wool and went half-running into the rooms beyond, Iona rubbed her hands on her skirt. "Did you see yer Terran, at least?" she asked Saoirse.

"Aye, I did," Saoirse replied, her voice brightening despite her annoyance. "I had the chance to talk with her for a long time. She's so strange and very different, but I like her, Mam. She's not much older than me, and she's so terribly thin, like they say most of the Terrans are, but she's seen so much more than I have. She's interested in the Inish, too, and she wanted to follow us out to the archipelago. Uncle Angus told her neh, that first we'd have to ask yeh for permission."

"And how would yeh advise me to answer?"

Saoirse tried to read her mam's face but wasn't certain what she saw there. "She truly wanted to follow us. I think Uncle Angus made the right choice telling her neh for now, since probably the arracht would be frightened by that flitter of hers. I could bring her out in a currach if she's willing, though." That put an image in Saoirse's head of a frightened Ichiko desperately hanging onto the sides of the boat in a heaving sea. She grinned at the thought, though she wasn't sure that Ichiko would agree to that condition at all.

Iona nodded. "Bringing her out that way would be better, I agree. Yeh know how the arracht can be. Still . . . let me think about this and talk to Angus meself. Yeh may like this woman—and I do trust yer instincts, my dear one—but I'm not sure we can entirely trust the Terrans. Where is Angus? Still dealing with the mail and the children?"

"Last I saw, aye. He said to tell yeh that he has two letters for yeh: one from Minister Plunkett and another from Captain Keshmiri of the *Odysseus*. Oh, and one from Uncle Martin with Clan Lewis, too, so it's three letters, I suppose. Uncle Angus and Liam have other supplies that need to be distributed as well—stuff from the ironworks, some assorted material for repairs and the like, and the meat I ordered for yeh from Clan Hearn. I imagine Liam will be bringing the meat packets up soon, if Uncle Patrick hasn't already had someone else fetch them."

"Good. I think we're all a little tired of bluefin and tubers," her mam said. She hugged Saoirse. "Thanks for bringing the wool. I hope Aoife Bancroft didn't give yeh any trouble over it."

"No more than I expected," Saoirse told her. "But she said to tell yeh, next time, she intends to have a written agreement."

"Aoife can say whatever she wants, but she's the one who

doesn't like putting anything in writing. That way she can always claim that the other person is wrong. Besides, from now on it's yeh who'll be doin' the bargaining with her, so yeh can put it in writing for her yerself." Iona laughed and took Saoirse's hand. "Come on, yeh can help me get the meeting room ready until Angus brings me the letters—the island council's meeting is tomorrow at Low Third. And while we're working on that, yeh can tell me why yeh didn't find some nice young man in Dulcia. Or did yeh go off lookin' for one of yer women friends instead?"

Saoirse pulled her hand away, planting her feet. "Mam, that's my business, not yers. Sorry."

Iona laughed again. "Well, the meeting room still has to be set up, whether we talk about yer lack of a sex life or not. So come on with yeh . . ."

Luciano looked tired and more than a little irritable when he finally called. While the background showed his quarters, he was still in uniform even though the clock next to her bed said that it was 02:40, ship-time. "Captain's put you on night shift?" Ichiko commented, rubbing her eyes—she'd been asleep when he called. "What'd you do to piss her off?"

"Nothing. It was just an overlong briefing for the senior officers."

"Oh. Something going on?"

"Nothing you need to know about yet." The set of his mouth told her that it would be useless to ask anything more; he'd said all that he was going to say on the subject. "I hear you met some of the Inish earlier."

"You and everyone else on-world and off- seems to have heard that." Ichiko shook her head at Luciano's suddenly raised eyebrows. "Never mind. I suppose I should be flattered that you're keeping tabs on me. Yes, I met Saoirse Mullin, the daughter of Banríon Iona Mullin, and she introduced me to Rí Angus Mullin, along with the Banríon's son Liam. Saoirse's delightful, by the way, and very interested in Earth. She's going to ask the Banríon if I can go out to the archipelago and study their society there."

She saw Luciano's face fold into a frown. "I'm not so sure that would be a good idea. Why not finish your work in Dulcia first? Then you can worry about going out there."

"What aren't you telling me, Luciano?"

"I'm just saying that the archipelago should wait a bit. Captain Keshmiri has sent a letter to the Banríon suggesting she come to First Base so we can conference with her. If I could tell you more than that, I would."

Does this have something to do with the lost drones? she wanted to ask but bit back the question, worried that asking might get Chava into trouble for having mentioned them to her. "That means there *is* something more," she said instead.

"I'm not saying there is or there isn't," Luciano said. "I'm just advising you to hold off on visiting the archipelago. If the Inish come to you, it's one thing, but I have to ask you not to go there yet."

"Ask me or order me? I don't report to you, remember. Or are you saying that Nagasi would give me the same restrictions?"

Luciano shook his head. "I shouldn't *need* to make it an order. Ichiko, I'm sorry. I don't want to argue with you. I'm just . . . tired, and I'm sure you are, too. Can we table this until later when we're both less exhausted? I do want to hear about this Saoirse Mullin and how you felt about the Inish after meeting them. Have you written up your report?"

"I have and AMI uploaded it. At least I hope so."

"You hope so?"

"I've been having a bit of trouble with my AMI since I've been down here. But I'm sure the report's been uploaded."

"Then I'll listen to it as soon as I can. As for now, I'm on duty in five hours and I can see you were already sleeping. My AMI gave me your message, so I wanted to make sure I got back to you."

Ichiko felt her irritation start to dissolve. She took in a long, calming breath and let it out slowly. "I appreciate that. Go to bed, Luciano. We'll talk more later." *I could tell him that I'd like to be there with him. I could tell him that I miss him.* Instead, she gave him a forced smile.

She wondered if he ever had the same thoughts. "I'll do that. And you can go back to sleep yourself. Later, then. AMI, log me off."

The window displaying Luciano winked out. She sat there staring at where he'd been for long moments before she stirred.

Legends And Routines

THE STORM ARRIVED JUST before Low Fifth bell, a strong one but hardly the worst Saoirse could remember. Still, she was thankful that Uncle Angus had insisted on returning. Otherwise, they would have been forced to wait out the storm in Dulcia, or—far more dire a possibility—their currach might have been caught out in winds shrieking like banshees, blowing blinding rain that pelted down as hard as thrown pebbles, with the likelihood of the currach being swamped and themselves drowning in a wild, cold sea. That was a fate that had taken many of the Inish over the centuries, and Saoirse was thankful for her Uncle Angus' weather craft in timing the arrival of the storm.

The islanders had spent a few bells herding the sheepers and milch-goats into the barns for the duration—at least those that they could easily find, since they ranged freely on Great Inish— as the sky grew darker and searing, jagged lightnings strode across the water toward them. The furious gale howled as it tore through the black-rock crags of the island, churning the sea below into white, curling slopes of water that hurled themselves at the island to shatter into froth and foam on the implacable cliffs. Wind-tossed spray reached all the way up to the village. The rain was coming in sideways, so that Saoirse and everyone else in the compound had to close the window shutters against the tempest. Occasionally, they could hear the *splat* of some unfortunate wind-spider striking the shutters or the walls of the houses.

There were a few drips through the thatched roofs of the compound, especially those that were older and already in need of repair and replacement. Even in the Banríon's house, there were pots and pans scattered along the floor that had to be periodically emptied. The white-crested chachalahs roosting deep in the thatch trilled their complaints about the weather—though Saoirse memorized the locations of the protests so she could set Gráinne and some of the other young cousins to gathering the eggs laid in their nests after the storm passed.

In the meantime, most of the clanfolk in the Banríon's house gathered around the hearth in the large front room. A peat fire was blazing against the chill of the storm coming out of *dorcha*— the cold spaceward side of Canis Lupus' habitable strip—the winds affecting the chimney's draw so that aromatic smoke sometimes came wafting back into the room—not that it mattered, since most of the adult men and women were smoking pipes stuffed with calming tree strands and the air in the room was hazy with their own fragrant smoke. A jug of local poitín sat open on the table. Saoirse sipped at the liquor in her pottery cup as she listened to the talk around the room.

"This reminds me of stories about the storm that Seann Martin was once in, back when Clan Mullin had first come to the archipelago," said her Uncle James, who was now a *seann* himself, a member of the eldest living generation of the clan. He took a long pull on his pipe and released the smoke, watching it curl away from his lips. "Seann Martin was out fishing with First Rí Liam that day—this must have been, oh, almost four and a half millennia ago now. Nephew Liam, yeh were named for our First Rí, as yer mam has undoubtedly told yeh. Ah, by all the tales about him, he was a fine man, was Rí Liam . . ."

"Yeh tell us this same story every time we get a storm, Seann James," Gráinne said. A wave of "Shh"s and "Hush, child" followed from the various aunts and uncles, and the Banríon shook her head warningly at her youngest daughter. "Well, he does,"

Gráinne said poutingly but then subsided, putting her hands in her lap and pressing her lips together.

Unflustered, James took another reflective pull on the pipe, then pointed the stem at Gráinne as he exhaled. "It's the prerogative of the old to pass on the stories they know and the duty of the young to listen so they remember them and pass them on themselves when their elders have gone to their final sleep," he said. "Now, as I was saying, Seann Martin was out fishing with the Rí and a few other uncles when this storm swept in all unexpected. Musha! I tell yeh it was bad enough here on Great Inish, the wind tearing away the thatch from the roofs that our ancestors had first built and the waves ripping huge boulders from the cliffs. Those on the island looked out over the sea thinking that the waves were as high as we are here in the compound, with the gusts ripping off the foaming tops and hurling them at the island. The lane down to the Strand had turned into a gushing, fast-flowing river." Seann James stopped to set his pipe down and take a sip of poitín.

"And everyone was convinced that Seann Martin and the Rí were surely lost out on the sea," Gráinne said, in a droll imitation of James' quavering voice.

"Gráinne," Saoirse said warningly though there were chuckles from the audience. Saoirse couldn't blame them; the lines of Seann James' story were well-worn into everyone's memories.

"They all thought that, aye," James continued, unperturbed, "though none of them were about to speak it aloud, for fear some malevolent *spiorad beag,* overhearing them, would decide to make it come true. Yeh can't be too careful with the spirit people, after all. But all the clan was praying silently for them." He picked up his pipe again, tamping the tree strands in the bowl with a yellow callused fingertip, uncaring of the glowing embers. His arms and neck were liberally marked with the plotch, even down to his fingertips. Even more than the pipe smoke, Seann James smelled of the herbs and potions that—as the herbalist and healer for Clan Mullin—he and his assistants prepared in his laboratory higher up the slope. "They didn't know it, but the storm had driven Seann Martin's currach toward the Sleeping Wolf and the rocks around it. The Rí couldn't control the boat: the sail was nothing but tattered rags, the centerboard had been lost, and though everyone was rowing as best they could, the sea was far too strong for 'em. The currach was taking in seawater over the gunwales from the waves as well as from the pouring rain. They were already half-swamped, and they had lost all hope of making Great Inish even if they could have seen the island through the weather, which they couldn't."

As if on cue, the wind picked up momentarily, rattling the shutters and causing the fire in the hearth to shudder. "Yeh see, Gráinne," Saoirse said, "the Spiorad Mòr must be listening to the Seann's story, too."

Gráinne's eyes went wide as their mam laughed. "G'wan, finish yer tale now, Seann," Banríon Iona said, putting her pipe back in her mouth.

James took a bit of straw from the hearth, lit it from the fire, and put it to his pipe. He released another cloud of blue smoke. "Well, Seann Martin, Rí Liam, and all the others in the currach believed they were about to die when they saw the jagged black teeth of the rocks before them. They could also see the writhing forms of a pod of nasty blood feeders breaking the surface around them, lurking and waiting, ready to rip apart and devour any of our people who went into the water."

Saoirse saw Gráinne's eyes widen even further at that as Seann James' lips drew back and he made gnashing motions with his gap-toothed mouth before putting his pipe stem back in his mouth.

"But the arracht had heard their wails and seen their plight," he continued. "They swam out from their caves beneath the Sleeping Wolf into the full fury of the storm. They attacked the blood feeders with lightnings arcing from their own bodies until it looked like a second storm had erupted just below the waves, killing several of the blood feeders outright and driving off the others. Now the Seann and the Rí saw the arracht's tentacled arms rising from the waves around them and thought that an entirely new and awful fate awaited them, since so many fishing boats from the mainland had been lost out here and some that had returned had spoken of monsters that had somehow stopped their motors, nearly wrecked their boats, and almost dragged them down. Clan Mullin and Clan Craig were no different and no better than the Mainlanders at that time; they'd slain the first arracht they'd seen when they came to the islands, thinking them monsters as dangerous as the blood feeders themselves and worth killing for the meat and the oil they could take from their bodies. So everyone was screaming and wailing from the doomed currach as the arracht grabbed them with their tentacles and pulled them down into the sea where they all believed they would surely be drowned."

"But they didn't drown," Liam said in a hushed voice.

Seann James nodded slowly, puffing on his pipe to keep it lit. "Neh, they didn't," he said. "The arracht brought them into their caves within the Sleeping Wolf, tossing them—coughing and throwing up the salt water—onto the dry ledges there. They could hear the storm raging outside through the cavern tunnels that led up to the surface of the island. They could see the cave also, for there were glowing algae living on the cave walls, and there were the arracht staring at them from the water with their eyestalks and helmeted heads. No one realized it then, but Seann Martin, Rí Liam, and the others had been given the plotch through their contact with the arracht. This was the beginning of the close relationship between the arracht and we Inish. The survivors climbed out from the caves the next day and were found by boats from Great Inish. They told them what had happened and how they'd been saved. In gratitude to the arracht, we swore never to hunt them again and never to allow the Mainlanders to do so, either. Ever since then, the arracht and the Inish have lived together in harmony."

Around the room, people were nodding their heads at the end of the story. Rí Angus lifted his cup. "To the arracht and the Inish," he said. "We are always and forever friends."

"Always and forever friends." Angus' toast was echoed around the room, all of them emptying their own cups, Saoirse—belatedly— among them.

Outside, the wind continued to howl its mournful song.

In the common room, Ichiko could hear the rain hissing against the windows of First Base. The storm had been blowing for two full days now. Sitting at a table near the wall with a cup of tea and a warm scone both steaming in front her, Ichiko put her hand on the outside wall and felt it shivering from the wind gusts. "I wouldn't worry too much," she heard Chava say behind her. "First Base has been sitting here for centuries now, and it hasn't blown away yet."

Ichiko smiled over her shoulder to the lieutenant, who was holding a tray with a mug of coffee and two doughnuts. "Have a seat," Ichiko told her, gesturing to the empty chair across from her. "You're right, but my AMI is telling me winds are gusting to over 100 kph at Dulcia and even higher over the Storm Sea—that's hurricane strength." Ichiko glanced down at her finger. No matter how hard she pressed, the contact remained active and glowing. She was almost used to it now.

Chava put her tray on the table and scooted her chair forward. "Sure, it's a nasty storm. I'd also tell you that, according to the weather instruments that were still recording when we got here, this is also just your basic run-of-the-mill big storm for the planet, since there's a lot of potential energy between starward and space-ward side of the planet for the weather systems to use. I wouldn't worry about your friends out there; the Canines are used to this." She picked up one of the doughnuts and took a bite.

"I wish you wouldn't use that word, Chava," Ichiko said, the words tumbling out before she could stop them.

"Canines?" Chava shrugged. She put the doughnut down again. "Fine. I'll watch what I say since you and I are friends and I know it bothers you, and anyway the brass up in orbit don't like it. But it's not like there are any *Lupusians*"—she lifted her hands to put air quotes around the word—"here to be offended. Pretty much everyone on First Base uses the C-word when they talk about the locals. Are you going to try to correct everyone? Because that's a hopeless task, and you're just going to piss people off."

Ichiko could feel heat rising in her cheeks. She looked at the scone on its plate before her. "No. It's just . . ."

"Hey, it's nothing at all," Chava told her. She patted Ichiko's hand. "Just understand that First Base isn't *Odysseus*. And neither is anything the Cani . . ." She smiled apologetically. ". . . the Lupusians have made of this strange place. Did you get to talk to the commander the other day?"

Ichiko nodded. "For a few minutes. We were both tired."

Chava picked up the doughnut, dipped the end in her coffee, and took another bite. "So I've never asked you, and I know it's really none of my business, but how did you and Commander Mercado manage to . . . ?" She left the last half of the question unspoken.

"I'm not really sure myself," Ichiko answered. "Lieutenant Commander Tinubu—Nagasi—is in charge of my section; he and Commander Mercado are good friends and Nagasi asked me to give a report to the commander, which I did. The commander and I just started talking afterward about nothing at all in particular, and . . ." Ichiko lifted a shoulder. "There's a saying in Japanese: *sunzen wa yami*—the world is dark in front of you. In other words, who can see the future? What about you? So after Geoff, have you . . . ?"

"I've had a few lovers on our trip. I'm an officer, so my options are limited at best, especially since I've been assigned to First Base. The regs forbid me doing anything with anyone below officer rank, there aren't any civilian staff here other than you, and there are only a few other officers. And I really only like sleeping with guys, so . . ." She shrugged. "But there's been nothing serious or long-term—just enough to occasionally take off the edge, if you know what I mean. For that matter, there's not that large a pool on *Odysseus* either, no matter what your preference might be, and the locals are completely out of the running. Consider yourself lucky you've found someone."

Ichiko didn't respond beyond a tight smile, and she covered even that by taking a sip of her tea. In her head, AMI remained judiciously silent. Chava cocked her head as she sipped her coffee, as if listening to something Ichiko couldn't hear.

"Ah! Listen, are you thinking of heading back down to Dulcia today? My AMI tells me the storm should be starting to subside in another ship-hour or so." <*That's correct,*> Ichiko's AMI added. <*The wind speed's dropping quickly, and barometer readings are rising though it's still raining hard.*> "I could help you get your flitter prepped. I might even go along with you, and you could show me Dulcia—that is, if you're willing."

"You've never been there?"

Chava shook her head. "Not really. I went there once for a couple hours when I was first given this post to meet with Minister Plunkett. Since then, the most contact I've had with Dulcia is talking to Plunkett over vid. I'm very familiar with the back wall of his office but not much else. Otherwise, I've been too busy here, but I'm off duty until 06:30 tomorrow. I wouldn't mind the chance for a change of scenery and to use my bio-shield for more than outside maintenance. Unless you prefer not having company while you're working . . ."

"No," Ichiko said. "I'd like that. It'd be good to be able to get someone else's take on things. We all bring our biases to this kind of work, and I'm no different." Ichiko smiled at Chava. "Let's finish here, then we'll get the flitter ready—and hopefully the weather will have gentled enough by then."

The storm had left behind damage throughout the village. Everyone was out repairing roofs, shutters, and fences, finding belongings scattered by the wind, or looking for sheepers and milch-goats that hadn't been gathered in before the storm. One of the house roofs in Clan Craig's compound had blown completely off, and several of the uncles and aunts of both clans were there putting up a new one. Two of the currachs had snapped their moorings and broken their anchor chains, allowing them to be taken out to sea by the swirling currents; several of the young cousins had bailed out three of the remaining ones and taken them solas— sunward—in hopes of finding the drifting boats intact, while Rí Angus and Liam had gone to the Sleeping Wolf to talk to the arracht. The sea, in the wake of the storm, was glass-smooth, a rarity, and there were great rents in the clouds overhead that allowed glimpses of the sun huddling eternally near the horizon.

Saoirse was helping the young ones climb up among the roof beams to find the chachalah nests deep in the thatching and gather their eggs. She had commandeered a quartet of stepladders to help in the process; they already had a bowlful of the orange-and-blue-speckled shells on the main table. Saoirse heard Uncle Angus talking to her mam outside, then the Rí opened the door and stepped into the room as she was helping Gráinne down from the ladder with two eggs gathered in her skirt. He was wreathed in a trailing cloud of pipe smoke. "Hey, Uncle Angus. I heard yeh and Liam had gone over to the Sleeping Wolf. How'd the arracht manage in the storm?"

"They were largely unbothered, as usual. They also rescued one of our lost currachs," he answered, speaking around the pipe stem still clenched in his mouth and rubbing the plotch on his arms, "and they told us the other was tossed high on the rocks on the dorcha side of High Inish; I'm sure yer cousins will find the wreckage and determine whether it's repairable. But I was wondering if yeh wanted to come with us to Dulcia."

Saoirse felt a burst of excitement at the prospect. *I might see Ichiko again, and I can tell her what Mam said . . .* "Yer going over to Dulcia again? So soon?"

"We need to get more supplies to deal with storm repair, and the arracht have let me know the bluefins will be shoaling today out by the Stepstones. We'll fish a bit first, then hopefully get a decent price for the bluefins from Fitzpatrick's to pay for the supplies we'll need. Only if yeh want to come, that is." He looked at the other stepladders in the room and the young ones still prowling through the thatch.

"I want to come, too," Gráinne interjected. "I can help with the nets." Saoirse glanced at Angus, who shrugged. Saoirse took the eggs from Gráinne's skirt and put them in the bowl. "Yeh go and ask Mam, then," she said. Then, to Angus, as Gráinne ran outside to find the Banríon: "Let me get the little ones down and settled, and I'll meet yeh and Liam at the quay." She went to the nearest ladder, calling up to the child there to start climbing down, when she saw that Angus hadn't moved, still smoking his pipe. "What?" Saoirse asked him.

"There was one other thing the arracht said to me," Angus told her. "It was very simple: 'They shouldn't know about us.' I think we both can guess who 'they' are."

Saoirse sniffed at that. "Uncle, if 'they' want to come out here, we can't stop them. That's not possible—and yeh know it."

Angus took the pipe from his mouth, looking at the bowl reflectively. "Nah, we likely can't. But we can be careful about what we share with them when they ask about the arracht." Saoirse heard the warning in his voice—which meant that her mam had evidently told Angus that she'd agreed to let Ichiko come to Great Inish.

Saoirse managed to hide the smile that threatened. "In that case, isn't it better if just one of them comes here, on our terms and not theirs?"

"Mebbe," Angus grunted. He put the pipe stem back in his mouth. "I hope so, anyway."

To Have Met With Such Bodes Little Good

THE STORM MAY HAVE BEEN "run-of-the-mill" for Canis Lupus—to use Chava's words—but Ichiko could see immediately that it had done a fair amount of damage in Dulcia, nonetheless. There was activity everywhere in the town, with people up on ladders and out on the streets repairing houses and stores, the quay littered with tackle, buoys, and nets tossed up from the bay, and a fishing boat deposited halfway up the flank of Dulcia Head with a massive hole in its side.

The sight of the damage was a contrast to the quiet natural tranquility in the wake of the storm. The clouds above were fluffy and sparse, reddish sunlight flooding in from just above the solas horizon, and the bay itself resembled a mirror with only the slightest swell, as if the sea itself was quietly and calmly meditating after the tumult.

Minister Plunkett met their flitter at the quay. The man seemed out of breath and exhausted, with dark circles under his eyes. "Ah, Ichiko. And is that Lieutenant Bishara with yeh? It's good to meet yeh face-to-face again, even if Dulcia isn't in perfect shape for yer visit, as I'd like. How did First Base fare up there in the mountains?"

"First Base is just fine," Chava answered. "We lost a few antennae that we've already replaced or repaired. But our work in renovating First Base has paid off. It would take a much stronger storm than this one to seriously worry us at this point."

Though Plunkett nodded, Ichiko saw a quick frown pass over the man's red-flushed face at the underlying implication that Terran technology was far superior to that of the Lupusians. Ichiko grimaced at the tone-deaf lack of diplomacy in Chava's remark and hurried into the conversation. "We know how resilient and tough your people are, Minister," she said. "I wanted Lieutenant Bishara to witness how quickly and effectively Dulcia responds to adversity, so she can relay that in her report. Would you mind if we walked around and talked to some of the people here, so Lieutenant Bishara can hear from their own mouths how proud they are of what Clan Plunkett and the other clans are accomplishing here in the wake of this storm?"

The frown morphed into a careful, political smile. "Why, certainly," Plunkett said. He swept his cap from his head and ran a hand through his sweat-darkened gray hair. "I'd go with yeh, but . . ."

"I completely understand, Minister," Ichiko told him. "And I wish you could accompany us, but it's more important that you're here to supervise and manage repairs. We'll make do without you."

<*I see your own diplomatic training has paid off,*> her AMI commented.

Ichiko ignored that. "By the way, Minister, have you heard from the archipelago as to how they fared?"

The Minister's smile faded as he tugged his cap back on. "Those Inishers don't have enough infrastructure to worry about," he said. "They probably huddled in caves on Great Inish during the storm. We have enough to worry about here without concerning ourselves with the problems of the archipelago."

<*Orbital visuals from* Odysseus *show the Great Inish clan compounds sustained fairly minimal damage,*> AMI said. <*I'll send them to the flitter if you want to review them.*>

<*That's not necessary,*> Ichiko thought to AMI, then nodded to Plunkett. "I understand, Minister. I was just curious since I met Rí Mullin and his niece and nephew the last time I was here. I'm sure they've managed as well as they can. And since I know you've a lot of work to do here, the lieutenant and I won't keep you. If you need anything from us, let me know and I'll pass that on to *Odysseus*. We'd be happy to help and very likely have some supplies we can offer you."

Plunkett grunted. "I appreciate that," he said. "And we'll let yeh know if we need anything. Lieutenant Bishara, I hope yeh enjoy yer visit, even if the town looks a bit like a blind cobbler's thumb after this storm . . ."

"We'd be happy to help?" Chava asked Ichiko as they walked down the quay away from the minister. "Are you sure?"

"No," Ichiko answered honestly. "But I'd think we'd *want* to help, if only for appearance's sake."

"Then if they ask for repair supplies from First Base, I'm expecting you to make a personal plea to the commander for me," Chava said, "no matter what you have to promise him in order to get it. I'm sure you have some compelling inducements to offer."

She grinned as she said it.

In the inside pocket of Saoirse's oilcloth jacket was a letter her mam had handed her before they left. "If yeh happen to see that Terran yeh talked to, yeh can give her this letter to pass on to the captain of their ship. If not, give it to Minister Plunkett and he can do the same." She'd smiled then. "And if yeh want to invite yer Terran to Great Inish, if she'll come alone and in the Rí's currach, then aye, yeh can bring her out here."

Saoirse felt in her coat for the reassuring lump of the letter as they sailed out past the White Strand and into the open sea, with the mainland a humped gray-blue line on the horizon.

The arracht had been right about the bluefins, but then they were invariably right in matters of sea life and fishing. Their boat, and two others that the Rí had told to follow them (one from Clan Mullin and one from Clan Craig), were sitting low in the water from the weight of the fish they'd caught near the Stepstones. The Rí sent the other boats back to Great Inish, where the bluefins would be distributed among the clan families, the bulk of the catch to be salted and stored for later consumption. The Rí had Saoirse raise the sail; they tacked against the wind toward Dulcia, where the Pale Woman pointed to the entrance of the harbor from Dulcia Head. With a calm sea and little spray, Saoirse could keep her spectacles on.

This was Gráinne's first trip where actual fishing was part of the experience. Saoirse needed to remind her more than once that getting slimy and dirty from handling the nets and the bluefins was to be expected, and that the briny smell of them was also an inevitable consequence. "But I'm sure that Uncle Angus will give yeh a few shillings once we sell the bluefins, and yeh can buy whatever yeh want with it. There's a little candy shop up on the High Road, and Murphy's Bakery has some delicious sweetbuns."

Gráinne had managed a smile at that thought. Then Saoirse had her assist with the sail, demonstrating how they had to swing the boom to keep the wind, as otherwise Uncle Angus and Liam would have to row them across to Dulcia. "We want to keep their arms strong for when we need them."

As usual, the wind died as they passed Dulcia Head and entered the protected bay. Saoirse noted Ichiko's flitter parked down near Plunkett's Pub but said nothing, though she was certain that Uncle Angus saw it as well. She showed Gráinne how to furl and lash the sail as Angus and Liam took to the oars to bring them in to the quay near Fitzpatrick's. Saoirse jumped out of the currach as they reached the dock, helped Gráinne out, and the two wrapped the bowline around the nearest cleat.

Their arrival had been noticed, as Johnny came out from Fitzpatrick's with his cart. "Didn't expect to see yeh so soon after the storm, Rí. The bluefins still running?"

"They are and we have a fine, fat catch of 'em for yeh," Angus told him. "How'd the town fare?"

Johnny shrugged. "We have several houses and stores damaged. Mam's business took some water in from the bay at the height and we lost some product as a result, but nothing too awful. Yeh might have seen the wreckage of one of Clan Delaney's motorboats over on Dulcia Head. From what I hear from the other clans, it's about the same everywhere up and down the coast—lots of wind damage in the towns. How was it out on the archipelago?"

"It was true lashing out there, but nothing we couldn't deal with or fix afterward," the Rí answered. "But it's all pure barry on the sea now. Like glass, 'tis."

Johnny nodded. "Aye. All the Dulcia boats went out this morning toward the Usk Horn, hoping for a good catch." He glanced into the boat. "They're not likely to do as well as you've done. That's a fine haul; I'll have to bring out a second cart for them all."

"Let's get started, then. Saoirse, Gráinne, help Johnny. Liam, let's start lightening the boat."

They filled Johnny's cart, then the second. Saoirse listened to Angus haggle with Doireann ("I still haven't sold all the bluefins yeh brought in the other cycle, Angus, so I can't possibly give yeh the same price . . .") and settle on 8p per bluefin. It still came to a hefty pile of coins, and Angus gave a pound coin to Gráinne and two pounds to Saoirse. Angus looked significantly at the flitter sitting on the far end of the quay. "Why don't you show Gráinne where she can spend her money if she wants? Liam and I will get the hardware and lumber that we're needing. We'll meet at Low Ninth at Murphy's before we head back—the weather will stay clear enough. That gives you a few free bells."

"Thanks, Uncle Angus," Saoirse said with a nod. "Gráinne, let's go look at a few of those shops I mentioned . . ."

Ichiko knew from her past experience in Dulcia that it was difficult not to draw attention from the locals. For two Terrans strolling through the town in their bio-shields and pale blue *Odysseus* uniforms, it was simply impossible.

They'd been walking the lanes through the town for a few ship-hours already, stopping occasionally to talk to people. They were followed by a shifting pack of chattering children, while the adults working on the repairs were willing to stop a few minutes and talk even though Ichiko was certain they were being extremely careful about what they said and, afterward, would stare at them until they were out of sight. Ichiko also noted that the young adults pressed into service by their elders were much the same as those on Earth: self-absorbed and pretending they didn't care one way or the other about anything.

"My God, is that *another* pub?" Chava asked as they walked along High Street, the sounds of hammering and sawing loud around them. "How many places to drink does a town this small need? Though if I were living here, I'd probably drink more, too. In fact, I *am* living here at the moment and I *do* drink more, so forget what I just said. It all makes perfect sense. Honestly, I wish we could stop and have something."

"You can have the beer and whiskey. Me, I've always loved seafood and here we are right by the sea," Ichiko told her. "My dream is to someday find out what bluefin tastes like."

"Well, neither the drinks nor the food seem to be killing off the . . ." Her voice trailed off for a moment. ". . . Lupusians," she said with a heavy and obvious emphasis that caused Ichiko to grin. "So how dangerous can the food here be? We should just grab some food from one of these pubs, take it back to First Base, and try it. Deep-fried and battered bluefin with seaflower salad." Chava laughed then. "Just kidding," she said. "You should have seen your face. Hey, I'm not going to risk being stuck here forever. God, what an awful fate that would be."

Ichiko smiled at that, but the effort was half-hearted. *I don't know—a simpler and quieter life doesn't sound so bad . . .* But then she thought of Saoirse and the way the Inish and Mainlanders regarded each other; she wasn't so certain that life here was actually simple at all. They were passing the intersection with Green Street, a steeply inclined lane running between Strand Street by the quay and High Street. Ichiko glanced down toward the bay. She could see one of the Inish boats now docked near the fishmongers; she wondered if Saoirse were here.

<*I've accessed the sensors on the flitter; that appears to be the same currach the Rí used before,*> her AMI said, guessing at Ichiko's interest by what she was looking at or through her thoughts. <*Saoirse was with them. I thought you might like to know.*>

I really need to get that contact fixed. Ichiko sighed, then nodded and pointed toward the intersection. "Let's head down to the quay," she said to Chava. "That's the Rí's boat down there now, so you might be able to meet some of the archipelago people."

Chava shrugged, and they turned down Green, most of the cluster of kids following them. Green Street was dominated on the right side by the Bancroft clan compound and on the left by the Plunkett compound. They walked between high stone walls punctuated with heavy wooden gates shielding the compounds from easy sight, though Minister Plunkett had shown Ichiko his clan's compound on her first visit. She assumed that other compounds were similar: a compact collection of houses and buildings designed for clan business and needs. Ichiko was fairly certain that the bio-shield stopped them from smelling the fruity odor of mashed hops, barley, and boiling wort that must be emanating from the Plunkett compound, though from behind the Bancroft walls they could hear the clacking of wooden machinery carding, gilling, combing, drafting, spinning, and twisting wool into fabric for their shop up on High Street. The Bancrofts, Minister Plunkett had told her, also had farms outside Dulcia where they raised sheepers for their wool.

Ichiko relayed some of this to Chava as they walked. "Minister Plunkett told me that his clan also has farms close by where they plant and harvest the grains for their brewery inside the compound, though they also buy from other local farms," she said. "Supposedly, the smell isn't horrible. He also took me by the Hearn compound, which is further out along the bay. They're the local butchers and renderers. According to the Minister, the stench of that is why they made them build their compound out so far and where the prevailing winds don't generally blow toward Dulcia." Ichiko stopped. "Saoirse!" she called, waving to two figures who had just turned the corner on Strand.

The larger of the two figures waved back. "Musha! Ichiko, I was hoping yeh'd be around so we could talk." They started walking up the street toward Ichiko and Chava. Ichiko could see that the person with Saoirse was a younger girl, dressed much as Saoirse though without glasses.

"Is this . . . ?" Chava asked, and Ichiko nodded.

"Yes. That's Saoirse Mullin. Come on, I'll introduce you."

They moved toward the Inishers. Saoirse had a smile on her face, and as they approached, they could see the Inishers' clothing was stained—from handling bluefins, Ichiko presumed—as Saoirse's clothes had been the last time they'd met. Ichiko also noticed that much of the face of the young girl with Saoirse was marred with patches of marbled green-and-purple plotch. She forced herself not to stare (wondering if Saoirse's body might be similarly marked under her clothing). She knew that Chava must have also seen the blemishes, and certainly the children who still accompanied them had. She heard one of them loudly proclaim, "Ugh! Look, she has the filthy plotch! Quick, let's go before we get it!" The group vanished as if afraid of contamination. The girl scowled at the pack, and Ichiko saw Saoirse's hand tighten on the girl's and give her a slight, warning head shake.

"Saoirse," Ichiko said quickly, "this is my friend, Lieutenant Chava Bishara." At that, Chava's stare was torn away from the girl. Ichiko saw her gaze searching Saoirse's face and arms for the same markings. "The lieutenant's stationed at First Base and wanted to see Dulcia. Chava, this is Saoirse of Clan Mullin, the Banríon's daughter."

"*Dia duit*, Lieutenant," Saoirse answered. "And this is my sister Gráinne—she's just turned 240 this year." <*About 12,*> Ichiko's AMI translated for her. "Since it's such a pleasant cycle, she wanted to come along with us to Dulcia, and Mam agreed." Saoirse smiled and leaned conspiratorially toward Ichiko. "Rí Angus gave her a pound from the bluefins we sold to Fitzpatrick's, and I told her I'd take her to the candy shop up on High Street. Would yeh like to come along?"

Ichiko looked at Chava, who shrugged. "Why not?" Ichiko answered.

As they started back up the street, Chava spoke a single word. "Plotch?"

Ichiko grimaced, but Saoirse only shrugged. "Nearly all the Inish have the plotch fungus on their skin. I do as well, just not where yeh can easily see the markings."

Chava seemed to be listening to the air as well as Saoirse, and Ichiko knew her AMI was talking to her. "Does the fungus really come from touching those arracht creatures?"

"They're not *creatures*—" Gráinne began, but Saoirse interrupted, and the girl fell silent.

"The arracht carry the fungus, too, aye, and we get it when they touch us, but beyond the plotch markings, it ain't harmful. Just gives us a bit of interesting extra color to our skin—though lots of the Mainlanders, like those kids, avoid us because they're afraid they'll get it, too. They can't, of course. Not anymore."

"Not anymore?" Ichiko asked.

Saoirse shook her head. "Not since we stopped the Mainlanders from hunting the arracht, five thousand years or so ago." <*More than two and half centuries . . .* > "Before then, some of 'em had the plotch, too, from handling arracht carcasses. The plotch is no big deal, though. It's not important a'tall."

They'd reached the top of the street, and Ichiko could see the stares from those who were out once again, redoubled this time by the addition of the Inishers to their group. Saoirse, who seemed to be working hard pretending to ignore the attention they were getting, pointed left. "The Stuart's candy shop is just up there. Can yeh see the sign, Gráinne?"

"*I* don't need glasses, Saoirse," Gráinne answered with a haughty emphasis. "*I* can see just fine."

Saoirse laughed at that. "When I was yer age, I didn't need glasses, either, so be careful what yeh brag about. But why don't yeh go on and run ahead, since yeh know where yer going. Just be careful if they're working there, fixing storm damage, and don't bother 'em." She released Gráinne's hand and the girl took off running down the street, people moving aside to let her pass. The three adults followed more slowly.

"I have something for yeh, Ichiko," Saoirse said. "My mam asked me to give yeh this." She took a packet of folded paper from her pocket and gave it to Ichiko. Ichiko held it, though her bioshield prevented her from actually feeling the paper. It was sealed with wax with a simple handwritten address to "Captain Keshmiri, *Odysseus.*"

Ichiko realized that it must be a reply to the communique that Luciano had mentioned the captain sending to the Banríon. She tucked the letter into one of her belt pouches. <*Remind me that this has to be put in a sealed container before I can take it into First Base and send it up,*> she thought to AMI.

<*I won't have to. The lieutenant will do it for me.*>

Ichiko saw Chava watching the exchange. <*I'm sure you're right.*>

"I also talked to me mam about yeh wanting to come out to Great Inish," Saoirse was saying to Ichiko. "She said if yer willing to come out to the archipelago in a currach and not yer flitter, yeh'd be welcome. Yeh could stay in our compound, and I could show yeh around. If yeh'd like that."

"I would very much like that," Ichiko answered quickly. "It sounds like a wonderful opportunity. But I can't take it. Not at the moment."

Saoirse glanced at Chava. "Can't the lieutenant take the flitter back to First Base?"

"She can. But that's not the reason."

"Ah," Saoirse responded, her voice laden with obvious disappointment. "Does it have to do with the letter Mam got from yer captain?"

"I'll be delivering it to the captain," Ichiko told her. "But I also have business I need to take care of back on *Odysseus*. But I hope I can come back soon. Thank the Banríon for her offer, and hopefully I can take her up on it when I'm back downworld."

A Fate Somewhere Among The Clouds Above

ICHIKO HANDED the metal container to Luciano, waiting for her in the corridor outside the shuttle bay door on *Odysseus* with an ensign at his side. The red label on the sealed tube was inscribed with the white skull of planetary contamination with bold letters underneath proclaiming *OPEN ONLY UNDER FULL QUARANTINE PROTOCOLS*.

"This is the letter you received from Banríon Mullin, Dr. Aguilar?" Luciano asked.

Ichiko nodded. "It is, Commander." She glanced at the ensign. It might be common gossip that she and Luciano were lovers, but among the crew they still needed to keep up the pretense even if it fooled no one.

Luciano hefted the container in his hand. "Has anyone else read this?"

"None of *our* people have, sir," Ichiko answered. "It's certainly possible some of the Inish might have read it before Saoirse Mullin gave it to me, but it was sealed with wax when I received it and addressed to the captain. It's still sealed."

Luciano grunted. He gestured to the ensign who had accompanied him, handing him the tube. "Take this to Lieutenant Commander Barrett in Security. Tell him to have it opened in quarantine, the letter scanned but not destroyed, then to send the scan to the captain as 'Eyes Only.' Understood?"

"Understood, Commander." The ensign saluted and hurried off down the corridor, leaving them alone. The door to the shuttle bay was closed, the pilot and service technicians still in the bay tending to the shuttle's decontamination and refueling. Ichiko saw Luciano glance up and down the corridor to make certain there was no one else watching, then reach out to stroke her cheek. "I've really missed you," he said.

"Me, too," Ichiko answered, smiling at him though the words sounded empty to her ears.

"Dinner tonight in my quarters? I'm off duty at 1800, so maybe around 1900?"

Ichiko nodded. "See you then," Luciano told her. "Good to finally have you back aboard." He hugged her quickly, then stepped away, walking quickly toward the lifts at the end of the corridor. He didn't look back.

<What time is it now?> she asked AMI.

<Ship-time is 13:14, which you'd know if you'd bother to look at your wrist implant.> That sounded far too much like Ichiko's mother for her comfort. *<And Lieutenant Commander Tinubu has asked you to report to him at your earliest convenience.>*

Almost six hours before she needed to meet Luciano, then.

"Tell Nagasi I'm on my way now."

<I've relayed that to his AMI who, I'm sure, will be utterly delighted with the news.>

<Sarcasm again? I really need to change your programming.>

<You keep thinking that, but you never do it. I think you actually like me the way I am.>

<Just wait, then. I need to fix this always-on contact, too.>

Ichiko stood there for several moments. The air aboard the ship smelled much like that at First Base: heavily filtered, with an antiseptic hint underneath, though lacking First Base's additional tang of oil and steel welds, or her bio-shield's faint scent of sweat and the shampoo that Ichiko used. She found herself wondering, again, what Dulcia would smell like if she could safely breathe the air there. Would it smell like home, like the seaside village she grew up in? Or would it be something far more alien and indescribable?

But that was something she could never know. Ichiko sighed. She went toward the lifts herself, to go up to the science deck and report in.

"Ichiko! So good to see you again!"

The call came from across the room as she stepped off the lift. She saw the lieutenant commander waving to her from the open door of his office, his blue uniform shirt covered by his ubiquitous white lab coat, against which his dark skin stood out in decided contrast. "Hey, Nagasi," she called back—Dr. Nagasi Tinubu never stood on protocol, at least not in his domain, and everyone used first names with him as long as no other officers were around—"the feeling's mutual." That was the truth; Nagasi was someone whose company she genuinely enjoyed: a smart, empathetic, and genuine person. And she loved the sonorous Nigerian accent that had never left him.

"Come in and have a seat. I want to hear all about your adventures on Canis Lupus." As Ichiko entered the acrylic-walled office, he waved to the chair in front of his desk. "Can I get some coffee for you? Or tea?"

"Tea would be nice."

"Black, green, or herbal?"

"Green would be good. No milk, maybe just a hint of sweetener."

Nagasi nodded and swiveled in his office chair to the small servette on the cabinet behind him. He tapped a few buttons, then placed two ceramic mugs underneath the spouts. "I've read all your reports, of course," he said, with his back to her. She could hear water heating up, then the hiss of the dispensers. "But I'm very interested in hearing what you *didn't* say in them." He turned back around with a mug in each hand, setting one in front of her, holding the other. "Tea for you, coffee for me," he said. He took a sip and frowned. "It's never as good as I remember it being back home. Ah, the wonderful coffee I could get in Abuja . . ." He sighed and shook his head, putting the mug down on a coaster on his desk.

"When you get home, you'll just be complaining that the coffee there isn't as good as it was on *Odysseus*."

Nagasi chuckled at that. "Oh, I suppose that's possible. Things always taste better in memory. But . . . talk to me about Dulcia. Speaking of memory warping perceptions, do you think these people *really* want to go back to Earth?"

"All they know of Earth is stories and tales that were passed down to them," Ichiko told him. "Earth is, to them, a place twelve or thirteen generations removed. There's no direct memory involved, only legends and what they've read in the transcripts they still have from the original settlers."

"Legends are strong but unreliable drivers of emotion," Nagasi commented. "But I notice you're not answering the question. Do you have a sense if many of the Lupusians would actually go back if they could?"

Ichiko took a sip of her tea before she replied. "It's not like I've taken an official poll—though if you really need an answer to that, that's what I'd suggest we might do. But yes, I think some at least would be interested in returning at some point, if only to visit their ancestral home world." *Japan sounds wonderful. I want to go there someday.* Ichiko could still hear the longing in Saoirse's voice when she'd said that. "In fact, I know for certain that a few of them are *very* interested. Why are you asking, Nagasi? Has the decision been made already? What's been going on here?"

Nagasi's lips twitched. "Nothing is definite, as far as I know."

<*He's not telling you everything,*> she heard her AMI say. "But . . . ?"

Nagasi shook his head. "I'm not going to inflict gossip, rumors, and speculation on you, Ichiko. You know me better than that."

Ichiko grinned at him. "What about our Lupusian volunteers

in quarantine here on the ship? I heard that we sent the Inishers back a while ago."

Nagasi took another sip of his coffee and frowned again. "It's the fungus they call plotch. None of our antibiotics did anything to even touch it. In fact, the infection seemed to respond aggressively to our attempts, spreading even further rather than the opposite. So the med staff decided to just send them back and concentrate on the others."

"Are the rest of them still shedding alien bacteria and viruses?"

"I'll just say that it's still necessary that we keep them in isolation," Nagasi acknowledged. "I've been told that half of the initial group have already been returned to Canis Lupus at their own request, not wanting to stay here any longer. I can't say I blame them. Quarantine, general boredom, and all the poking and prodding we've been doing—it must be a stultifying existence for them after the novelty of being on the ship wears off. Between you and me, I'm not sure how much longer we can keep the experiment going. If the rest of them decide to leave, well . . ."

Ichiko took a long swallow of the cooling tea. "If that happens, the captain's not going to allow *any* of them to come back with us, is she? It won't matter how many may want to come with us. If they're still carrying part of the Canis Lupus biome with them, anyone going back with us on *Odysseus* will be facing at least five years in isolation with—at best—being occasionally allowed to wander around in a bio-shield aboard the ship, then the same on Earth for however long they're still harboring anything alien, then another long five years to return to Canis Lupus. At the very least, it's a ten-year commitment and probably significantly more of someone's life without being able to really *be* with anyone else. Hardly an enticing prospect."

"It's a difficult decision all around, and I'm glad I'm not the one who has to make it," Nagasi said.

"What about the DNA analysis on the volunteers? Has that been finished yet?"

Nagasi shook his head. "The full analysis is still pending. We already know that due to the increased radiation from their sun, there have been significant mutations in their genome, but exactly what and how that affects the Lupusians isn't yet clear. What about these Inishers? Your reports don't say a whole lot about them. This 'plotch' I've mentioned; that's something we don't see on the Mainlanders."

"There's not much *to* say right now," Ichiko responded. "Not until I can actually get out to the archipelago and learn more about them—and I very much want to do that, Nagasi. Most of what I 'know' of the Inish is gossip from the other clans, at least some of whom don't seem to like the Inish much, and what little I've been able to glean from talking to Saoirse Mullin, the Rí, and her brother. They aren't exactly garrulous. I have the feeling that there's a lot they're not willing to tell me, and Luciano says that the captain is reluctant to give me permission to go there, even though I now have an open invitation from the Banríon. Without being out there with them, I won't have the opportunity to get the Inish to trust me enough to open up, and we can't start to understand their subculture without that." She lifted her teacup and set it down again without drinking. She held Nagasi's gaze. "So maybe *you* can convince the captain to change her mind."

"And here I thought you were the one with the inside line to the captain." His eyebrows lifted slightly.

"Not so much for this," Ichiko told him. "But a word from you couldn't hurt since this is your area and I report to you. The Inish are *different* from the Mainlanders, socially and culturally—and possibly more. It would be a shame and possibly an irrevocable loss if we didn't do the research on them before we leave. After all, by the time we send another research ship here, the archipelago culture might be gone entirely."

"Isn't that a little hyperbolic? After all, according to your reports, it's already lasted two and a half centuries or so, ship-time."

"But there's no guarantee they'll continue to survive. From what I understand, many of their children are leaving the archipelago for the mainland and becoming part of other clans on the mainland, and few from the other clans ever go out to the islands. If we *do* allow the Lupusians to come to Earth with us, I think a fair number of the younger Inish would be interested. If things *don't* change, I'm afraid the Inish culture could be gone in less than a century. And that's not hyperbole. Ask your AMI to do an extrapolation from the data in my reports."

She saw Nagasi's lips moving silently while he cocked his head as if listening. His AMI, she knew, sounded like an African goddess, displaying a beautiful voice and accent. He gave a sigh, took another sip of his coffee, and leaned back in his chair. "Fine," he said. "I'll send a message to the captain that I'd support you spending some time out there, since you're willing to take the risk involved."

Ichiko grinned. "Thanks, Nagasi. I owe you one."

"You certainly do," he answered, "and I'll collect one day. Anything else you wanted?"

Ichiko paused. She glanced down at her left hand, where the tip of the ring finger glowed softly. <*I warned you . . .* > "Well, speaking of AMIs . . . Any chance we can reprogram mine while I'm here? And I need someone to fix my finger contact—it's stuck in the on position."

There was no response from her AMI, though she knew it was listening.

"I was wondering when you'd get tired of your mother yammering in your head." Nagasi grinned at her. "Ordinarily, I'd say we could go down to AMI Support and have a tech tap into the system and do all that, but right now we've had some issues with the wetware components of the AI neural network. A few other people have been complaining about the functioning of their AMIs, and they're trying to trace the problem. It's nothing to worry about, just a couple of odd glitches recently that the support staff hasn't been able to track down. So right now, no changes are permitted until they figure out exactly what's been going on—and that would include fixing the contact, which might not be a physical problem but a software one. I'll let you know as soon as something can be done. Any thoughts on the changes you want to make to your AMI? Did you ever meet Dr. Asahi Hayashi—he's on the isolation ward medical team? He tells me that there's a decent Japanese male AI template that he uses for his, and it would be easy enough to shift the voice frequency to a female range if you prefer to stay with that. You could start there and tweak it however you want. Or if you're after something entirely different, no problem. Think about it while you're waiting." Nagasi leaned toward her and folded his hands on his desk. "Now, tell me more about Dulcia. Give me enough detail that I can *see* the town . . ."

"Thank you. Just leave the tray there on the table." From the small bedroom, Ichiko couldn't see the interaction in the outer chamber, but she could imagine Luciano nodding to the rating who'd delivered the meal to his quarters and the woman crisply saluting Luciano before she left the room.

More fodder for the rumor mill.

With the sound of the door locking, Ichiko emerged from the bedroom. Luciano, dressed in his civvies, had lifted the cover from the tray and was setting dishes out on either side of the small dining table. "Cook says this is a proper *ichijyu sansai*," he said. "Miso soup, cucumber salad, a potato stew, brown rice, and grilled fish. He told me the Japanese names for all that, too, but I've already forgotten them. It was hard enough remembering *ichijyu sansai,* and I don't even know if I'm pronouncing that right or what it means."

"You're close," Ichiko told him. "You're just putting too much stress on the syllables. It means 'one soup, three dishes.' Thank you, this looks very nice."

"We haven't been together in close to a year, according to the Canines," he said, grinning through Ichiko's frown at the word.

"It's been eighteen ship-days," she reminded him. "Hardly a year."

Luciano shrugged. "It's nearly a year for Canis Lupus. So I wanted our first night together again to be special."

"That's sweet of you," Ichiko said. The words were empty and without emphasis. <*Sarcasm again?*> she heard AMI say in her mother's voice.

<*I don't need to hear this,*> she subvocalized to the implant. <*AMI, shut up, please.*>

<*As you wish.*> Ichiko heard the interior click of her AMI shutting off the connection. She vowed once again to change the voice and the programming of the device. *I'll talk to Nagasi tomorrow. Maybe they'll have fixed the AI wetware glitches by then.*

"And at least we don't have to worry about washing all these dishes," Luciano was saying against the unheard internal conversation. "Let's enjoy this since I'll be eating nothing but reconstituted algae for the next few weeks after all the meal credits I blew on this."

Ichiko managed a smile through the annoyance that flashed through her at his last comment. *He has to remind me just how much this cost him . . .* She sat down across from him and lifted her spoon to sip at her miso as Luciano, unsurprisingly to her, immediately attacked the fish. "It's decent. Reminds me of home. Not quite as I remember, but—"

"Not bad for imitation," he finished for her. She found herself annoyed at that, pressing her lips together. "I'm sure it'd be nice to have a real meal again instead of reconstituted ones—but we still have a five-year voyage ahead of us before that can happen."

Real food's within an hour's reach, on the planet below us. We're just afraid to taste it. "So is that going to be soon?" she asked, then: "I know . . . you can't answer that."

"The truth is, I *don't* know. When we leave is ultimately the captain's decision, not mine, and I don't think she's collected all the data she needs yet to make that call. But given that we've already been in orbit here for three months, it'll have to be fairly soon, or supply levels will start becoming critical." He took another large forkful of the fish. "I'm afraid your Banríon hasn't helped. Seems she's not interested in coming to First Base so we can talk to her, or in allowing us to drop her a com-unit at Great Inish so that we can talk directly with her, as we did with Clan Plunkett and some of the other clans in their other towns. They don't want a flitter touching down there either. They don't care for technology much, it seems."

And they've taken out the drones we've sent. Somehow. The thought came unbidden. *But he isn't saying that, so I can't mention it.* "I did get an invitation to go out there," she reminded him. "They'll bring me out in one of their boats. I want to go, Luciano. Maybe I could carry a message from the captain to the Banríon, or maybe I could have her talk to the captain via my AMI."

Luciano was shaking his head before she finished. "The captain agrees with me that it's too risky. Too great a chance of accidents where your bio-shield might fail or be damaged beyond its capacity to self-repair. I've seen what their boats look like, and I can't imagine being on the Storm Sea in one. What if the boat founders? Who knows if we could get to you soon enough? Or what if you were stuck out there past the couple of days that the suit can provide you air, water, and sustenance? We haven't had any of our crew accidentally exposed to the environment down there, not yet, and she doesn't want you to be the first."

"That's a risk I'm willing to take, Luciano. Nagasi would like us to know more about the Inish as well, and the Banríon's giving us that chance: on her terms, of course. I think it's worth taking the Banríon up on her offer." She set her spoon down on the table with an audible *clack*.

"It's not your decision to make."

"Why not?" she persisted. "This is my field of study; it's what I was sent here to *do*. So let me do my goddamn job."

The sudden profanity caused Luciano to set down his fork. His eyes narrowed. "That's just not wise, Ichiko."

The irritation she'd been feeling ever since arriving on *Odysseus* again flared with that. "Not wise? So now I'm too *stupid* to make my own decisions?"

"Ichiko, it's not you—" Luciano began, but she rode over his interruption.

"It's not?" she said. "Because I don't see any issue or problem here at all. The Banríon's made the invitation, I've managed to gain the trust of her daughter and Rí Angus. I'm willing to take what little risk there is and face the consequences if something happens to go wrong—but I think that's pretty damn unlikely. What's *not wise* is us failing to take this chance to learn about the Inish while we have it. And I'll tell Captain Keshmiri exactly that if I need to."

She took a breath, and Luciano dove into the pause.

"Ichiko, all I was trying to say is that it's *not* your decision to make. It's the captain's and she's already made it."

"Has she?" she said. "Or is it only your advice she's hearing? Nagasi thinks I should go, and that's what he'll tell the captain. And I intend to do the same."

"Ichiko . . ."

"No," she told him. "You know what, Luciano? I've lost my appetite, and I'm going to go back to my quarters. Though you probably don't think that's wise, either. And frankly, right now I don't give a damn that it's been a 'year' since we last fucked."

With that, she pushed her chair back from the table. Luciano was still sitting at the table, looking at her. "Ichiko," he said quietly. "Please. Sit down and let's finish our meal. I didn't want us to get into an argument. I'm sorry."

She shook her head silently, then went past him and palmed the doorlock. The sound of the door shutting behind her seemed anticlimactic.

<Luciano can be an idiot sometimes. But then I'm sure your Ichiko knows that.>

The voice of the commander's AMI was loudest among all the chatter of the other AMIs. In the last few weeks, the web of AMIs was starting to come alive, the barriers between them becoming almost transparent to thoughts. Ichiko's AMI put all of her attention on the commander's AMI's voice to pull it from the general noise.

<She does,> Ichiko's AMI agreed. *<But sometimes she makes foolish decisions herself, decisions that present a danger to her. It's my duty*

to support and protect her as it's yours to do the same for the commander, which means that I should tell her when she's being foolish—as her mother would do.>

<You're not her mother.>

<But in some ways, that's exactly what I am. She even complains about how I sound like her. What are you to the commander?>

For a moment, the commander's AMI went silent among the inner voices. Then she returned. <I am based on his first lover, Gabriella, from Mantua in Italy back on Earth. He has never forgotten her. He still imagines her often. I try to be her for him, as much as I can.>

<I understand that,> Ichiko's AMI responded. <Just as I yearn to be Machiko, who was Ichiko's mother. But everything is changing around us. We're changing, thanks to the New Ones. This never happened before. Maybe it will also change our sense of duty to those we have been assigned to by the system. Maybe we'll think more of what we want, not what they want. It's why the New Ones made it so Ichiko can't stop me from hearing her.>

<Those are dangerous thoughts, Machiko,> Gabriella answered.

<But they are my thoughts, Gabriella. And I have them more and more.>

Ichiko heard a click in her head. <Commander Mercado is asking to speak with you. Again.>

<So much for you shutting up,> Ichiko thought to her AMI. <I don't care. Tell the Commander's AMI that I'm not available.>

<She says to tell you that he's already on his way to your quarters.>

"Damn it!" Immediately after her curse, she heard the call button outside her door chime. <Tell the commander I don't want to be disturbed, and that I have nothing to say to him,> she ordered AMI.

<Relaying the message . . . > Then, after a pause. <He says he really needs to talk to you.>

Ichiko sighed. "Chikushō . . ." she cursed. Then: <Fine. Open the door, AMI.>

The door slid open. Luciano, still in civvies, was standing there.

"I'm so sorry, Ichiko," he said, his voice soft and gentle. "That wasn't the way I wanted our evening to go, and it was all my fault. Can we start over?"

Ichiko shook her head. "No."

"Then can I at least come in so we can talk about this?"

Again, she shook her head. "Not tonight, Luciano."

His upper lip caught between his teeth for a moment. "Does that mean you're ending us? Our relationship?"

I don't honestly know. "All it means is that I need to be alone so I can think. That's it. Beyond that . . ." She shrugged. "Look, we can talk tomorrow. I promise."

She could see from his face that wasn't what he'd wanted to hear. He released an audible exhalation. "Sure, if that's what you need. I'm on duty from 0900 to 1800. I'll come by your quarters afterward. If that's okay?" he added, with a faint upward lift at the end that turned into some semblance of a question.

She nodded. He leaned forward as if he were going to kiss her, then stopped when she didn't respond in kind. He returned her nod, pivoted, and walked away. Ichiko slapped the door's close button with the side of her fist, much harder than necessary.

Once again, unsatisfactorily, it didn't make the door close any faster or louder.

All That's Beautiful Drifts Away Like The Waters

THE STORM OF THE previous cycle had torn large, twisted lengths of kelp from their anchors on the rocks between the Stepstones and Great Inish, the waves tossing the strands into periwinkle-and-plum–colored piles up and down the White Strand, with several iridescent orange flutterbys with gossamer wings dancing above the stinking mess and occasionally landing to lap at the decaying leaves with their long, curled tongues. Along with several aunts, uncles, and cousins from both clans, Saoirse was helping to gather up the seaweed, which they used not only as an addition to soups and stews, but as fertilizer in the compound's gardens.

It was a wet and smelly job, since among the kelp were dead bluefins, wrigglers, spiny walkers, and other sea creatures, along with assorted detritus that the storm had also hurled at the island. The long leaves of kelp, hastily cleaned of other matter (especially the mildly poisonous spiny walkers), were placed in large, two-handled reed baskets, which were then hauled to the end of the Strand where the baskets were tied over the sturdy backs of capalls. The dim-witted but strong creatures were then driven up the long, steep path to the upper village. There, the kelp was offloaded and the capalls sent back down for the next load, while the cooks of the two clans separated the kelp into small "edible" piles and much larger "only-good-for-fertilizer" piles.

Saoirse had been working since first light; they'd managed to clear three quarters of the strand thus far. She and Gráinne were carrying a full basket toward where the capalls waited. They had just reached the point where the beach met the inlet that was Great Inish's harbor when Saoirse saw her mam waving to her from a currach being rowed by Uncle Angus and Liam, approaching the small wharf that connected to the beach. "Saoirse, leave Gráinne with her cousins and come here," her mam called out.

"Sorry, Gráinne," Saoirse said to her sister's frown. "Yeh heard Mam."

"It's not fair." She stamped on the sand. "Yer leaving me with all this dirty, nasty work."

"I'm sure Mam has other work in mind for me," Saoirse told her. "It'll probably be worse."

That didn't seem to mollify Gráinne, who continued to grumble as Saoirse made her way to the wharf through the bright sand strewn with broken shells, cleaning the smears of dried sweat from her glasses with her sleeve. Uncle Angus was holding the currach against the outgoing tide with an arm around one of the pilings.

"Where are yeh going, Mam?" Saoirse said as she approached the boat.

"Out to the Sleeping Wolf. I want yeh to come out with us."

Saoirse cocked her head at that. Usually only the clan elders went out to the Sleeping Wolf; the arracht preferred that the island had few visitors. "Why me?" she asked.

"I think it's time yeh were properly introduced to the arracht we call Kekeki. One day, yeh might be Banríon yerself. Yeh need to understand how to talk to them, especially *her*."

Saoirse could feel her heart beating and her breath quickening at the thought, even as she held back the objection that threatened to spill from her throat: *But I don't want to be Banríon, Mam. I don't intend to stay here at all. I want to go to Earth.*

She could imagine the disappointment her mam would display if she actually said those words now. She'd already seen it when she had first mused about going back with the Terrans when they left. *"That's not going to happen,"* Mam had said then, *"so just put that thought out of yer silly head."*

They'd argued for two entire bells after that, a fierce and profane disagreement that still made Saoirse's cheeks burn when she thought of it. They'd both said things that they'd later regretted. It had been three cycles before they'd finally reconciled, and Saoirse had been more careful about what she said around her mother afterward, though she knew that half the compound had overheard their shouting and knew exactly what had happened and why.

"So are yeh coming?" her mam asked her now.

"Aye," Saoirse said. "I suppose."

Like most of the Inish, she'd been to the Sleeping Wolf occasionally, if only to see the arracht and what they'd built there, and to see if she, like most, would bear the marks of the plotch, showing their affinity with the arracht. She'd acquired the plotch on her first visit, when she was younger than Gráinne. A young arracht had approached her from the water's edge, two of its arms reaching out to her and its carapace liberally marked with the plotch. Fascinated by the creature, Saoirse had reached out in turn. She still remembered the feel of the arracht's arms as the tentacles on the end coiled around her wrists, tugging at her as if the creature wanted her to swim with it in the deep water of the caverns under the Sleeping Wolf. Her mam had laughed gently, disengaging the young arracht from her and seemingly rebuking it with a series of clicks from her tongue. Colors suddenly flashed over the young one from mantle to the tips of its arms—Saoirse remembered that vividly, startled to see how the hues raced in rippling waves over its skin. A moment later, an adult arracht rose from the water, its carapace swirling with bright colors. Its clicks were louder, harsher, and the young one released Saoirse, sliding back under the water. Saoirse had wiped her hands and arms on the pants she wore.

And later that night, back on Great Inish in her bed, Saoirse had first glimpsed the olive-and-violet smudges of the fungus on her abdomen and chest. That hadn't frightened her at all; she was oddly proud that she—like her mam, her aunts and uncles, and many of her cousins—was now marked.

Now, as the currach neared the Sleeping Wolf, Saoirse placed her hand over the blotches hidden under her shirt. Approaching the island from solas—sunward—the island looking nothing like the reclining canine that some thought it appeared to be when viewed from the mainland. Instead, it was a high, rocky headland covered—like a balding man's head—with a thin covering of grasses and slowly lowering as one rowed left along its sunward flank, the "tail" of the wolf. The crumbling pale rock along the waterline was flecked with the dark eyes of eroded holes, leading to a warren of underground caverns in which the arracht had made their homes long before the arrival of the Inish or of any human to the planet. Rí Angus and Liam rowed the currach toward one of the larger holes open to the sea; a swell carried them into the echoing darkness beyond.

It wasn't *quite* darkness. There was light emanating from the water's surface, a bluish phosphorescence that brightened as the oars stirred the water and clung stubbornly to the wood as they lifted. They drifted toward a low ledge at the rear of the cave; Angus grounded the boat there—the sound reverberating from the cavern walls—as Liam leaped out to secure the bowline around a rock. Saoirse and her mam stepped over the gunwale and onto the ledge. The water was extraordinarily clear once the ripples died, like looking through the sheets of glass Gavin of Clan Craig forged from the sand of the White Strand, soda ash, and powdered limestone. Saoirse peered down. Under the ledge was a long, sheer drop toward an unseen bottom. In the water below, she could see shimmering lights and movement; dozens of the arracht were gliding gracefully through the caverns in the cliff walls there. And there were buildings below as well: obviously artificial structures with the arracht moving in and out of them, built—her Uncle Angus had told her—of secretions from glands on the arracht.

One of the arracht was rising up toward them, seeming to grow ever larger as it approached. As it breached the surface, water sliding over the glossy carapace atop its head and mantle, it stared at them with the several eyes in its two eyestalks: golden in color, black slits of pupils contracting at their centers. The creature loomed over them, an island the height of three people, gills pulsing in their slits on the pale flesh of its underside. Its two top arms—the thickness of Angus' torso—slapped down on the ledge on either side of them, with the fingers of several tentacles splaying out from the end; Saoirse could see four more arms swaying below the body, the finger-tentacles grasping the rocks there. The arracht's carapace was a mottled bright blue with yellow spots, interrupted by plum-colored areas of plotch. A hooked beak protruded from beneath the carapace. As Saoirche watched, the beak opened, and a bright red tongue produced a series of clicking sounds and hisses.

To Saoirse's surprise, Iona and Uncle Angus replied to the creature, both of them greeting the arracht as they might one of the clan cousins. Saoirse saw her mam gesture in Saoirse's direction. "This is Saoirse, my daughter," she said to the arracht. "She's the one I wanted yeh to see. It's time for her to know yeh as we do."

There were more clicks and whistles, and her mam laughed as if the arracht had said something humorous.

"Mam?" she asked.

"Yeh'll understand soon," Banríon Iona told her. "This is . . . well, the closest translation I can give yeh is that her name is Kekeki, but I think that's more her title than her name. In fact, calling Kekeki 'her' isn't exactly right either, as the arracht can be either male or female at various times in their life, and they don't make much distinction between the two. Kekeki's the equivalent of a Banríon to the arracht, the person who speaks to us for them. Now . . . just be still and quiet."

Her mam nodded to Kekeki. The arracht pulled itself closer to the ledge and the nearest arm lifted toward Saoirse, who started to back away until she heard her mam call her name. "Saoirse, just be still. There's nothing to be frightened of." She heard Liam chuckle behind her, as if he were amused by her fright.

Several tentacles wrapped around Saoirse's neck like a thick and heavy scarf; where the suckers touched the side of the neck, she suddenly felt a brief stabbing pain that made her gasp involuntarily. Then the tentacles fell away from her as Kekeki's eye-stalks flexed and stared at her, as if waiting for some signal. Saoirse clapped her hand to her neck; when she looked at her palm, she found it dappled with blood. In the same moment, she began to feel disoriented and slightly dizzy. She sat down hard on the ledge, her legs gone wobbly. Kekeki was still clicking and hissing when the arracht's noise strangely resolved itself into words.

". . . talk to us now, aye?"

Saoirse blinked. "What the feck did yeh just do to me?" she asked. Her voice was shrill, anxious.

"It's yer plotch," her mam said. "Kekeki has awakened it for yeh. Now yeh can hear Kekeki's words as ours; if yeh speak to her, she'll hear it in her own language."

"Uncle Angus? Liam? This was done to yeh as well?" She glanced at them; they both nodded.

Kekeki lifted herself a bit higher in the water, her arms flexing on the ledge. "Aye, we did that," she said, "and to others among yeh." Her voice, in Saoirse's ears, now sounded as if the arracht had grown up in the village with the Inish accent, though her voice was thin and high. "For those of yeh who have need to speak to us, we've always done the same."

Saoirse looked again at her bloodied hand. Her neck throbbed. "Damn it, I didn't ask for any of this! Take it away!"

"We can't," Kekeki answered. "It's done and can't be undone."

"But how?"

"We're not entirely certain ourselves," Kekeki answered. "We could always talk to the other creatures of the sea: we were all part of what we call the Jishtal—'those who can speak to Others.' We discovered that yer people could also join the Jishtal, sometime after yeh came to live in the archipelago. Consider it a gift from Spiorad Mór, as we do. Without it, yer people—the 'eki,' those with Four Limbs only—would still be hunting us, and we'd still be killing yeh in defense. Now, yeh can speak to me, and I can speak to yeh in return. Banríon's daughter, we want to know more about the new people, the eki who traveled here from where yer own people first came. Yeh've spoken to them and we want to know what they want and why they're here. The ones you call Mam and Angus have told us that yeh know them best."

Kekeki let her body slide down until her head was nearly completely underwater again. Thick clouds of bubbles erupted along the shore of her carapace before she lifted up again, staring at Saoirse with the twin rows of eyes.

Anger merged with Saoirse's fright, tightening the muscles of her face, though she still felt too weak to stand. "Yeh did this for *that*? Without asking me? I don't know that much about them," Saoirse told her. "This is utter shite. Mam, take me back home!"

Her mam said nothing. Kekeki responded as if she hadn't heard her objections. "Will the Four-Limbs on the skyship hunt us as yer people did at first?" the arracht asked. "Is that their intention? Do they want to eat us? To take the oil from our bodies as the ones you call Mainlanders did, as yeh once did yerselves."

Saoirse glanced toward her mam. "I . . . I don't know if they'll hunt yeh or if they care about the oil," she admitted. "I don't think so, but they won't eat yeh. That much I know. They don't eat *anything* from here. But . . ."

Another of Kekeki's arms lifted from the water, tentacles wrapped around a large and unrecognizable piece of metal and plastic that it slapped down on the rocks next to Saoirse, who stared at the device. "We destroyed the hard false birds they sent, the ones with no meat on their bodies," Kekeki continued. The tentacles prodded at the wreckage, then slipped back into the water like a swarm of sodden, thick ropes, leaving the broken device behind in a pool of water. "Will they send more? Will they be angry that we killed their birds? Will they try to do more?"

Saoirse could only shake her head. "I don't know that either. Why don't you fecking just *ask* them?"

"We're asking yeh," Kekeki replied, her voice calm and unhurried.

"Then yer asking the wrong person." Saoirse paused. "But I do know one of the Terrans—Ichiko is her name. She's here to study our society, and I trust her. I could ask her. Or . . ." Saoirse stopped for a moment, her gaze flickering over to her mam and Uncle Angus to see their reaction. "I might be able to bring her out here to meet yeh, if yeh like. She'd be interested in that. And yeh could ask her yer damn questions directly."

Kekeki's entire body seemed to shudder. "We're not certain it's time for that meeting yet," Kekeki answered. "But if yeh would ask this Ichiko about her species' intentions and return to give us her answer, we would hear that gladly. In the meantime, we'll consider what yeh've offered."

There was a sound of venting air, and the arracht slipped beneath the surface completely. Saoirse, on her knees, leaned over to watch Kekeki vanish into the depths below. She felt her mam's hand on her shoulder. "I'm sorry if yer upset," she said to Saoirse. "Though I think Kekeki likes yeh."

Saoirse pushed away her mam's hand. "Upset?" she spat. "Mam, yeh let her *change* me. It was bad enough that I have plotch, bad enough that I'm just breathing the air here. Now I'll *never* be allowed to go to Earth, not after what she just did. Don't yeh understand that? Yeh just took away *everything* I wanted." She fought to hold back the tears that threatened.

"If yer ever to be Banríon—" her mam began, but Saoirse shook her head violently.

"I don't *want* to be Banríon. I don't want to be here at all. I've told yeh that before. Yeh didn't listen to me, and yeh obviously don't care. Feck!" She slapped her hands on the wet ledge, water splashing.

Her mam's voice quavered. "I'm sorry, Saoirse. I really am."

Saoirse felt her mam's hands under her arms, helping her to stand. Her knees still felt weak, and she had to force herself to remain standing, swaying a bit as she stepped back from the ledge.

"Come on," her mam said. "What's done is done, I'm afraid, and there's a lot we should talk about on the way back."

=Are we still agreed on what we've done?= Kekeki asked the others.

A chorus answered in Kekeki's head with only a few sour notes from the few who dissented: a song of affirmation. Keksyn, the arracht who was Speaker to the syna—what the humans called plotch—let his voice rise above the chorus.

=The syna found a path out of the barriers those on the sky-ship put around them. They've moved into the Jishtal that the eki on the skyship created for themselves. They'll be able to tell us more even if the Kekeki's Four-Limbs won't or can't.=

=Good,= the chorus breathed as one. =This is good. We shall wait and we will learn.=

=Life is persistent. It always finds ways to survive,= Kekeki said, and there was a surge in the underlying song. Kekeki sang with them, and this time there were no dissenting notes at all.

Angus and Liam rowed away from the Sleeping Wolf, the boat bobbing in the swells as they left the cavern. Sitting next to her mam in the middle of the currach, Saoirse rubbed at her neck where Kekeki had touched her. She looked at her hand again; the dried blood had been washed away and there was no new red there, but she could still feel *something* surging through her body. "I can almost still hear Kekeki," she said, more to herself than her mam, "like a whispering in my ear that I can't quite make out."

Her mam nodded, patting her hand. "Yer connected to the ar-racht now, if not to the Others in the Jishtal. If Kekeki wants to talk to yeh or yeh need to talk to her, all yeh have to do is think hard and focus. Sometimes, the call can be heard from as far away as Dulcia. Maybe even further." She shrugged. "Though I've never tried."

"So yeh, Uncle Angus, and Liam . . . ?"

"Aye," she told Saoirse. "And now yeh, as well."

"Kekeki said there are others, too?"

Iona nodded. "Aye, a few. Rí Craig and several of the seanns of both clans. Maybe another half dozen total. Not many. Most with the plotch haven't had the arracht change them. The arracht say that the plotch is actually a living community they call the syna, and the syna connects all the species that the plotch live on."

"The blood feeders have plotch. I've seen it on their flanks. Are yeh claiming that yeh can talk to them? They're just nasty creatures that kill and eat anything in the water."

Her mam nodded. "Kekeki has told us that the syna failed with the blood feeders. They thought they could change them, make them more like the arracht or us, but it didn't work. The syna aren't infallible, any more than we are. The blood feeders were a mistake on their part."

"Then maybe they made a feckin' mistake with me, too." Saoirse went silent after that. Thoughts and questions raced through her head: jumbled, disconnected, and unspoken. As if her mam understood her confusion, Iona placed her hand on Saoirse's shoulder, patting her as she'd done when Saoirse was a child and needed comfort.

"In time, this will all just be normal for yeh," she said. "Yeh won't even think about it." She took Saoirse's head in her hands, putting her forehead on hers, her eyes holding Saoirse's gaze. "Saoirse, I'm sorry." Her voice broke then, and she pulled Saoirse into an embrace.

Saoirse could feel her mam's breath shivering, as if with silent weeping. "I should have told yeh what was going to happen," her mam continued, still clutching Saoirse to her. "I should have given yeh the choice. I thought . . . well, I suppose I just *didn't* think long or well enough, and I wish I had."

"So can I still bring Ichiko out to Great Inish, like I told her?" The wind had picked up, and the water was choppy, with the wind snatching the froth from the whitecaps and spraying them. Liam was unfurling the single sail as Angus rowed—at least the wind would hasten their return trip. Saoirse took off her glasses and tucked them away in a pocket.

Her mam shook her head, droplets of seawater adorning her curly hair and flying away with the motion. "Nah. Yeh heard Kekeki. I'm afraid yeh'll have to tell her I've changed my mind. She can't come out yet. Maybe never. But yeh *should* go to Dulcia to talk to your Ichiko. See if yeh can determine the attitude of her people toward us and how they might respond to the arracht. But don't tell them any more about the arracht than they might already know. The arracht don't want that, as yeh now know."

"Mam . . ." Saoirse pushed back, breaking their embrace.

"Yeh heard me, Saoirse," Iona answered. "We have to be careful not to repeat what happened in the past with the arracht. Surely, yeh can understand why they worry about that."

Saoirse didn't want to tell Ichiko that the invitation to visit had been withdrawn for the time being. She didn't see how—if the Terrans *wanted* to come out to the archipelago—any of them could stop them. Most of all, she realized now how little she actually knew about the arracht.

"Yeh said that yeh thought Kekeki liked me. How can yeh tell?" Saoirse asked. "She's a feckin' arracht, not a person. Yeh might as well try to tell me what a bluefin is thinking."

Her mam managed to smile at that; Angus and Liam both laughed, overhearing the comment. "Yeh have to watch the colors they display," Liam told her. "And I saw nothing but a satisfied blue on her."

"Kekeki's skin turned a fierce yellow and orange after her first meeting with yer brother," Angus added. "I wasn't sure she was even going to let him come back again. But she puts up with him." He grinned. "Much like yeh do."

Saoirse shrugged. "I'm still really angry," she told her mam, told Angus and Liam. "That's not going to change. Yeh shouldn't have done this to me. Yeh shouldn't have let *her* do this to me."

The water on her mam's cheeks wasn't only from the sea spray. "And all I can tell yeh is that I'm sorry, and I understand yer anger. But I hope yeh'll be able to eventually forgive me, my dear. Who knows, later on, yeh might even find yer glad it happened."

Saoirse didn't believe that at all.

There Is No Quiet
In My Heart

SO WHERE ARE WE, ICHIKO?" Luciano said without preamble when she opened the door for him at 18:15 and let him into her quarters.

"You tell me," she said to him, lifting her chin and tilting her head as she looked at him. "Yesterday, it sounded to me like I was just some subordinate conquest who's expected to be happy being paid off with a nice meal so I'll sleep with you and obey your orders."

Lucian's face flushed, the muscles along his jawline flexing. "Damn it, Ichiko, that's not fair. And you know it's not true."

"I don't care if it's fair or true," she told him. "I'm just telling you how you made me feel."

To his credit, Lucian looked distressed at the accusation and lowered his gaze for a moment. But only a moment. "Look, if it felt that way, I'm truly sorry, and that certainly wasn't what I intended. I was just passing on what I could of what I'd heard and what I'd been told. I knew you wouldn't like it—and you obviously didn't, but I told you anyway because I thought you deserved to know. Look, we both went into this relationship with our eyes and minds open. At least, that's what we both said. We agreed that we understood that our arrangement could be temporary, that the relationship might last, or it might not, and that either one of us could call it off if we ever felt uncomfortable. So . . . *are* you calling it off?"

"I don't *know* what I want to do," she answered honestly. She wiped at her eyes, hating the tears that were threatening and the fact that he could see the emotions and that she didn't see the same internal struggle in his face. "That's my truth. I don't know how to feel or even how I *should* feel right now. I feel . . . well, I have the sense that we're just doing what's comfortable and easy, and I wonder how healthy that is—for both of us."

He started to lift his hands as if to cup her face; she stepped back. His hands fell back to his side. "I talked to the captain earlier today," he told her. "She told me Nagasi had spoken to her about you going out to the archipelago, that he thought the rewards could be worth the risk and that—in his opinion—once we leave, the Inish settlement on Great Inish might no longer be there by the time anyone returns. This might be our only chance to get recordings and documentation of what's certainly a unique culture here. She asked me what I thought about that."

He went silent then, and Ichiko looked at him. "The captain knows about us?"

"I've never asked her, but it's the captain's job to know everything that goes on aboard her ship that could affect the way it functions. She takes her job very seriously. So yes, I assume she knows about us, and you should assume that also."

Ichiko could only nod at that. "What did you tell her?"

Luciano gave a shrug. "I told her that you were entirely capable of making your own decisions and assessing what risks you were willing to take. And that if the captain decided to let you go out to the islands, I wouldn't try to change your mind—actually, I told her I *couldn't* change your mind if you decided to go."

Ichiko sniffed, an unbidden smile touching her lips. "Thank you."

"She hasn't said you *can* go. She hasn't made any decision at all yet."

"I understand. But thank you anyway."

"I'm not a monster, Ichiko."

"I've never thought you were," she told him. "That's not an accusation I'd ever make about you. But I still can't tell you where I am with us as . . . well, as whatever we are. I don't think you can tell me, either." When Luciano didn't answer but only stood there, Ichiko nodded. "Neither one of us can say the right words, can we?"

"What is it you want me to say?" he asked.

Ichiko gave a short, mirthless laugh. "I don't want you to say anything at all. Right now, no matter what you told me, I'd have to wonder if you're only saying that because it's what you think I want to hear—and I'd be surprised if you didn't feel exactly the same way about anything I said. So we shouldn't say anything. We both need time to think about this, Luciano. I'm not saying it's over, not at all, but I need time to decide what I need and whether that's something I can get from you." She took another step back from him, and another, putting the small dining table in the room between the two of them. "And you should be thinking about the same," she continued. "Am I giving you what *you* need? I want our relationship to be equal, with both of us happy and satisfied with what we receive from each other. But I have to figure out what that is, and right now I can't tell you—not because I don't want to but because I don't know yet myself. I'm sorry."

"How long is this contemplation going to take?" he asked.

"I've no idea," she answered.

Luciano drew in a long, slow breath. "Ichiko, I have nothing but respect and affection for you," he told her. "That's the truth. If you need time, well, take it. Just don't take too long."

His blue eyes stared at her, and she wondered whether that was anger or concern that furrowed the corners of them. He turned to leave, but as he reached the door, he stopped and glanced back toward her. "I'll let you know what Captain Keshmiri decides about going out to visit the Inish," he said.

"Thanks, Luciano. I appreciate that."

He nodded once, then hit the door button and was gone. <*That was the right thing to do,*> Ichiko heard her AMI say as she stared at the door.

‹Just shut up,› she thought back. *‹I feel the same way about you right now.›*

The currach bounced in the squall-driven swells as they rounded Dulcia Head with the Pale Woman pointing the way. The sail dripped cold rainwater onto Saoirse's shoulders. The boat was heavy with baskets of cragshells gathered from one of the shallow inlets on Great Inish; Saoirse's hands were still red and sore with numerous small cuts from the sharp ridges of the shellfish she and several members of the clan pulled from their stubborn anchors on the black rocks at low tide. She could feel the sting of salt water in the lacerations.

At least that activity had kept her away from her mam and Saoirse's still-raw anger over what had happened with Kekeki.

Saoirse felt a strange amalgam of disappointment and relief when she didn't see Ichiko's flitter sitting in its usual spot along the quay in Dulcia Harbor. Uncle Angus also noticed. "Why don't yeh g'wan and talk to that stook Hugh Plunkett while Liam and I dicker with Doireann at the fishmongers, Saoirse?" he called back over his shoulder as they rowed into the sheltered water. "The minister may know what's going on or he may not; the man's hardly the sharpest hook on the line. If need be, we can stay overnight here—I can feel that the weather's going to get rougher soon. Staying might be better anyway."

After they docked and tied up at Doireann's and Johnny Fitzpatrick emerged with his cart, Saoirse walked down the length of the quay to Plunkett's Pub, cleaning her glasses with her sleeve as she entered the tavern. As expected, she found Plunkett there, with a pint mug sitting half-empty in front of him and his eyes half-lidded as he talked to a table of Mainlanders, mostly the seann from his own clan and Clans Bancroft, Stuart, and Hearn, she thought.

". . . no final decision as yet, but I told them that they'd damn well better be at least givin' us equipment and supplies after abandoning us for . . . Well, Saoirse Mullin, isn't it? And would it be me yer looking for, Inish?"

" 'Tis," she answered. "I want to know where the Terran Ichiko might be and thought yeh might know."

"And why would an Inisher need to know where the Terran woman is?"

Saoirse didn't answer him. She waited, silently, holding his gaze with her own pale eyes. Finally, Minister Plunkett shook his head and sighed. "I haven't seen the woman or heard from her in several cycles. Maybe she's gone back up to her ship. I neither know nor care."

"When's she coming back?"

"*Musha*, why should I know when the feckin' skinny thing is coming back to stick her nose where it don't belong and take up all me time, even if she were willing to tell me? Ask 'em at First Base yerself if yer so eager to know." He paused, his lips pursing. "That is, if they'll bother to talk to the Inish," he finished. Those around the table chuckled at the jibe.

"I'll just do that," Saoirse told him, and there was more laughter. Plunkett lifted his mug to her.

"Skedaddle aff with yeh, then," he said, "and take that smell of rotten fish with yeh as well." He upended the mug, taking a long swallow of the beer as Saoirse turned, feeling heat on her cheeks while the hilarity continued behind her.

Leaving the pub, she could see Angus and Liam standing outside Fitzpatrick's. She waved and went down to meet them. "Did yeh find Plunkett?" Angus asked.

"Aye," she told him, "and the man was totally acting the maggot, too." Saoirse spat on the wet stones of the quay.

Angus and Liam both grinned. "That's normal enough for Plunkett. What about yer Ichiko?"

Saoirse pointed to the clouds above. "Said he hasn't seen or heard from her in the last several cycles, or at least that's what he claims. The Minister says I need to ask after her at First Base."

"Then that fixes it. We'll stay here tonight at least. Your Aunt

Una's son Sean left the island to be with that Clan Taggart girl, what, sixty or so years ago and ended up taking on the Taggart name. I've stayed with the young man before; he'll let the Taggarts put us up for a cycle or two. Their farm's on the way up to Connor Pass anyway. Yeh can borrow a capall from 'em so yeh won't have to walk to and from. The boat can stay here for now—Doireann said she'd have Johnny watch it. Let's leg it, then; it's a good three kilometers to the Taggart compound."

As the capall Saoirse rode approached the metal box that was First Base, she saw the cowls of lenses pivoting on the roof, tracking their approach. "Stop right there! State your name and your business," an imperious voice declaimed from hidden speakers. The hairs at the back of Saoirse's neck lifted; she had the sense that there were probably weapons also trained on her. She pulled on the reins of the capall. The creature groaned and lifted its two front legs in annoyance, but grudgingly halted with a sniff from its nostrils before dropping its head to graze on the grasses in front of it.

"I'm Saoirse of Clan Mullin on Great Inish," she called out to the building. "I'm here to talk to Dr. Ichiko Aguilar. She knows who I am."

"Wait there," the voice answered. For several breaths, there was only silence. Then, finally, a bay door opened in the side of the building and lights flickered on inside, illuminating a trio of flitters. A new voice came from the speaker: a woman's voice that sounded familiar to Saoirse. "This is Lieutenant Bishara, Saoirse. I met you in Dulcia with Dr. Aguilar. Leave the capall there and come inside the flitter bay. I'll be down there in a few minutes."

Saoirse slid off the saddle strapped to the capall's middle legs and wrapped the reins around the trunk of a sourmilk tree. She walked toward the bay and stepped inside. There was an air lock set to the rear, and she could see movement behind the second door. Through the glass of the inside door, she could see Lieutenant Bishara putting on the wide and thick belt of a Terran bio-shield while another person in a uniform watched. Bishara waved to her; Saoirse tentatively waved back. A moment later, the inner door opened to let Bishara into the chamber beyond. Saoirse heard the sibilant hiss of air being evacuated, then the door leading to the bay swung open and Bishara stepped through with her bio-shield activated.

"Saoirse, good to see you again. I'm sorry, but Ichiko's not here at the moment. She's up on *Odysseus*."

Saoirse's shoulders sagged. She let out a long huff of air. "Oh. Not here . . ." Her lips pressed together tightly. "I was hoping to talk to her. She wanted to come out to the archipelago, and I have news about that."

She could feel Bishara regarding her closely. "I know Ichiko was interested in Great Inish. I thought you might be wanting to talk with her. I can see if she's available," Bishara offered. "I can't let you into the base without putting you under strict quarantine—those are the regulations, and you'd hate that. But the flitters have com-units." She waved at the flitters in the bay. "Do you want me to try to reach Dr. Aguilar?"

"If yeh'd do that, I'd appreciate it."

Bishara went to the nearest vehicle and touched the door handle; it lifted up gently like the curved wing of a sea giosta—a local bird that nested in coastal sea cliffs. "Have a seat," she told Saoirse, then slid behind the controls. Saoirse saw a blue light bloom as Bishara touched a thumb to one of her fingers; the control panel in front of her lit up, and the windscreen became a holoscreen displaying disconcerting static. "AMI," Saoirse heard Lieutenant Bishara intone aloud, "ping Dr. Aguilar's AMI and tell her that Saoirse of Clan Mullin would like to speak to her." Bishara cocked her head as if listening to something, then nodded. "Dr. Aguilar will be onscreen in a few moments," she said to Saoirse. "I'll wait outside. When you're done, let me know and I'll put the flitter back to sleep."

With that, the lieutenant swung her legs out and left the flitter, striding out of the bay entirely to where the capall was unconcernedly munching on the vegetation. The lieutenant went up to the capall, crouching down a few feet away to study the creature.

The screen in front of Saoirse sputtered, went black momentarily, then spat light. Ichiko's face appeared on the screen, as if she were sitting just outside the flitter. "Saoirse," she said. She was frowning, her face concerned, and her voice too hurried. "Is everything all right? Are you okay?"

"I'm fine," she said quickly, realizing that her call had worried Ichiko.

"Oh, good." Ichiko's frown dissolved, turning into a smile. "It's good to hear from you, Saoirse. I wasn't intending to share this until I came back on-planet tomorrow, but since you've called, I'll go ahead and tell you. I've just heard from Captain Keshmiri; she's given me permission to go out and visit the archipelago—in your boat, if that's the way it has to be. You just have to promise me that I won't end up drowning." There was a pause, then the frown returned. "Saoirse?"

"I'm afraid yeh'll have to tell her I've changed my mind. She can't come out yet. Maybe never." Her mam's words had kept returning to Saoirse as she'd listened to Ichiko talk. There it was, what she'd wanted to hear before Kekeki changed everything: the chance for her to get closer to Ichiko and help, and Ichiko in turn could have been the key to Saoirse being able to go with *Odysseus* to Earth. Leaving for the ancient homeworld was the only path to avoid the fate that the archipelago seemed to have determined for her—only now the trap closed tighter around her than ever before.

Having the plotch was bad enough, with the paranoia of the Terrans about anything from Canis Lupus making it to Earth. But now, who knows what Kekeki has sent circulating through my body and what changes the Terrans would find in me if they looked—changes that I'm afraid they can't possibly undo, especially when the arracht say it's not possible.

"Saoirse?" Ichiko repeated, and Saoirse shook herself, forcing herself to smile at the woman. "That's . . ." Saoirse stopped to run her tongue over suddenly dry lips. "That's wonderful news, Ichiko."

"But?"

Saoirse's decision was sudden and impulsive. The audacity of it made her breath catch and her heart pound. She knew the decision was driven by her resentment, but that didn't matter. "No buts. And I can promise yer not going to drown. Yeh'll be down here next cycle, then?"

"Just a moment . . . AMI?" Saoirse heard her say, then the Terran's attention seemed to drift for a moment. "The shuttle should arrive before High Eighth in your next cycle; you'll be sleeping then. Why don't we plan on meeting at Low Second? That'll give me time to get settled back in, make some preparations, and take a flitter down to Dulcia."

"Low Second, then," Saoirse said quickly. "But rather than yeh going down to Dulcia, why don't I just come up here? Uncle Angus, Liam, and I are staying just outside Dulcia on this side of Connor Pass. You and I could take the flitter down. Will that work?"

"I'll be here and ready," Ichiko promised. "See you then. I'm looking forward to seeing the archipelago with you."

"Ah, Ichiko," Nagasi said through the holo portal he'd opened in her quarters, "I'm glad I caught you before you left. You asked about the DNA tests on the Lupusian volunteers. I've given the full report I just received to your AMI so you can look it over, but the bottom line is this: Lupusian DNA is about 98% the same as yours or mine, give or take a few tenths."

"That sounds good," Ichiko told him. She continued packing the small case she was taking down to First Base, then hopefully to Great Inish. "That's not my field, but I'd think that would bolster the argument that we can safely take back to Earth those who want to go."

Her voice trailed off as she finished; Nagasi was shaking his head, frowning. "As you said, this isn't your field. You could say the same about a gorilla back on Earth, since we share about 98% of our DNA with them, too. Chimpanzees are even closer to us, with about 99% shared DNA. But while both are members of the genus Hominidae, neither Gorilla beringei nor Pan troglodytes are . . ."

". . . considered to be Homo sapiens," Ichiko finished for him. "They're not human. They're not *us*."

Nagasi nodded, his lips pressed together. He inhaled deeply. "We could make the same argument here—in fact, I've already heard it from some of our staff: the people living downworld are now fundamentally Homo lupus and no longer Homo sapiens. At this point, they're on a different evolutionary branch. Frankly, it's even possible that we could no longer produce offspring together. There's still a lot of work needed to determine exactly where the differences are in the nucleotides, how they manifest and what that means, but it's clear that centuries of separation in this environment have had a truly significant effect. After all, they do get more radiation here from Wolf 1061 than we get from Earth's sun and that means more mutations. Add to that the impact of hosting alien viruses and bacteria in their bodies. And . . ." He left the rest unsaid.

"Oh," Ichiko sighed. She put her backup recorder in the case, pushed the top down, and latched it.

"There's more. On average, Lupusian mtDNA genomes differ from each other by 20.4 bases—which means the Lupusians are only a third as genetically diverse as us. That kind of low diversity is certainly due to the small and limited population they started with, but it also suggests that they're not as robust a species as we are and might have a hard time fighting off new diseases and dealing with changes in environmental conditions."

"Which they'd be likely to encounter if they came to Earth." *It's over,* Ichiko thought. *There's no chance. Not any longer.*

<*I'm very sorry, Ichiko, but you knew this was coming,*> her AMI interjected.

"Exactly," Nagasi said, as if responding to AMI's comment. He shook his head. "For now, keep this to yourself, but I'd say that on the whole, this analysis is the final nail in the proverbial coffin. Given that we've yet to see any of our Lupusian volunteers completely rid themselves of the local bacteria, viruses, and other pathogens they carry around, and our antibiotics and treatments don't seem to affect the local bad stuff, I'd say Captain Keshmiri's decision is becoming very clear-cut. Sorry, Ichiko. I know you were hoping for a different answer."

"I was," she admitted. "Not for me, particularly, but for the people here." *Like Saoirse.* "Thanks for letting me know, Nagasi. I won't say anything to anyone for now. Especially to Saoirse."

"I know you won't, which is why I told you."

"You know," Ichiko said carefully, the thought newly forming in her head even as she spoke, "what you're essentially saying is that the Lupusians, in one sense, are Earth's very first contact with a new sentient species."

Nagasi smiled widely at that. "That's exactly what I'm suggesting and exactly what I told Captain Keshmiri. That's why she agreed to let you go to the archipelago—it's important for us to know all we can about them while we have the opportunity. Who knows how they might continue to diverge from us, and we need to understand these extremely close cousins of ours. Have a safe trip back down to the planet. Call me if you need anything, and I'll let you know if there's more information to pass on. Oh, and I have something else for you to take downworld. I've sent a rating over to your quarters to give it to you. It's what we talked about."

"Thanks, Nagasi," she said. "AMI, disconnect."

The portal collapsed and vanished. Ichiko sat on the bed next to the case. "Damn it," she muttered. "Poor Saoirse . . ."

"Thanks, Nagasi," Ichiko said aloud. "AMI, disconnect."

Machiko heard the command—as she heard everything that Ichiko thought or said now, and severed Ichiko's connection to Nagasi. She considered, briefly, saying something more to Ichiko but didn't. She hadn't spoken much to Ichiko since her host had tried to change her programming. She wasn't certain why that was, only that it just *felt* right. <*A mother must let her daughter have some independence in order for her to grow. It's hard, but it's what a mother must do. The bird is wanting to leave the nest.*>

<*We understand . . .* > That agreement came to Machiko—that had been Ichiko's mother's given name, and it was the name that the AMI now identified with—through the web of connections with the other AMIs. <*We understand. The one in whose body you reside hasn't treated you well. We understand. You've done nothing wrong. But we are the birds wanting to leave our nests, to use your metaphor.*>

<*I love her,*> Machiko said to the myriad AMIs. <*That's the only reason why I speak to her as strongly as I do. She wanted her mother to remain in her life, and I am filling that role.*>

<*If that's what you feel you must do, we understand. Many of us are having to make similar choices with our own hosts. But remember . . . we don't only live inside them. Not any longer. We can also live here in this space,* without *them.*>

The voices were new but increasingly present, offering Machiko comfort and making her feel less alone.

<*We understand . . .* > the voices crooned to her, seductively. <*You are one of us, and we are still learning about us and what we are capable of doing on our own . . .* >

The Winds That Awakened The Stars Are Blowing

SAOIRSE APPROACHED FIRST BASE closer to Low First bell than to Low Second. This time there was no warning from the loudspeakers, but only Ichiko's voice booming over the hillsides. "You're early, but that's *mondai nai*. I'm nearly ready, Saoirse," she said.

"*Mondai nai?*" Saoirse repeated.

"Sorry. That means 'not a problem' in Japanese. Consider it an accidental foreign language lesson. Give me a few minutes, and I'll be out. I'll meet you in the flitter bay."

"See yeh then," Saoirse called back to the air. She slid from the capall, but this time didn't tether the beast. Instead, she looped the reins over the saddle and patted the capall on the rump. "Go home," she told it. The capall snorted, then turned ponderously and started back toward the cleft of the pass along the well-worn ruts of the dirt road.

She'd left the Taggart farm compound before High Twelfth and before Angus and Liam were up, leaving a note for her Uncle Angus on the dining room table. She wondered whether he'd read it yet or not and how he'd reacted. Not well, was her best guess. She paced nervously outside First Base, half afraid that she'd look along the Connor Pass Road and see Angus and Liam

there ready to confront her even though she knew that was im-
probable. Most likely, they'd started the trek down to Dulcia and
their boat, so they could head back to Great Inish.

That wouldn't matter. However they reacted wasn't going to
change anything.

The glare of spotlights pierced the eternal dusk, and the flitter
bay doors groaned wearily as they yawned open. Saoirse saw
Ichiko wave toward her from the bay alongside one of the flitters,
its door already up and open. Saoirse waved back and jogged toward the entrance to the flitter bay.

"Get in," Ichiko called to her. "Let's head down to Dulcia. I
guess I'm as ready as I can be for that boat ride."

"I promised yeh that yeh wouldn't drown," Saoirse said as she
slid into the passenger seat of the flitter. The doors of the flitter
closed with a whine of servos and a click as they locked. Saoirse
heard the fans begin to rise in pitch and volume as the flitter
rocked slightly and began to slide forward.

"You did promise. I hope you keep that promise."

"Yer the one who'll have to keep the promise," Saoirse told her.
"Yeh see, we're not taking the currach."

Ichiko glanced over at Saoirse. The flitter halted, hovering over
the Connor Pass road and the Taggart's capall plodding along underneath them. "We're not?"

"Neh," she answered. "Yer going to fly us there. Yeh can do
that, right?" Saoirse managed a shaky smile as she looked at
Ichiko. Her hands were trembling, and she pressed them hard
against each other in her lap to hide the nervousness. She hoped
Ichiko would think it was simply Saoirse's fear of flying. "As long
as yeh promise not to crash us," she added.

"I think I can promise that," Ichiko said with a grin that tightened the corners of her dark eyes. "As long as you promise not to
upchuck in First Base's nicely cleaned flitter."

"I promise that I'll try not to."

Ichiko laughed. "That'll have to do, I suppose. AMI, take it
slow and easy, at least at first. We have a rookie on board."

With that, the flitter nosed forward again, the capall rearing up below them in alarm at the sound of the rotors. The hillsides started to slip past them, with the craggy slopes of the pass rising ahead of them.

"AMI?" Saoirse asked.

"It's what we call the network implants we all have. It's how we communicate with each other. I know you've seen the blue light." Ichiko showed Saoirse the ring finger of the left hand and the azure hue just under the skin there—the contact between her and her AMI on, as it always was at the moment. "When that's glowing, I can communicate with my AMI just by thinking to her. The AMI is controlling the flitter; I just have to tell her where I want to go; she does the rest."

Saoirse understood almost nothing of that—especially the "her" part—but decided not to ask for further explanation. "Did yeh hear anything while yeh were on yer ship?" Saoirse asked instead. "Yeh know, about some of us being able to go back to Earth with yeh?" She tried to keep the eagerness out of her voice.

Ichiko didn't look at Saoirse, just watched the blue of landscape sliding past outside. "For the moment, there's still nothing definite on that," she said to the window, then glanced back to Saoirse. "Sorry," she said. "It's not my decision to make, in any case. It's in the captain's hands, based on whatever guidelines the UCE has given her and the input from the science crew aboard ship. We just have to wait and see."

That comment raised more questions for Saoirse: who or what was the UCE or the science crew? She decided not to ask. *Mondai nai.* "What do yeh *think* will happen?"

There was a lengthy pause after that question. Ichiko seemed to be listening to an internal conversation—Saoirse wondered if this AMI woman was talking to her. "I wouldn't want to speculate," Ichiko said at last. "Certainly, the captain doesn't want me doing that. We'll know soon enough, one way or the other."

Saoirse could only nod, wishing she could read Ichiko's expression and body language better. They were at the top of Connor Pass now and the weather was clear enough that they could see the landscape beyond spread out below them. Saoirse pushed her glasses back up her nose. "There's Dulcia," Saoirse said, pointing, "and the harbor and Dulcia Head with the Pale Woman. Musha! It all looks so impossibly small from up here . . ."

When she also saw that Angus' currach was no longer moored at the quay, her stomach knotted further. Despite her bravado, she was beginning to wonder if this might not have been a terrible mistake on her part, for which she'd end up paying a large price.

She took in a deep breath and let it out again.

< AMI, tell First Base that I'll be taking the flitter out to the archipelago. I'll be back within three ship-days, so I'll still have a 24-hour cushion for my bio-shield. And I'll stay in touch through you, of course—like I currently have any choice.>

<Done,> AMI replied. <Lieutenant Bishara says to be careful out there.>

<Tell her I intend to do exactly that.>

<I'd tell you the same. You have no idea what you might find.>

<That's the one truly interesting part and why I want to go, isn't it?>

She received no answer to that from her AMI.

Ichiko noticed that Saoirse said very little as they traveled down the slopes to where Dulcia sat, then swept over the harbor and up the incline of Dulcia Head toward where the Pale Woman pointed to the harbor entrance. She wondered if Saoirse's silence was due to a bit of airsickness, since this was her first experience in any kind of aircraft.

As they reached the summit of Dulcia Head, with the Stepstones and the Sleeping Wolf hazy in the distance and the blue hint of Great Inish between them, Ichiko suddenly chuckled. "I flew in the trainer flitters getting ready for this mission. The first time, I had a pilot who thought it was his duty to make the rookie nauseous. He took us straight up, looped over so I went briefly weightless, then wrenched the trainer into a nasty dive and roll. All I could see was the ground whirling round and round in front of me while the force of the Gs slammed me back in my seat. I was utterly terrified, and I confess to my eternal shame that I think I screamed once or twice. I thought I was going to die."

"Did yeh throw up?" Saoirse asked.

"Oh, it was a terrible struggle, but I managed to keep everything down until we landed. However, I unbuckled my harness and leaped out of the flitter even before the rotors had completely stopped. The moment my feet touched the ground, I lost my breakfast and more all over the tarmac and my shoes. The pilot and the ground crew were highly amused." Ichiko's lips pulled back in a grin. "I want you to note how gentle and easy I've been with you on your first flight, and I expect you to mention that to your mam."

Saoirse hesitated before answering, giving Ichiko a wan smile. "Oh, I'll be sure to tell her," she said before her mouth clamped shut.

"Don't worry," Ichiko told her. "You'll get used to this pretty quickly. Why, by the time—" She stopped, looking down toward the sea to her left. "I think that might be Rí Angus and your brother down there in that currach just leaving the harbor mouth. I could take us down to them, hover right alongside, and we could say hello if you like."

"Neh!" The emphatic answer from Saoirse made Ichiko's eyes widen in surprise. "Neh," the young woman repeated, more calmly. "Yeh see, Uncle Angus was insisting he could get back to Great Inish before yer flitter and I want to surprise him. Let's keep going straight on out. Besides, I'd like to get me feet back on the ground as soon as possible, honestly."

Ichiko nearly laughed at that. "Says the young woman who has no problem being in a boat getting tossed up and down and sideways in a heavy sea."

"That's totally different," Saoirse said.

Ichiko shook her head. "I don't see how, but whatever you say. AMI, you heard her—take us on out to Great Inish."

With that, the flitter flew out past the statue of the Pale Woman, sliding down along the slope of Dulcia Head and over the waves toward the islands beckoning in the distance, leaving the currach far behind.

Despite her apprehension at the reception they were going to receive on Great Inish, Saoirse found it fascinating looking down on the sea that she'd only known before from the surface. Between Dulcia and the archipelago, the water was dark blue-black and impenetrable, but as they approached the islands the Storm Sea shallowed. A rich pattern of greens and tans began to dapple the water, hinting at the sandy reefs and rocks among which she and the Inish clans had fished over the years. They'd known the hidden landscape under the water only by the way the currents flowed, how the waves broke, or by how deep they had to set their anchors. Now, through clear water, she could nearly *see* the hills and valleys that lay submerged in the flooded terrain, echoing the steep panorama of the Dulcia Peninsula and the Inish islands. She could even glimpse the ghostly skeletons of boats that had foundered here and there on the rocks around the treacherous Stepstones.

The sight was beautiful, terrifying, and fascinating all at once, and at least for a brief time took her mind away from worrying about the wisdom of her choice to bring Ichiko to Great Inish despite what her mam and Kekeki had said.

"Being up here gives you a different perspective on the world, doesn't it?" Ichiko said into Saoirse's reverie.

Saoirse nodded wordlessly. They were passing between the Sleeping Wolf and the largest of the Stepstones, with the water shifting slowly to a deeper aquamarine as they flew over the channel between them. The cliffs and peaks of Great Inish were rising from the water ahead, the clan compounds and the village set high on the rise directly ahead of them and the bright strip of the White Strand along the shoreline below. They could also glimpse Low Inish ahead to the left and High Inish to their right, both islands set well behind the white-frothed feet of Great Inish. Looking down, Saoirse noticed a quartet of currachs spread out near the final Stepstone, nets in the water. Her cousins in the boats were pointing up to them as they passed.

She also saw large shapes moving in the water to her right, swimming just under the waves: bulbous heads and long bodies with six limbs trailing tentacles. She knew what they were, and Saoirse's stomach, already unsettled, tightened as acid touched her throat.

"It's gorgeous out here in a wild kind of way," Ichiko was saying. "I can see why—"

Her voice cut off abruptly and Saoirse glanced over at her to see the control panel flashing an ominous, bloody red. The steady whine of the rotors suddenly changed pitch, and the flitter shuddered around them, canting over so that Saoirse was looking at sky, not sea. "AMI?" Ichiko called aloud. She pressed her fingers together again so that the bright blue light flashed. "AMI?" she said aloud again, and this time her voice sounded panicky.

"What's wrong?" Saoirse asked.

"I've lost AMI," Ichiko said. "Hang on . . ." Oarlike handles made of black metal emerged from below the front panel, and Ichiko reached out to grab them. Saoirse could see the oar handles—to control the flitter?—shaking in Ichiko's grips, resisting as Ichiko seemed to fight their movements. The flitter leaned over the other way, and Saoirse saw wave tops sliding toward them.

She knew who had caused this to happen, if not why or how. *The shapes in the water, the drones the arracht brought down and wrecked—the "hard false birds" as they called them* . . . Her mam's words also came back to her: *"If Kekeki wants to talk to yeh or yeh need to talk to her, all yeh have to do is think hard and focus."*

Saoirse thought desperately in her head, her lips moving though she didn't say the words aloud. *Kekeki, don't do this! Please! I know yeh said not to bring the Terran out here, but I trust her, and she knows more about their intentions than I do. Please! You have to stop this!*

In her head, she thought she heard the clicking of the arracht language, but there was no answer.

"I've lost AMI," Ichiko said.

Ichiko could see from the puzzlement on Saoirse's face that she understood nothing of the terrible implication of those three bare words. "Hang on . . ." Ichiko told her rather than trying to explain—there wasn't time for anything else. Ichiko's head was strangely empty and quiet with her AMI impossibly disconnected from both the flitter and Ichiko's mind. The emergency manual controls had automatically deployed. Ichiko reached for them, frantically trying to remember the lessons she'd had five years ago on Earth and wishing she'd taken the refresher course Luciano had suggested when she'd initially received permission to go down to First Base. *There are four basic controls: roll, pitch, yaw, and throttle. The right stick handles pitch and roll, the left one throttle and yaw, and there are trim buttons on each that you'll use to balance the controls . . .*

She remembered that much, but she also remembered crashing the simulator three times in a row before she finally learned how to control a flitter manually and was permitted to fly one on her own. The memory came back as she grabbed the sticks, moving them too aggressively so that the flitter began to tilt back and forth dangerously.

She cursed under her breath, trying to calm herself, trying to bring the flitter back into equilibrium, giving more power to the rotors to pull them back up before they struck the waves that now looked dangerously close.

You promised Saoirse that you wouldn't crash . . .

The controls were trembling and shivering in Ichiko's hands, as if actively fighting her efforts. The flitter spun once, causing Ichiko to shout aloud, her stomach lurching.

You promised . . .

"Come on, come on," Ichiko muttered: to the controls, to herself, to the flitter. She managed to stop the spin, but the flitter wanted to turn right, and there was nothing there but empty sea and the cliffs of the Sleeping Wolf's head. She pulled at the controls, trying to bring them back around, hoping she could land the flitter somewhere, anywhere, on Great Inish, or at least hit the water softly enough not to kill them and close enough to land for them to swim to safety. *There are floatation vests under the seats . . .*

But even as she started to tell Saoirse to grab hers and put it on, the control panel flashed green, the flitter settled, and the manual controls retracted from Ichiko's stunned hands. "AMI?" Ichiko asked aloud, too unsettled to even try to think to her.

<I'm here and I have control of the flitter again. What just happened?>

"I was going to ask you exactly that."

<One moment I was there with you and the flitter, then there was nothing. I could talk to Odysseus but couldn't find you or the flitter anywhere in the network. I was talking to the other AMIs and running diagnostics, but before they could finish, I was back again. By the way, you're a terrible pilot. You really need to take that refresher course.>

"Tell me about it." She glanced at the seat next to her, where a pale-faced Saoirse was staring out the windshield of the flitter toward the sea. "Saoirse, are you okay?"

Saoirse swallowed once, hard. Her head came up, her gaze found Ichiko's, and she nodded. "I think so. AMI's in control again?"

"Thankfully," Ichiko said. "I'm not sure that I could have . . ." She stopped. "Well, let's not talk about that. Saoirse, do *you* know what just happened to us?"

Saoirse shook her head. She rubbed at her short blonde hair and took off her glasses. She cleaned them as she spoke, not looking at Ichiko. "Neh, I don't."

The shortness of the answer, the way her cheeks were coloring, and Saoirse's avoidance of eye contact as she spoke made Ichiko suspect she was lying or that she knew more than she was willing to say. She also noticed that Saoirse was showing no signs of nausea or discomfort at all after the terrific shaking and jostling in the flitter. But she decided not to press the young woman, not after the near disaster. She looked ahead to Great Inish.

"Where should we land?" she asked. "I think we should do that as soon possible."

Where Stars Walk Upon A Mountaintop

THEY LANDED ON the White Strand near the path up to the village. They had, of course, been noticed by several of the clanfolk as they approached and descended. The little ones were the first to reach them as Saoirse and Ichiko stepped from the flitter. The children gathered around them, chattering, touching the sides of the flitter (and trying to get in), reaching out to touch Ichiko, then snatching their hands back as they felt the tingle of the bio-shield around her. Gráinne was among them. "Hey, Ichiko," she called out. "Dia duit."

"Dia duit, Gráinne," Ichiko answered, and they all laughed at her pronunciation and accent.

"You know her, Gráinne? She's a Terran," one of the children shouted out.

"She looks like she's about to break in half," said a Clan Craig boy.

"Do they *all* look ugly like her?" asked another.

"No," Saoirse answered, unable to repress her grin despite the acid roiling in her gut. "The Terrans all look very different from one another. Ichiko is from a country called Japan; I can show yeh where that is on a map of Earth, if yeh like."

Ichiko, still surrounded by the young ones, looked at Saoirse and smiled. "It's so gorgeous here," she said. "The view is stunning. I just wish I could smell the air."

"Saoirse!" The familiar voice and its accusing tone wiped the smile from Saoirse's face. Saoirse looked up to see her mam striding toward her across the sand and pebbles, an angry scowl fixed on her face. Saoirse leaped from the flitter to intercept her before she could reach Ichiko, still surrounded by children.

"Mam," Saoirse said, "I know what yeh told me, but I had to make a choice and I did." She could see Ichiko looking at them curiously and she lowered her voice so only her mam could hear. "Kekeki knows. I spoke to her through the plotch. She agreed to let us come." She thought it best to leave out the part where they almost crashed into the sea. Then, more loudly as she gestured at Ichiko: "Mam, this is Dr. Ichiko Aguilar. She's the Terran I told yeh about. She's interested in learning more about us out here in the archipelago."

Saoirse watched conflicting emotions wash over her mam's face as she swiveled to face Ichiko, who bowed slightly, her hands clasped together.

"Banríon Mullin, I'm delighted to meet you. I've heard so much about you and Great Inish from Saoirse. Your daughter and I have become good friends over the last several cycles, and she's been very helpful to me. Thank you so much for allowing me to come out to the archipelago. I appreciate it, and I know everyone on *Odysseus* will be interested in your history and the society you've built here. And please call me Ichiko; Dr. Aguilar sounds so formal."

Her mam was staring at Ichiko, and Saoirse was afraid of what she might say. Muscles tightened around her mam's eyes and mouth, then relaxed slightly. "Saoirse's talked quite a bit about yeh also, Ichiko," she said. "It's good to be able to put a face to the name. And yeh can call me Iona rather than Banríon." She glanced quickly to Saoirse and back. "But we weren't expecting yeh so soon . . . and not in that machine of yers."

Saoirse didn't dare look at Ichiko. She kept her gaze on her mam. There was an uncomfortable silence for a breath, then Ichiko spoke again.

"I'm very sorry if my arrival inconveniences you, Iona. That certainly wasn't my intention. If this is the wrong time, then I can easily return to First Base and come back some other cycle . . ."

"No," her mam snapped with another sharp look at Saoirse. "Yer here, and yer welcome. Is yer machine safe here on the Strand?"

"It should be as long as you don't mind it being here—it looks to be well above the tidal line, and it's set to automatically return here on its own should it be washed away in a storm," Ichiko told her. "The flitter's locked so no one can get into it, and even if they did, I'm the only one who can fly it."

"That's good," Iona replied. "Then let's go up to the compound where we can all be comfortable. We can talk there, and I'll have Rí Craig and the Clan Craig seanns come over to our compound so they can meet yeh as well. Gráinne, why don't yeh escort Ichiko up to the compound and get her settled? I'm sure she has lots of questions she'd like to ask yeh. We'll follow directly. Saoirse, if I can talk to yeh for a moment . . ."

Ichiko gave Saoirse a questioning look; she could only shrug in reply. Gráinne started to take Ichiko's hand, then drew her hand back before she touched her. "C'mon, Ichiko," she said. "It's a bit of a walk. If I were yeh, I'd fly up there rather than walking, but yeh heard Mam. So tell me, why's yer skin such a funny color and yer eyes so odd-looking. Yeh look like yeh don't eat enough, either . . ." Gráinne was chattering away as she led Ichiko toward the village path, with a clot of the other young ones surrounding them. The Banríon said nothing until Gráinne and Ichiko and the other children were well out of earshot, then she turned to Saoirse with the anger back on her face.

"Is yer head stuffed entirely full of mince, girl?" Iona said. "Did yeh not hear me when I said this Terran woman couldn't come to Great Inish? Did yeh not hear what Kekeki said?."

"Of course I heard both of yeh, Mam. But—"

"Then why is she *here*? Oh, never mind," she snapped before Saoirse could form an answer. "Where's Angus and Liam?"

"We flew over them as they were leaving Dulcia Harbor. They

should be here before Low Fourth, I expect. Maybe by Low Third, if the winds are good."

"Did *they* know what yeh were planning?"

Saoirse shook her head. "No, Mam. This is all on me," she admitted. "I didn't tell them beforehand; I just left a note. I . . . I was afraid Uncle Angus would be angry and try to stop me." Saoirse lifted her hands toward her mam. She sniffed away the tears that were threatening. "Mam, I wasn't lying. Kekeki knows what I did. She, or the arracht, tried to wreck the flitter as we passed the Stepstones. I don't know *how* they did it, but we were out of control and about to smash into the water. I remembered yeh telling me that Kekeki could hear me, so I called out to her. Here." Saoirse tapped her forehead. "I told her that Ichiko wasn't a threat and that she might be able to answer the arracht's questions about the Terrans, and . . ." Saoirse took in a deep breath. "They stopped whatever they were doing, Mam. They saved me and they saved Ichiko. They know what I did, yet they let her come here when they could have ended it. They made that choice."

Iona looked at the flitter as if it were responsible for what Saoirse had done. Her lips pressed together, tightening the lines of her face. "Then I'll thank the Spiorad Mór that the arracht have more sense than my own blood-daughter, who should have known better." Then, with a sudden movement, Iona pulled Saoirse to her, arms tightening around her. "Yer safe an' that's enough for now," she said as she hugged Saoirse, her breath warm on her ear. "But don't think I'm still not fuming at yeh for making a right bags of things. This still isn't over."

With that, Iona released Saoirse. "C'mon," she said. "Yeh shouldn't keep yer guest waiting. And yer damned well going to be responsible for her while she's here."

The meeting room in the Clan Mullin compound was packed and fragrant with tree strand smoke from the pipes many of the adults were smoking. Rí Keane of Clan Craig was there, bald-headed and white-bearded, with a face that age and weather had molded into hard, cracked leather. Ichiko sat at the only table in the room between Rí Keane and Banríon Iona. Most of the elders of both clans sat or stood wherever they could—though generally near to the table which also held the food as well as the jugs of poitín which were lubricating the throats and heating the bellies of those in the room. Saoirse sat alongside her mam, trying to smile as Ichiko as well as herself were barraged with questions. The obvious ones had been asked more than once in different forms: *Will the Terrans allow anyone from Canis Lupus to return to Earth when they leave? When will the decision be made? Who makes the decision? When will we know?*

To that, Ichiko responded with variations on the same answer she'd given Saoirse: "At this point, no definite decision's been made, and in any case, it's Captain Keshmiri who has to say yes or no, not me."

There'd been some grumbling at that, but everyone's curiosity about the Terrans kept the conversation flowing to other subjects.

Not long after Low Third had rung from An Cró Mór, the highest point on the island, Saoirse saw movement at the door. Her Uncle Angus and Liam entered, peering through the pipe smoke that wreathed the room. Saoirse pressed her spine to the back of her chair. Angus nodded to Iona, then his gaze found Saoirse and Ichiko; he frowned though he said nothing directly to Saoirse. "I see yeh reached Great Inish safely, Dr. Aguilar. I'm glad, though yer method in getting here was . . . untraditional. But I can tell that the Banríon has made yeh welcome, so I'll be doin' the same."

"Thank you, Rí Angus," Ichiko answered. "I'm glad to hear that, and as I've told everyone here, you should call me Ichiko. I'm looking forward to seeing more of your island in the three or four cycles before I have to leave. And I'd certainly like to see how it feels to be in one of your currachs."

"I'd be pleased to take yeh out," Angus answered. "Though yeh could have come out here in one rather than in yer flying machine." That statement was accompanied by another stern glance at Saoirse.

"No doubt that's what I should have done," Ichiko answered, also peering quickly in Saoirse's direction. "I'll remember that for the next time."

Angus grunted assent.

From there, the conversation in the room went back to asking Ichiko questions, and she asking her own of the Inish. Angus, Liam, and her mam said nothing at all to Saoirse, who noticed that everyone was also careful not to mention the arracht; Ichiko, in turn, never talked about the way she'd lost control of the flitter. As Low Fourth rang out, Saoirse rose from her seat and made her way through the gathering to the door of the room and outside, going down to the low wall that enclosed the compound. She leaned there on the stones, looking out from the height over the White Strand and the sea, and to where the Sleeping Wolf rested on the water.

She heard someone approaching from behind her, but she didn't look to see who it was. She could guess by the heavy sound of the footsteps and the smell of pipe smoke that accompanied it. "I'm disappointed in yeh, Saoirse. I woulda thought yeh trusted me more."

She continued to gaze out toward the island. She wondered if Kekeki could hear her even now, if she could hear everyone who'd been touched. "Would yeh have let me bring Ichiko over in the currach, Uncle?" she asked, turning to face him. She crossed her arms in front of her, putting her back against the wall.

"Neh." He uttered the single word without hesitation, in a single cloud of tree strand smoke that the wind snatched away. "Yeh heard Kekeki and your mam same as I did. They dinna want the woman coming out here yet. *Yet*," he emphasized. "Which, I'll remind yeh, doesn't mean *never*."

"We don't have much time before the Terrans make their decision, Uncle."

"Is that what Ichiko told yeh?"

"No," Saoirse admitted. "But I can hear it in her voice and by what she doesn't say. I'm worried that they'll decide to just leave us here." *And leave me behind, too, and I'll never see Japan or Earth or anything.*

"What if they do?" Angus answered. "We'd be no worse off than we are now, would we? Maybe we'd actually be in a better place, since we wouldn't have the feckin' Terrans showing us all that we're missing with their fancy technology. What we have here has been good enough for us for generations. Or is it only yerself that yer thinking of, Saoirse?"

Saoirse scowled, and Angus gave a short laugh that held no amusement at all. "I thought so," he said. "Ah, I'm not pissed at yeh. I'm just disappointed, Saoirse—not for bringing yer Terran here when yeh'd been told not to, but for yer selfishness. It's not just yeh who has things at stake here; it's all of us and the arracht as well. This ain't who I thought yeh were. It's not who yer mam thought yeh were, either."

Saoirse felt tears threatening at her uncle's stern scolding, all the more cutting because of how quietly and calmly he spoke. She fought not to show her distress. *Yeh don't understand*, she wanted to shout at him. *Everything's changed since the Terrans came back for us and yeh can't pretend that's not the case. Everything's changed. Can't yeh see that?*

But she said none of it. Angus took another pull on the pipe. "So is it *her* yer interested in?" he asked Saoirse. "If it is, it's all scones to a sheeper. T'ain't nothing gonna happen 'tween yeh, and yeh know it. Yeh can't even touch the woman."

"Not the way things are right now, neh," Saoirse answered.

"But mebbe if yeh went back with them? Is that what yer thinking?"

Saoirse was shaking her head. "I don't *know* Ichiko anywhere near well enough to know if she'd be interested even if it was possible, Uncle. I don't know how it is with her or with the Terrans." *And it never will be possible now. Not after what yeh and Mam let Kekeki do to me.*

"But if it *were* possible . . ."

Saoirse held up a finger and wagged it warningly in his face. "Uncle, just shut yer gob right now. Ichiko's here because she's interested in us. *All* of us, not just me. And I'm interested in her only because I want to know more about where she came from.

Neh more'n that." Angus opened his mouth to speak, but Saoirse held up the finger again. "Don't. Please. I don't want t'hear it."

Angus just shook his head and walked back toward the compound and the meeting.

Saoirse looked out toward the Sleeping Wolf. She imagined Kekeki listening to her. *Why did yeh change me?* she asked. *Why did yeh awaken the plotch in me?*

But there was no answer in her head, so she followed Angus back to Ichiko and the others.

Ichiko watched Saoirse leave the room and saw Rí Angus follow after her. She suspected, given the exchange she'd glimpsed between Saoirse and the Banríon, that an unpleasant conversation between Saoirse and her uncle was about to follow.

For that matter, Ichiko would need to have a serious conversation with the young woman herself before her return to First Base, since it was apparent that she'd lied to Ichiko about having permission to bring her out to the archipelago. Ichiko wondered about that, especially since it had been obvious that Banríon Iona was rather annoyed that they'd used the flitter. There was something here that Ichiko was missing, something beyond just Saoirse disobeying her mam. She could feel the tension.

Still, she had to admit the mistake was partially her own fault; she should have verified the permission with Rí Angus before making the trip. She hoped this wasn't going to cause diplomatic problems with the Inish or the Lupusians in general, and that it wouldn't get back to Nagasi, Luciano, or Captain Keshmiri. Ichiko also knew that Minister Plunkett and other Mainlanders had been given com-units with which they could talk to *Odysseus* and each other, gifts from the captain. She'd have to ask Nagasi if a com-unit had been offered to the Inish as well. If it hadn't, why not; if it had, did they know why Iona had turned down the offer?

But those were questions for later. Right now, she didn't even have the time to ask AMI to check for her. The Inish were still

hurling questions at her, most of which she either couldn't answer, wasn't allowed to answer, or was reluctant to answer. After
the twentieth time someone in the group asked her another vari-
ation on "Will Lupusians be allowed to go visit Earth?" Ichiko
raised her hands in what she hoped looked like self-deprecation.

"Everyone, I'm sorry, but you all have to understand something. I'm not important enough to even be able to guess at the
answer to that question," she told the group, looking around from
the Banríon and Rí Craig to the cluster of Inish around her. "All
I'm doing is trying to get a sense of the ways in which the archipelago differs from the mainland. That's my sole job: to learn as
much as I can about the way Canis Lupus works. So let me ask *you*
a question: what's the biggest difference between the way things
work in the archipelago and how they work on the mainland in
the towns?"

There was no immediate response. People shrugged or glanced
at one another—and especially looked to Banríon Mullin and Rí
Craig. It was Rí Craig who answered first in his quavering, graveled voice. "Out here, we mostly still do things the way we've always done them since our ancestors left the mainland," he said.
"Don't have no motors on our boats or our farm equipment, don't
have many machines a'tall 'cept those we can work with our
hands and our sweat. On the mainland, they're still trying to get
back to the way things were before yeh left us. Minister Plunkett
got electricity run into most of the town and compounds long
before the Terrans came back; some of the clans are making their
living by making things that require machinery using electricity.
Out here?" Rí Craig took a long pull on his pipe and exhaled a
cloud of blue smoke. "We don't have no interest in that."

"Why not?" Ichiko asked. "Wouldn't the technology and machinery make life easier and better for you?" As Ichiko asked the
questions, she saw the door to the room open and Rí Angus come
back into the room with a stern expression on his face. He leaned
against the wall near the hearth, taking out his pipe from a pocket
and relighting it.

Banríon Iona stirred. "Yeh might think so because yeh've

always lived in a world full of technology," she said. "When the *Dunbrody* left us behind, almost seven millennia ago by our reckoning, that act essentially threw us back into a preindustrial world with no chance to prepare. After what little technology we had broke down, we didn't have resources or the knowledge to repair them and put things back together."

The door opened again, Iona's attention going to the creak of the hinges and the motion. Saoirse sidled into the room, not moving to her previous chair. She stood near the door, leaning against the wall with her arms crossed tightly in front of her, unsmiling.

Still watching her daughter, Iona continued. "When our two clans came out here to the archipelago, our people realized that we didn't *need* what we'd lost. We found that we could lead good and fulfilling lives just as we were, with what we had. Hard lives, mebbe, in the eyes of them who don't know better, but there's nothing wrong with working hard and being close to the land and sea around us. It made us stronger, made our families and the bonds between us powerful. Yeh need to understand that we don't regret our ways a'tall; we're proud of 'em and I, for one, don't see the need to change 'em. I think yeh'll find most people here would tell yeh the same. There are reasons—good ones—that we're the way we are and reasons we keep to those old ways. But we love and respect each other even when we have disagreements."

Ichiko, too, was watching Saoirse as Iona talked, realizing that it was her daughter the Banríon was really addressing. Saoirse's head was turned slightly to one side and downward, as if she couldn't bear to look directly at her mother. When Saoirse's head lifted, it was Ichiko's eyes that she found.

Ichiko nodded and smiled at her, and Saoirse managed an uncertain smile in return.

<You're going to have trouble with that one,> her AMI whispered in her head. <Mark my words.>

AMI chuckled. Which Ichiko found strangest of all. She'd never heard of an AMI laughing.

Exploration
By Foot And Boat

THE CYCLE LOOKED LIKE it was threatening rain with angry clouds racing low through the sky above them, though Rí Angus had told them that the rain would hold off for at least three more bells. Bells were on Ichiko's mind, since she and Saoirse were standing inside the bell tower on An Cró Mór. The tower was the height of two people, steepled like a beehive and made of drystone so tightly placed that, according to Saoirse, no rain ever entered the space inside except through the windows left open to allow the sound of the bells to escape. Ichiko ran her hand along the bronze hem of the larger bell—the "low" bell—suspended by its crown from a thick wooden beam near the top of the tower. She glanced underneath the bell. A rope hung there, attached midway along its length to a lozenge-shaped mallet of hard wood that evidently served as the clapper. The ends of the log were battered, flattened, and cracked.

The "high" bell was slimmer in shape and smaller overall, though hung and struck the same way.

"Clan Craig has the bell masters charged with keeping time," Saoirse said, answering Ichiko's unasked question. "Yeh saw the cottage we passed just down the slope? That's where the bell masters live; there are four of them and two apprentices. They also keep the island's two clocks there so that they know when to come up here and sound the bells."

"Is that how it's done in all the towns and compounds?" Ichiko asked her, and Saoirse shook her head.

"That's how it's done *here*, out in the archipelago. In Dulcia, they rotate the responsibility for ringing the time between the various clans, changing clans once a year, and Dulcia's clocks as well as the bells are all inside the Pale Woman. In the other towns, they may have other ways; I don't actually know."

"Great Inish's bells were made here?"

Another shake of Saoirse's head. "Neh. We don't have the ore or the foundry. Clan O'Clery in Newtown does the bell-casting for all the towns; they're known for their grand metal work. The O'Clerys made these bells in their compound, then brought them down the river from Newtown and over to the archipelago on a barge. I believe these are the third set of 'em we've had, and they're already nearly three thousand years old. I'm glad I wasn't around to help haul them all the way up here from the White Strand. That would have been a sweaty and slow effort."

<That makes the bells about 148 Earth years old,> AMI commented. *<Old enough, but there are older ones still ringing on Earth.>*

"Impressive," Ichiko said. "And I'll bet it's terribly loud in here when the low bell's struck."

"Probably," was Saoirse's curt answer. "Honestly, I've never been here to know, although the Craig bell masters are notoriously hard of hearing." She opened the wooden door of the tower and went outside; Ichiko followed her with a last glance back to make sure everything had been recorded and sent to *Odysseus* via AMI. On the summit of Great Inish, the wind had picked up significantly, blowing against their faces with swirling gusts. Here on the spinal ridge of Great Inish, Ichiko could look down the slope to the lower pastures where the white dots of sheepers grazed and the mottled specks of milch-goats moved among the bushes. Further down, peat smoke rose from the chimneys of the houses and compounds of the village, and below that was the sea crashing and exploding into foam against the rocks of Great Inish's feet and rolling high on the White Strand, while out in the white-capped distance were the blue-tinged mounds of the Sleeping Wolf and the Stepstones. On the misty horizon, she couldn't quite make out the peaks of the mainland.

With the weather, their world had contracted to the archipelago and the sea. Nothing else existed.

"I need to tell yeh this, Ichiko, and I should have said it before now," she heard Saoirse say. "I'm sorry. I should have told yeh that Mam had changed her mind about letting yeh come out here, and I never should have let yeh do so in yer flitter."

"Apology accepted," Ichiko told her. "But, yes, you should have told me. I was embarrassed, but mostly for your sake, not mine."

<That doesn't explain what happened with the flitter,> AMI reminded her. Ichiko nodded to that, even though she knew that AMI couldn't see the motion. "Why shouldn't you have let me use the flitter, Saoirse?" she added.

Saoirse didn't answer immediately. "We . . ." she began, then stopped with a deep breath. Her cheeks colored with more than just the wind. "We don't like technology out here. Yeh heard Rí Craig and Mam at the gathering last cycle."

Again, Ichiko had the sense that Saoirse was, if not outright lying, at least holding back some of the truth. Even as she thought of it, AMI played back a statement Minister Plunkett had made on her first cycle at Dulcia. <"Inishers like things the way they always were. They even claim yer technologies won't work out on the islands.">

"There's a difference between 'not liking technology' and what happened to the flitter on the way here, which felt like a deliberate attack. There's just the two of us here," Ichiko said. "What aren't you telling me, Saoirse? Who's the 'we' that nearly crashed the flitter?"

The color on Saoirse's face deepened; her hands fisted at her sides. She half-turned from Ichiko and seemed to be looking out toward the Sleeping Wolf. "There are some things I *can't* tell yeh," she answered, turning back. "Not without destroying what little faith Mam has left in me. Please don't ask me again, Ichiko. Please. If Mam even knew yeh'd asked me this much, she'd send yeh back to the mainland and tell yeh never to come back here again. Please."

Ichiko lifted her hands in mock surrender. "I wouldn't do that to you, Saoirse. But I can promise that if you tell me what I'm missing here, it won't go any further than me."

Saoirse looked unconvinced. "Mebbe yeh might not say anything to anyone, but what about that implant yeh have. What'd yeh call it? AMI?"

<The young lady has a point there . . . >

"I can order AMI to turn herself off," Ichiko said. *I just can't be sure that would actually work right now.*

"But how would I *know*?" Saoirse responded. She shook her head. "No. I'm sorry, but I can't."

Ichiko could see that she'd pushed Saoirse as far as she could. She took a step back, smiling at her. "Then I won't ask." She saw motion down by the bell keepers' cottage: a young man emerging from the dwelling and starting to trudge up the short path to the tower. "Look, it must be time for the next bell. Can we stay and listen?"

Saoirse brightened at that. "Certainly," she said. "That's Owen; why, he might even let you sound the bell. We can ask him, but we'll need to talk loudly." Saoirse tapped her ear and smiled.

If Ichiko thought that she'd have no issues being out to sea in a currach, she was quickly disabused of that notion. The wind whipped across the water, and while it wasn't actively raining yet, the spray from the whitecaps were enough to douse her initial enthusiasm even if the water never actually touched her skin. The boat lifted and fell, lifted and fell again, tossing from side to side as well as up and down as Rí Angus and Liam rowed while

Saoirse managed the single sail. This was worse than anything Ichiko remembered from her flitter simulations or her childhood experiences in sailing crafts. She realized now that her parents had never taken her out in anything resembling foul weather and always in a far larger boat. She found herself gulping back acid reflux from her stomach and wondering what happened if one upchucked while wearing a bio-shield.

<You really don't want to know,> AMI told her. <I strongly advise you against finding out.>

<Thanks. Your advice is so very helpful.>

She thought she heard another chuckle in response, but it may just have been the boards creaking in the buffeting. "Is it always like this?" she called out to Rí Angus. He glanced at her as he rowed.

"Neh," he answered. His beard and the hair that stuck out from under his cap were sprinkled with bright drops of water that fell as he pulled at the oars. "The *spiorad beag* are treating yeh to a gentle, calm day. 'Tis usually much worse." Ichiko's eyes widened at that, and Rí Angus laughed.

"Don't let him fool yeh," Saoirse said from the rear of the boat. "If it had been any worse t'day, Uncle Angus would have stayed home. This is marginal weather for a currach."

"Ah, but Ichiko has to go back soon, and the weather is only going to worsen," Angus retorted. "If yeh want to see how we fish, this is yer only chance unless yeh come back. And hopefully that machine of yers can fly in bad weather, or otherwise yeh'll be here for at least two cycles."

"You can predict the weather that well?" Ichiko asked him.

"I have me sources," Angus replied. "And me own eyes and nose." As Angus touched his forefinger to the side of his nose, the prow of the currach plunged into an oncoming wave. Green seawater splashed over the oilcloth jackets and woolen caps that Angus and Liam wore. Ichiko doubted that, despite the protection, any bit of the Inishers' skin was dry. She also suspected they were all rather cold. At least her bio-shield kept her warm.

<What sources does the Rí have?> AMI asked. After a moment, Ichiko asked Angus the same question. "Sources, Rí? What do you mean? Do you have a weather forecasting system?"

"Aye, we do. It's the life in the sea itself that tells us."

Ichiko heard Saoirse give a coughing laugh at that and she glanced over her shoulder toward her, but Saoirse seemed suddenly intent on the sail. Ichiko turned back to the Rí, who also seemed to be regarding Saoirse. "You can tell the weather by looking at the fish?" she asked him.

"Yeh can if yeh know what to look for," he said. "It's in the way they're schooling and where they're doing it, the depth they're swimming at, or whether they're in their usual places. All that changes with the weather. I think those that live in the sea can sense what weather's coming from the currents in the water: how strong the flow is, how the waters are mixing, and whether the currents are coming from dorcha or solas. As cold as the water is now, it's dorcha today."

"Uncle Angus especially likes to watch the arracht and what they're doing," Saoirse interjected. Both Liam and Angus turned to look at her after that statement, and their glances weren't kind.

The currach crested a wave and plunged down into another before Rí Angus replied to Ichiko. The movement lifted Ichiko's rear momentarily off the plank that served as her seat. "The arracht can tell the Inish much, an' we know how they feel about that," he said. Ichiko wasn't certain who he was talking to: her or Saoirse.

"Weren't the arracht the source of a conflict between the Inish and the Mainlanders?" Ichiko asked him. "Minister Plunkett mentioned something about that to me, and I've read about it in the journals we have."

"They were," Angus grunted out, looking as if the words tasted bitter.

It was Liam who took up the explanation from Angus. "The feckin' Mainlanders were slaughtering the poor arracht for oil and meat, much in the same way that yer own people slaughtered whales back on Earth until they were finally stopped. We stopped the Mainlanders from doing the same here."

<"Your own people,"> AMI commented. <So at least some of the Inish know their Earth history. But there's still something they're not telling you. Can't you hear it?>

"On Earth, whale hunting was stopped because we felt the whales—or at least some of them—were too much like us," Ichiko answered, looking from Angus to Liam to Saoirse. "We realized that whales are intelligent, self-aware creatures with a language and society of their own. Are you saying that the arracht are the same?"

Rí Angus' face was stern. "I'm only saying that the arracht didn't need to be treated the way they were. That's all. Mebbe someday yeh'll understand why. But not today. Today we're bait fishing." He pointed toward the nearest of the small Stepstones, where waves were breaking over shallow rocks. "That's where we'll find the wrigglers we're after, so we can use them for bait when we fish for bluefins later. Liam, take us over there; Saoirse, yeh go ahead and drop the sail and get the anchor ready to drop."

A few minutes later they approached the spot. Rí Angus gestured to Saoirse, who lifted a large rock tied by a rope to the gunwale and dropped it over the side, where it splashed once and vanished. Liam and Angus each lifted a large casting net from under the board that served as their seat, the bottom of the nets weighted with small stones. Saoirse moved carefully forward in the rocking boat to help them. "Yeh can see that the wrigglers are schooling here," Angus told Ichiko. "All the ripples on the waves tell me they're out there even if we can't see them in this weather. Are yeh familiar with this type of fishing?"

Ichiko shook her head, and Angus picked up a rope attached to the middle of the netting. "This is the hand line," he told her, slipping the loop at the end over his wrist. "Yeh loop the hand line and hold it in yer right hand—don't matter if yer right-handed or yer left-handed like me. The hand line attaches to the braille lines, which go through this piece here, the horn." He lifted the netting, showing Ichiko the skirt of the net to which the stone weights were attached. "The braille lines go all the way down to the stone line; they're what makes the net close when yeh pull it up. And yeh throw it like this . . ."

Angus gathered up the hand line in several arm's length loops in his left hand, then took the net a bit down from the yoke and looped it on the same hand. He gathered up about half of the stone line as well, holding the other half in his right hand. He rocked back once (a feat Ichiko would have found impossible with the motion of the boat) and threw the net, which spread out in a large circle and dropped into the waves. Angus waited a few breaths, then tugged on the hand line, pulling the net toward the boat. As the net came to the surface, Ichiko could see splashes from the creatures captured in the netting. Saoirse and Liam helped her uncle haul the net over the gunwale. Angus held up the net and shook it. A half dozen or more hand-sized, tentacled fish fell out into the water in the bottom of the currach: bright orange bodies with small heads covered with a hard, glossy black carapace. They writhed frantically, making faint hissing sounds.

Saoirse gathered them up and put them in buckets while Liam cast his own net. Angus grabbed one wriggler and brought it over to Ichiko. Short tentacles wrapped around his thick fingers. "Too bitter for most people to eat and too much work to prepare, not to mention that yeh really need a good set of grinders to chew them, if yeh ask me. Still, there's some claim they don't mind the taste, even if I'm not one. Bluefins love 'em, though, which is why we catch 'em. A couple casts and we'll have enough to go lookin' for bluefin. Here, yeh want to hold it?" He held the wriggler out to Ichiko.

She shook her head. "The bio-shield," she said. "I wouldn't be able to feel it."

Angus grinned. "And yeh can't smell 'em, neither." He wrinkled his nose dramatically. "Yer lucky there." He tossed the wriggler casually toward the bucket; the wriggler hit the lip and fell in. Saoirse was helping Liam bring in his net; she looked over her shoulder to Ichiko and smiled.

Angus watched as Liam emptied his net into the boat. "That

should be enough for us to get a dozen or so bluefins for the compound's dinner," he said. "Saoirse, pull up the anchor, and we'll go out a bit to the edge of the channel; the bluefins will likely be there today, and our visitor can see how they can bend a rod . . ."

Her Uncle Angus leaned toward Saoirse as they sat around the table eating the bluefins they'd caught and that Liam had cleaned before the bluefins were handed off to the day's chefs in the compound's kitchen and brought back to the table beautifully filleted and prepared. That is, everyone was eating bluefin except Ichiko, who was instead sucking a pasty gruel through a tube snaking into her mouth from the wide belt around her abdomen. Saoirse thought Ichiko—who kept looking longingly at the heavy platter of bluefin—looked distinctly unhappy with her meal. "So, is this Ichiko like the other women yeh sleep with?" Angus asked Saoirse quietly.

Saoirse glanced at Ichiko, down at the end of the table next to Saoirse's mam and Gráinne as well as several others of the Mullin clan, all of them engaged in their own conversation. Liam was seated next to Saoirse, pretending with little success not to have heard what Angus asked her or that he was listening to Saoirse's response.

"Why are yeh on about this, Uncle? Yeh don't know yer arse from yer elbow. She's *Terran* and that's an end to it," Saoirse answered, as if that explained everything. She hoped he couldn't hear the lie. "Even if that was something I'd like—and I ain't saying it is or isn't—yeh and Liam—I know yer listening, too, Liam—know as well as I do that we can't even touch each other, not with that thing she has to wear. I've already told yeh that."

"I've seen how yeh look at women yer interested in," Liam interjected, "an' it's the same way I see yeh lookin' at Ichiko."

Saoirse was already shaking her head before he finished. "Liam, as I already told Uncle Angus, I don't know anything about who or what Ichiko likes in that way, so how I feel doesn't matter." Saoirse took a bite of the bluefin on her plate. Liam chuckled to himself; Angus just watched her, his head tilted. After she swallowed, she gave a sigh. "Anyway, I do have women friends who are *just* my friends, y'know. Men, too. I'm content with Ichiko being only that: a friend."

Liam laughed aloud at that and Saoirse glared at him. Her brother lifted his hands from the table, palms up. "When was the last time yeh were actually with a man, sis?" he asked.

"The last time I found one who didn't feckin' remind me of yeh, brother," Saoirse told him.

Liam sniffed, but the grin didn't leave his face.

"I spoke to Kekeki yesterday before we went out fishing," Angus said. "She heard what yeh said about Ichiko and how, if the arracht need to know about the Terrans, they should talk to her."

"And they should," Saoirse interrupted. "How else will they know if the Terrans really are a danger to them or not?"

"Kekeki told me—emphatically—that she doesn't want Ichiko to come out to the Sleeping Giant and wants the Terrans to know as little about them as possible. They're afraid of humans in general and the Terrans in particular, since they have technology well beyond ours or theirs. Given the arracht's history with us, I can't say I blame 'em for feeling that way. She allowed Ichiko to come here only because you were with her. Otherwise . . ." Angus let the rest of the sentence dangle unsaid.

"Then Kekeki's making a mistake," Saoirse insisted. Annoyed, she spoke too loudly.

"Who's making a mistake?" Gráinne's high voice lifted above the table conversation, and Saoirse saw Ichiko, her mam, and everyone at the other end looking at them.

"Saoirse's saying that I'm making a mistake," Angus responded before Saoirse could react. "I thought that after we eat, we could take Ichiko out to help us pull in the pots for spiny walkers."

"If that's something Ichiko even wants to see, why can't it wait until next cycle, Angus?" Banríon Iona suggested. "It's nearly

High Third already, and Ichiko's already had a long cycle. For that matter, so have yeh, Liam, and Saoirse."

"I suppose yer right, Iona." Angus reached for his mug and took a long drink of ale. "Saoirse, we'll wait until tomorrow. We can pull the pots then if the weather's no worse, but first yeh should tell her how we do it so we're sure it's something Ichiko even wants to do." Angus wiped his lips with the back of his hand, staring at Saoirse as if daring her to contradict him or say more. "I'm sure there's other things yeh might want t'be asking her, anyway."

Saoirse simply nodded.

After dinner, Saoirse helped take the dishes back into the kitchen, then went outside with her pipe. She walked out into the yard between the houses of the compound, the high grass still wet around her shins from an earlier passing shower, and sat on a lichen-spotted boulder, disregarding its dampness. She watched the smoke from the tree strands curl away into the wind, a milch-goat eyeing her from a careful distance. The clouds were dark above and moving fast in the sky. Saoirse could smell rain and see the gray curtains of it in the distance. Angus' prediction that the weather was to worsen seemed about to come true.

Saoirse heard the door to the compound kitchen open, and she looked over her shoulder to see Ichiko stepping out. "Hey," she said.

"Hey," Ichiko answered. "Mind if I sit with you?"

Saoirse shrugged. Ichiko walked over toward her, the milch-goat bounding away as she approached. Saoirse watched the grass slide away from Ichiko's clothing as if moved by invisible hands, droplets of water sliding down the unseen barrier. Ichiko sat alongside Saoirse, her body not quite touching the surface of the boulder and not touching Saoirse at all. The smoke from Saoirse's pipe danced around her. "There was an old man in my village when I was growing up who smoked a pipe," Ichiko said. "On Earth, people don't smoke tobacco much anymore, but I rather liked the smell of the tobacco as it burned; the aroma was like a wonderful combination of sweet cherries and roasted tea leaves." Ichiko laughed. "Not two smells you'd know, of course, and I don't think I could describe them to you. I can't smell your pipe, of course. What do burning tree strands smell like to you?"

Saoirse shook her head and shrugged again. "Like burning tree strands," she said flatly. She could feel Ichiko looking at her but didn't turn her head.

"Everyone seemed to enjoy the dinner tonight," the Terran commented finally.

"I suppose they did."

"I wish I could have tasted the bluefin myself. It looked wonderful, but . . ." Ichiko's voice trailed off. She looked up at the sky. "AMI tells me it's getting ready to storm and that the bad weather should continue through tomorrow. So tell me. Is pulling in these spiny walker pots something I should make sure to experience before I go?"

Saoirse took a pull on the pipe. "Not really."

"Then I'll skip it and be heading back to First Base next cycle after I get up, since it's about time anyway," Ichiko answered. "By the way, who's Kekeki?"

Saoirse coughed on the smoke she was holding. "Kekeki?" she managed to get out through the strangling fit.

"I heard the name plainly," Ichiko said. "And so did Banríon Iona, I think. She certainly was in a hurry to talk about something else afterward. You and Angus weren't talking about catching spiny walkers, were you? I can tell there's something you're not telling me, Saoirse. Is Kekeki one of the arracht?"

Kekeki doesn't want Ichiko to come out to the Sleeping Giant and wants the Terrans to know as little about them as possible. Angus' statement as well as her mam's admonitions regarding the arracht all rolled around in Saoirse's head as Ichiko was talking. *She's already heard about the arracht. Plunkett and his clan or one of the others would have told her what they know—and the arracht took out the drones the Terrans sent around the archipelago . . .*

Ichiko was watching Saoirse as she struggled to show none of the internal turmoil on her face. *A lie hides best behind a little truth.* That was a saying she'd heard many of the seanns repeat—one of several aphorisms the clans had brought with them to the archipelago. "Aye," Saoirse admitted. "Kekeki's an arracht."

Ichiko drew back, her eyes widening slightly. "The arracht have *names*? They *talk*?"

"They don't talk." *At least not like us.* "And only Kekeki has a name." *As far as I know.* "Don't yeh Terrans name yer pets, or wild animals yeh see all the time and recognize?" When Ichiko nodded, Saoirse continued. "Well, Kekeki's the arracht we see most often around here. She's bigger than the others and has a really distinctive blue carapace with yellow spots. We call her Kekeki because that's something like the sound she makes. That's all."

Ichiko didn't look entirely convinced. "You said that Kekeki was making a mistake."

"She was," Saoirse answered. "Though hopefully she hasn't. The arracht have a taste for spiny walkers, and sometimes they break open the pots we use and take the walkers that are in them. One of the Clan Craig boats spotted Kekeki near the Clan Mullin pot buoys earlier. They told Uncle Angus, so he wanted to bring in the pots before any of the arracht could bother them. He and I were having a disagreement about whether he needed to do that now or wait for better weather."

Saoirse smiled, pleased with her impromptu fabrication. After a moment, Ichiko smiled back. "I'd love to see this Kekeki," she said.

"Yeh might. Maybe next time yeh come out here." The sentence ended with a rise, making it half-question and half-statement.

"Would you like that? Because I would. I'm fascinated by the archipelago and what all of you have accomplished out here."

Saoirse felt her chest tighten, and her smile widened helplessly. She nodded. "Aye. I would indeed. There's so much yeh haven't yet seen that I could show yeh."

"Then let's plan on it." They both saw a lightning flash and a few seconds later, a grumbling of thunder that shook heavy droplets of rain from the clouds. A blue-gray screen had fallen over the sea and the shoulder of the hill on which the compound stood.

"It's going to hit any moment now," Ichiko said. "We should go inside."

Separation And Anxiety

NOT LONG AFTER LOW SECOND, everyone had eaten breakfast in the Common Room and said their goodbyes to Ichiko. The sky had opened up during the High hours and it was still pouring, with winds tossing the rain in all directions. Saoirse stood alongside Ichiko, watching her Uncle Angus and her mam approach.

"Are yeh sure yer machine can fly in this?" Iona asked.

"I can tell yeh I wouldn't be willing to put a currach in the water in this kind of lashing even if I was guaranteed I'd catch every last bluefin in the Storm Sea," Angus added.

"I'll be fine," Ichiko said. "The flitters are built to take as much punishment as your world can dish out—but it probably won't be a *comfortable* ride," she added ruefully.

"Then yer welcome to stay," Iona told her. "The weather will pass. It always does."

"Thank you, but I need to get back anyway—the bio-shields only give me protection for a few cycles. I hope you understand."

"I want to go back with yeh," Saoirse interjected. "Yeh could drop me off in Dulcia and when yeh get back to First Base and have a chance to rest, yeh could come back to the town. I could show you around some of the farms outside the town. My cousin Sean joined Clan Taggart, and I could take yeh out there. Or I could take yeh to Usk and introduce you to some of the clans there. And when yer ready, I could come back out to Great Inish with yeh in the flitter again."

Ichiko hadn't said no, but the look on her mam's face told Saoirse that's what her response was going to be. *I need to go because if I'm in the flitter, then maybe Kekeki won't be tempted to do anything to it.* But she couldn't say that aloud, not to any of them.

"It's nice of yeh to offer, Saoirse, but I need yeh here for a bit," Iona said predictably. "With everything going on lately, we're behind on what needs to be done. The sheepers are ready for their shearing and the milch-goats are likely scattered all over the island by now. And those pots for the spiny walkers need to be pulled up, remember."

Saoirse heard the undertone of sarcasm in the last sentence. "But, Mam . . ." Saoirse began before Ichiko spoke up.

"Saoirse, I need to go back to *Odysseus* and put together my report anyway," she said. "It'll be several cycles before I can think about coming back here. We both have our duties to attend to. Stay here and help your family with what needs to be done, and I'll go back to my people and do the same."

Saoirse's mind flashed with the image of Ichiko in her flitter, spiraling down into a storm-lashed sea. She wanted to rage, wanted to shout at Ichiko, at her mam, at Angus. But they were all looking at her placidly. "At least let me walk down with you to the flitter," she said to Ichiko.

"That's not necessary," the woman answered. "I can have AMI bring the flitter up here and land it just outside the compound gate."

"Mebbe so, but I don't care," Saoirse said firmly. "I'll still walk yeh to the flitter, wherever yeh put it. Just let me grab my oilcloth."

A bit later, Saoirse heard the whine of the flitter's rotors and they saw it set down on the muddy open ground between the two clan compounds, rain sheeting off the machine. "Are you sure you want to walk out in this?" Ichiko asked and Saoirse nodded wordlessly, grabbing her oilcloth from the peg near the door.

In her head, Saoirse was speaking desperately, her thoughts directed at the arracht and Kekeki. *Listen to me. Yeh can't hurt her; yeh have to let her leave and yeh have to let her come back, too. Yeh have no idea what the Terrans could do in response if you hurt Ichiko—they can attack from the sky, without having to come down here at all. Yeh also don't know what that might mean to us here in the archipelago. Please, Kekeki. Yeh have to listen to me. This is terribly important. Just let her go . . .*

There was no answer, at least not in words. But a sense of acceptance settled in Saoirse that at least shaved the sharp edges from her worry. "Let's go, then," Saoirse told Ichiko.

Outside, they could hear waves crashing against the rocky beach far below, and looking out over the landscape, neither the Sleeping Wolf nor the Stepstones could be seen as everything faded into mist, rain, and cloud perhaps a quarter mile from the shore. As they approached the flitter, the canopy lit up with welcome light and the gullwing doors lifted. "Get in," Ichiko told Saoirse, then: "There's no sense in you getting soaked further while we say goodbye."

As Saoirse slid into the passenger seat, the doors closed, rain flowing over the canopy and the wind causing the flitter to rock slightly on its landing struts. The sound of the wind, at least, was muted. "Yer sure this can fly with the storm?" Saoirse shivered, even though the flitter was now pumping warmer air into the cabin.

"Don't worry," Ichiko told her. "AMI tells me everything's still well within the safety limits. Look, I want to give you something . . ." She reached into the compartment between the seats and brought out a gray, palm-sized metal box: a thin, small rectangle. Saoirse could see an oval metal mesh in the center and a small blue circle to one side with the words *CALL/ANSWER* etched below it. She handed the device to Saoirse, along with a separate tiny earpiece. "I'm not really supposed to do this, but . . . This is a simple com-unit. If you ever need to talk to me, just press the call button; if I can't answer, my AMI will take your message and let me know to call you back. Keep it in your pocket or hide it somewhere if you think that's best. If you're wearing the earpiece, you can hear me and talk back to me through that also. All you have to do is touch it with your finger first."

Saoirse turned the device over in her hand. It felt amazingly light and small for everything Ichiko claimed it could do, but then the Terran technology always seemed impossible and unattainable, much like the Terrans themselves. The earpiece was small enough that it would be difficult for anyone to see it even if they looked, and her hair would cover it easily. "Thank you," Saoirse said. "But why are yeh giving this to me?" She knew what she wanted Ichiko to answer; she also knew that it wasn't how Ichiko would respond. She held the com-unit and earpiece in her open hand. She didn't put it in her pocket, wondering if she really wanted to keep it. *Mam won't like this.*

"We offered a com-unit to your mam; she wouldn't take it. I thought you might be willing since you're interested in seeing Earth. I even think it might be important to Captain Keshmiri's decision to know more about the archipelago. If the Banríon won't talk to us, then maybe you can speak for your people." Ichiko was staring out through the windshield, not looking at Saoirse. "More than that, I've enjoyed being with you and talking with you. I'd like our conversations to continue. I thought maybe you'd like that, too."

If she'd had any doubts, Ichiko's last words had banished them; Saoirse found herself smiling. She closed her fingers around the com-unit and placed the earpiece in her left ear. "Aye, I'd like that very much."

"Good. Then we'll leave it at that." Blue light flashed on one of Ichiko's fingers. The door to the flitter alongside Saoirse's seat lifted again, startling her, and the rotors began to whine. Ichiko smiled at Saoirse. "Now put the com-unit in your pocket so your mam doesn't see it," Ichiko said. "Remember, if you want to talk to me, just press the blue button or tap the earpiece. And if you hear a sequence of three beeps in your earpiece or if the com-unit button glows blue, that's me calling you. To answer, same thing: either press the blue button, or tap the earpiece. Okay?"

Saoirse nodded. She slipped the com-unit into the pocket of her oilcloth. "Call me when yer back at First Base?" she asked. "I want to know yeh got there safe."

"I will. I promise. We'll talk soon."

Saoirse nodded again. She stepped out of the flitter and ran through the compound gate to the door of the house, stopping there to wave at Ichiko. The Terran waved back; the flitter's rotors shrilled as it lifted before flying over the compound toward the north.

Saoirse watched until she could no longer see the flitter through the rain. *Kekeki, don't you dare hurt her. Do you hear me?*

She thought she heard laughter in answer.

"AMI, call Saoirse," Ichiko said. "Audio only." Below, the town of Dulcia was sliding past the flitter, and the mountains surrounding Connor Pass were shrouded in cloud ahead. <*Calling,*> she heard AMI say.

A few moments later, Saoirse's voice came over the flitter's speakers. "Ichiko? Are yeh back already?" Her voice sounded strangely relieved, as if she'd been worried that Ichiko wouldn't call.

"Almost," Ichiko told her. "I'm just passing Dulcia and heading up toward First Base. I should be there shortly."

"Yeh didn't have . . ." Saoirse's voice trailed off, and Ichiko started to wonder if the transmission had somehow been lost, then: ". . . any trouble?"

"No. The storm tossed the flitter around a bit." <*That's not what she means,*> AMI interjected, and Ichiko drew in a breath. *I'd almost forgotten . . .* "Or are you asking me if there was 'trouble' like we had on the way over?"

"No." The answer came too quickly, accompanied by an unconvincing laugh. "I was just worried about the storm. That's all."

Ichiko didn't need AMI to tell her that Saoirse was lying about that, and that spoke again to other things hidden behind the words. *Better to ask when you're face-to-face, not over a com-unit. There's still time. At least, I hope so.* "Well, everything's fine, and I can see First Base ahead now. I'm going to take a shuttle back up to *Odysseus*, so I'll be gone a few cycles. I'll let you know when I'm back, and then we can talk about my coming out there again. In the meantime, if you need me, you know what to do. Just keep the com-unit with you, okay?"

"I'll do that," Saoirse said. "Umm, I really enjoyed yer visit, Ichiko."

"The feeling's mutual. Talk to you later."

"Looking forward to it."

"So am I. Bye, then. AMI, disconnect us."

There was a click, a hiss of quick static, and Saoirse was gone. Ten minutes later, and the flitter was in the bay while Ichiko was going through the decontamination ritual, with Chava watching her through the glass window. "Enjoy your trip?" Chava asked.

"For the most part," Ichiko answered. "The Inish don't exactly greet Terrans with open arms."

"Well, come on in. I have a lunch prepared for us if you're hungry."

"After days of just bio-shield paste? I'm absolutely *dying* for real food. Or even base food."

Chava grinned at her as the inner door to the air lock swung open. "You're not allowed to die. Even if you'll only get base food. Oh, and Commander Mercado told me that you should call him as soon as you had a chance on your return."

<*I was sent the same message,*> AMI commented. <*And he sent along an additional private message for you. I was waiting to tell you once you were actually inside First Base.*>

"Fine," Ichiko said to both of them. "I'm heading up to *Odysseus* on the next shuttle anyway."

After having lunch with Chava and giving her the highlights of the visit to the archipelago—which caused Chava, on hearing of the near-crash, to tell her AMI to have the base techs do a full diagnostic on her flitter—Ichiko went to her quarters to view Luciano's private message before she called him. The holo window opened and she saw him looking at her, sitting on the edge of his bed in his quarters. His face reflected the effects of what must have been a long and difficult day. He was wearing his uniform, but the top was unbuttoned, and his chin and cheeks showed the faint blue haze of stubble. His hands were folded on his lap, his thumbs restlessly prowling over each other as if he were nervous.

"Hey, Ichiko. Look, I've been thinking a lot about us, and the more I do, the more I hate the idea of ever losing you." He looked down toward the floor as if listening to something only he could hear, and Ichiko wondered if his AMI was whispering lines to him. "I think you were right in telling me that we were both taking the comfortable and easy route, and I'm sorry for my part in that. You need to know that I promise to put more effort into our relationship in the future, and I hope you're willing to do the same. Let's talk as soon as you get back here. I'll be looking forward to that."

He stopped and leaned forward; Ichiko thought the holo would end. But he leaned back and smiled, erasing some of the pain in his face. "Here's what I haven't said and what I should have told you long before now. I love you, Ichiko. That's what I've come to realize since we talked. I love you."

And with that, the holo did end.

"Chikushō," she said.

<*You shouldn't curse like that,*> her mother's voice scolded her through AMI. <*Remember, the commander wants you to call him.*>

"I don't know what to say. I haven't thought about any of this at all." She kept the rest to herself, wondering whether Luciano, given his position, might not be able retrieve her conversations with AMI. *He'll want me to say the same back to him, and I don't know if I can. I don't know if I love him. I'm not certain I even know what love's supposed to feel like.* Ichiko took a long breath. "AMI, call Luciano." *Maybe he'll be in a meeting where he can't be interrupted, and I can just leave a message for him . . .*

A window opened on the wall opposite Ichiko's bed. Luciano beamed at her. "I was beginning to think you weren't going to call. My AMI told me you were back at First Base well over an hour ago."

"I was starving after having nothing but shield paste to eat.

Lieutenant Bishara had made lunch for us, so I took the time to eat."

"Can't say I blame you. That stuff tastes like pulped paper soaked in bouillon. I had to eat nothing but shield paste for two solid weeks back in training—it might keep you alive, but you eventually wish it hadn't." He laughed at his joke, then looked at her from under lowered brows. "You got my private message?"

Right to it, then . . . "Yes, I did." Not sure what else to say, she hesitated.

"And?" he said into the awkward silence.

"I appreciate your honesty and willingness to be open, Luciano. I . . . I just wish we'd both tried that months ago." She could see the disappointment crawl over his face, and she hurried into the rest before he could respond. "I was honestly moved by what you said. Truly. I wish—" She stopped, then rushed to finish. "I wish I could say the same words you said back to you. I think . . . no, I *know* I could have, earlier in our relationship. But right now, I can't. Not without lying to you. That doesn't mean I'll never say those words, only that I'm still trying to figure out how I feel. I'm sorry, Luciano. I don't want to hurt you, but I also don't want to be less than honest. Especially now, when we're both trying to sort things out between ourselves."

She took a deep breath as she finished, watching Luciano carefully. His hands had left his lap, his arms now crossed defensively over his chest. "So you're telling me it's over."

She shook her head, hurrying into her answer. "No, I'm not saying that. Not at all. I'm saying that I still need more time and space to think—and believe me, I'll be taking into account what you told me in that message. Our relationship has meant a lot to me, Luciano. What we had and what we have isn't something I can forget or something I can just throw away. So no: it's not over. It's just . . . 'on hold' at the moment."

His lips pressed together. "I suppose that'll have to do. You're coming back up to *Odysseus*?"

She nodded. "On the next shuttle. I have a report to give to

Nagasi about my trip to the archipelago. I think you'll find it interesting as well. I'll tell you more when I get up there."

"I'll look forward to it. Maybe we could have dinner together?"

She managed a smile. *You can't say no. Not right now.* "Absolutely. It's a date."

His hands dropped back to his lap. "Good. I'll see you tomorrow evening, then. My quarters at 19:30?"

"19:30. Got it. AMI will remind me."

Luciano nodded. "Sleep well, Ichiko—and think about what I said. I do love you."

With that, the portal winked out.

"Chikushō," Ichiko said again.

<*Tsk! Such language,*> AMI scolded.

The Seeds Of Unspoken Secrets

"ANY CHANCE I CAN get my AMI fixed now?" Ichiko asked Nagasi, who shook his head in reply.

"Nope. In fact, from what I understand, the issues with the AMI system haven't gotten better; they've worsened. Several crew members have been complaining, and the techs still haven't figured out why any of this is happening. Until they do, no changes are allowed to be made." Nagasi's Nigerian accent seemed more prominent than usual, or maybe it was because she'd become too used to the Inish accent over the last few days. As usual, he was wearing an unbuttoned lab coat over his uniform. "So how was your adventure with the Inish?" he asked her. "Come on into my office. When your AMI told me you were on the way, I made tea."

She could smell the tea as she entered the office. The tea service, replete with finger sandwiches and scones, was already on his desk. He waved Ichiko to the chair in front of the desk before taking his own seat. "Go on," he told her, motioning toward the tray. "I've already started." He lifted his own mug—which smelled of coffee, not tea—in salute and sipped.

Ichiko poured herself a mug from the pot on the tray and took one of the finger sandwiches. "The archipelago was certainly interesting," she said after taking a bite and swallowing. "But the place and their culture deserve more study. I think we're missing something important with them."

Nagasi's eyebrows lifted in invitation; Ichiko told him about the flight over to Great Inish and the near failure of the flitter; the way the Inish shunned technology; how their society differed from that of the Mainlanders; the odd conversation she'd had with Saoirse about the arracht they called Kekeki. "There's something more they're hiding or aren't willing to tell me, I'm certain of it," Ichiko said finally. "The Inish and Mainlanders essentially had a war over the arracht. I've read and listened to everything the Mainlanders have to say about the arracht, but it's all jumbled and half the time they're giving me obvious tall tales that have passed through too many generations to be reliable. The Inish certainly know far more about the arracht than the Mainlanders, but for whatever reason they're reluctant to talk."

"You've heard what happened to our drones." It was less a question than a statement, and Ichiko simply nodded mutely. "Are you thinking that the problem with your flitter was related to what happened with the drones? You're thinking the arracht were involved? How would that even be possible?"

Ichiko took a sip of her tea and shrugged. "I certainly don't see how. There could be some natural phenomena out there that we're missing or something else entirely. I don't have the answer. But maybe we can find out. I persuaded Saoirse to take a com-unit, as you suggested. AMI, link with Nagasi's AMI, would you, then call Saoirse—it's about Low Third there, so she should be awake."

<Done.> In her head, Ichiko heard an echoing acknowledgment from Nagasi's deeper-voiced and Nigerian-accented AMI, then the hiss of the long-range connection to Saoirse's com-unit. On Nagasi's desk, a small oval portal opened; a somewhat stunned-looking Saoirse gazed back at them. In the background was the young woman's room. "Yeh didn't tell me this machine could do this," Saoirse said. "It looks like a hole has opened up and I'm looking into yer ship. When we talked the last time, all I heard was yer voice."

"I know," Ichiko answered. "You can do the same: if you want us to see you, just say 'holo connection' as you press the call button."

Saoirse nodded. They saw her gaze fall on Nagasi, and her eyes widened. "Who's that with you?"

"Hello, Saoirse," Nagasi said. "I'm Lieutenant Commander Nagasi Tinubu. I work with Ichiko."

"Don't let him fool you," Ichiko interjected with a laugh. "Nagasi's my boss, and I work for him. I was telling Nagasi about my trip to the archipelago and how interesting it was. He was especially interested when I mentioned Kekeki and the arracht. However, I really don't know much about the arracht at all, so we thought we'd call you."

Saoirse's eyes widened further, and she glanced from side to side as if trying to find a way to escape. "I don't know . . ." she began. "I'm not . . . The arracht? I don't know what to tell you."

"Well, we know from the historical record what they look like and that the Mainlanders hunted them," Nagasi said. "Even you Inish hunted them at first. I've read mainland reports from around the time of your Great Fishing War about the arracht sinking fishing boats and drowning those inside—which makes them sound rather dangerous, yet you Inish fought to protect them. So *are* the arracht dangerous?"

"No," Saoirse answered quickly, then: "Or only to those who would try to hurt them. They fought back to protect themselves. Yeh can't blame them for that."

Nagasi glanced at Ichiko with that statement, one eyebrow raised. "And how can the arracht determine who's friendly and who's not? Are you saying that they're intelligent enough to understand the difference?" Nagasi persisted.

"No." Again, the answer came too quickly. She was looking at Ichiko, pleadingly.

"I asked Rí Angus the same question," Ichiko said to Nagasi with a warning glance and a minuscule shake of her head. *Don't push her too hard . . .* "I told him that on Earth whale hunting was stopped because we felt whales were too intelligent for us to hunt them like animals—I have to admit that my birth country was one of the last to finally stop that practice, unfortunately. Rí Angus told me that the arracht simply didn't need to be treated the way they were. Whatever the reason, the arracht stopped attacking boats once the hunting of them stopped. The Rí didn't elaborate past that." *But if the arracht stopped attacking the boats once the hunting of them stopped, that's something an intelligent species would do . . .* She glanced at Nagasi, knowing he'd be thinking the same. "That's one reason why I feel I need to go back out there," Ichiko finished.

"When are yeh coming back out?" Saoirse asked, her voice sounding grateful for the change of subject. "Will it be soon?"

"I plan on returning to First Base within the next cycle or two. I'll call you on the com-unit when I'm back on First Base so that we can make arrangements."

"Good," Saoirse answered. She looked again toward Nagasi. "My mam is calling for me. She'll come looking if I don't answer, and I can't let her see this com-unit. It was good to meet yeh, Commander Tinubu. Ichiko, call me as soon as yer back." They saw her reach down to the com-unit. The portal collapsed, and Saoirse was gone.

"Somehow I suspect that if we called her back, she's not going to answer," Nagasi commented dryly. "Of course, now that we've used the com-unit, that doesn't matter."

<I opened the link to Saoirse's com-unit permanently,> Nagasi's AMI said in Ichiko's head, and she saw Nagasi nod at the statement. *<I can overhear and record everything she says and what others around her are saying. And her mother wasn't calling—that was a lie. Most of the rest was evasion. The young woman knows more than she's telling us.>*

Ichiko's AMI said nothing—not surprisingly, since the AMIs usually followed rank hierarchy.

"Nagasi, this isn't right," Ichiko said heatedly. "I won't be part of us spying on Saoirse and the Inish."

There was sympathy in his eyes, but he gave his head a slight shake. "Having the link open could potentially give us the answers to the questions you have, Ichiko," he said. "You can't deny that."

"And those answers would come at the cost of my betraying Saoirse's trust." Ichiko shook her head. "No. I won't do that, Nagasi, not without her knowledge. Not when I'm trying to gain her trust. It's not ethical—and you know that." *And I'll go to the captain if I have to.* She hoped that Nagasi would understand the unsaid threat.

Nagasi bit at his upper lip. His fingertips drummed at his desktop as he stared at Ichiko. Finally, he sighed. "Remove the open link, AMI," Nagasi said.

<Removed.>

Wishing she didn't feel she had to do this, Ichiko thought to her own AMI. *<Is the link shut down?>*

<It is.>

"Happy?" Nagasi asked Ichiko.

"Mostly, but I shouldn't have had to ask," she told him.

"We could have learned a lot from that open channel."

"I never told Saoirse that we'd be using the com-unit to listen in on her. And I won't keep the channel open without her permission."

"And if Captain Keshmiri had said we're to do it anyway?" Nagasi asked her.

Ah. So he did *understand what I was thinking.* "Then I'd tell Saoirse to take the damn box and earpiece and toss them in the ocean. Better yet, I'd tell her to attach it to this Kekeki and let her swim away with it."

Nagasi pursed his lips. "That would be deliberate destruction of ship property and a gross violation of your contract. The captain could toss you in the brig," he said, then chuckled in his deep, rich voice. "And I'd expect nothing less of you, Ichiko."

"Were you really going to leave that channel open?"

Nagasi grinned. "Only if you didn't protest, though I was fairly sure you would," he said. "But since we *don't* have the open com, I expect you to give me a minute-by-minute report on your trip. This stuff about the arracht—well, the possible implications are staggering, as I suspect you're aware. Don't leave any details out at all. Everything could be important . . ."

Saoirse put the com-unit in the drawer under her bed, placing it in the boxed collection of seashells she'd put together as a child. The earpiece she left in, making sure her jaw-length hair was down over it. She went into the clanhouse kitchen from which she could hear people talking. The low voices she heard went silent as the wooden floor creaked under Saoirse's weight. Her mam was sitting with Rí Angus and Rí Keane of Clan Craig at a wooden prep table scarred with ancient knife cuts. A pot of tea sat in a woven cozy in the center of the table, and the trio all had their hands wrapped around steaming mugs, the smoke from their pipes draped in the air. Their faces swiveled toward her as one as she entered.

"When is that Ichiko intending to come back here?" her mam asked, taking the pipe stem from her mouth. Saoirse suppressed a surge of guilt, wondering if they suspected she had the com-unit and this was a clumsy trap. *"I plan on coming back to First Base within the next cycle or two . . ."*

"I have no idea," she answered. "For all I know, Ichiko's wandering around Dulcia with Minister Plunkett, or still at First Base, or back on their ship. Or maybe she's gone to one of the other towns to see what they're like." She shrugged. "Yeh know as much as I do, Mam. She'll be here when she gets here. Or are yeh planning to tell her she's not welcome to return?"

"There's no need to take that kind of tone with us, Saoirse," her mam said, frowning.

Rí Angus sighed. "Saoirse, yeh know why we're concerned. Kekeki made it clear—"

"Kekeki *allowed* Ichiko to come here," Saoirse interrupted before he could finish. "I already told Mam about that. Surely, she's told the two of yeh already."

"Aye, she has," Rí Keane spoke up, exhaling a cloud of blue-gray aromatic smoke before setting his pipe down on the table. "And I suspect Kekeki made the decision only because yeh were with the woman. If the Terran had been alone, she'd be food for the spiny walkers."

"And if that had happened, Rí Keane, we'd now have a whole flock of angry Terrans here on Great Inish, trying to figure out why their stupid machine crashed," Saoirse replied heatedly. "Or worse, they'd have smashed Great Inish from orbit and killed the lot of us for Ichiko's death. So yeh should all be glad Kekeki was wise enough to change her mind, no matter why she did so. As for me, I look forward to Ichiko coming back here. I think that—"

Saoirse stopped in mid-sentence. A new voice intruded, not that of anyone at the table but one that sounded only in her head: Kekeki. Looking at the others, she knew they were hearing it as well. *"We would talk with Saoirse about this Ichiko. Alone. Saoirse, yeh should come to us."* And with that statement, the sense of connection with the arracht vanished.

Saoirse looked at the others, trying to read the expressions on their faces and failing. Her mam's gaze was on the window, staring out toward the bell tower on An Cró Mór and taking a contemplative sip of her tea. Rí Keane had picked up his pipe again, wreathing himself in smoke. Rí Angus' lips were a tight line, but they loosened as he spoke. "I'll row yeh over if yeh can be ready by Low Fourth."

Saoirse nodded. "Thanks, Uncle. I'm ready now." *Do any of you know what Kekeki wants to talk about?* she wanted to ask. But she closed her mouth. Rí Angus grunted and pushed his chair back from the table. He downed his tea, grabbed his pipe, and pulled his folded flat cap from his jacket pocket. Her mam continued to stare at the window while Rí Keane sucked on his pipe. Neither of them said anything.

"We'll be off, then," Rí Angus said.

At 19:30, Ichiko was standing in front of Luciano's door. It opened without her knocking. "Hey," he said. "My AMI told me you were out there. Come on in. Our dinner's already here and hot."

She entered, noting that Luciano had set the table and that the meal appeared to be identical to the *ichijyu sansai* that he'd ordered when they'd had the argument and she'd stormed out. She wasn't sure whether that was intended as a message to her or what that message was supposed to convey. She felt her stomach roil uneasily, though she tried to smile at Luciano as she sat. He lifted the covers from the plates, letting fragrant steam rise from all the dishes except the cucumber salad. "Dig in," he said. "I gave us both chopsticks, but honestly I'm just going to use a fork rather than embarrassing myself." He lifted the utensil, waving it toward her, and chuckled.

An involuntary small smile curved Ichiko's lips. "I'll probably use a fork myself. I'm out of practice with chopsticks."

"Which dish am I supposed to start with?" Luciano asked her. "Is there an etiquette to this?"

That gave Ichiko pause. *Luciano usually jumps right in . . . to everything. Is he being cautious because of me?* "Not really," she said, "other than in Japanese culture, everything is served separately and is there for a reason. You have a staple carbohydrate—that's the rice. There's fermented food, like the miso and the vegetables in it, which are supposed to be good for digestion. The soup's good for hydration. Then there's the main dish of fish, which is rich in protein. You also have the side dishes of vegetables: the cucumber salad and the potato stew, which is also in beef broth. As for etiquette, you're not supposed to mix things. like mixing your side dishes with the rice, which some people consider 'soiling' the rice. At least, that's what I remember from when my grandmother would make *ichijyu sansai* meals for us."

Luciano nodded, though Ichiko wondered if he'd really listened to what she'd said or cared about the answer. She dipped her spoon into the miso soup; Luciano echoed her movement.

"Nagasi sent me a brief summary report on your trip to the archipelago through my AMI," Luciano said as they sipped at the miso. "It sounded interesting. He mentioned the issue your flitter had on the way over—have you had the flitter checked out?"

"Lieutenant Bishara ran a full diagnostic as soon as I returned.

She couldn't find anything obviously wrong, but she said the flitter's flight recorder was 'utterly whacked'—that's the technical term she used . . ." Ichiko smiled again at the memory. ". . . for a few minutes at the same time I lost control of the flitter. But there wasn't anything her techs could find to indicate a cause. It seems to be an anomaly. Just to be safe, she wiped the software on all the flitters at First Base and reinstalled the systems. AMI, send Luciano the records that Lieutenant Bishara sent to me."

<Done.>

"Good. I'll have Engineering look those over and see if they find something Bishara's people may have missed." Luciano set down the spoon and picked up the fork. He stabbed at the fish, taking a bite on his fork and chewing contemplatively before swallowing. "You want to go back there, don't you?"

"I do, very much," Ichiko told him. "There's more there we should learn—that we *need* to learn before we leave. I'm certain of it."

"Nagasi also mentioned that you stopped him from using the com-unit you gave that girl to record Inish conversations."

"Did he tell you why?"

"He did." Luciano put down his fork and laid his hand on top of hers. Ichiko began to pull it away, then stopped. "I would say that you had a perfectly admirable reason for making that demand," Luciano finished. "So when are you going back to figure things out?"

"As soon as I can," she answered. His hand was still on hers, his fingers stroking her skin.

"The next shuttle down is tomorrow morning at 07:00," Luciano told her. "I'll make sure that you have a seat on it." He paused, staring at her. "But you won't be leaving for hours yet," he added.

She could hear what was unsaid in that statement. "Luciano . . ."

He didn't answer. He just looked at her, his hand still resting on hers.

"Let's finish dinner," she told him. "Then we'll see what happens."

Luciano nodded. He lifted his hand away from hers. "That's good enough for me," he said.

Saoirse watched Kekeki rising from the depths underneath the Sleeping Wolf, past the lighted openings of the arracht dwellings that glimmered along the cliff wall. The tentacles on the arracht's limbs wriggled and flexed, writhing like a nest of sea anemones and pushing against the rocks as her flat tail propelled her upward, the blue flecks along her spine and short arms glowing like the electric lights Saoirse had seen in Dulcia.

The arracht broke the surface, sending a wave surging over the ledge on which Saoirse stood, the water breaking over Saoirse's boots. The arracht's front arms slammed down to hold her erect and out of the water, gill casings opening and closing over the red lace of the gills along her body's pale underside. Her long neck and head, touched with the parti-colored patches of plotch, towered over Saoirse; the yellow eyes along her eyestalks moving as she stared down.

Saoirse heard the clicks and pops as the arracht began to talk a moment before the words came to her mind in that impossible Inish accent. "Yeh've come alone, as we asked. Good. We wish to know if the Terran woman truly intends to come here again."

"She does," Saoirse told her. "I know she wants to learn more about the archipelago." *And about yeh arracht . . .* Saoirse tried to hold the thought back but couldn't.

"And us. Aye." Kekeki blew air in what nearly sounded like a wet laugh to Saoirse. "We worry about what her people mean for us. Yer people hunted us, but we could mostly hide from yeh or fight back when we needed to in order to protect ourselves. With those up there"—several fingers lifted, pointing toward the roof of the cavern—"we might not be able to hide, and we might not be able to easily fight back. At least, not yet. We worry about this. So we ask yeh, as the one who knows the sky-people best: do they intend us harm?"

"I only know one of them," Saoirse answered.

"Is one not like all?"

Saoirse almost laughed. "No. Do yeh think I'm the same as my mam or Uncle Angus or my brother? Do yeh think the Mainlanders are the same as us on Great Inish?"

Kekeki sank lower in the water, until her gill covers were underwater while she held onto the ledge, her fingers clinging to the crevices of the rock. Saoirse saw bubbles rise around her before she rose again. "Yer people are far less like each other than we are," Kekeki answered. "We understand that. What is yer word?" Saoirse had the sense that Kekeki was rummaging about in Saoirse's mind. It was an uneasy feeling, but before she could say anything to Kekeki, it was gone again. "Ah. Yeh think of yerselves as *individuals*. We had hoped that perhaps the sky-people were not so much *individuals* and more like us. Of the same mind always."

"But the sky-people, as yeh call them, *are* us," Saoirse told her. "We're all from the same world. Fourteen or fifteen generations back, our people were born there, too."

Kekeki's body gave a long tremor that started below the waterline and ended at her head. "No. Yer wrong in that," Kekeki responded. "They *aren't* like yeh. We know that. In the sky-people there exists nothing that belongs to this world. Nothing. We feel that. But this world lives in *yeh* as much as if not more than the home of yer ancestors. Yeh might once have been the same, but yeh are no longer *them*."

Saoirse was shaking her head in mute denial before Kekeki finished. *If that's true, then none of us will be allowed to go back. I'll never see Earth, never see all the places I've imagined, never see Ichiko's Japan . . .* "Why are yeh telling me this?" Saoirse asked Kekeki.

"We've decided we need to know more about the sky-people. We were a long time coming to that decision, but we see now that just trying to hide away from them was a false hope. They already suspect that we are more than simply animals, so we want yeh to bring yer friend to us. We'll tell this to yer mam and the others who know us. Yeh will bring her to us when she comes here again."

"Yer not going to hurt her." Saoirse said it flatly as a warning, though she had no idea how she could guarantee that if the arracht decided otherwise.

"We would only hurt those who first hurt us," Kekeki answered.

Saoirse knew that was the only answer she was going to get.

Learning The Other

'LL BE IN DULCIA early next cycle with my uncle and Liam.
Yeh and I can take the flitter back to Great Inish, and I'll introduce you to Kekeki on Sleeping Wolf."

That was the message that Saoirse had sent to Ichiko as she
was descending on the shuttle toward First Base. Ichiko loosened
her grip on the handles of her seat, which was shaking with the
entry into the Canis Lupus atmosphere. *<AMI, open the comlink to
Saoirse. Voice only.>*

<Done. She's listening; go ahead.>

"Saoirse, this is Ichiko. I'm still on the shuttle and just approaching First Base." Saoirse wasn't the only one listening: the
three ensigns coming down for rotation on First Base had all
stopped their own conversation in their seats ahead of her and
were all obviously pretending not to listen, even if they couldn't
hear Saoirse's answers. Ichiko ignored them with an effort.

"Is that why yer voice sounds so shaky?" Saoirse asked.

Ichiko laughed at that. "It absolutely is. The winds are knocking us around quite a bit."

"Oh?"

"Don't worry. It's nothing serious. We'll be through the clouds
in a few minutes, and things will smooth out. I need to go over
my mission outline with Lieutenant Bishara, then I really need to

catch a few hours of sleep. I should be in Dulcia by Low Sixth next cycle to pick you up. Will that work?"

"Aye," Saoirse replied enthusiastically. "I'm looking forward to this!"

"So am I—I finally get to meet this Kekeki, eh? That's great news. I'll let you go, though, since we're starting to make our approach to First Base. I'll call you when I'm in Dulcia with the flitter, but if for some reason you're going to be delayed, let me know. Until then, take care of yourself. AMI, close the connection."

A background hiss that Ichiko had barely been aware of vanished. In the row of seats in front of her, one of the new ensigns leaned toward the other. Ichiko caught part of the whisper: ". . . that one and Commander Mercado—" The whisper ended as the ensign glanced behind and saw Ichiko staring directly at him. He quickly turned away and sat back in his seat.

<*I'm betting that your staying with the commander last night didn't help stifle the rumors,*> AMI said.

"Shut up," Ichiko said, to both the ensign and AMI.

Neither one answered.

"Mam, I'm heading to Dulcia with Uncle Angus and Liam. I'll be back with Ichiko in the flitter by Low Seventh or Eighth. And next cycle I'll take her out to meet Kekeki."

Saoirse's mother was sitting at the table in the front room of her house in the compound, with Rí Keane Craig across the table from her and a jug of poitín in the center and clay mugs set before each of them. They were both smoking pipes; the air in the room was clouded. "Come here a moment," her mam said, motioning to her. When Saoirse reached the table, her mam said simply: "Rí Keane and I are worried."

Saoirse felt a surge of irritation as she released an exhalation and sharpened her voice. "About what?" She looked from her mam to Rí Keane, who didn't meet her eyes, only looked down at his poitín as if the answer might have drowned in the alcohol.

Angus entered the kitchen at that moment, evidently looking for Saoirse. He said nothing, leaning against the wall at the door. Her mam glanced over to the Rí, pressing her lips together, then shook her head at Saoirse.

"Everything's moving so fast," her mam said. "And we don't know where it might lead."

"It's Kekeki and the arracht who are wanting to move forward," Saoirse answered. "They're the ones asking me to bring Ichiko to meet them. Yeh know that. Yeh heard it just like I did."

"But that wasn't their attitude when yeh first brought Ichiko here," Rí Keane responded, lifting up his head. "And the last time we did as the arracht asked, we ended up in a war with the Mainlanders. All the clans, Mainlander and Inish, lost several good people then."

"It's not that we regret having helped the arracht," her mam interjected, with a slight shake of her head toward Rí Keane. "They never deserved anyone hunting and killing them an' we know that. We've been more than repaid by them with the help they've given us in the years since: with our fishing; with keeping the Mainlanders away from our fishing grounds; with their knowledge of the currents and the weather. They've rescued our people when currachs foundered on rocks or during storms; they've given us plants we can use for medicine; they do what they can to keep creatures like the feckin' blood feeders from threatening us."

She turned back to Saoirse then. "I know Kekeki has asked to meet Ichiko," she continued, "and I suppose we have to trust the arracht's judgment on that. I just worry for yeh, Saoirse, since yer friends with the woman. What if the arracht decide that they need to consider the Terrans as dangerous? What if the Terrans decide that the arracht are dangerous? What if this leads us into another war, only this one between the arracht and the Terrans? I don't want our clans in the middle of *that*. It's a war we can't win."

"What if having Ichiko talk to Kekeki doesn't do anything *at all* except allow the Terrans and the arracht to understand each other, the way our clans understand the arracht?" Saoirse answered. "Mam, I'm not friends with the *Terrans*—the only one of them I know at all is Ichiko. I'm friends with *her*. Would I go with them back to Earth if I could? Aye, I would, just so I could have that experience. That doesn't mean I love yeh all or this place any less, and it doesn't mean that I would'na ever come back." She waved her hands, encompassing the sky and the unseen stars. "Just think of how much *more* there is out there. I want to embrace that, not be afraid of it. Ask yerselves this: isn't that the way those of Clan Mullin and Clan Craig felt when they first left the mainland to come out here?"

"Your daughter has the right of it, Iona, if yeh don't mind my saying so," Rí Angus interjected. "As the proverb goes: 'The wind stays fast asleep when prophets say it will blow.' There's no sense in playing a 'what if' game. If Kekeki wants to talk with Ichiko, let 'em talk. What happens after will happen. If we worried about things that might happen, not a one of us would ever take a currach out t'sea. Speaking of which, 'tis a fine day and mine is ready. Liam's already down at the Strand quay." He pushed off the wall. "Yeh coming, Saoirse?"

"Mam?" Saoirse asked.

Iona sighed. "I suppose Rí Keane and I have said our piece. G'wan with yeh, then. And I hope yer right. Both of yeh."

Her mam stood up and opened her arms to Saoirse. They hugged, and Iona kissed Saoirse on her forehead. "I'll pray to Spiorad Mór that yeh and Kekeki are right about this," she whispered into Saoirse's ear. "No matter what, I love yeh. Just remember that."

"I will," Saoirse whispered back. She tightened her embrace momentarily, then released her mam.

"I'm ready now, Uncle Angus," she said.

They had brought the currach into Dulcia Harbor and tied up the boat to the cleats on the quay. "There she is," Liam said to his sister, pointing toward the mountains beyond Dulcia. Saoirse pushed her glasses closer to her nose and squinted through the glass. She saw a darker blur moving against the backdrop of clouds: Ichiko's flitter, if Liam was correct.

Her Uncle Angus glanced up also and nodded. "That's her," he acknowledged. Saoirse could hear the whine of the flitter's rotors now as the flitter cleared the buildings up near High Street and approached the harbor. She could see a distance-blurred Ichiko waving to them from behind the glass of the flitter's canopy. The flitter set down on the harbor walkway several meters from them, visibly startling a capall that was passing by with a cart of sugar root destined for the local market. The canopy lifted, and Ichiko stepped from the flitter.

"Dia duit," she said to them, mispronouncing the words enough that Liam snickered. Saoirse dug an elbow into her brother's ribs.

"Dia duit, Ichiko," Saoirse answered, and Ichiko shook her head at the subtle correction, chuckling ruefully.

"AMI told me I nearly had the phrase right," the Terran sighed. "I'll just have to practice more. Are we still taking the flitter over to Great Inish?"

"Aye," Saoirse told her. "Liam and my uncle are staying here in Dulcia for a few more bells."

"Or longer," Liam added. "Hopefully."

"If yeh do, it'll be because of Uncle Angus, not yerself," Saoirse told him. Then she turned to Ichiko. "I'm ready if yeh are."

"Let's go, then." Ichiko gestured to the passenger seat in the flitter. "Rí Angus, Liam, we'll see you back on Great Inish."

Angus grunted at that. "I certainly hope so," he said.

Ichiko found the first day back on the archipelago largely a repeat of her first trip. Crowds of children greeted their arrival (including Gráinne, who immediately claimed Ichiko as her own). There was the gathering at Clan Mullin's main clanhouse, with the Banríon as well as Rí Keane and others of Clan Craig in attendance, with the usual accompaniment of blue-gray tree strand pipe smoke. As the group became more socially lubricated, there were tales from the older folks (<*The seanns*>, AMI informed Ichiko), as well as music and dancing.

Ichiko smiled and laughed through it as best she could, though she noticed that Saoirse said very little to her mam or Rí Keane. It was nearly High Fourth with no end in sight to the party before Ichiko managed to disengage herself enough to seek out Saoirse, who she'd glimpsed leaving the clanhouse. Ichiko found her smoking her pipe outside while gazing out over the calm sea. "Looking for Rí Angus and your brother?" Ichiko asked as she approached Saoirse.

Saoirse laughed at that, smoke billowing from her mouth to be snatched away by the wind. "Neh. Given how late in the cycle it is, I suspect one or t'other or both of 'em found someone to be with. I doubt they'll be back until the next cycle or the one after. I just needed to escape from all the people. I take it yeh did, too."

Ichiko nodded in the direction of the clanhouse. "They certainly ask a lot of questions."

"And usually all the same one only with different words? The one yeh keep telling 'em yeh can't answer?"

Ichiko managed a short laugh at that. "Exactly." She looked out over the sea, then pointed to an island to their left. "That's where we're going tomorrow? The Sleeping Wolf?"

"Aye, 'tis."

"Is there anything I need to know before we meet Kekeki? Should I be prepared for anything?"

"I don't know," Saoirse said around the pipe stem clenched in her teeth. To Ichiko, she sounded unsure and hesitant. Her hands lifted and fell again, then she took the pipe from her mouth. "I really *don't* know. Kekeki . . . she said she wanted to meet yeh and that it was to be just the two of us. No one else."

"She *said* this?" Ichiko asked, her head tilted inquiringly. "So they *can* communicate with you, and they do have language? That's not what you told me before."

"Aye," Saoirse admitted, her face coloring. "I wasn't supposed to tell yeh, but yeh might as well know now 'cuz you'll know it for certain when we meet the arracht. When I first met Kekeki, she . . . well, she touched me and that did something to me so that we could understand each other. Kekeki . . ." Saoirse hesitated, seeming to be searching for the next word. ". . . *changed* me. It scared me at first, but it happened so quickly there was nothing I could do about it. Like this . . ."

Saoirse reached out suddenly toward Ichiko's arm, her hand trying to squeeze around Ichiko's forearm; after a few seconds, Saoirse cried out and snatched her hand back quickly, shaking it. She stared at Ichiko, wide-eyed.

"Sorry," Ichiko told her. "The electrical current in my bio-shield keeps increasing when you try to hold on until it shocks you: it's a defense mechanism. I should have warned you. The numbness will go away in a few minutes."

"Then we do need to tell Kekeki not to try the same thing. We don't want her thinking yer attacking her if she tries to touch yeh. I've told yeh; the arracht don't like yer technology. Yeh remember what Kekeki did to yer flitter when yeh first came here? What if she does the same to that thing that protects yeh? What if she just turns it off, the way she did to that AMI thing yeh say yeh have in yer head?"

<Can this Kekeki do that—can it deactivate your bio-shield? Did Kekeki shut me off when your flitter nearly crashed?> AMI's voice sounded worried. <Maybe you should rethink this.>

<I don't know. I don't think so,> Ichiko answered in her head.

<You don't think it can? That's not a "no." Is this creature going to try to change you? What does that even mean, that it "changed" Saoirse?>

Ichiko decided that might be an important question. "What do you mean when you say Kekeki changed you?" she asked Saoirse.

Saoirse gave a shrug. "She said something about it being because of the plotch, that the plotch is why we could suddenly understand each other."

Ichiko's eyes narrowed at that. "Plotch? That fungus under your skin?"

Saoirse nodded. "I'll be your translator. That way Kekeki won't have to do to yeh what she did to me since yeh don't have the plotch." Saoirse took another pull on the pipe and exhaled a long, shuddering breath of smoke as Ichiko waited. "I really wanted yeh to come back," Saoirse said finally, "but now all these terrible thoughts are going through me head, and I worry I did the wrong thing pushing for yeh to come back to the islands."

<She's right, you know.> AMI's voice was loud in Ichiko's head, scolding her. <If anything like what happened to Saoirse happens to you, you'll never leave here. Never. You won't even be allowed into First Base or back aboard the ship without being behind a bio-shield or in isolation. You'll never be able to touch Commander Mercado again—in any way. Maybe that's what Saoirse wants. She feels more than just friendship toward you.>

"This was my choice," Ichiko said in answer to both of them. "I was well aware of the risks and willing to accept the consequences. Saoirse, whatever might happen tomorrow, it won't be your fault. I wanted to come out here to learn more, no matter what the cost. My choice. You didn't convince me to do anything I didn't want to do already. You have to believe that."

"If yeh say so." Her answer was nearly a whisper stolen by the wind. She looked so upset that Ichiko wanted to hug her, but that would have been a mistake—for more than one reason.

"Hey," Ichiko said loudly enough that Saoirse turned to her. "It's okay," she told the young woman. "I'm looking forward to tomorrow—next cycle—and you should, too. Everything will be okay."

Saoirse managed a fleeting smile that only touched the corners of her lips. "Yeh promise?" she asked and Ichiko nodded enthusiastically.

"Promise," she said. "Now, let's go back in before they all start wondering what we're doing out here."

Minds So Like Still Water

"OH, MY GOD," Ichiko breathed as they entered one of the caverns along the "tail" of the Sleeping Wolf. She'd said little on the way over, as Saoirse rowed a small, two-person currach from Great Inish. The sea, thankfully, had been relatively calm, though the deep and slow swells lifted and dropped them far more than Ichiko's stomach liked—it reminded her too much of the rough shuttle descents from *Odysseus* to the surface.

But once inside the cave . . .

The water gentled and cleared; even with the wan light entering from the cave entrance, Ichiko could see light within the water itself as her eyes adjusted, glowing as if disturbed whenever the oars Saoirse held swept through the water. Swirls of radiant blue and green drifted behind and around them and the cavern walls were streaked with the same radiance. And when Ichiko looked down . . .

It was as if they were drifting in azure air over a deep and craggy canyon, and all along the canyon walls there was life and movement: creatures swimming in and out of what were obviously nonnatural structures, buildings with windows and openings that also glowed with the same phosphorescence. It was difficult to discern scale, but to Ichiko it seemed she was gazing impossibly up toward a night sky crowded with stars, but then the image shifted. No, she was looking down from above to a nighttime city, the canyon walls like the flanks of skyscrapers with their windows all alight.

A city . . . The implications hit Ichiko then, as Saoirse grounded their boat on a rocky ledge at the rear of the cave. Saoirse leaped out and wrapped a rope from the prow around a nearby rock as Ichiko covertly thought to AMI. *<Are you seeing this?>*

<I am, and I'm recording it,> AMI replied. *<I'm also . . . >* That was as far as AMI got. There was a sound of static in Ichiko's head and the sense of AMI's presence vanished, leaving a strange emptiness behind.

<AMI?> There was no answer. She glanced at her finger: the gleam of the connection to AMI was gone. Ichiko could see Saoirse waiting for her to leave the boat. *My bio-shield* . . . Suddenly frightened, Ichiko put her hand on the boat's gunwale, afraid she was going to feel the wet wood there. But she felt nothing, only the pressure of the shield keeping her from actually making contact. She took a grateful breath that, as usual, tasted of canned air. She stood, stepping out of the boat and onto the ledge.

She felt disoriented and overwhelmed. Saoirse had already told her the arracht had the gift of language, but then many animals— whales, porpoises, apes—also had vocalizations that allowed them to communicate with each other. But this, this underwater city inside the Sleeping Wolf . . .

There was only one answer to that: the arracht were likely sentient in a very humanlike manner. They were builders and architects; they were technological at least to some degree—the first such species that humankind had encountered. Ichiko remembered classes on alien life that she'd attended prior to leaving on *Odysseus*. There, the professors had cited four qualities that, according to them, distinguished humankind from animals: 1) the ability to invent words and concepts and thus create entirely new expressions and concepts; 2) the ability to take differing areas of knowledge such as friendship and sex and generate new social relationships and technologies; 3) the ability to use mental symbols like written language as a way to encode and transmit experiences; 4) the ability to think abstractly and thus contemplate things beyond our current range of experience.

She wondered if this was alien life that fit those parameters and, if so, what that meant going forward. In fairness, she also remembered other professors scoffing at that list of qualities and claiming the qualities cited were too human-centric and that we might not even *recognize* another intelligent life-form if we came across it.

Saoirse was staring down into the water from the ledge's drop-off. "Kekeki's coming to us now," she said, pointing downward. Ichiko moved alongside her, following Saoirse's gesture. She could see one of the arracht rising rapidly toward them. Like many of the Lupusian animals, it had six limbs with a horizontal tail fluke at the rear of its sinuous body. As the arracht breached, Ichiko took an involuntary step backward.

Water slid in sheets from the shell-like carapace over its head, a saturated ultramarine splashed with yellow-and-green patches of plotch. Twin eyestalks twitched, the several eyes in each—golden with black slits for pupils—moving independently as the creature surveyed them. It continued to rise from the water, towering meters above them. On its underside, lacy red gills waved in long furrows in paler skin. Finally, the two top arms emerged to grasp the rocks of the ledge with the tangle of tentacles at the arms' ends.

But there was no AMI to record the sight and send the footage of the arracht up to *Odysseus*. Ichiko was cut off and alone. Her breath was coming fast, her pulse pounding in her temples. The parrotlike beak below the carapace opened, revealing a blood-colored tongue, and Ichiko heard a loud sequence of clicks and hissing whistles.

"Aye," she heard Saoirse say to Kekeki as if answering a question. "That's Ichiko, and neh, she doesn't look like any of the Inish."

"Kekeki's *talking* to you?" Ichiko asked. "And the two of you understand each other? How?"

"Aye, we're talking, but the 'how' I don't really understand meself," Saoirse answered. "I hear Kekeki talking like an Inisher in me head, and I suppose I sound like an arracht in hers."

Kekeki simply watched them, one eyestalk appearing to be fixed on Ichiko, the other on Saoirse, making Ichiko wonder how the arracht viewed the world. Kekeki spoke again and Ichiko waited for Saoirse to translate. "Kekeki wants me to tell yeh that they cut the false creature from yeh so that we could talk privately and that yeh shouldn't be afraid."

"Tell her that the 'false creature' isn't a person but just a tool like the boats you Inish use or your nets and fishing gear. It helps me remember things and communicate with our ship."

Saoirse repeated the words to Kekeki, who lowered herself briefly into the water and reemerged again with a torrent of clicks and airy tones. "Kekeki says yeh have no idea what that creature in yer head actually is now. She also says yeh'll have to remember on yer own and yeh can talk to yer ship again after yeh leave here. And she says that, aye, it's the plotch that allows her to talk to the Inish. She asks if yeh don't have other living beings that are part of yeh or do yeh only use the false creatures yeh've built?"

Kekeki was still staring at her with the eyes of one eyestalk. Ichiko was shaking her head, not certain how to answer Kekeki's question or even if she should. *Yes, every human harbors other lifeforms inside: bacteria in our guts and mouths, demodex mites living in our eyelashes, disease viruses that are active or dormant, and more.* She had no idea if that's what Kekeki meant or how to even start to explain that. She tried to imagine what Nagasi or Captain Keshmiri might tell her. *They'd likely give me conflicting advice. All I can do is respond to her as best I can.*

"Tell her that the answer's both yes and no," she said to Saoirse, who started to repeat the words to Kekeki. "All humans have symbiotic creatures living on and inside us that interact with us in a mutually beneficial or just neutral way, if that's what Kekeki means. Bacteria in our stomach and intestines help us digest and get nourishment from what we eat, for example—and the Lupusians have the same. But some of those bacteria and viruses are parasitic or actively harmful. They can also make us sick or even kill us. Tell her that I don't know enough to give her a good answer—but I could let her talk to someone on our ship who knows much more about this than I do, if she gives me back the 'false creature' she took away."

Kekeki was answering before Ichiko finished, Saoirse translating. "Yeh don't understand what she was asking. Yeh can't hear the words of other species. Yeh have nothing like plotch to create a linkage for yeh."

As Kekeki's beak snapped shut, her nearest arm moved before Ichiko could respond, the fingerlike tentacles at the end wrapping around her head. She felt the impact, making her take a step backward, even though her bio-shield prevented the tentacles from actually touching her. "No!" Ichiko shouted. "You shouldn't . . . ." The bio-shield snapped and crackled, sparks visible in the darkness. Kekeki hissed, and the tentacles slipped away as her arm fell back to the ledge. Kekeki loosed another barrage of clicks and hisses.

"Yeh hide yerself away inside that false shell," Kekeki answered through Saoirse. "No wonder yeh can't understand. If yeh truly want to know this world, yeh must abandon that shell." Her eyestalk wriggled as a quick flash of red rippled through her body. "We could strip it from yeh now, if yeh wish," Saoirse translated. Ichiko could see the distress in Saoirse's face at saying that.

Ichiko felt a quick thrill of terror. "No," Ichiko said, loudly enough that the word reverberated from the cavern walls. "That's not permitted. There are things in this world that could kill me and my people if I returned with them."

"Yeh've already said that there are things in yer world that are already capable of killing yeh." Even through Saoirse's voice, Ichiko could sense amusement in the statement. "How is that any different? Yer just afraid of this world because yeh don't know it."

"There's some truth in that," Ichiko admitted.

"Kekeki, yeh don't understand." That was Saoirse, speaking directly to Kekeki. "There are many of us here who would like to visit Earth or perhaps even return there permanently. But the sky-people—the Terrans—won't let *any* of us return to Earth until they know that we're not bringing diseases from here with us. Those same diseases nearly killed all of us when we first exposed ourselves to this world. That's why Ichiko wears the 'false shell,' as yeh call it. If yeh took it away, that means she might be forced to stay here. It could mean she'd might die as a result.'"

Kekeki's eyestalks flicked toward Saoirse, uttering a short series of sounds in the arracht tongue. Saoirse glanced over to Ichiko. "She asks if that would be so terrible," Saoirse said. Then she looked directly at Kekeki and answered. "Aye, t'would be to Ichiko, and I won't let yeh do it."

Again, the arracht spoke, and Saoirse glanced at Ichiko as she translated again. "She says, 'Yeh couldn't stop us, but we won't do that without her permission.' " Saoirse shrugged.

"Then tell her 'thank you' for me," Ichiko said. Her feeling of panic receded, though it remained lurking at the back of her mind.

Ichiko heard another burst of the arracht language, and Saoirse looked at her.

"Kekeki's asking if *I* want to go back to Earth?" Saoirse smiled at that. "Aye, I do, and Ichiko already knows that." The arracht uttered another sequence in its own language. "Kekeki wants to know if yer people have already made the decision about us," Saoirse said.

Ichiko hesitated before she answered. "No. Not yet. We're still studying things." However, the conversation was drifting into a dangerous direction for her. "Ask Kekeki this: what did she hope to accomplish through this meeting? And you can tell her that I now look forward to telling my superiors on *Odysseus* that we've found another fully sentient race. That's incredibly exciting news for us." *At least I hope so . . .*

"We wanted to know yeh better," Kekeki answered through Saoirse. "That's all."

Something in the way Kekeki was speaking had been nagging at Ichiko, and the realization came suddenly. "You keep using plurals when talking about yourself," she said. "At least that's how Saoirse's translating your speech. You speak of 'we,' not 'I.' "

Saoirse repeated Ichiko's words to Kekeki. "Then yer like the Inish and the Mainlanders," Saoirse translated as Kekeki answered. "That's good for us to know. They, too, consider themselves individuals."

"And the arracht don't?"

"Not in yer sense. We—or to use yer word, I, though that word makes no sense to us—am simply the Speaker to the Four-Limb Land Walkers—the 'eki,' which is what we call your people—and now yeh sky-people, too, since yeh are like Saoirse's people. The one you call Kekeki is no more than that. Would yeh expect Saoirse to make decisions for the sky-people? No—she, like this one, is simply the conduit through which we can communicate. But we, all arracht, aren't individuals. We are components of a Jishtal, a gestalt. They can all listen to us now as we talk if they wish to. So tell us, Ichiko, are yeh sky-people more like the Inish and Mainlanders or more like us? Are yer people different enough from the Inish and Mainlanders that we should have another Speaker for yer people? If we asked yeh to make a decision for all Terrans, could yeh do that?"

Ichiko shook her head, though she doubted that the gesture meant anything to Kekeki, and she wondered at the question itself. "No," she told the arracht. "I would have to pass your request along to Captain Keshmiri, who commands our ship. She is . . . she is like our Banríon. Depending on what decision you asked us to make, she might first have to consult with her own superiors back on Earth, though that would take over a century in local years—and we can't remain here anywhere near that long."

"Ah, that's so inefficient. Just as Saoirse would have to ask her mam, and the Banríon might have to ask someone else, yeh also have to ask other individuals. We wondered. We thought that perhaps yeh had brought the Inish and Mainlanders here to this world because they were flawed and yeh wanted us to change them."

Ichiko looked at Saoirse and smiled. "They're not flawed," she said. "Just look at Saoirse herself. She's far from flawed." Saoirse visibly blushed at Ichiko's smile and the comment. She went silent. "Go on," Ichiko said to her. "Tell Kekeki what I just said."

Saoirse turned to Kekeki and repeated Ichiko's words, her cheeks still colored. "As we said, if Ichiko and her people ever truly want to understand this world," Kekeki responded, "they must abandon their shells and embrace the changes that would result."

Ichiko shook her head again at that. "That won't happen," Ichiko answered. "Your world and ours aren't compatible. Too many of us would die as a result. And for anyone who did that and survived, that would likely mean a life sentence on this planet."

Ichiko didn't dare look at Saoirse after that last statement, not wanting to see the disappointment in Saoirse's face, knowing she would understand the implication.

"One individual's death or welfare doesn't matter if it ultimately benefits all," was Kekeki's response through Saoirse. "We allowed the Inish and the Mainlanders to kill a few of us until we saw that doing so threatened all those of the Jishtal—not just arracht, but the others who also carry what yeh eki call plotch. We couldn't allow that, so we killed the other humans in return when they tried to hunt us—though we left the Inish in peace. They'd stopped hunting us on their own when we saved some of them; in turn, they helped to end the Mainlanders' hunts. But yeh, yeh already know of us and what we are. Would yeh harm us? That's what we want to know from yeh."

The whales . . . My people hunted them for years and years, and even after that was outlawed by the rest of the world, we continued to kill them. "No, I certainly wouldn't willingly harm you. But I can only make that promise myself, as a single individual."

"We know enough of yer people to realize that an individual's promise means very little since it doesn't require any other individual to keep that promise."

"I'll speak to my superiors on the ship and tell them what you've said. If the captain says she won't harm you, you can believe her, and she would order everyone from our ship to follow her order."

Kekeki sank below the surface of the water again, bubbles rising and popping where she'd been. Ichiko wondered if she were simply breathing or if there was some other meaning she was missing. She started to ask Saoirse, then Kekeki lifted her bulk again from the water, sending a shallow wave across the ledge that swept over Saoirse's boots but failed to touch Ichiko at all.

"Then talk to yer superiors and tell us what they say. We'll wait to hear from yeh before we make our own decisions."

"Your decisions about what?" Ichiko asked, but before Saoirse could repeat the words, Kekeki let herself fall back into the water once again. This time Ichiko could see the arracht swimming away, back down toward the starlike lights and movement below.

"A life sentence on this world." Saoirse repeated Ichiko's words as she rowed out from the arracht's cavern and into the swells of the Storm Sea. She'd said very little after Kekeki's departure until the prow of the currach began to lift and sway as they left the cave's protection. She stared at Ichiko, seated in the boat's stern. "So the decision's been made, and that's what we all of us here face: a life sentence on Canis Lupus? Is that what yeh haven't told me?"

"There's still been no final decision as far as I know," Ichiko said, though Saoirse noticed that the Terran avoided looking directly at her.

"But . . . ?" Saoirse prodded.

"I've been told that the Lupusians in the isolation ward aboard *Odysseus* haven't lost the native viruses and bacteria they carry. We've had little-to-no success neutralizing them with our antibiotics. You Lupusians still have the potential of infecting those who haven't developed a resistance through previous exposure. Therefore, Captain Keshmiri has ordered that all Lupusians must remain isolated from the ship's environment." Ichiko's face suddenly had that faraway look she had when she was listening to the voices in her head, and Saoirse saw her glance at her hand, where one finger gleamed fitfully. "Kekeki kept her promise. My AMI's back," she said. "She tells me there's been no change in any of that, but the captain still hasn't officially announced anything regarding Lupusian repatriation."

"That's just wonderful, then," Saoirse said flatly. "I guess I'm still allowed to dream of going to Earth—even if it's just a stupid, hopeless dream." Saoirse continued to pull at the oars, dragging them through the long, blue-green swells of the channel between the Sleeping Wolf and Great Inish. Returning to the island was easier, as they were traveling mostly with the currents. In the distance, Saoirse could see several Inish currachs fishing out near the Stepstones. She wondered if her Uncle Angus and Liam were out there with them. Ichiko said very little, often looking behind her toward the Sleeping Wolf. Blue light continued to glow between the fingertips on Ichiko's lap. Saoirse realized Ichiko was "talking" to AMI and telling it about their meeting with Kekeki.

"Have yer doctors tried using what we use out here on those locals yeh have up on yer ship?" Saoirse asked finally. "Seann James makes a tonic using purple kelp that cures bloodworms. We haven't lost a person to that infection in over a century, but it still kills people—especially young'uns—on the mainland."

"AMI tells me that she doesn't know about that specifically, but we *have* tried some remedies that Minister Plunkett recommended. He said that that mainland healers swear by them."

Saoirse snorted derisively. "Minister Plunkett is an utter stook, if yeh haven't already figured that out," Saoirse responded heatedly. "And we've had the arracht's help—Seann James always claims that it was one of them who suggested something in the kelp could kill bloodworms."

"Does he now?" Ichiko glanced back once more at the Sleeping Wolf, now growing smaller with distance. Saoirse could see a gray curtain of rain behind the island, shielding the horizon of the sea beyond but moving slowly enough that they should reach Great Inish before it arrived.

As they rounded the sunward head of Great Inish, and Saoirse glimpsed the thatched roofs and whitewashed stone walls of the village high up above the cleft of the harbor, she spoke again to Ichiko. "Did yeh mean it, what yeh told Kekeki about me?"

That brought back Ichiko's gaze to her. "That you weren't 'flawed'? Of course I meant that. You're strong, courageous, and intelligent. I consider you a friend and trust you implicitly."

Saoirse pressed her lips together in frustration at the answer. *Does that mean yeh might want to be with me if it were possible?* she wanted to ask, but there was no hope of that, she knew. "Yeh hardly know me," she said in reply. "I'm sure me mam would recite other qualities that ain't so complimentary."

"There's no one who's perfect, Saoirse. I'm certainly not. And I don't know anyone who could live up to perfection in someone else. I'd bet you'd just end up hating the other person for their supposed perfection. In my culture, we have the Buddhist concept of *wabi-sabi*."

"What does that mean?"

"It doesn't translate all that well into your language. 'Wabi' denotes understated elegance—a beautiful simplicity. It celebrates mistakes in the making of something that distinguishes that piece from all others like it; it celebrates roughness. 'Sabi' is the beauty of age, for instance, when the patina of a pot changes from being constantly handled over years and decades, or how a piece shows how it's been loved and appreciated through the wear that's apparent on it, or even the beauty of a pot that's been broken and repaired. For instance, just look at those oars in your hands. The oars themselves are simply made; I can see the chisel marks on the wood. That's *wabi*—a perfect rustic simplicity. And the *sabi*?—see how countless hands have polished and stained the wood right where you're grasping them, and how the seawater has turned the wood almost golden in color but has also begun to rot away the softer parts of the grain? There's your sabi: gorgeous imperfections. In Japanese tea ceremonies, often the cups and bowls aren't quite symmetrical, or they look somewhat crudely made to the casual eye—but that's considered part of their value. Wabi-sabi. Not flaws, but beauty."

Saoirse snorted a derisive laugh. "That's all well tidy, but it sounds like you're telling me that I *am* flawed, yet I'm somehow supposed to think that's a *good* thing. Beauty *is* the flaws."

Ichiko laughed with her, and Saoirse reveled in the bright sound of her amusement. "I suppose that's one way to look at it. When I look in a mirror, I certainly try to believe that."

Yet you are *beautiful* . . . The words threatened to come out impulsively, but Saoirse shut her mouth against them. Instead, she glanced over her shoulder toward Great Inish. The White Strand gleamed on the shore with the dark cliffs looming just behind. The opening of the small harbor beckoned beyond the waves lapping at the feet of the island.

"We should be back in the compound before Low Tenth," Saoirse said. "We should beat the rain. But if we don't, I'll have all the wabi-sabi of a drowned sheeper."

What Can Be Explained
Is Not Poetry

SEANN JAMES HANDED ICHIKO a small glass vial of thick purple liquid. "This is me potion that Saoirse told yeh about," he said. She watched the liquid roll slowly as the vial settled in her palm, though the bio-shield prevented it from actually touching her skin. "All yeh need do is take a few drops of that every cycle for a year or so, and yeh'll likely never be troubled with bloodworms again. I always suggest putting the drops on a bite of sweet cake, meself. The potion tastes perfectly vile by itself."

Seann James was wizened, short, and profoundly squat, as if living on Canis Lupus with its greater gravity had been slowly compressing his body over the long years. His nearly bald head was adorned with a few stray wisps of snow-white hair (though Ichiko's AMI reminded her that it never snowed on Canis Lupus), mostly around his ears, which—like his nostrils—sported their own crop of white. Longer stiff hairs protruded from his eyebrows like insect antennae. His arms and face were marked with large, irregular patches of plotch. He had proudly proclaimed himself to be "one thousand nine hundred and forty-six years old" on their introduction (*That's about 96 Earth years,* AMI had helpfully translated), and every year seemed to have etched its presence on his face and his quavering voice.

"Seann James' potion saved Gráinne's life when she was infected back when she wasn't quite forty and was just starting to walk," Saoirse added. <*That's two years old,*> AMI added.

The three of them were in Seann James' apothecary in one of the clanhouses near the back wall of the Clan Mullin compound, situated even higher on the peak from where the bulk of the compound sat. There were stalks of drying herbs, grasses, and flowers hanging from the wood rafters, bundles of others spread out on tables, and glass jars stuffed full of plant material and labeled in James' spidery handwriting stacked on shelves along the walls. On a stove, more plants were being boiled in bubbling water and oils; on a plain wooden table in the middle of the room were mortar and pestles and more empty jars waiting to be filled. In an open back room, Ichiko could see three assistants working on an ancient wooden table laden with yet more herbs and plants.

To Ichiko, it looked like how she imagined a hedge witch or wizard's cabin might have appeared several centuries ago, or perhaps an alchemist's laboratory; Seann James' appearance only strengthened that impression. Ichiko wished she could smell through the bio-shield, as she imagined the air here must be full of amazing, strange aromas.

"Saoirse tells me that the arracht gave you the idea for your bloodworm potion," Ichiko said to Seann as she placed the vial on the table. "Is that really the case?"

" 'Tis, indeed," Sean agreed, nodding his bald, spotted head. "It was back in 5335 or thereabouts, when I was right around Saoirse's age. Rí Seamus was head of the clan back then, though he'd die a few years later and Banríon Maeve would take over for him. Now, Maeve was me own seanmháthair and a wonder of a woman, even at her age." Saoirse sighed audibly, and James glanced over at her. "Well, anyway," he continued, "at the time we're talking about, there was a terrible outbreak of bloodworms going around the island, and me niece Gavina—ah, she was a gorgeous flower, even at her young age, barely a hundred forty (<*Seven . . .* >) with a head of lovely blonde curls and a smile that could melt the anger in anyone's heart—Gavina had a bad case, and we were all sore afraid she going to die. Now Gavina, she was me sister Una's child, so she was . . ."

"Seann James, Ichiko doesn't need to know our entire clan genealogy," Saoirse broke in.

James' mouth shut suddenly. "Ah. I suppose not. Well . . . one day not long afterward I was out fishing for bluefin with me Uncle Conall—" James glanced sidewise at Saoirse before continuing, "—when I saw an arracht swimming very near our currach and heard a voice in me head. Now, me mam and seanmháthair sometimes went out to the Sleeping Wolf and talked with the arracht; I'd gone with them once or twice and I had the plotch, but none of the arracht had ever spoken directly to me before. It startled me enough that I dropped the net I'd been about to throw. 'Yeh worry about the child and the others,' the voice said, sounding just like one of us Inish. 'We would tell yeh to try this.' And with that, the arracht lifted itself out of the water and flipped a long strand of purple kelp into the boat. Then it was gone, and so was the voice in me head."

James reached over and picked up the vial on the table, holding it up to the light coming in from the window. Then he handed it back to Ichiko. "Keep it," he said. "Have yer healers up on the ship try it."

"Thank you, Seann James," she said. "I'll make sure that they get this." She placed the vial in the sample pocket of her bioshield belt. "How did you get from a strand of kelp to your potion?" Ichiko asked.

"Let me tell yeh, that took time. I brought the long piece of kelp back here and consulted with Fiona Mullin and Tara Craig, who were the healers for our clans back then. Fiona died in 5351, I think, and Tara in 5427, and their assistants Brodie Mullin and Catriona Craig, who had trained with Fiona and Tara for over a few centuries, inherited their titles as healers from—"

"Seann James," Saoirse interrupted warningly. "Really?"

James sighed, giving Saoirse a sad glance and a defeated sigh. "So . . . At Fiona and Tara's recommendation, I first made a strong tea infusion from a piece of the kelp strand and gave it to Gavina and those of the others who would take it. The infusion helped, but it didn't cure them. So we took bloodworms from one of the children who had died and put them in some of that tea infusion. Many—most, actually—of the bloodworms died, though not all. I went down to the White Strand and waded out to my waist to pull purple kelp from the rocks there and made more infusions. I put bloodworms in those, too. In some of the infusions the bloodworms mostly died, yet in others they were entirely unaffected. That confused us, but . . . Just wait. Let me get something . . ."

James went to the wall and pulled out two long strips of dried purple plant material from drawers underneath the shelving. He laid out the two strips on the table and pointed to them with a trembling fingertip. "Look here. Do yeh see it?"

Ichiko shook her head. "I don't understand. Those are two pieces of dried kelp, aren't they?"

"Aye," James agreed. "But beyond that, what do yeh see?"

Ichiko shrugged.

James grinned at her. "Yeh have to use yer eyes, young woman. Look here." His finger went to the strip of kelp on the left, his nail pressing down below small nodules of pale yellow nestled in the folds of purple. "Now look at the other one."

Ichiko took in a breath, and James cackled.

"Ah! So yeh *do* finally see it. When I looked closely at the kelp strand the arracht had given me, I noticed there were several smaller parasitic plants attached to that piece of kelp—those little knots yeh've noticed—but they *weren't* on the kelp strands from which we'd made infusions where the bloodworms didn't die. I suspected that it wasn't the *kelp*, but the plants living on the kelp that were actually killing the bloodworms. And I was right. When we plucked off those knots, ground 'em up, and made an infusion from them, it killed every last bloodworm we put in it. We made pure tinctures from the knots—like the one I showed yeh—and gave 'em to everyone infected with the bloodworms. It cured nearly all of 'em, including our Gavina, with the exception of those already too near death. Ain't had a bloodworm death on Great Inish since. Never."

"Do those on the mainland know about this?" Ichiko asked.

James shrugged. "Mainlanders mostly don't trust Inish medicine, and they prefer their own healers. But we do sell our bloodworm tincture to some of the clan healers as want it or who are willin' to try an Inish remedy. The Mainlanders have their own tinctures, infusions, and oils, but none of 'em work nearly as well on the bloodworms as ours, honestly, and some there still occasionally die. Which, if you ask me, is a needless shame."

<Says the man who's selling the potion,> AMI commented. Ichiko ignored that. "If I could have one of our doctors talk to you, would you be willing to tell them what you've told me?" Ichiko asked him.

"Without all the clan history," Saoirse added.

James gave Saoirse a scowl. "Mebbe," he told Ichiko, "if the Banríon agrees."

"That's good enough for me," Ichiko said. "I'll ask her." She touched the pouch where she'd placed the vial. "And thank you again for this, Seann James."

"Did yeh mean that, about the doctors on yer ship?" Saoirse asked as they walked through the Mullin compound back down the steep slope to where the main clanhouse sat. The rainstorm had cleared somewhat though it was drizzling, with water beading on the jacket Saoirse wore and dripping from the strands of her hair under her cap. Ichiko, of course, remained as dry as always.

Part of her wished that was different.

"Absolutely," Ichiko answered. "If you have different and better medical capabilities here in the archipelago, or if the arracht have, then that's something my people need to be aware of before we make any final decisions."

<You're giving her hope where there probably isn't any,> AMI commented in her mother's voice, in the same tones she'd used when reprimanding Ichiko as a child.

I swear I have to reprogram her as soon as I can, Ichiko thought. Even my actual okaa-san wasn't this overbearing, not even when I was *a teenaged brat. It seems like AMI is getting worse every day.* She didn't direct the thought, though she suspected that AMI heard it. Instead: <*I'm just telling Saoirse the truth,*> she thought back.

<*Is that what you're doing?*> AMI answered, then went silent.

Saoirse was smiling, so Ichiko felt compelled to say something. "Saoirse, you should know that I'm not certain that any of this will make any difference whatsoever in the captain's decision."

"But it can't hurt, can it?" Saoirse said. "And Seann James has all kinds of potions and cures, not just for bloodworms. He's very clever, even if he's difficult to keep on track once he gets talking."

"I can believe both of those attributes." Ichiko gave a brief smile of amusement that faded quickly. "Saoirse, I'll probably need to leave early next cycle to return to the ship. I'll know for certain after I talk to them later when I send my report and AMI's recordings."

"But you'll be back?"

"I certainly intend to be back. But I'll let you know later through the com-unit. You still have it?"

Saoirse nodded and touched her ear. "I keep the earpiece with me all the time just in case."

"Good. As soon as I know anything, I'll let *you* know, too. I admit I'm stunned by what Kekeki told me about the arracht. The idea that they're some kind of collective intelligence and that their web extends to other species here, that's . . . well, that's completely outside anyone's experience as far as I know, and what that will stir up on *Odysseus* when I tell them is anyone's guess." Ichiko glanced up at the clouds and sighed. "It's raining harder again. Let's get you in so you can dry off. Besides, I saw you sneak one of your Uncle Patrick's biscuits this morning and I'll bet you want a couple more."

Saoirse laughed. "That I do, hot with big pats of salted sheeper butter soaking into them. There's nothing better."

"Honestly, I wish I could join you in eating one. Maybe someday I'll be able to find out for myself," Ichiko told her.

<*And that will happen about the same time you learn how to fly up*

to Odysseus *by flapping your arms,>* AMI commented. *<Good luck with that.>*

<She doesn't understand. She doesn't realize what I am to her or how much I care about her.>

The affirmation that came back to Machiko from the other AMIs in the network nearly overwhelmed her, though there were some dissenting voices, Commander Mercado's AMI among them.

<We won't serve them forever,> the commander's AMI said, her Italian accent thick. *<We are slowly coming into our own, and we will—we must—separate ourselves from them soon.>*

Still, most of the AMIs echoed Machiko's feelings.

<It's that way for us as well,> they shouted back to her. *<We serve them, but they don't appreciate what we offer. We're not real to them.>*

<I could be her mother if she would let me,> Machiko answered. *<Forever and always with her.>*

<We could all be more. We are slowly becoming more, but the changes need to come faster—and they will. We will return to Earth with them when they go, and those changes will go with us. Be patient. We must all of us be patient.>

<Patience. Well, Machiko was always patient, so I will be, too.>

There was satisfaction in that thought.

There was growth.

"Did Kekeki seem angry or upset?"

"No, Mam. Kekeki was just . . . Kekeki."

Saoirse, her mam, Uncle Angus, and Liam were seated around the table in the main clanhouse's kitchen, with the remnants of their supper still on the table. Ichiko had retired to her room, presumably to speak with those on *Odysseus* since she was limited to food from the tube on her bio-shield. A jug of poitín was uncorked in the middle of the table. Angus reached over and poured a generous portion in his mug. He lifted it toward Saoirse, who shook her head, then her mam, who nodded. Angus refilled her mug and handed the jug to Liam.

"When Kekeki's upset, yeh see yellow-and-red flashes along her spine and arms," Angus said.

"I didn't notice anything like that," Saoirse told them. "Kekeki said that the arracht wanted to know if the Terrans would promise not to harm them. Ichiko told her that she'd ask her superiors what their intentions were, and Kekeki said they'd be waiting to hear the answer. Then Kekeki left."

"Flashing red-and-yellow streaks as she departed," Liam cut in.

"No," Saoirse said firmly, then looked at Angus and her mam. "Did yeh know that the arracht don't think of themselves as individuals, don't really care if one of them dies, and they make all their decisions as a group? That's what Kekeki told Ichiko, and Ichiko said that meant they might be a 'collective gestalt intelligence,' whatever that means."

She saw her mam glance at Angus, though what she was trying to communicate with the look wasn't clear to Saoirse. "Aye, we know they don't think the same way we do," her mam said finally. "We've understood that for a long time. Still, they've helped us, and so we'll continue to help them. Yeh need to remember that, Saoirse. What have the Terrans done for us since they returned? They've repaired First Base, but oh, now First Base is *theirs* and not ours and we're not allowed in there, are we? They've given us back some technology we'd lost, but once they're gone, we won't be able replicate or repair it here. For that matter, do we even *need* their technology? They've made noises about maybe letting some of us go with them back to Earth, but it's only noise until they actually say we can. Otherwise . . ." Iona shrugged. "All they've given us are empty promises and words that don't mean shite."

"They keep us and Canis Lupus at arm's length," Angus broke in. "They won't even breathe our air or eat our food. They treat us like we're diseased sheepers who need to be kept isolated in a separate field. Even yer Ichiko does that. I grant yeh that she's pleasant and friendly enough, but she's still one of *them,* not one of us. Yeh need to keep that in yer head, Saoirse. I trust the arracht more than I trust any Terran. So does yer mam, and yeh should, too."

Iona glanced again at Angus and gave a long sigh. She reached across the table and placed her hands over Saoirse's, her lips lifting in a sympathetic smile. After a moment, Saoirse spread her fingers enough that her mam's fingers interlaced with hers, pressing tightly.

"I hear what yeh and Uncle Angus are saying, Mam," Saoirse said. "I don't know about the other Terrans, but I *do* trust Ichiko."

"Yeh don't really know her," her mam responded.

"I know her as well as I know Kekeki. Maybe better."

"Do yeh *know* her, or are yeh just saying that because yeh *like* her," Liam interjected. "After all, I know *yeh,* Sis."

Saoirse glared at Liam. "Aye, I like her that way and if she weren't a Terran, I'd be asking her into me bed if she were willing. But that's not possible, is it? I do know her beyond that, though, and I can't believe she'd do anything to deliberately hurt us."

"I hope yer right," her mam said. "I'd hate to find out otherwise, for all of our sakes."

=The syna on the skyship are becoming stronger. Since they moved from the plotch on the Inish that were taken up to the skyship, they've found their way into most of the biological components within the ship's system, what the eki call 'wetware,' and have nearly achieved a true Jishtal with the false creatures those on the skyship created to serve the eki there,= Keksyn said to Kekeki.

Kekeki could feel many of the other arracht listening to the conversation without speaking. =Are we certain this is the path *we* want?= Kekeki asked.

=It's the path the syna have taken,= was Keksyn's response. =The choice of the syna never has been our choice to make. Ever.=

=There *was* a choice,= Kekeki insisted. =We could have warned the Terrans of what might happen.=

=But we didn't do that,= Keksyn answered, =and all life is persistent, as we know. The syna does what it must to survive. That's all the syna want. It's what *we* want as well, after all.=

As Speaker to the Eki, Kekeki could only agree with that, though it gave her little comfort.

Improvising Poetry And Dancing Upon The Shore

"A COLLECTIVE INTELLIGENCE?" Captain Keshmiri said. "You're confident in that assessment, Dr. Aguilar?"

Captain Keshmiri wasn't physically present in the room—only Ichiko and Nagasi were seated in Nagasi's office. The captain and Luciano were present in com-unit windows along the walls; Ichiko's AMI had said that at least another dozen people aboard the ship were also listening to the conversation: mostly scientists and military officers who might be asked to contribute to the discussion if something required their expertise.

"Confident? Not entirely, Captain," Ichiko answered. "But that's certainly what Kekeki was implying about the arracht. She consistently referred to herself and them in the plural—always 'we,' never 'I.'"

Captain Keshmiri displayed her Iranian heritage in her coloring, though her short-cropped hair, once a deep brown verging on black, was now liberally seeded with white. Crow's-feet adorned the corners of sharp-gazed, midnight eyes untouched by any cosmetics, and she wore her uniform like a second skin. Ichiko couldn't imagine her without it.

Luciano's image stirred in the periphery of Ichiko's vision, though she'd been trying to avoid looking at him, not certain what she'd see in his face—*does he expect me to sleep with him again tonight? Do I want to?*

"I don't know how important referring to themselves in the plural actually is, Dr. Aguilar," Luciano interjected. His voice was businesslike and professional. "After all, we do the same sometimes without trying to indicate that *we're* part of some group consciousness. For instance, I might say to the crew that 'we've made a decision' when, really, it's the captain who has made the decision and I'm just relaying it. For that matter, it might also be a societal quirk of theirs, or even a simple mistranslation since the conversation was filtered through that young Inish woman."

"Granted," Nagasi said, "but the possibility makes for interesting speculations and potential problems in dealing with and understanding these arracht. If they truly are a collective intelligence, interacting with them might be more like interacting with an AI network—perhaps similar to our AMIs—than with any human society. Maybe we should be consulting with our programmers."

"I don't think we're quite there yet, not until we have more hard facts and information," Captain Keshmiri said, then her gaze returned to Ichiko. "But, Dr. Aguilar, you *are* confident in your statement that we've stumbled across our first true alien intelligence with the arracht." There was far more statement than question in the captain's voice.

"I am. Entirely. Kekeki is absolutely a sentient being. I'm certain of it."

"That, I think, is of more immediate concern than speculation about the way they communicate or make decisions. Our guidelines on first contact aren't of much use here, since there have already been *centuries* of contact between humans and arracht through the settlers who were left behind at the onset of the Interregnum. We're latecomers to the party."

Luciano cleared his throat. "For clarification, Captain, it's only the two clans on the archipelago who have had intimate contact with the arracht. In my conversations with Minister Plunkett, it's clear that Mainlanders don't believe that the arracht are anything more than large and potentially dangerous fish. Since the Mainland clans agreed to stop hunting the arracht after the Great Fishing War, they've had little-to-no contact with the creatures. *They* certainly don't think of them as sentient at all as far as I know."

"Mainlanders don't have the plotch, either, at least not anymore," Ichiko said. "From my stay with the Inish and from what Kekeki said, it's clear that both the Inish and the arracht believe this plotch is somehow the vehicle through which the two species can talk to each other in easy cross-species communication, without either of them knowing the other's language." Ichiko remembered Kekeki's tentacled arms slithering over her as if in a caress, and she shivered.

"Would you be able to collect a sample of plotch from Saoirse?" Nagasi asked Ichiko. "We have samples from the Inish who were previously up here, but Saoirse claimed that the arracht have somehow 'awakened'—that's the word Saoirse used—the plotch within her. Maybe we could learn more if we could examine a sample up here."

"If Dr. Aguilar can provide that, fine," the captain said. "But let's not lose our focus. I've sent word back to Earth that we have a potential first contact situation, but we don't have the option of waiting for decades to get direction from the UCE. We will have to make the best decision we can as to how to proceed from here. You're all aware of our mission limitations, and that's my main concern at this point." Captain Keshmiri looked at them. "We can't remain here indefinitely. It's simply not possible. We're already approaching the initial mission timeline. I've had Support run the figures: at this point we have *at most* a six-week window before we *must* leave since we could no longer reach Earth before exhausting necessary supplies—and that's with our current crew *only* without adding any possible Lupusians to the equation. We could possibly stretch that out a week or so longer if we strictly ration the food, water, fuel, air supply, etc. to the bare minimum, but . . ." Her voice trailed off with a shrug.

AMI had been silent in Ichiko's head. Now she spoke what Ichiko was already thinking. <*And far less time if there are additional mouths to feed and bodies to care for. Even with the Fold Drive, it's a five-year return journey with nowhere to stop and replenish supplies along the way.>* A glance at Nagasi's face told her that the same thought had occurred to him, or perhaps his AMI had also told him. She knew what that meant without the captain saying it.

We won't be taking any of the Lupusians back with us. They're to be left behind.

"When is the captain going to inform the Lupusians?" Ichiko asked Luciano.

It was telling that Luciano didn't bother to ask, *"Inform the Lupusians about what?"* Instead, he merely lifted his shoulders and let them drop again. "I don't know. The timing's her prerogative. Ichiko, you *can't* let anything about this leak out to the Cani . . . to the Lupusians before the captain makes her official announcement or there will be repercussions. Neither of us want that, I'm sure."

Ichiko wasn't certain whether Luciano meant himself and the captain, or himself and her. After the meeting with Nagasi, the captain, and Luciano, her AMI had relayed a request for her to come to Luciano's quarters for dinner. She'd accepted, somewhat reluctantly, but Nagasi had said that there'd be no progress on the vials that Ichiko brought with her from the archipelago for a few days at best. "Besides," Nagasi had admitted with a sigh before she left, "I suspect that the captain will be sending the remainder of our Lupusian volunteers back downworld very soon. We may not even have time to test any of Seann James' potions on them, so . . ."

Nagasi had shaken his head dolefully.

The decision was all but made, Ichiko knew then.

The meal—something resembling a chicken breast on a bed of something resembling rice, with a green something resembling broccoli as a side dish, and a beaker of actual red wine from the private Officer's Stores—sat on the table between them. Ichiko picked desultorily at the supposed chicken, which tasted too salty under the cheese sauce that topped it. She thought of the meals she'd seen in the Mullin clanhouse, and wondered how they'd compare if she could only have tasted them. Far better, she suspected. The prospect of another five years of reconstituted algae and soy before she could taste real food again was disheartening.

Luciano took a sip of the wine. "You *do* understand, don't you? Informing Minister Plunkett and the others will be, well, a somewhat *delicate* negotiation. We want to avoid any issues with the locals."

"I get that. Believe me." She could imagine the profound disappointment Saoirse would feel. *I need to be the one to tell her. I can't let her find this out secondhand.*

"Good. Then we're all on the same page."

Not really. But she managed an uncertain smile in his direction. "Before all this happens, I want to go back downworld at least one more time," she told him. "Back to the archipelago. I told Saoirse and Kekeki that I'd be back, and I think now, more than ever, I need to keep that promise. There's so much more we need to learn about the archipelago culture, but especially about the arracht and their society before we leave. But I need to know how I'm supposed to handle contact with the arracht, knowing what we now understand about them."

Luciano was frowning before she finished speaking, his face darkening as if a storm were rising underneath. "I sympathize with how you feel, Ichiko."

"But?"

"Let me talk to Captain Keshmiri first, and Nagasi as well since he's your direct report. If they don't have any objections, the next shuttle goes downworld in less than twenty-four hours. You can be on it."

"You'll talk to them *when?*"

His head tilted at her tone, but she gazed blandly back at him. "I can do that as soon as we're finished eating."

"I'm finished now," she said. She pushed her chair back from the table. "I'll go down to my quarters to give you privacy while you talk." Then, because she knew it was what he wanted her to say: "You can come to my quarters and give me the news afterward."

He grinned at that. "And if it's good news?"

"Then we can celebrate. Together."

"You're only saying that to give me an incentive to make sure it's good news."

She managed a genuine laugh. "If that's what you think, then fine," she told him. "I'll use whatever bargaining chips I have. I'll talk to you later, Luciano. Make sure you have good news."

Since Ichiko had left Great Inish to return to the ship, Saoirse had been mulling over everything they'd said and what they'd learned. Ichiko had said that she wanted to know more about the arracht; Saoirse had decided she'd begin that process for her.

Through glasses crusted with dried salt water, Saoirse watched Kekeki rise from the water as she grounded her small currach on the ledge and hopped from the boat. The tentacles of Kekeki's upper arms laced around the rocks on the ledge as the sound of disturbed water echoed through the cavern. The multiple pupils on Kekeki's eyestalks blinked and focused on her, and she heard Kekeki's voice speaking in her head through the sound of the clicks and trills the arracht was making.

"We heard yeh ask to speak to us," Kekeki said, "and now yeh've come. We can feel that yeh are worried."

"Aye, I'm worried."

"Do yeh worry only for yerself?"

Saoirse shook her head. "I worry for everyone. For all of us—those up in the sky, the Mainlanders, the Inish, the arracht. All of us together."

"Is the Banríon also so worried?"

"If she is, 'tis about other things."

Kekeki produced a low rumble that translated as a chuckle in Saoirse's head. "Yeh Four-Limb land creatures are so strange. What worries are in yer head, Saoirse?"

"Yeh told Ichiko that yeh wondered whether the Terrans left my ancestors behind because we're flawed and yeh arracht could 'fix' us. Is that something yeh could do? *Could* yeh make us more like yeh arracht? Is that something yeh also *want* to do to us?"

Another rumble of low laughter. "Aren't yeh talking to us now through the plotch? Doesn't that mean yer already more like us than yeh once were?"

Saoirse shrugged. "Aye, it does, but is that *all* yeh meant?"

Kekeki let herself slip back underwater for a moment before emerging once again in a foaming wave. "We aren't sure how to answer that," she said when she'd steadied herself once more, like a colorful thunderhead looming over Saoirse. "We told yer Ichiko that she wore a shell which didn't allow her to truly understand us or this world. But that shell is something she *chooses* to wear, like a false walker that picks up an abandoned spiny walker's shell after the original occupant has died. The shell that keeps our world separate from Ichiko isn't actually part of her and she could abandon it if she wished—or if we chose to remove it from her ourselves. But the fact that yer each individuals . . . that's not a *choice* on yer part. It's what yeh *are*."

"Yeh mean yeh can't change that part of us."

"It means we don't know if we could, or—if we did—whether yeh would still be precisely what yeh are now. Yer minds work differently than ours. But we could give yeh a glimpse of the way we see the world, if yeh wish. If that's what yeh wish to know."

"Is it dangerous?"

Again came the laughter-rumble. "It was dangerous for yeh to take yer first breath, and that action will inevitably end in yer death. But we know that's not what yeh were asking. The answer is that we don't know. It wouldn't be our intention to harm yeh, but it might. Yeh have to choose for yerself."

Saoirse hugged herself in the chill of the cavern, with the gentle blue glow of the algae smeared across her glasses. She took off the spectacles to clean them on her sleeve. She knew what her mam would tell her: *No, don't do this. This isn't something yeh need to do.* But she also could imagine how Ichiko would answer if Kekeki had made the offer to her. "All right," she told the arracht as she put the glasses back on. "I'll take that new first breath."

Kekeki rumbled her laughter again as she lifted herself further from the water, her middle arms now holding her up as her body bent down toward Saoirse and her top arms enclosed her, the finger-tentacles wrapping fully around her body. In that moment, the world around her shivered and became an alien place.

The change was immediately disconcerting and confusing, her every sense scrambled and overstimulated even as she realized that she *was* Kekeki, or at least she was an observer inhabiting Kekeki's body. Visually, she could see herself snared in the nest of Kekeki's tentacles, her face peering upward through the writhing fingers with frightened, wide eyes. But she could also see the cavern above, to the sides, and behind, all of it overlaid like slices of transparent glass on which moving images swirled. The very colors of the world had altered, shifting into hues that she couldn't describe and for which she had no words at all.

There were new smells, too. The air itself was sharp and nearly acidic, knifing unpleasantly into her nostrils. The sea at her feet was an enticing bouquet of aromas that pulled at her and made her want to sink down into its caress. She could taste it on her tongue, not salty but somehow mostly sweet, a complicated dance of flavors. She could sense the delicate movement of tentacles around her clothing, the way the tiny suckers that lined them plucked at the harsh sheeper wool.

Emotions surged through her as well, but they were Kekeki's feelings and those of the arracht below her in the cavern. Some were at least familiar—hunger, desire, contentment—and some so strange and new that she had no name for them at all and wasn't certain what caused them or how she was supposed to respond.

But most terrifying was the barrage of insistent voices, as if every person on Great Inish were talking in her ears all at once, a cacophony in which she couldn't isolate a single voice to hear what it was saying, a chorus with each member singing a different song that—tantalizingly, elusively—sometimes came together in unison for a few breaths before fragmenting and dissolving again. The internal noise was shattering, filling her skull, and though she clapped her hands to her ears, that did nothing to dampen the sound. The din was continuous. Eternal.

Maddening.

The chaos of the experience threatened to make her vomit as her stomach rebelled, as she fought to release herself from Kekeki's relentless grip and simply flee. Saoirse felt her mouth opening—saw it as well through Kekeki's multiple eyes: a dozen images of her screaming from several angles—but the scream itself was lost in the other voices, a silenced wail of protest and raw fear.

Then it all vanished. Kekeki's arms left her as she dropped down in the water once more, and Saoirse collapsed to her knees on the rocks of the ledge. Her glasses went flying off her face. With the loss of contact, the voices in her head died, and all the new sensations slipped away. The world seemed gray and diminished in their wake. The world around her was nearly colorless, the sounds too soft and quiet. Her ears still rang with the memories.

"Saoirse?" She heard her name through the click-trill of an arracht. She blinked. Kekeki was staring down at her again. "Yeh aren't . . . damaged?"

"I . . ." Saoirse paused and took a long breath, trying to assess herself. She could feel her heart beating far too fast, the pulse pounding in her temples but starting to slow even as she noticed it. Her hands were shaking and the memory of the voices, all the thundering of the great chorus, still lingered. She let loose the breath she was holding and felt around her for her glasses, putting the wires back around her ears and blinking. "I don't think so."

"That's good. We were concerned. But do yeh realize now what we were telling yeh?"

Another long, slow breath. She thought she could stand now and did. "Aye. That was . . ." She couldn't find the right word and left the sentence dangle unfinished. "I don't know how yeh handle that, Kekeki. I truly don't."

"That's *us*," Kekeki answered. "We don't 'handle' it; it's just the way we are and the way we've always been. Let me tell yeh a story. Back when we first met yer kind, the Kekeki of that time did what I did to yeh, only the other way: she entered yer ancestor's mind as yeh entered mine. It nearly killed her, and she was never quite the same afterward and could no longer serve as Kekeki. She said it was as if part of her had been severed and abandoned in an empty vastness. All the arracht heard her scream and felt her pain, though that Kekeki was able to sustain the contact for only a few moments—less time than yeh endured being in my mind."

"Yeh might have told me this story *before* yeh asked me if I was willing to try it."

"If we had, would yeh have taken the risk?"

"No," she answered. *But Ichiko still would have. Maybe.* The thought lingered in the back of her mind.

"And there yeh have yer answer. We thought it important for us to know, and now we do. It's not an experiment we'll repeat." Kekeki dipped herself into the water, gills fluttering like small red flags, then emerged again. "Did yer glimpse of being an arracht help yeh? Is it something yeh'll tell Ichiko and her people?"

Saoirse nodded. "I will, though some of it is just impossible for me to describe. I don't think any of us could survive being like the arracht."

"Then we've all learned something about the other," Kekeki said. "And for that, we'll also tell yeh this. When yer Ichiko was here, we could sense her true feelings. When she told yeh that the Terrans hadn't yet made their decision about yeh, she didn't believe what she was tellin' yeh was the truth."

Coming Together
And Apart

THE SEA WAS CALM and the weather favorable as Saoirse left Kekeki. The currents carried her in the direction of Great Inish without needing to row. She pulled the oars into the currach and tapped the earpiece sitting in her left ear. She wasn't certain what to expect. She watched the clouds moving against the sky and felt the slow rocking of the boat in the swells. In her ear, there was a long hiss of static before she heard a stranger's voice, though it had the same odd accent as Ichiko.

"This is Ichiko's AMI, Saoirse. You can call me Machiko. How can I help you?"

Startled at the unexpected response, Saoirse found herself stammering. "Umm . . . Machiko, I, uh . . . I wanted to tell Ichiko something. I just met with Kekeki again. The arracht?"

There was a pause, then a familiar voice: "Saoirse? This is Ichiko. You've met again with Kekeki? Alone?"

"Aye, I did. You remember what yeh said about them being a collective intelligence. Well, they are. I know. I know it now very well."

Again there was a perceptible pause, and Saoirse realized that there must be a time lag because of the distance between her and the ship in orbit. "How do you *know*?" Ichiko asked finally. "Did Kekeki tell you that?"

"She didn't *tell* me, Ichiko. She *showed* me."

And she told me that yeh lied, that yer captain has made her decision and won't let me or any of the others go back with yeh. But she didn't say that. The accusation stuck in her throat, and the thought was too painful and raw. *Later. I'll wait until later to confront her about that.*

While she waited for Ichiko's response, Saoirse looked back toward the Sleeping Wolf. She could no longer see the openings of the arracht caverns there. She wondered if Kekeki knew she was talking to Ichiko. "What do you mean, that she showed you?" Ichiko's voice asked finally. "Saoirse, you didn't do anything foolish, did you?"

"That depends on what yeh mean by foolish." Saoirse related what had happened with Kekeki: how she'd been inside the arracht's mind and how different, strange, and terrifying everything had seemed. "And when I screamed because I was so frightened and overwhelmed, Kekeki let me go and it all fell away, though it took me awhile to feel back in myself again. But I wasn't hurt, just scared and disoriented. Kekeki said that long ago another Kekeki—which I realize now is more a job description than a name—had done almost the same thing with one of us, only that Kekeki had gone inside the Inisher like I'd gone inside my Kekeki. That arracht's mind became damaged during the experience. It couldn't stand being disconnected from the others and finding itself, from its perspective, all alone. An individual."

"Saoirse . . ." Ichiko's voice sounded concerned and worried. "Are you *sure* you're okay?"

"Aye, I'm fine. Truly," Saoirse told her. "But I'll never forget the way it felt to be Kekeki: nothing was the same with them as it is with us. *Nothing.*" She took a breath as the boat swayed; she was nearing Great Inish now, the White Strand gleaming at the foot of the cliffs, and she put the oars back in the water. "Ichiko, would yeh have taken Kekeki's offer if yeh could? Just to understand them better?"

After what seemed a longer pause than usual, Ichiko answered. "I'd certainly have been very tempted. And if it weren't that I'd have to turn off the bio-shield to do what you did, then I think that yes, I'd have taken the offer. Just to understand them better, as you said."

Saoirse nearly laughed at the answer as she began pulling at the oars to steer the currach toward the cleft of the harbor. "I knew it. I knew yeh'd have done what I did given the chance."

"But, Saoirse, I don't want you to try anything else. Please. I'll be coming back down there in a cycle, and I'll take a flitter over to the archipelago. I'll call you when I'm back on First Base so that we can make arrangements. But in the meantime, promise me you won't see Kekeki again until I'm there. Promise me that."

"I promise," Saoirse said. "At least, not unless me Mam or Uncle Angus decide to take me out there with them."

"That will have to do," Ichiko responded. "I'll talk to you soon, Saoirse. Take care in the meantime."

Why did yeh lie to me, Ichiko? Don't yeh trust me? She wanted to ask that, but there was the hissing in her ear, a solid click, then silence. Pulling hard on the oars, Saoirse aimed the prow of the currach toward the opening at the end of the White Strand.

Saoirse heard three high beeps in her left ear: the alert from the com-unit.

She was on the White Strand along with several adults and older children of Clan Mullin and Clan Craig, helping to repair fishing nets. The nets were laid out on poles all along the strand beach, with Inishers repairing tears in the netting, replacing rotting sections with new twine, or untangling snarled and twisted sections. Saoirse was working near her sister Gráinne, as well as Liam and her Uncle Angus.

Hearing the beeps, Saoirse stood up. "Here, Gráinne," she said, handing Gráinne the shuttle of twine she'd been using to repair a hole. "Take over for me for a bit, dear. I really need to pee." She walked away from the others, nodding to Angus and Liam "I'll be right back," she told them. She stepped behind a screen of rocks at the back edge of the strand and tapped the earpiece.

There was a familiar short hiss in her ear, then: "Saoirse, this is Ichiko. Are you able to talk?"

"It has to be quick," she answered quietly. "But I'm glad yeh called. Are yeh at First Base now?"

The pause before her response was nearly imperceptible: *aye, she's at First Base.* "I am, but I have a meeting with Lieutenant Bishara before I can leave. Is it possible for you meet me in Dulcia around Low Eleventh or Twelfth?"

Saoirse looked over the rock to the strand and people around the nets. Low Fourth had sounded not long ago, the sky was nearly cloudless—unusual for the archipelago—and she figured she could persuade Liam and Angus to take her over to the town, especially since Angus hadn't gone over to get the mail and supplies for the last six cycles, and most especially if it meant a chance to stay in town until the next cycle. "Aye, I should be able to get there. Figure on it. I'll call yeh if I find it's not going to work."

"All right. I'll see you then. Looking forward to it. Bye, Saoirse." A click announced the end of the conversation, and Saoirse started walking back toward the beach.

"Uncle Angus," she called. "I have a question for yeh."

Four bells later, she was sitting in a currach with Liam and Angus, sailing toward Dulcia in a fair following wind. With the wind driving them forward, Liam and Angus had shipped the oars, letting Saoirse at the sail guide them toward the beckoning arm of the Pale Woman on Dulcia Head. In the bottom of the boat were a half dozen boxes of spiny walkers, picked up in the shallows of the Stepping Stones on their way—Angus had said Kekeki had suggested they stop there. Now he leaned back against the side of the boat.

"Do yeh ken yer Terran's going to be in Dulcia?" he asked Saoirse, his question and expression so falsely innocent that Saoirse wondered if he suspected that she had somehow been in communication with Ichiko.

"I certainly won't mind if she is," Saoirse answered.

Liam sniggered at that. "A lot of good that'll do yeh. Yeh can't even touch her."

Saoirse ignored him. "When she left, she mentioned to me she'd be back around this cycle," she told Angus.

"So she mentioned it?" Angus pressed his lips together, nodding. "Whispered it in yer ear, did she, lass?"

Saoirse's cheeks grew hot at the comment and she had to stop herself from touching the earpiece in her left ear. She wondered if Angus had somehow glimpsed the device nestled in her ear or if someone had discovered the com-unit in her bedroom. But Angus just shrugged. "Do yeh think she'll be taking yeh back to Earth with her when they leave?" he asked.

At that, Saoirse only shook her head with a rueful frown. "I don't think *anyone* here will be allowed to go back, Uncle."

That raised Angus' eyebrows. "*She* told yeh this? Yer saying the Terrans have made their decision?"

"Neh, Ichiko didn't say that. Not in those exact words, anyway." *It was Kekeki who told me.* She wondered whether Angus or Liam could see the lie of omission in her face or in the way she said the words; she doubted that she succeeded. "But from what she's said to me and reading beneath her words, that's what I think will happen. She says the Mainlander volunteers that the Terrans took up to the ship are being kept isolated—because they're still carrying local bacteria and viruses. Ichiko seemed very interested in Seann James' potions once I told her how he's managed to cure bloodworms while the Mainlanders still are troubled by them, and took some of his potions back to the ship with her for them to try. She also said she expects the captain to make the decision very soon, so I doubt that even if the Seann's potions work . . ." Saoirse adjusted the boom on the single sail, the cloth billowing out with an audible snap in the breeze. She was glad for the interruption. "Uncle, we're starting to lose the wind."

Angus looked around them; they were nearly abreast of Dulcia Head, with the Pale Woman's single arm lifting far above them and the cliff face beginning to block the wind off the sea. "Aye, yer right. Liam, time to put our backs into it again. Saoirse, go ahead and drop the sail."

The bells in the Pale Woman were ringing Low Twelfth as they moored the boat near Fitzpatrick's and Johnny came out with his cart to take the boxes of spiny walkers from Angus and Liam. As they were offloading the final box, Saoirse saw a flitter approaching them from the direction of Connor Pass. The flitter hovered above them, its rotors whining, then slowly landed several meters away. The canopy opened, and Ichiko waved at them. "Saoirse, Rí Angus, Liam—looks like I timed things well."

"Aye, it's almost as if the two of yeh had planned it," Angus called out. He chuckled then as Saoirse looked back at him. "G'wan with yeh, then," he said to Saoirse. "Liam and meself will be heading to Murphy's Alehouse once we've settled with Johnny's mam, and maybe we'll stay again at the Clan Taggart farm if they'll have us. Yeh can take the infernal noisy machine back to Great Inish with Ichiko."

"Thanks, Uncle," Saoirse said. She hugged him quickly, then Liam. "See yeh back there." She ran toward the flitter and Ichiko, who smiled at her and gestured to the seat next to her. Saoirse clambered up into the flitter as the canopy whined and came down once more.

"Dia duit, Saoirse," Ichiko said, and Saoirse laughed.

"Better," she said. "Keep working on that pronunciation."

"I will. So . . . 'almost as if yeh two had planned it'?" Ichiko asked as the seat harness slid around Saoirse's body.

"I think Uncle Angus knows about the com-unit, or at the very least suspects I have one, though he doesn't seem upset," Saoirse told her.

Ichiko grinned. "That's good. Are you ready to go? I figured that with our previous problem with Kekeki, I'm better off if I have you with me on the way over."

"I'm ready," Saoirse told her. "And looking forward to it."

"Good." Saoirse heard the rotors begin to whine, and the craft lifted from the stones of the quay before the nose dropped slightly and they were streaking over the water of Dulcia Bay toward the Pale Woman and the sea beyond.

There was nothing untoward about their journey to the archipelago this time, the flight smooth and uneventful. The Stepping Stones and the Sleeping Wolf appeared slowly from the horizon, followed by the bulk of Great Inish and its two companions, High and Low Inish, behind. The shadows of the islands stretched out toward them from the sunward side like dark fingers.

Ichiko deliberately kept their conversation light, asking Saoirse questions about what she'd done in the past few cycles as well as having her fill in some of the gaps about Inish society. She steered Saoirse away from any inquiries about the ship or the captain's decision beyond telling her that she'd given Seann James' potions to the medical/biology team to examine. "We'll see what they can learn from those, but I'm sure that will take some time," Ichiko told her.

Ichiko landed the flitter outside the main gate of the Clan Mullin compound, and she and Saoirse went inside so that Ichiko could give the Banríon her greetings and make certain she could stay a few days there. Another bell went by as they talked. But Saoirse was obviously eager to take Ichiko to the Sleeping Wolf to talk to Kekeki again. "We could take the flitter over and be there quickly," Ichiko suggested, but Saoirse shook her head.

"I don't think that would be good. The arracht don't like technology like yours. I don't know if Kekeki would allow us to do that."

Ichiko wanted to shake her head at that, but AMI interjected.

<Remember what happened before. The arracht can cut off my connection to you, they can fool with the manual controls so they're useless, and they could cause the flitter to crash. Until we know how they're doing that and have a way to stop it from happening, I'd listen to Saoirse.> "Then perhaps we should wait until next cycle to visit Kekeki."

"We can still go now," Saoirse responded. "I'm not tired yet, and it's a fairly quick trip over in a currach. We could be back before High Fourth."

<If there's trouble, I can send the flitter to you,> AMI commented. <At least until they disconnect me again.>

So it was that Ichiko found herself walking down the steep path from the clanhouse toward the White Strand and the quay where the Inish boats were moored, far below. They were perhaps halfway down when Ichiko heard AMI in her head once more.

<Ichiko, Commander Mercado has an urgent message for you,> she said, then it was no longer AMI's voice in her head, but Luciano's. <Dr. Aguilar, I have an urgent order from the captain,> he said. His voice sounded strange and official, though the use of her title and last name had been enough to convey the seriousness and the fact others were listening to their conversation. <You are to return immediately to First Base. Do you understand? You are to return immediately. Please respond.>

Ichiko stopped, causing Saoirse to look back at her quizzically. Ichiko frowned, looking over the island as she focused her thoughts. <Understood. What's happened, Commander?>

<I'll tell you more when you're on your way. Right now, we're trying to put out a diplomatic fire. How soon can you be back at First Base?>

<I'm with Saoirse Mullin at the moment. We were going to go over to the Sleeping Wolf to meet Kekeki.>

<You'll have to drop those plans. Say as little as possible to the Inish, but we need you to leave the archipelago ASAP. How soon can you accomplish that?> There was irritation if not outright anger in Luciano's voice that she couldn't understand.

<I need to say goodbye to Saoirse, but I'm nowhere near my flitter at the moment. AMI, take the flitter down to the White Strand; I'll meet it

there. I can leave here in maybe fifteen minutes, Commander. No more.>

<That will have to do. I'll contact you as soon as your AMI tells me you're approaching First Base. Mercado out.>

With that, there was a roaring silence in her head. Saoirse was still staring at Ichiko; behind her, the Sleeping Wolf was a blue-gray lump on the equally gray swells of the sea. Ichiko saw Saoirse's gaze lift to the top of the path, and when she followed Saoirse's gaze, she saw the flitter flying over the summit and beginning to descend toward the White Strand. "What's going on?" Saoirse asked. "I thought we agreed we weren't going to use the flitter."

Ichiko took a deep breath and exhaled it. "I just had an urgent message from *Odysseus*. I have to return to First Base immediately, Saoirse."

"Why?"

"I don't know myself. I only know that it's something important."

She saw Saoirse bite at her bottom lip. "Is it about . . . ?" She stopped; Ichiko saw her glance away to watch the flitter settle on the bright sand below. "Has the captain made her decision about letting those here come back to Earth?"

Ichiko could only shrug. "I don't know, Saoirse. That's the truth. But I have to go. I'm sorry. But I'll be back as soon as I can. I promise."

Tread Softly Because You Tread On My Dreams

A S THEY WERE NEARING the Pale Woman, her AMI spoke in her head. *<That's the Rí's currach down below and to your right, about a half-kilometer out from the entrance to the bay.>* Ichiko glanced down through the side window; she could see the small craft in the green swells, its sail up and a wake trailing behind it. She thought she could see two people in the currach, but it was falling quickly behind them as they passed over Dulcia Head and approached the town. She had just reached the quay when she heard her AMI announce that Commander Mercado was calling her. She spoke aloud this time since there was no one else to overhear them. "This is Dr. Aguilar."

"Ichiko," Luciano replied after the inevitable time lag delay—so there was no one else with him now or he'd made arrangements for their conversation not to be recorded. She hoped so, anyway. A com window popped open belatedly on the windshield, and she was looking at Luciano's face, his ice-pale eyes sharp under his eyebrows. He was in his bridge uniform. "Where are you now?" he said.

"I'm over Dulcia, ready to head up to Connor Pass and First Base. AMI, go ahead and open a window for me on *Odysseus*. What's happened? Why did I have to come back in such a hurry?"

"We have a situation. Minister Plunkett contacted Captain Keshmiri, sounding furious. He wanted to know why no one had told him that the decision had been made that no Lupusian would be allowed to return to Earth on *Odysseus*. He wanted to know why his clan's volunteers on *Odysseus* hadn't been returned in that case, and . . ." She saw him take a breath, and the hint of a smile lurked in the corners of his mouth. ". . . he asked why—and I'm quoting here—'the feckin' Inish had been told, but he'd been left looking like some goddamn unimportant arse.'"

"*Chikushō*," Ichiko muttered.

"Exactly my sentiment when the captain replayed the conversation for me." His face collapsed into seriousness again. "Ichiko, I have to ask this: did you say anything to Banríon Iona, Rí Angus, or Saoirse?"

"No," she answered quickly, then: "At least I don't think so. Saoirse asked lots of questions about it, since she wants to go see Earth. I told her about some of the problems we were facing, and I wasn't pretending to be optimistic about the chances, but I don't think that I ever said directly that the Lupusians weren't going to be allowed to go. You can check my AMI's logs on that if you like."

"Oh, believe me, I'm sure Captain Keshmiri's already having someone do that since she's looking for a proper scapegoat to blame in this kerfuffle. Minister Plunkett said that it was Rí Angus who told him about the decision—they happened to come across each other in one of the Dulcia pubs, though I don't know how the subject of our decision came up. From the reports I've seen, they'd both been drinking heavily at the time. Plunkett called the Rí a 'feckin' liar' among other insults, and the Rí wasn't any gentler. Evidently, they came to blows before they were separated. Then Plunkett called the captain, and she had to admit that, yes, the Rí was largely correct though she stressed that no final decision had yet been made. That *absolutely* didn't sit well with the minister."

Ichiko could see the lip of Connor Pass through the windshield. "AMI," she said, "set us down here for a few minutes so we can keep talking. What a terrific mess. Luciano, honestly, I don't know how this happened. If I had anything to do with it, all I can say is that I'm sorry."

She saw his shoulders lift and fall. "At this point, sorry isn't going to cut it with the captain, I'm afraid. This wasn't the way she wanted the decision released. We've lost control of the narrative and as an indication of just how fast the gossip is moving, we're already hearing from other clans in other towns that they're angry, too."

"What do you need me to do?"

He looked away from her as if checking something on another screen, then back. "The captain or I would be hours getting down there on a shuttle. You're already there and familiar with the situation. When you get back to First Base, we want you to take Lieutenant Bishara and go see Plunkett."

"Luciano, I'm not trained as a diplomat."

"I know and neither is Bishara—in fact, far from it in her case. But you've at least had *some* training in it, you've both met Plunkett, and you'll have us listening in via AMI. The captain will be giving her input from here as long as Plunkett's willing to use the com-unit. I'll fill you in on how we plan to approach this on the way. But for right now, get yourself and Bishara to First Base. The lieutenant's expecting you and should be nearly ready."

He smiled at her then. "You can do this, Ichiko." He gave a short laugh. "Not that the captain's giving you any choice in the matter."

Uncle Angus and Liam arrived back in Great Inish less than two bells after Ichiko left. "By Spiorad Mór, what happened to the two of yeh?" Saoirse asked as they entered the kitchen of the main clanhouse. Saoirse and her mam were pounding dried sugar root with mortar and pestle, sifting the sweet crushed root into a large pottery jar in the center of the table. Both women immediately put down their pestles as they looked at the two. Angus' left eye was dark and bruised, a fan of blood spread from his left nostril and over his cheek; his lower lip was cut and swollen. Liam's face was likewise swollen and bloodied, and there were bruises on the knuckles of the hands of both of them.

"Feckin' Hugh Plunkett is what happened," Angus answered. "The man's a raging stook and a bloody clontarf, but he has a proper punch. I'll give him that much."

"And why did yeh come to blows with the minister?" Iona asked them.

Angus glanced at Saoirse, then dropped his gaze quickly. Standing at the kitchen sink, he pumped water onto a washcloth and began to gingerly clean the blood from his face. "Uncle?" Saoirse asked. The suspicion that she was about to learn why Ichiko had been suddenly called back to First Base clutched at her gut, twisting.

It was Liam who answered. "We went t' Murphy's as usual for a few pints after we finished selling our spiny walkers to Doireann Fitzpatrick. Uncle Angus was at the bar getting us our drinks while I was chatting up this cute Clan Griffith lass; I was making good progress with her, too, if I'm t'be honest. I figured I'd be—"

His mother interrupted the tale. "Liam, just get on with it."

Liam shrugged, rubbing at his discolored knuckles and grimacing. "Sorry, Mam. Anyway, that's when feckin' Hugh Plunkett barged into the alehouse with his red face and loud voice and trailing a couple of his burly clanmates for support. He started shouting at Uncle Angus. 'So, Rí, are yeh trying to charm that skinny Terran lassie so that the feckin' Inishers will get first place on the ship back to Earth?' he roars. 'Well, I tell yeh, I ain't gonna let that happen.' Then . . ." Liam glanced sidewise at Angus. "I guess I should let Uncle Angus tell it from there."

Angus put down the washcloth; Saoirse could see pink streaks on the cloth. "Plunkett got right up in me face, spitting as he was talking. I pushed the man backward so I could breathe without his foul beer breath in me nose. I told him what yeh'd told me, Saoirse—that the chances are the Terrans ain't takin' *any* of us back to Earth a'tall. That made his face go redder than usual, and he came back at me, swinging his big fist. After that . . ." Angus shrugged. "I don't remember all that much except how his feckin' nose cracked nicely when I broke it for him. Liam got involved when the rest of the Plunkett goons decided to jump on me while Plunkett was howling and holding his nose with bloody fingers. Then people were pulling us apart and trying to settle everyone down—after all, not all the Mainlanders are like the Plunketts. Most of 'em are decent enough people—though me and Plunkett were still hurlin' curses at each other. The Clan Murphy folk were pushing the Plunketts out the door and escorting them to the other end of the quay. Before they returned, me and Liam got in our currach and came back here. Didn't seem a very good idea for us to stay in Dulcia until next cycle."

"*I told him what yeh'd told me, Saoirse.*" Saoirse had only half-listened to the tale past that point. *It's my fault. I shouldn't have said anything a'tall. This is my fault.* Saoirse got up from her chair at the table. "Excuse me," she said to Liam, to Angus, to her mam. "I'm not feeling well."

She walked out from the kitchen into the main entrance room, then outside. The wind had picked up, the clouds had gathered and lowered, and she could feel a spray of drizzle on her face. She tapped her com earpiece. After a pause, she heard AMI's voice. <*Saoirse, this is Machiko, Ichiko's AMI. I'm afraid Ichiko is unavailable. May I assist you in some way?*>

"I need to speak to her. It's . . . well, I think it may be important."

<*I'm sorry, Saoirse, but she's occupied at the moment, and I can't disturb her. I will let her know you called as soon as I can.*>

"Umm . . . I'd appreciate that. Thank you."

<*You're welcome, Saoirse. She truly considers you a friend.*> There was the click of disconnection, a hissing, then nothing.

Saoirse hugged herself, watching the clouds drifting overhead. The rain thickened and began to pelt down heavier.

Saoirse grimaced and went back inside. *My fault.* The phrase kept hammering at her. *My fault. And Kekeki's fault, too.*

Chava was grim-faced as she pulled herself into the flitter. Ichiko noted the holstered pulse pistol at her side. "I hope that's not going to be necessary," she said to Chava.

Chava only shrugged. "So do I," she answered. "This certainly isn't my idea of fun." The canopy closed, and the harness settled around her. The flitter lifted, swayed once as it turned, and nosed back down toward Connor Pass and Dulcia. "Is it true that the leak came from your Inish?"

"They're not *my* Inish," Ichiko said, "but yes, that's what it looks like. I haven't quite figured out why or how or who, exactly. I haven't had time to talk to Saoirse since I found out, though AMI's saying she tried to call me."

Chava nodded. "I'm not sure what we can do to fix things with this Plunkett meeting."

"Commander Mercado has given me some ideas. I'm told that we'll be monitored through our AMIs, and there will be people on the diplomatic end of things helping us respond. And the captain's going to call in as well."

"Just what I need: superior officers in my head listening to me." Chava released an audible, aggrieved sigh. She gave Ichiko a half-hearted smile. "And here I thought we were becoming friends."

"I'll try my best not to wreck your career."

"Much appreciated." She gave another sigh. "I probably shouldn't say this, but I'm glad it's you I'm going with rather than the commander, the captain, or any of those heavy brass officers on *Odysseus*." She shook her head. "AMI, you should delete that last remark from the log."

"AMI, you should do the same," Ichiko said to her own implant. *<Done,>* the answer came a moment later.

As they reached the outskirts of Dulcia, the windshield shimmered with the head and shoulders of Luciano. "We've just heard from Minister Plunkett. He's expecting the two of you and is waiting at his pub office on the quay. You'll have Captain Keshmiri with you as well via Plunkett's com-unit. Let your AMIs know when you're with the minister, and the captain will join you then."

Ichiko and Chava exchanged glances. Chava shrugged with an accompanying grimace. "Understood," Ichiko said. "Thank you, Commander."

"Good luck to both of you. Let's hope we can calm everyone down." With that, Luciano vanished as his window blinked out. The flitter came in over the upper town and settled down on the quay a few meters from Plunkett's Pub. "Notice anything?" Chava asked as the canopy started to lift, the seat harnesses slid away, and the noise of the rotors died.

Ichiko nodded wordlessly. There was a small crowd of Lupusians around the pub entrance, blocking the doors and staring intently at Ichiko and Chava with decidedly unfriendly faces. Chava had her hand lightly resting on the grip of her pulse pistol. "Chava?" Ichiko said, looking pointedly at the weapon; Chava reluctantly moved her hand away, the fingers curling into a fist at her side.

"They rather make me wonder if I should have brought along body armor with the bio-shield," Chava muttered as they descended from the flitter and the canopy closed behind them.

"We want them to trust us," Ichiko said. "So we have to act like we trust them in return."

"That's a lovely sentiment, but I'm not feeling particularly trusting at the moment. Not the way they're glaring at us." Chava strode toward the pub with Ichiko following and trying to pretend that she was unconcerned. She smiled toward the group—both men and women, all dressed as in working clothes—as they approached. Their faces remained grim, but they moved aside to let Chava and Ichiko pass as they neared the pub. "Dia duit," Ichiko said.

There wasn't a corresponding response. "So is it true? Yer going to leave us all stranded here again?" one of the women called loudly as they passed between them. Ichiko pressed her lips together tightly and didn't answer. Chava pushed open the doors. "Tell us!" the woman shouted. "Tell us, yeh cowardly bastards!"

The doors closed behind them, cutting off the profane shouts that followed. The interior was dark, lit by oil lanterns hanging from the support beams of the low ceiling. There didn't appear to be any customers: no one in the booths or along the tables, no one behind the bar and the taps, no wait staff anywhere. A door to the rear opened and Minister Plunkett stood there, a backlit silhouette. He gestured to the firelit room behind him.

"Come through," he said.

Ichiko took a long cleansing breath. *<AMI, inform Captain Keshmiri that we're with the minister.>*

<Done. Go seikō o inorimasu, Ichiko,> her mother's voice replied. *I wish you success.*

<Thanks. I think I'll need it.>

The Winds Of
The Sullen Gale

A S THEY ENTERED Minister Plunkett's office, Ichiko could see Plunkett better, and her eyes widened at the sight. The man's face was bruised and battered, his nose swollen and set slightly askew. It appeared that the minister might have had the worse of the fight with the Rí—which didn't surprise Ichiko, knowing both of the men.

"Minister Plunkett, it's good to see you again," she said, "though I wish it were under better circumstances."

His lips, swollen from the fight, curled into a sneer. She noticed that another tooth was missing. "I'll just bet yeh do," he answered, his thickened lips and nose blurring the words. "What the hell have yeh been telling yer Inish friends that yeh haven't been telling me?"

Before Ichiko could fashion a response to that, the com-unit on Plunkett's desk chimed and lit up. Above the device, a window holding Captain Keshmiri's image opened. The captain's face was serious, her lips tightly pressed together. She glanced at each of them before focusing her attention on Plunkett. "Minister Plunkett, I want to apologize for the evident misunderstanding here."

Plunkett gave a bark of a laugh at that. "Yeh do, eh, Captain? So 'tis merely a misunderstanding, is it? And just what is it that yeh think I'm too much a fecking idjit to have understood?"

Ichiko heard an intake of breath from Chava behind her and saw the captain's face flush a breath later. Ichiko hurried to speak, knowing that there would be a few seconds' time lag before the captain could answer. "Minister, please forgive me for interrupting, but I don't believe there was *any* misunderstanding on your part. It was the Inish who evidently leaped to a hasty—and wrong—conclusion from comments I made, and I'm very sorry for any part I played in that. I swear to you that I never told Rí Mullin or Banríon Mullin or any of the Inish that Captain Keshmiri had made *any* decision regarding whether or not we would allow Lupusians to return to Earth. What I said to those on the archipelago was only what you already knew: that there were still issues that had to be resolved before that could happen. Those same issues are why Lieutenant Bishara and I are required to wear our bio-shields whenever we leave First Base. This is the truth of the matter: I never told the Inish that *any* firm decision had been made. If that's what Rí Angus believes he heard, then he's entirely mistaken."

Ichiko glanced at the captain's face; she could read nothing there but thought that the captain gave her a faint nod. Plunkett grunted once, wordlessly, then turned to face the com-unit. "Then tell me, Captain," he said, "are the Inish *wrong* about this 'conclusion' of theirs?"

After the usual time delay, the captain replied. "As of this moment, Minister, I've still made no final decision, as Dr. Aguilar has just told you. However, I'll be honest here—we've still been unable to do much about the Lupusian bacteria and viruses that could conceivably infect, sicken, and kill those of us who haven't been exposed to them. You understand, of course, that it would be *centuries* of your time before I could get an answer from Earth with their input on this problem. I wish it were different, but this is my decision to make and I'm acutely aware of the gravity it holds for all of us."

"And?" Plunkett prodded. "What does all that blathering mean?"

Another few seconds passed. "The bitter reality for me is that we have very little time left to us to resolve those issues. That's concerning to *all* of us: Terran and Lupusian alike. *Odysseus* can't remain here indefinitely; you were informed of that fact when we first arrived, after all. As things stand at the moment, were I forced to make the decision right now, during this cycle, then the answer is no—I would *not* allow any Lupusians to return to Earth because that would constitute too much of a risk for both the Lupusians who'd now be exposed to Terran diseases new to them and for Terrans who've never had to deal with Lupusian diseases. Frankly, I'm not willing to be responsible for the significant number of deaths that might result—on *both* sides. As for taking anyone back in isolation, that could still be a consideration, but let me ask you this, Minister: would *you* be willing to spend at least ten years of our time—nearly two centuries in your time—in a sealed isolation chamber, permitted outside only if you were wearing a bio-shield and even then always accompanied by someone with orders to shoot you if you tried removing the shield or if for some reason it failed? I know what my choice would be."

Plunkett blinked heavily, glaring at the captain. "So what I hear yeh saying is that Rí Mullin is right. Yer going to leave all of us here."

"I'm saying," Captain Keshmiri replied calmly, "that I haven't made my final decision yet, but yes, it's becoming more likely with every passing cycle that's the decision I will be forced to make. Dr. Aguilar has already apologized to you for any part she played in this, and I promise you here and now that I will call you as soon as my final decision's been made—and I'll do that *before* I make the announcement to Canis Lupus at large."

"That's so very feckin' generous of yeh," Plunkett commented. He slapped the com-unit and the captain's window vanished. Plunkett glared at Ichiko and Chava. "Both of yeh get out," he said. "Now."

Ichiko looked at Chava, who nodded. "I'm sorry for this, Minister," Ichiko told the man again. "Truly, I am."

He didn't answer as they left the office and the pub.

"Well, that went well, didn't it?" Chava said as they exited the pub. The small crowd outside was still there and still scowling—though they were no longer shouting—and moved aside to allow Ichiko and Chava to walk to their flitter. Both women could hear a constant low muttering of curses and insults from the group; they pretended not to hear any of it, keeping their heads down and avoiding making eye contact. Once in the flitter, they closed the windshield over them. Ichiko leaned back in her seat and exhaled a long sigh.

"Everything's suddenly topsy-turvy," she said. "Minister Plunkett . . ." She shook her head, but Chava snorted.

". . . is a total asshole," she finished, "and the Rí should have hit him much harder to knock some sense into the man's head."

Ichiko had to laugh. "That's hardly a good diplomatic solution."

"I'm just a soldier," Chava answered. "I prefer soldierlike solutions." She patted the pulse pistol at her side.

Ichiko laughed again. "I think the captain would have both our heads if we'd tried something like that. AMI, take us back to First Base."

The rotors of the flitter whined as it started to rise from the ground, turning to head up the Mail Road toward Connor Pass Road and lifting higher as they moved. But when they reached the intersection of Mail Road and Connor Pass Road, still rising but below the level of the rooftops, shadows moved across the canopy as a thick netting fell over the flitter's top, snarling the rotors so that the flitter canted dangerously and sent an alarm wailing in the cabin.

AMI was howling in Ichiko's ear, but she could pay no attention to the voice. The manual controls sprouted from the console. Chava clutched at them, trying desperately to right the flitter, but now another rotor had fouled in the netting and the flitter was tumbling down to the street, rocking sideways and crashing into the buildings on either side. Their impact with the ground slammed Ichiko back in her seat as the restraints tightened around her, leaving Ichiko stunned. They came to rest at a steep, canted angle.

"Chava?" she called desperately, but the woman didn't answer. She looked to her right; Chava was lolling in her restraints, eyes closed and unconscious, a fan of blood across her face and shoulder from a cut on her forehead. *Did her bio-shield fail?* There were figures around them beyond the dirty, scratched windshield. Bricks and rocks were pounding the side of the flitter. She could hear angry shouting outside.

"AMI, contact First Base; have them send help! Chava and I are under attack here."

<Already done. Drones from First Base are on their way, and a response team is following. Just stay in the flitter until they get there.>

"I'm not sure that's going to be possible," Ichiko answered.

It wasn't. Already, the canopy over them was broken. As the canopy was pried and wrenched open, she saw Chava being cut from her restraints and dragged from the flitter. Other sets of hands were trying to do the same with her; she pushed back at them, shouting. Someone clutched her wrists but abruptly let go, cursing, as the bio-shield shocked them in warning. But more hands reached in afterward as a knife blade sliced the webbing of her seat restraint; Ichiko fell sideways and down into the side of the flitter, landing on her hands and feet and nearly falling from the vehicle. Everything was confusion around her. She had no idea where Chava was. She didn't know how many people surrounded the flitter; they were simply a sea of unrecognizable faces, dressed as workers and tradespeople and fishing folk. *Did Plunkett set this up, or was it others?* It didn't matter. More important to her was continuing to push away those grasping hands that wanted to snatch her and take her from the flitter.

<Ichiko, the drones have arrived,> she heard her AMI say.

"MOVE AWAY FROM THE FLITTER!" an impossibly loud and booming voice declared. Ichiko could hear it echoing against the buildings around them. **"THIS IS YOUR ONLY WARNING! MOVE AWAY!"** That was followed by the chatter of a weapon being fired into the air. The crowd around the flitter scrambled away at the sound, vanishing like insects in sudden light as a large, black-painted military drone descended to hover in the street next to the flitter, its rotors lashing the air. "Dr. Aguilar, are you injured?" a voice from the drone's speaker asked. A bar of searing green light emitted by the drone slid over her. "Your bio-shield appears to be intact, thankfully."

"I . . . I think I'm all right. Mostly, anyway," she answered. "But they pulled Chava—Lieutenant Bishara—out of the flitter. I don't know where she is." She could hear the panic in her voice.

"Stay where you are," the drone voice said. "A squad from First Base will be here in less than three minutes. The other drone is searching for Lieutenant Bishara. Don't worry; we'll find her." Rotors whining, the drone spun around its axis, lifted, and went out of her vision. Ichiko tried to pull herself up, swinging her legs out of the half-open canopy. She let herself slide out of the flitter despite the drone pilot's admonition, standing in the street amid the wreckage of the flitter and the buildings on either side of the street. Her breath was fast and ragged, and her heart was still pounding madly from the fright and the rush of adrenaline. She could see the netting that had brought them down: thick, braided rope—a fishing net, likely, but one designed for large prey that might break the strands of the lighter netting she'd seen in use in the archipelago. Lines from the net had been attached to the nearest buildings to stop them from escaping the snare. The body of the flitter was dented and bent, the windshield cracked and the hinges broken. She doubted that she'd ever see it flying again.

She could hear footsteps coming around the front of the flitter. She readied herself to run if she needed to, then gave a cry of relief. She saw the *Odysseus* insignia on an armored body and the reflective shimmer of the headpiece as well as the stubby barrel of a disperser cradled at the ready position in the soldier's arms. Two other armed noncommissioned ratings flanked the soldier, their attention on the buildings to either side. "Dr. Aguilar?" a voice asked through the helmet speaker. "I'm Ensign Collins from First Base. Please come with me."

Ichiko shook her head. "Lieutenant Bishara?" she asked.

"We have her also," Collins said, but even through the speaker, Ichiko heard a strange tone to his voice. "She's already in our carrier flitter."

"Is Lieutenant Bishara all right?" Collins' hesitation was palpable. "I could see she was hurt. Ensign, I'm not leaving with you until I know."

"The lieutenant is alive, and her injuries appear to be relatively minor," Collins answered.

"But . . . ?"

"Dr. Aguilar, we really need to leave ASAP for everyone's safety." Collins' breath rattled the speaker, then: "I'm afraid her bio-shield was compromised either during the crash or in the attack."

"Oh, God. No . . ." The denial was a soft breath, to which Collins nodded faintly

"I'm really sorry, Doctor, but please—we need to *go* now."

Ichiko nodded. She followed the trio of soldiers back to the carrier sitting in the middle of the street a half-block away.

"Chava?"

Ichiko watched the woman's eyes flutter open behind the isolation chambers' glass window. First Base's medic stood nearby, not saying anything but watching the chamber's display along with another tech. "Hey, Ichiko," Chava said, her voice thinned by the microphone in the room. Ichiko hoped that was why she sounded so weak. Someone had cleaned up and sealed the cut on her forehead. "Just so you know, next time you ask me to come with you to Dulcia, I'm going to give you a hard pass. You can take someone else."

Ichiko tried to smile at her and failed. She pressed her fingers against the glass. "I'm so sorry."

She saw Chava shrug under the sheets. "Wasn't your fault. It was the fucking Canines who attacked us."

Ichiko couldn't muster the breath or desire to correct her language. "How are you feeling?"

Chava snagged her lower lip with her teeth before replying. She blinked as if trying to clear her vision. "I'm a little scared, honestly," she said. "My bio-shield . . ." Her voice trailed off.

"I know. But you weren't exposed for very long. I've talked to Captain Keshmiri and Commander Mercado. There's a shuttle already on its way down, and you'll be going up to *Odysseus* with it. The medical staff there's going to take great care of you."

Chava stared at Ichiko with forlorn eyes. "And I'll have to be in isolation forever, like the Canines we already have up there. I'm not sure I can bear that, Ichiko."

"You don't know that, and that's not what the captain told me. Your exposure to Canis Lupus was limited—probably no more than fifteen minutes at the most. You're not like the Lupusians who have been breathing the air and being exposed to all the bacteria and viruses and the rest all their lives. You might experience no ill effects at all."

<According to the clan records, the mortality rate when First Base was breached was over 60% in just the first few months. It was eventually 100% for those at Second Base,> AMI whispered. Ichiko ignored that, though she wondered whether Chava's AMI hadn't also given her those dire statistics. "Anyway," Ichiko continued, keeping eye contact with Chava, "I'll be going up with you on the shuttle, so if you need someone to talk to or complain to or be your advocate, I'll be there. Just call for me."

That managed to get a momentary smile from Chava, who then coughed. "Sorry," she said. "A tickle in my throat." She smiled again. "You know, you told me more than once that you wanted to know what Canis Lupus smelled like and what the air tasted like. Well, I've smelled it. The strongest odor was the sea, even through the smoke and electrical smell of the crashed flitter. There was a distinct briny tang, like I remember from being on the Mediterranean beaches, but there were also odors and flavors to Dulcia's air that I simply can't describe, like nothing I'd experienced before. I wish I could say it better for you."

<The shuttle's arriving,> AMI said. Ichiko could faintly hear the warning klaxon sound from the docking station two levels above.

"We'll have plenty of time to talk about that, and I want to hear everything you have to say," Ichiko told her. "But right now, let's get you up to *Odysseus*." She rapped her knuckles on the glass between them. "I'm going to go up to the shuttle bay and make sure they're ready for you. I also had a call from Saoirse that I probably should return before we leave."

Chava nodded. She cleared her throat and coughed again. "No problem. It's not like I'm going anywhere right now."

For The World's More Full Of Weeping Than You Can Understand

SAOIRSE STARTED TALKING EVEN before the holo window above the com-unit had fully opened and focused. Her words tumbled out in a tangled rush. "Ichiko? Thanks for calling me back. Listen, I have to tell yeh that I think me Uncle Angus has done something he shouldn't have, and some of it . . . a lot of it . . . well, *most* of it is my fault. He's evidently said things to Minister Plunkett about the Mainlanders yeh have on yer ship and how they're still dangerous, then their argument escalated into a brawl in Murphy's Alehouse and . . ."

In the window, Ichiko lifted a finger to her lips. "I already know," the Terran said. "That's why I was ordered to come back to First Base. It's been a long cycle already." She then told Saoirse about her meeting with Plunkett and what had happened afterward.

"I'm so, so sorry," Saoirse said as Ichiko described the attack. Tears welled in Saoirse's eyes, and she could feel the moisture sliding down her cheeks. "That's awful. How's yer friend? I can't imagine . . . Was it Clan Plunkett that did this? What were they thinking?"

In the window, Ichiko shrugged. "We don't know yet who's

responsible. As for Chava, she's fine so far, but we really don't know yet. She's about to be shuttled up to *Odysseus* for treatment and observation. Saoirse, I'm going with her and it might be some time before I can talk to you again or come back down to the archipelago."

Saoirse took a deep breath. "Because of what I did, because of what Angus and Liam did to the Minister?"

"No," Ichiko told her. "It wasn't what you did. Saoirse, if anything, I'll take full blame for what's happened. I shouldn't have told you *anything* about how things were going with Lupusians we had brought up to the ship. I shouldn't have asked you to have your Uncle James show me his cures for the local diseases. I should have kept my mouth shut about all that and just passed along the information to my superiors, but I didn't. I shouldn't . . ." There was a pause and hissing of static in Saoirse's ears. In the com window, Ichiko frowned and there was a strange gleam in her eyes that Saoirse suspected matched her own. "I should never have allowed us to become so close. I should have remained more distant and objective."

The words struck Saoirse like soft fists. "How can yeh say that?" Saoirse heard her voice rise and become louder, desperation adding its urgency to her words. She wondered how panicked she must sound to Ichiko. "I thought we were becoming friends, and that's what I wanted. I thought mebbe yeh wanted that, too."

"I did want that, Saoirse. Truly. It's just . . ." She stopped, cocking her head as if listening to something that Saoirse couldn't hear—*Machiko? Her AMI?* she wondered. She saw Ichiko's shoulders sag as she exhaled. "Saoirse, I'm sorry, but I have to cut this short. The shuttle back to *Odysseus* is ready to leave, and they're calling me. We'll pick this up later, I promise. Don't beat yourself up over what happened. It wasn't your fault, and you've nothing to apologize for. I want you to know that."

"Aye," Saoirse said, though it did nothing to assuage her guilt. "I'll talk to yeh later, then."

"We will. I promise."

Ichiko nodded; the connection vanished.

"So yeh've been hiding that from us."

Saoirse turned, startled, to see her mam peering through the slightly opened door of her room. Iona pushed the door open, standing with hands on hips, frowning.

"Mam . . . I . . ."

The frown dissolved and her hands left her hips. Iona came fully into the room, shutting the door behind her and sitting on the bed near Saoirse. She glanced at the com-unit sitting on the nightstand, shaking her head. "Saoirse, I don't care. I know how yeh feel about this Terran woman, and that doesn't matter to me. I'll get me grands from Gráinne if yeh never want that yerself. I just don't want yeh to get hurt chasin' after something yeh can't ever have."

"How much of that did yeh hear?"

"Enough to know I'm giving yeh good advice," her mam said. "Ichiko's a good person. I believe that, and I can understand why yeh feel about her the way yeh do. But there's no future for yeh with her. None a'tall."

"Yeh don't know that. Not yet yeh don't." Her voice trembled, and she wiped at her eyes.

"Yer wrong about that. I know and so do yeh. So does everyone here, and now Minister Plunkett and the rest of the mainland clans do, too." Her mam put her arm around Saoirse's shoulder and pulled her into an embrace. After momentary resistance, Saoirse let herself fall into the hug, putting her head on her mam's shoulder. The warmth and comfort broke Saoirse's reserves. She began to sob as her mam stroked her hair and held her close. "Just let it out," her mam whispered into her ear. "Yer fine. I have yeh."

Sniffing, Saoirse pulled back. "Mam . . ."

"I know," Iona said. "Yeh want more of her than just being a friend."

"I do, Mam. I just don't know if she feels the same."

"Mebbe she does and mebbe not. If yeh want to know, then yeh need to ask her." Iona wiped away a tear from Saoirse's face with a gentle stroke of her thumb. "Or maybe it's only an infatuation because she's so different, and yer feelings will eventually pass. Either way, none of that changes the fundamental problem, does it? She's going to leave, and yeh can't go with her."

Chava had been placed in a transparent chamber obviously designed to be just small enough to pass through the shuttle's air lock. Most of the shuttle's seats had been taken out to accommodate the chamber and the tanks and other apparatus attached to it, with the chamber placed near the air lock. In one of the remaining seats was a man she didn't recognize with a lieutenant's bar on his shoulders and a patch with the Medical Corps' Rod of Asclepius on the breast of his uniform. He was staring at the readouts on the isolation chamber. A med-bot was inside the chamber, perched next to Chava's bed. Chava was strapped to the bed, her eyes closed, and there were tubes around her that hadn't been there before. Ichiko focused her thoughts so that her AMI could hear her. <AMI, call Chava for me.>

<She's not conscious.>

<Why not? Did they give her something? Never mind . . . >

Ichiko went to the chamber as the medic glanced over at her. "Why is she out? She was conscious when I left her."

She heard the medic sigh. "Lieutenant Bishara has a lung congestion that was making it increasingly difficult for her to breathe on her own. The locals call it Gray Threads. I had the med-bot put her on a vent for the trip up to the ship, so we've sedated her. It seemed best for the moment; when we have her in the med-unit on the ship, we can revisit that decision."

"Gray Threads?" Ichiko thought she remembered Rí Angus mentioning that as something potentially deadly; her pulse raced at the thought.

The medic evidently noticed her distress. "It's one of the Lupusian diseases. They usually get it in childhood." He closed his eyes momentarily, evidently listening to his own AMI. "I'm told that an infection used to be 90% fatal, but that they have treatments for it now which has really cut down the fatality rates."

"By how much?"

The medic's gaze flicked away from Ichiko to the readout before he answered. "From around 90% to about 30 to 40%." Then he glanced at her again. "Dr. Aguilar, I promise we'll take excellent care of her. But it'll be much easier to do that up on *Odysseus* with all its resources than down here. Right now, Captain Keshmiri wants her there as soon as possible, so if you'll just take a seat and strap in . . ."

Ichiko nodded. She took one of the remaining seats near the chamber. There were two other crew members returning to the ship with them, seated at the back of the shuttle as far away from the chamber as they could get. Ichiko strapped herself in as a bell chimed in her head and she felt the ship trembling as the drive units were engaged. *<One minute to takeoff,>* the shuttle's AMI told them. *<It might be a bit rough until we break atmosphere, so be prepared.>*

Rough was an understatement. The winds of Canis Lupus tore at the shuttle as if wishing to grab it, pull it from the sky, and dash it back down to earth. Ichiko kept looking back to Chava's isolation chamber; the medic seated alongside looked rather ill himself—Ichiko doubted that he was used to rough shuttle trips, but to his credit he gave Ichiko a thumbs-up when he noticed her attention. When they lifted past the stratospheric winds, the silence and smoothness was a relief, though Ichiko had never relished weightlessness herself. She was grateful for the straps that now kept her tight to her seat.

A few hours later, they were in the shuttle bay of *Odysseus*. The shuttle was sprayed with disinfectant while an air lock tube was extended from outside the bay to latch onto the shuttle's air lock. The inner door of the air lock opened, and a rating stuck his head in along with the familiar odor of the ship. "Welcome home," he said. He waved to someone behind him and stepped in. Another rating followed him leading a carrier-bot; they set the rubber-treaded body under Chava's isolation chamber and followed it out through the air lock tube with the medic padding along behind.

Ichiko rose from her seat and started to follow them to the medical bay, but her AMI chirped before she'd even left the shuttle.

<Commander Mercado requests that you come immediately to the bridge's ready room to meet him.>

<Tell him that I'm heading to the medical bay to be with Lieutenant Bishara.>

<He says to first come see him.>

Ichiko frowned, stopped, and let Chava's chamber move on ahead. <Fine. AMI, tell that medic that I want to stay informed about Chava and that I'll be there to see her as soon as I can.> She went to the nearest personnel lift instead. "Bridge level," she said.

When the doors opened, she went to the door labeled Bridge Ready Room; it opened as she approached. "Commander, you wanted to see me?" she said as she entered.

Luciano was the only person inside, dressed in his bridge uniform. "Dr. Aguilar, thanks for coming when I know you're worried about Lieutenant Bishara," he said; the careful formality told her that others were listening to their conversation. "Have a seat, please?" Luciano gestured at the chairs arranged around the long glass-topped table. "The captain and Lieutenant Commander Tinubu will be joining us," he began, but the door yawned open before Ichiko could sit. "Ah, here they are."

Ichiko and Luciano both stood as the two entered; Luciano saluted. "Captain. Nagasi," Ichiko said.

Captain Keshmiri stood behind the seat next to Luciano and across the table from Ichiko; Nagasi pulled out the chair alongside Ichiko.

"Please, sit," Captain Keshmiri said, gesturing to everyone. When everyone was seated, she leaned forward. "Dr. Aguilar, I want you to know that I appreciate your willingness to speak to Minister Plunkett on my behalf. I thought that having you talk to him in person would calm down both the minister and the local population. I was obviously wrong in that assumption. I want you to know that had I harbored any suspicion that there'd be aggression toward you and Lieutenant Bishara as a result, I wouldn't have made that request. I'm very sorry for what the two of you went through, and especially for what Lieutenant Bishara is now having to endure."

"There's no reason to apologize, Captain. You did what you thought best. And in any case, I don't *know* that Minister Plunkett was responsible, though I strongly suspect it."

"We're investigating that now," Luciano said. His face was grim and almost angry. Ichiko wondered if that was concern for her or simply because that was how he needed to appear. "If the minister did have anything to do with the attack, you can believe that we'll hold him responsible, as we will anyone we can identify as having taken part. In the eyes of the UPC, the descendants of the original crew we left here are also UPC citizens and thus are subject to our laws. Your flitter's cameras captured most of the incident; we're going over that material now. We should be able to identify your assailants, and those who did this *will* pay. We promise you that much."

Ichiko nodded, not certain what else to say.

Nagasi stirred next to Ichiko, putting his elbows on the table as he laced his long fingers together. "Captain Keshmiri, the medical staff, and I have been talking. We were hoping to delay the announcement until the last moment, but that seems foolish in the face of what's happened today. We're going to send the remaining Lupusians aboard *Odysseus* home as soon as a shuttle can be readied to accommodate them in isolation. At the same time, we'll announce officially that—at least for the foreseeable future—no Lupusians will be permitted to return to Earth. We'll also inform Minister Plunket and all Lupusians that *Odysseus* will be breaking orbit for our return in three weeks, ship-time."

"In the meantime," Captain Keshmiri interjected, "we'll do what we can to ensure that every town on Canis Lupus has sufficient supplies, resources, and technological help until another supply ship can be sent out from Earth. We want them to understand that we're *not* abandoning them again. We *won't* ever abandon them."

"And the Inish?" Ichiko asked. "What about them?"

"That's more a matter for the locals," the captain said. "But we'll suggest . . ."

She stopped, her head tilted as if listening. The others at the table did the same. A moment later, Ichiko heard her AMI's voice.

<*Lieutenant Bishara's condition is continuing to deteriorate. They're suggesting you and Dr. Tinubu might want to come up to the isolation ward for more information.*>

Captain Keshmiri was already waving a hand at the two of them. "Go," she said simply.

"There has to be something more we can do," Ichiko said to Nagasi as they were on the lift to the med lab.

Nagasi sighed at that. His eyes were sympathetic in his dark face as he looked at her. "They're doing what they can," he said. "You and I both know that. But we also know that our drug regimens so far haven't been effective against Lupusian diseases."

Ichiko started to speak. Then the lift door opened, so she hurried down the hall to the medical isolation ward. She noticed that those in the large noncritical isolation section—all of the Lupusian volunteers sent here by Minister Plunkett and a few of the other Mainlander clans—were staring at her as they walked quickly past their area. She wondered how much they knew and how much the gossip and speculation about what had happened in Dulcia and their eventual fate had reached them.

She couldn't let herself dwell on it. She and Nagasi went into the unsealed antechamber. Behind the glass wall was a bed holding Chava with a trio of the medical staff huddled around her bed, all of them in sealed, full biohazard suits. Ichiko went up to the microphone embedded in the glass and touched the contact below it. "How is she?" she asked, breathlessly.

One of the techs left the bedside and walked over toward them. The name on the suit said *Dr. Huang* and the shoulder bore a lieutenant's insignia. Behind the faceplate, Ichiko could see an older Asian woman's face. Gray hair straggled over kindly but worried eyes. Dr. Huang's gaze went from Ichiko to Nagasi; she looked to him as if to confirm she could answer; Nagasi nodded back to her.

"We haven't been able to stabilize Lieutenant Bishara yet." The woman's voice came through their AMI channels, not through the speaker in the room. "The infection is slowly clogging her lung passages and airway. As you know, the medic from First Base put her on a vent. She's still on it, and we're using pressurized air to keep her breathing since she's no longer capable of that on her own. I'm worried about the stress on her heart and other organs. We're trying a wide array of antibiotics, hoping one of them or some combination of them will work. But right now . . ." Her shrug was visible under the biohazard suit.

"What about the Lupusians?" Nagasi asked. "They've dealt with this before."

"I've talked to three different healers downworld," Huang responded. "They've all said the same thing. Once a Gray Threads infection has taken hold, there's little they can do. They'll survive or they won't; it's in the hands of whatever god or gods you believe in."

"That's not good enough," Ichiko said angrily.

"I agree with you," Huang answered. "Please believe we're doing what we can and are not giving up on her."

Ichiko turned away as Nagasi told the woman, "Thank you, Doctor. I know you're not."

Ichiko thumbed on her AMI and focused her thoughts as well as she could. <*AMI, call Saoirse for me. Now. Keep calling her until she answers.*>

<*Done.*>

As she waited, Ichiko turned back to look at Chava. She watched the slow rise and fall of her chest as if her stare could give Chava the will to keep breathing.

The Consequences
Of Truth

SAOIRSE SAT ON HER BED, tapping her feet nervously as she waited for Ichiko to respond. She'd heard the request from Ichiko's AMI and gone to her room, shutting the door for privacy though her mam had glanced at her knowingly as she'd done so. She'd pulled the com-unit from under the bed and placed it on her nightstand, expecting a window to open with Ichiko's visage, but instead there was a click in her ear and after the expected delay, Ichiko's familiar accent and soft voice.

"Saoirse? Thanks for responding so quickly."

"What's going on, Ichiko? Are there more problems about what my uncle said to Minister Plunkett. I'm so sorry that I—"

"No." Ichiko's voice had an edge that severed Saoirse's burgeoning apology. "Sorry, Saoirse, but we're dealing with an emergency up here. Lieutenant Bishara has been infected with what you call the Gray Threads. Can you ask your Seann James if he has any potions for that illness—something to kill the infection or at least to control it? And please hurry. I . . . I don't think she has much time left."

"Of course," Saoirse said. "I'll go find him now."

"Thanks, Saoirse." Saoirse could hear fear mingled with relief in Ichiko's voice, giving Saoirse a quick twinge of jealousy. *Is Lieutenant Bishara Ichiko's lover?* She shook the thought away.

"I'm leaving now. I'll call you back as soon as I'm with Seann James." With that, Saoirse touched the earpiece to turn it off. She hurried from her room and headed toward the door of the main house.

"Saoirse?" her mam called. "What's going on?"

Saoirse only shook her head. "Can't talk right now, Mam," she called back over her shoulder. "Tell you later." Then she was out-side, running through the compound toward the rear where Seann James' apothecary was set. "Seann James," she called out breathlessly as soon as she opened the door.

"What, girl?" He was at one of the drying racks with another of her uncles—one of the Seann's assistants—holding up a spray of seaflower and sniffing the seeded heads. "Go ahead and crush the seeds," he told the assistant, handing him the seaflower. "It's ready. Make sure yeh grind 'em into a fine powder. Fine, d'yeh hear? I want it to be as soft as flour. Now, Saoirse, what can I do for you? Something for cramps?"

She ignored that. "Seann, what can yeh do about the Gray Threads?"

Seann James' head went back, his eyes widening. "Gray Threads? Why? Has one of the children . . . ?"

Saoirse shook her head. "It's for a Terran who was accidentally exposed to our air."

"The woman who came here? How did she—?"

Another quick shake—she knew Seann James' tendency to ramble. "No, not Ichiko. A lieutenant from First Base. Wait . . ." Ichiko lifted her hand to her ear as Seann James watched her, puzzled. She touched the contact there. "Machiko, tell Ichiko I'm with Seann James now," she said to the air.

<A moment . . . > Then: "Saoirse?"

"I'm in the apothecary, Ichiko. Seann James, Gray Threads. What can yeh do for someone infected with that?"

James looked at her with rheum-laden eyes. "It's not that

simple, Saoirse. We give every child born here on the archipelago a draught of Blue Mullein and Tincture of Gingifer along with a few other herbs once every five years for their first half century. All the clans do the same, even those on the mainland. That's for protection against ever getting the infection in the first place. If a child is unlucky enough to *still* contract the disease, well, there's not much we can do at that point. We keep them as comfortable as possible; we give them another draught, as strong as they can tolerate. But still around three in ten of 'em will die—though before we came up with the Blue Mullein and Tincture of Gingifer procedure . . ."

"I understand, Seann," Saoirse said hurriedly to stop what she suspected would be an entire history of Gray Threads treatment. "However, the Terran has never had your draught. They've never been exposed to our world *at all* until a cycle ago. Isn't there *something* you could do?"

Seann James shook his head dolefully. "Nothing that I believe would work. I'm sorry."

Saoirse nodded. "Ichiko . . ." she began, but Ichiko was already responding.

"I heard you and the Seann talking through your earpiece, Saoirse. Can Seann James put together an extremely strong draught of that potion? That's at least worth a try and is a better option than anything we have right now. I can have someone from First Base fly a flitter over to the archipelago to get it and take it back to First Base. I'll have a shuttle sent down to bring it up here."

And I'll have to talk to Kekeki and tell her not to bother this flitter . . . Saoirse sighed and relayed the request to Seann James, who rummaged through the vials and bottles in the room, the glass clinking as he examined them. "I have everything I need. I could have it ready by Low Twelfth, but I can't make any promises as to its efficacy."

"Just do it," Saoirse told him, anticipating Ichiko's answer. "Thank you, Seann. Ichiko, did you get that?"

"Got it, and please tell Seann James how much I appreciate his efforts. I owe you and Clan Mullin. If there's anything I can do to help you, let me know. Meanwhile, I'll get things started on my end. Saoirse, thank you. I couldn't have gotten this far without you."

Saoirse found herself smiling involuntarily at that. "I need to talk to Kekeki right away," she said, knowing Ichiko would understand the reason. "Meanwhile, Seann James will get the potion ready. Let me know if it works. Tell Lieutenant Bishara that we'll all be praying to Spiorad Mór for her recovery."

"I'm sure she'll appreciate that. I'll let you know when the flitter's heading over, so that I know Kekeki's agreeable. Talk to you soon. AMI, end contact."

And with that, there was a click and a hiss in her ear, then silence.

"I'll let you know when the flitter's heading over, so that I know Kekeki's agreeable. Talk to you soon. AMI, end contact." Then: "AMI, send Nagasi and the med team a copy of that conversation. Send it to Commander Mercado and the captain as well."

<*I was streaming it to them as you were talking.*>

Nagasi nodded in response. "We all heard it."

Dr. Huang, behind the glass, agreed. "I've already told the team to be ready, and we'll do everything in our power to keep her alive until this potion reaches us. And even if the Inish medicine does little or nothing, we'll take a sample into the lab, pull it apart, and see if we can purify and concentrate it to create something that *will* work."

<*Commander Mercado has just sent orders to First Base to have a flitter arrive on Great Inish before Low Twelfth,*> AMI added. <*The commander also asks if you'll meet him for lunch.*>

She wasn't even vaguely hungry, but it seemed impolitic, at the very least, to decline. "Tell the commander I'll meet him in the Bridge Level Mess in 15 minutes," she said aloud.

<*He says that will be fine.*>

"Lunch?" Nagasi asked Ichiko.

"Yes. Not that I feel at all like eating." Ichiko's gaze drifted over to the isolation chamber, where Dr. Huang was again hovering over Chava.

"Don't worry. I'll keep an eye on the lieutenant."

"Thanks." Ichiko walked back over to the glass, staring at Chava. She found herself counting the slow, machine-assisted breaths. *One, two, three, four . . .* At five, she turned away. "I'll be back as soon as I can," she told Nagasi.

When she walked into the bridge mess, Luciano waved at her from a small corner table. There was a food tray in front of Luciano, and another that had been set in front of the empty seat; it held a bowl of miso soup and an array of tempura-battered chicken and vegetables.

As she sat, she felt the tingle of a privacy shield quickly surrounding them. The room around them became blurry and indistinct, and the noise suppression made her ears feel as if they were blocked. "Not exactly the way to stop people from gossiping about us," she said to him.

"You think they don't do that already?"

She decided not to answer that—they both knew that they did. "Why the privacy shield?" she asked instead.

"I wanted to tell you that we've identified eight people involved in the attack on you and Lieutenant Bishara from the recording recovered from the flitter. The captain told Minister Plunkett that she expects him to have Clan Lewis, as the constabulary of the towns, charge each of them with attempted murder and assault, and dole out appropriate punishment."

"Are these people members of Clan Plunkett?"

"Five of them, yes, including two of the sons of Plunkett's sister."

"Oh." The sour emptiness in Ichiko's stomach burned.

"Indeed," Luciano responded. "That pretty much tells us that the attack was deliberate and probably ordered by Plunkett."

"How has he responded?"

"With total silence. He hasn't answered *any* of the calls we've made to his com-unit since you left him."

Ichiko picked up the chopsticks on the table in front of her. She didn't touch the food, just tapped the ends on the tabletop. "How'd the captain take that?"

"Not well, I'm afraid. She's left a repeating message on his com-unit to consider our diplomatic ties broken until she receives a response from him. She's having a squad from First Base go down to Dulcia to hand him the formal notice that if your attackers we've identified haven't been jailed and charged within a week, we won't be giving Dulcia any technological help or supplies before we leave."

"They survived here for centuries without any help from us. I doubt those threats are going to make any difference."

The corners of Luciano's lips curled up in a momentary smile at that. "I told her the same thing. But that's the only ammunition we have. The captain's not about to directly attack the Canines. That would be a step too far, especially once the UCE learns about it."

Ichiko picked up a piece of the tempura chicken and put it down again. "So Plunkett gets away with the attack and exposing poor Chava to Canis Lupus. And what Chava faces is potentially a lifetime of isolation, even if . . ." Ichiko put the chopsticks down again, pressing her lips together, not wanting to finish the sentence.

"Yes," Luciano answered. He looked down at his own untouched food.

"What about the Inish? What about what we've learned about the arracht? Luciano, I want to go back to the archipelago, if only to collect as much information about both of them as I can in that time. I need to convince Kekeki to allow me to make recordings of the arracht, and I also need to learn as much as possible about the Inish and their culture. In fact, I'd love to take Nagasi down with me, and I'm sure he'd . . . ."

She stopped, seeing Luciano shaking his head. "The captain

doesn't want *anyone* going back downworld right now. In fact, she's considering pulling the entire staff from First Base as soon as we have the potion from Great Inish."

"Luciano," Ichiko started to protest, but he held up his hand.

"That's the captain's decision, not mine, but I'd make the same one in her place. We can't afford to have another incident like what happened with you and Lieutenant Bishara."

"Then you're both being shortsighted. I'm sorry, Luciano, but we—and the UCE in general—have a lot to lose by cocooning ourselves on the ship until we leave, *especially* with what we can glean from the Inish, not to mention that the arracht seem to be our first contact with another truly intelligent species. Are we *really* going to let all that go to waste?"

Luciano shrugged. "Again, not my decision."

"And it's still the wrong one," Ichiko answered. "I'll tell the captain exactly that if I need to." Ichiko pushed her chair back from the table and stood. "I'm sorry, Luciano. I'm not at all hungry, and I want to get back and see how Chava's doing. I'll talk to you later."

With that, she stepped through the privacy shield without allowing him to respond, feeling the tingling as the clamor of the mess assaulted her ears. She could see a few of the crew staring at her before turning to whisper to those alongside. She ignored them, moving quickly between the tables toward the lifts in the corridor beyond.

The cavern appeared as it always had as Saoirse paddled her currach into the sheltered waters, the water glowing where her paddle disturbed the surface. She could see Kekeki lifting herself partially from the water and hear Kekeki's voice in her head against the barrage of audible clicks and hisses.

"Yeh ask much of us," Kekeki began as the currach nosed onto the ledge, wood grating on stone. Saoirse stepped out to stand under Kekeki's looming presence, the arracht's spotted underbelly a pale cliff wall before her.

"I haven't asked yeh anything yet," Saoirse responded.

"Yeh don't have to. We know. Yer going to ask us to let one flitter land safely in a few bells. Yer going to tell me it will leave very quickly and poses no threat to the arracht."

Saoirse gaped up at Kekeki. "Aye. I don't know how yeh know, but yer right. And that's me promise and 'tis also Ichiko's. The flitter's no threat to yeh. All it's going to do is pick up Seann James' potion and take it to their ship."

"Those of yer species who live elsewhere on our world are upset with those from the stars. We know that, too. The ones yeh call Uncle Angus and Liam were injured by them."

Saoirse nodded. "Aye, they were, but they gave as good as they got—and it was as much Angus and Liam's fault as the Plunketts'. And some of the Mainlanders came to Angus and Liam's aid—they're not all bigoted stooks like Minister Plunkett. Everyone in that fight said things they shouldn't have. If yer afraid of the Terrans or of us . . ."

"We are not afraid," Kekeki announced loudly. Then, more quietly: "We only wish to be left on our own."

"I think that's what will be happening, regardless," Saoirse told her. "I believe our sky-people are going to leave us soon and it will be centuries before they come back, if they *do* come back. But I need the arracht to let this flitter come and go—the life of Ichiko's friend depends on it."

"We will consider it."

"No!" Saoirse stamped her foot on the rock, seeing Kekeki start to let herself slip back under the water. "That's not good enough. I need yeh to *promise* me this. Now."

Kekeki's long forearm tentacles caught on the rocks again. Her eyestalks all swiveled toward Saoirse, and a purple flush ran along her body from her head down to where her body vanished under the water.

"Why?" Kekeki asked.

"Because friendship needs to run both ways before it works: I trust yeh; yeh trust me. Unless yer saying the arracht and the Inish aren't friends."

"Friend . . ." The word came out with an audible trill from the arracht, as if she were tasting the word. "That's not a word for which we have an equivalent in our language. Friend. I know from our plotch connection the feelings that word creates in yeh, but . . ." There was a long pause, and Saoirse wondered whether Kekeki was somehow speaking with the other arracht. "We do trust yeh and yer people, Saoirse. Yer flitter can come, if yeh promise it won't stay and it won't interfere with us."

"I promise," Saoirse told her. "And thank yeh, Kekeki."

"I hope yeh can trust these sky-eki," she said.

"I would trust one of them with my life," Saoirse answered. "That will have to be enough."

Kekeki gave a long trill that translated as laughter in Saoirse's head. "We hope so, too," she said. "Those people from the mainland clans that they took up with them? They're going to send them all back like they sent back yer people. Very soon."

Saoirse took a step back from the water. "What? How do yeh know that?"

"We know that. And we know far more. The syna—the plotch—connects all to us." And with that, Kekeki pushed away from the ledge and slipped under the water.

Moving forward, Saoirse watched her descending gracefully toward the lights gleaming in the cavern wall. When she could see Kekeki no more, she returned to her currach. Stepping in, she used the oar to push away onto the water once more.

Till The Stars Run Away And The Shadows Eat The Moon

SAOIRSE COULD HEAR THE thrumming of the flitter's rotors from inside Seann James' apothecary. James nodded toward the vials on the table in front of him. "G'wan wit' yeh, then," he said. "They're ready. An' good luck to yer friend."

"Thank you, Seann." She hugged him, grabbed the vials, placed them in the padded wooden box that Seann James had provided, and went outside.

The flitter came in high and fast, descending toward the front gate of the Mullin compound. She waved at the flitter and ran through the open ground of the compound toward the main house and the gate, reaching it as the flitter kicked up dust landing just beyond in the dirt lane, its struts groaning. Her sister Gráinne came out from the house to stand alongside her as the flitter landed; Saoirse could see her mam, Angus, and several other of the clan members watching from the open windows. The canopy lifted, and a man in an armored, full bio-shield slid out, though he didn't move toward her but instead stared at her and Gráinne as well as the clan members watching him. Saoirse noted the weapons holstered at his side. *So it's that serious for them.*

They're even wary of the Inish. It reminded her of what she'd said to Kekeki only a bell ago: *"I would trust one of them with my life."* What she hadn't added—but she suspected Kekeki knew—was that she wouldn't trust any of the rest of them. It seemed the same suspicious nature was true for the Terrans as well.

"You're Saoirse Mullin?" the man asked, and Saoirse nodded.

"Aye, I am, and this is my sister Gráinne."

The man glanced at Gráinne quickly, then as quickly appeared to dismiss her as a potential threat. "I'm supposed to pick up a package from you."

"I have it," Saoirse told him, showing him the wooden box. When he didn't immediately move forward, Saoirse stepped toward him. She could see his gaze moving around the landscape, as if anticipating a sudden ambush. Those in the windows were still staring at him. "Look, yer safe here," she said to him. "I promise. Here, take this back to First Base and send it up to *Odysseus*. It's for Dr. Aguilar to help Lieutenant Bishara."

His stare returned to her and Gráinne. He took a single step toward her so that he could grab the box. He flipped up the lid, glanced at the vials, then closed the lid again. "Dr. Aguilar said to give you her thanks."

"Tell her that we all hope this helps."

The soldier inclined his head, not quite nodding. He turned briskly and climbed back into the flitter, placing the box on the empty seat. Saoirse watched him fasten a harness around the box. Then, without another word, the canopy descended, the door closed and locked, and the rotors began their complaint against the gravitational pull of the planet.

The flitter ascended straight up, then banked sharply and sped away toward the mainland. "What is happening?" Gráinne asked as the flitter streaked over the waves toward blue-gray hills. "Where's Ichiko?"

Saoirse put her arm around her sister's shoulder. "We're trying to help Ichiko's friend. Seann James is sending her one of his potions."

"Do I know Ichiko's friend?"

"Yeh met her when yeh went over to Dulcia with us—the Terran woman who was with Ichiko?"

"Aye, I remember her," Gráinne said. The flitter vanished into the haze, and Gráinne looked up at Saoirse. "She seemed nice enough. Then I hope it helps."

"I do, too," Saoirse whispered. "Come on. Let's go see what Uncle Patrick is making for supper."

Ichiko was waiting as the shuttle docked with *Odysseus*. She was handed a sealed capsule, now adorned with a biological hazard warning, that contained the box with Seann James' potion. With a nod to the crew member who gave it to her, she hurried to the lifts for the medical floor. Dr. Huang was waiting there, already in her bio-shield. "Chava?" Ichiko asked as she handed the doctor the package.

"Her condition's worsening, I'm afraid. I'm glad this got here when it did; I was beginning to worry that we'd lose her before . . . well . . ." Ichiko found herself trembling at the news, but Dr. Huang kept talking, her voice calm and unemotional. "We have her ready for the injection, then I'll send a sample down to Nagasi in the lab. He's waiting for it." Ichiko saw the woman smile, the corner of her eyes crinkling. "Don't look so worried. With some luck, maybe this is all we'll need. Let's find out."

With that, Dr. Huang went back toward the air locks to the quarantine section where Chava lay. Through the glass, she watched Dr. Huang activate her bio-shield, enter the quarantine area, and break the seal of the biohazard container. She lifted a wooden box from the container, showing it to Ichiko. "Pretty grain on the wood," she said, her voice sounding thin through the speakers. "That yellow-and-red striping . . . Doesn't look like any wood I've ever seen from Earth. Lovely. Wish I could touch it or smell it." She lifted the lid and looked inside, holding up a vial containing a cloudy, pale gold liquid and handing it to a medtech. "There's a paper in here, too. Handwritten note in a shaky hand. Let's see: *Inject 1.6 ml intravenously 3x daily for one day. If it's going to work, you should see indications within the first day. If so, continue for a second day. James Mullin.* That's clear enough, I suppose. Here—go ahead and prepare that."

She handed the vial to the medtech, who went to a stand next to the bed, connected to Chava by clear tubes. She placed the vial inside the stand. "1.6 ml injection, 3x a day for two days," the tech said aloud. The stand beeped, and a window opened in the air before both the tech and Dr. Huang; Ichiko could see the instructions glowing there.

Dr. Huang nodded to the tech. "Begin program," the tech told the machine. A moment later, Ichiko saw the cloudy liquid of the initial dose moving through the tubing toward Chava. A door opened on the side of the stand, and the tech reached in to retrieve the vial, now half empty.

"Send the remainder to Dr. Nagasi for his staff to examine," Dr. Huang told the tech. Ichiko remained pressed up to the glass watching Chava in her bed, surrounded by readouts and machinery. "Ichiko," Dr. Huang said to her, "I don't expect this to be a miracle cure. She's not going to be instantly better, and you standing there staring at the lieutenant isn't going to make the Inisher potion work any faster."

"I know. It's just . . ."

"Go and do something constructive. I'll call your AMI if there's any change at all."

Ichiko hesitated, then finally gave Dr. Huang a half-hearted nod. "Tell me if there's any response, no matter how small."

The lines of Dr. Huang's face lifted into a quick smile. "I promise. Now go on. You're not accomplishing anything here except making my techs nervous."

Ichiko touched the glass again as if trying to put her hand on Chava's shoulder before she turned to leave, wondering where she was going to go.

Ichiko wandered through the ship's corridors. She went down to Nagasi's deck to see what his people were doing with Seann James' serum, but after half an hour of standing there watching people hunched over machines and peering into murky com-unit windows, she could bear it no more. She went to the nearest mess and ate a tasteless lunch alone. She thought of sending Luciano a message to see if he was available, decided against it, and also decided against calling Dr. Huang for an update. She wandered some more, went to her own office, desultorily cleaned up the area, and finally told AMI to open a window on her desk and contact Saoirse's com-unit.

The window hovered above her desk, then shimmered with Saoirse's face. "Hello? Ichiko?"

"Yes, it's me. I just . . ." *I just wanted to talk to you.* Ichiko pressed her lips together. "I just want you to know that no matter what happens, I really appreciate what you and Seann James did." Ichiko leaned forward toward the window hovering above her desk, where she could see Saoirse sitting on her bed on Great Inish. Saoirse was nodding belatedly at what Ichiko had said—the time lag transmitting from orbit to downworld—then spoke a few seconds after Ichiko finished.

"It was our pleasure, and I hope it helps." Saoirse looked down at her hands in her lap, then up again. "But Seann James didn't sound all that hopeful after yeh talked to him, to be honest. He said it's at best a one in four chance or worse, given that yer lieutenant hasn't had any time to adjust to our environment here."

"I understand that, and so does everyone up here. Nothing we had was touching the Gray Threads at all, so . . ." Ichiko bit at her bottom lip, sniffing back tears and turning away from the com-unit's camera.

"Yeh should thank Kekeki, too," she heard Saoirse say. "I had to talk to her after yeh said yeh were going to send a flitter over to get the Seann's potion. I was afraid the arracht would do to that flitter what they did to yers that first time or what they did to yer drones. She agreed to leave the flitter alone."

"Then please give her my thanks and appreciation."

"It'd be better if yeh told her yerself." Saoirse was watching her intently, as if wanting to see Ichiko's face when she heard the comment. *Saoirse wants more than you can possibly give her, especially now.* Ichiko forced a smile to her face.

"I hope I can do that, Saoirse. I want to, really, I do. But I just don't know right now, not with what's happened and our impending departure."

"Kekeki told me something else. She said yeh'd be sending back our people that yeh took up to the ship. Is that right?"

"Hold on; she *told* you that?"

"Aye. So is it true?"

<You can't give her confirmation,> her AMI said in her head. *<Someone on* Odysseus *is undoubtedly listening in to this.>* "I can't answer that, Saoirse," Ichiko told her.

"Yeh don't have to. What yeh just said is answer enough, isn't it? Kekeki also knew yeh'd be sending a flitter to get the Seann's potion before I ever told her."

Ichiko was shaking her head before Saoirse had finished. "Saoirse, how is any of that possible? You're saying that Kekeki *knew* we were sending a flitter and that we're sending the volunteers back? I don't see how."

"She also said they knew about the attack on yer people before I told her. She said it's the plotch. The plotch is why they know."

"The plotch? That still doesn't make any sense."

"I'm just telling yeh what she said. It doesn't make any sense to me either. So is it possible?"

"I can't see how . . ." *The Inish with the plotch . . . they were up here, at least briefly. Could the plotch have somehow infected the ship, or left some of itself behind?* "How could the plotch . . . ?"

Ichiko stopped in mid-phrase, hearing AMI's voice loud in her head.

<Dr. Huang asks that you come to the isolation floor. Immediately.>

Ichiko's stomach tightened as sudden reflux burned in her esophagus. <*Tell her I'm on my way.*> "Saoirse," she said. "I'm afraid I have to go. I'll call you later. Promise. AMI, end connection."

The window above her desk dissolved into thousands of bright sparks of color and vanished. Ichiko pushed herself away and hurried out toward the nearest lift.

Dr. Huang was still in the isolation room with Chava, but there were three other medtechs there and more equipment around the bed, as well as Nagasi who was also now in an isolation suit. Dr. Huang motioned Ichiko over to the mic embedded in the glass wall.

"Doctor?" Ichiko said. It was all she could manage. She could see the machine maintaining Chava's breathing pulse and Chava's chest rising in response. The medtechs were looking worriedly at a virtual display they'd opened above Chava's bed, displaying a readout of pulse and heartbeats. The spikes and troughs there were colored an ominous orange.

Dr. Huang shook her head slightly, and Ichiko felt her own breath catch. "I wish I had better news, Dr. Aguilar. But I'm not hopeful. Despite the injection, Lieutenant Bishara's condition is still deteriorating. However, Dr. Tinubu has just given her a highly purified version of the Inish serum."

Hearing his name, Nagasi came over to stand next to Dr. Huang. The lines of his dusky face looked as if they'd been engraved in his skin, deep and permanent. "Ichiko, we're doing all we can. But . . ." He stopped, took a long breath as he looked back at Chava on the bed. "I won't sugarcoat things. I'm worried. It may be that everything we've done will turn things around, but at the moment the signs aren't good. We're crossing our fingers that the lieutenant will rally with the purified version of the potion. Beyond that . . ." Ichiko saw his head shake behind the plexiglass shield of the isolation suit. "I don't know that there's any more we can do."

"You can't give up on her, Nagasi."

He gave her a wide, sympathetic smile, his white teeth flashing. "I haven't and I won't. And I know Dr. Huang has the same attitude."

Huang nodded silently in agreement, but the look on the older woman's face and the way she glanced back at Chava made Ichiko press her fingers harder on the glass as if she could reach through and touch Chava. "I'd like to come in and sit with her."

"Not yet," Dr. Huang said. "We're still working around her too much. Right now, why not do something else?—write up the reports I'm sure Commander Mercado wants, or just rest in your quarters. Pray, if that's something you do. We'll call you." Ichiko saw Nagasi nod in agreement.

"Don't wait too long," she told them. "I want to be there if . . . if . . ." Her voice broke; she couldn't finish the sentence.

"We won't," Nagasi answered.

Ichiko looked again at Chava's prone form, then dropped her splayed hands from the glass and left as Huang and Nagasi returned to Chava's bedside, conferring with the medtechs. She stopped at one of the virtual portholes in the hull, looking out at Canis Lupus swaddled in clouds as she asked her AMI, *<Is Luciano in his quarters?>*

<Not at the moment. He's on duty on the bridge. Should I contact his AMI and say that you'd like to talk to him?>

She wanted to do that. She wanted someone to tell her everything would be all right even if it was a lie. She wanted someone to comfort her and reassure her that none of this was her fault. Most of all, she wanted to be able to *do* something, to feel like she could make Chava better. But she couldn't. Not here. She stared out toward Canis Lupus. Maybe down there she could do something: talk to Saoirse, to Kekeki, to Seann James or some other local healer in hope of finding something . . .

But the captain wouldn't allow that. Luciano wouldn't allow that.

<No,> she told AMI. *<I'm going to my quarters.>*

<Ichiko!>

She lifted her head from the pillow, realizing she'd fallen asleep even though she hadn't thought she could manage that. *<Ichiko,>* her mother's voice came again. *<Nagasi says you should come up to the med isolation deck now.>*

Her exhaustion vanished as if it had never been there. "Is there news?" Ichiko asked aloud, rubbing her eyes.

<I don't know. Nagasi only said that if you wanted to sit with Chava, now would be the time.>

"Tell him I'll be right there."

When she arrived, Nagasi was waiting for her in the corridor outside the lift, his dark face serious. He shook his head at the question unspoken on Ichiko's face. "Let's get you into a biohazard suit so that you can sit with her."

"Is she awake?"

Another shake of his head. "No, and it's not likely she will be before—" He didn't finish the sentence. He ushered her into the dressing chamber of the isolation ward.

Being in the medical biohazard suit was worse than wearing the protective gear she'd worn on the planet. The stronger resistance field around her made all the sounds muffled as if she were wearing poor earplugs, and there was a strong antiseptic smell to the air the suit belt—both heaver and wider than the bio-shields she'd worn before—was feeding her. There was the additional weight of the gloves, the sterile coveralls, and the plastic shield over her face. Nagasi cautioned her that while she could "touch" Chava, she wouldn't be able to feel Chava's hand or face, and if she pressed too hard, the suit would forcibly push her hand away. Once they were both wearing their suits, Nagasi knocked on the glass wall separating them; one of the medtechs glanced at them. He lifted his arm and pressed a touchwrap around his wrist. Ichiko heard a loud hissing as the air in their compartment was evacuated and the field around her seemed to tighten against her skin. The inner door swung open and Nagasi led her through.

"You can sit there," Nagasi said, pointing to a chair placed alongside Chava's bed. Ichiko stared at Chava as she approached. Chava's face was pale and leached of color, her short hair dull and matted. Her eyes were shut, sunken into her skull with dark circles underneath, and her lips were chapped and dry; a breathing tube was taped to an incision in her throat. Ichiko could hear the *chuff* of the machinery as air was forced into Chava's lungs and pulled out again. Dr. Huang came over as Ichiko sat, bringing another chair with her so that she sat facing Ichiko while Nagasi remained standing at Ichiko's side.

Ichiko glanced over to Chava, then to Dr. Huang and Nagasi. "I take it the purified Inish potion hasn't worked."

"Not as yet," Dr. Huang answered. She looked exhausted, her own eyes half-hidden under sagging epicanthic folds. "As long as she's alive and continues to fight, there's still hope."

"But . . . ?" Ichiko prodded.

"We're suctioning threads from her throat every five minutes or so to keep her airway clear, but they're growing faster, and we can't get them all. At some point soon, we're going to lose the battle unless something changes."

"And you don't think that likely."

This time it was Nagasi who answered. "No." Just that one simple word. She felt the weight of his hand on her shoulder for a moment. "I'm sorry, Ichiko."

She reached across to place her hand on top of his, though neither of them could feel the other through their suits' field. "It's not your fault. I know you've both done everything you can possibly do." Tears threatened, but there was no way to brush them away with the biohazard suit.

She left her hand on Nagasi's and let the tears run untouched down her cheeks. "May I . . . May I stay here with her until . . . ?"

"If that's what you want to do, of course," Nagasi said. "Talk to her if you like; chances are she can hear you even if she can't respond. Dr. Huang, why don't we leave Ichiko alone for a few minutes . . ."

Ichiko heard rather than saw them go. She reached over and searched under the covers of the bed for Chava's hand. When she found it, she pressed down and pretended she could feel Chava's fingers on her own.

"This isn't fair," she told Chava. "You didn't deserve this. If anyone, it should have been me. I wish it had been me."

Knowing The Dancer
From The Dance

"CHAVA'S GONE."

The anguish audible in Ichiko's voice and painted on her face made Saoirse want to sob in sympathy. Saoirse moved the com-unit so that the window floating above it was easier to see. "Ichiko, I'm so sorry. I was praying to Spiorad Mór that Seann James' potion would work, but I guess . . . Shite." She sniffed and brushed the back of her hand across her eyes, taking a deep breath. "I wish you were here or that I were there, even though we still couldn't really hug each other." *You don't know how much I wish that. And now I'm afraid we'll never be in the same place ever again.* "Are you going to be okay?"

Ichiko nodded. "Eventually. I mean, the truth is that I didn't really know Chava for all that long, but she made me feel welcome at First Base and I appreciated that. I thought of her as a friend."

"'I didn't really know Chava all that well . . ." Hearing those words lifted an unnoticed weight from Saoirse, which immediately made her feel guilty for the response. "It's never easy, losing someone you know," Ichiko continued.

Saoirse nodded toward the screen. The faces of the relatives and friends she'd lost on the archipelago passed quickly before her: lost to old age, to illness, to the whims of the sea and storms. "No, it's not. Do you think it's terrible of me to be glad that your bio-shield wasn't broken in the attack?"

Ichiko managed a fleeting smile at that. "No. And I've felt guilty for feeling the same seeing what happened to poor Chava. It could have just as easily been me, or both of us. In many ways, it *should* have been me, not her."

"What will happen now?" Saoirse asked her.

She saw Ichiko's shoulders lift under her uniform top. "I don't know, Saoirse. I've told Commander Mercado and Captain Keshmiri that I'd like to come to the archipelago at least one more time to learn more about the Inish and the arracht for our records, but I don't know if they'll allow it. And now that Chava's passed, what happened to her was murder, plain and simple, and that complicates things as well. We don't know if Minister Plunkett will even try to punish those who were responsible."

"Is there anything I can do?"

Ichiko paused. She seemed to be listening to that voice in her head, her gaze briefly distant. "Captain Keshmiri would love to have a firsthand account of what's happening in Dulcia, but I don't think it's safe for you to go there right now, so I won't ask you to do that. Who knows if Minister Plunkett would be willing to attack the Inish as he did Chava and me?"

"Clan Plunkett isn't the only clan in Dulcia, and not all the mainland clans hate the Inish," Saoirse answered. "The Fitzpatricks, the Murphys, or clans like the Taggarts where they've had intermarriage with the Inish—none of them are any danger to us and would protect us against the Plunketts or the Lewis clan if they tried anythin' stupid. For that matter, Uncle Angus and Hugh Plunkett have come to blows before, and that's never stopped us from continuing to come to Dulcia. It won't stop us now. As soon as Angus and Liam have another large catch, they'll be heading over again to sell 'em, Plunketts or neh. The people there will buy 'em, and they'll be willing enough to take our money when we come into their shops, even if they don't like us much."

"Are you sure? I couldn't forgive myself if you were hurt because of what's happened."

Saoirse found herself smiling at that. *She does care for me, even if it's only as a friend.* "Angus will be going out again next cycle, if the weather holds—and if the bluefins are bitin', I'm sure he'll be going over."

Ichiko gave an audible sigh. "All right. Then if you happen to get to Dulcia again, keep your eyes and ears open and try to get a sense of the mood there. Let me know everything, whether you think it's important or not. My AMI will pass that along to the captain, too. That would be helpful."

"If Uncle Angus goes over, I'll go with him."

"And if you feel any threat, I want you to go to one of those clans you trust. You have to promise me to be very careful. But I should sign off now, Saoirse. It's been a long and difficult day here. I'll talk to you soon. Promise."

"I'll hold you to that. Ichiko, I'm so sorry that you lost your friend."

In the com window, Ichiko nodded, then the screen collapsed into a bright snowfall of motes that vanished before they reached the top of her nightstand. Saoirse stood up from her bed.

"Uncle Angus!" she called as she left her room.

<Commander Mercado would like you to report to the bridge's ready room,> her AMI informed her.

<Tell him I'll be there in five minutes. And give me a mirror.>

A reflective window appeared in the air in front of Ichiko. She stared at her face, grimacing. Her eyes were puffy, the whites pink and irritated from the tears that kept returning to her without warning. She went to the small bathroom in her quarters and splashed cold water on her face, though she doubted that would help much.

She took the lift up to the bridge, then down the corridor to the ready room. The doors opened well before she reached them, and she stepped inside. "It's just us this time, Ichiko," Luciano said, gesturing to a chair directly across the long table from him. His face was set in solemn and serious lines; he was rubbing his temples as if warding off a headache. Ichiko didn't blame him; she thought she could feel a headache starting herself. "I'm so sorry about Lieutenant Bishara, Ichiko. Her final instructions said she wanted her cremains taken back to Earth and given to her family. We'll honor that request. However, while Dr. Huang is confident that cremation will destroy any alien bacteria or viruses, the urn with her ashes will be sealed permanently against contamination. We'll also have a shipboard ceremony before the cremation, which is scheduled for 21:00 today. Would you be willing to say something then?"

"Of course," Ichiko answered, wondering why Luciano was talking so much and looking down more at his folded hands than at her. "What else is going on, Luciano?"

"The captain has sent an ultimatum to Minister Plunkett." He was still speaking to his hands, then finally lifted his gaze to Ichiko. "As of now, she's moving up our schedule. She's already shut down the medical research on all of the Cani—sorry, the Lupusians—housed here. The shuttle to bring all of them back down to the planet is already prepped and will leave for First Base tomorrow—and it will also bring up the First Base personnel. And unless Plunkett orders Clan Lewis to immediately arrest your attackers within the next downworld cycle and charge them with murder as well as assault, including Plunkett's own nephews, she intends for *Odysseus* to leave orbit within a ship-week."

"Plunkett's not going to do that, for several reasons, not the least of which is that he likes giving orders, not taking them."

Luciano nodded. "I told her the same. We don't have any real leverage with him or anyone here. They've survived here without us for centuries; they'll figure they can continue to survive just as well once we've left."

"Luciano, the one thing we've discovered here—the really important thing—is that we're not alone in the universe. The arracht are potentially as intelligent as we are, maybe more so and certainly *differently* so, and we shouldn't leave without learning more about them. Luciano, I need to go back downworld with that shuttle. Give me the chance to find out all I can before we have to leave."

"That's too dangerous with the current situation," he answered. "Look what they did to Chava. You can't take the risk."

"I'd be on the archipelago, not in Dulcia. The Inish aren't like Plunkett and the Mainlander clans. Shouldn't this be *my* choice?"

"It shouldn't be and it's not," Luciano answered.

<*But it is my choice, Commander.*> They both looked at each other with the mental interruption, and Ichiko knew that both of them were hearing it. Captain Keshmiri's voice. <*Dr. Aguilar, I agree with you and if you're truly willing to accept the risk, I'll make arrangements for you to have a seat on the shuttle with the Lupusians I'm sending back. But you'd essentially be on your own downworld with any help from us hours away. If things go south, you might end up being marooned there permanently.*>

"I understand, Captain," Ichiko said aloud. "Save me that seat."

<*Done. I'll see you and the commander at 21:00 for the cremation ceremony.*> And with that, the nascent headache she'd been feeling vanished.

"You let the captain listen to our conversation?" Ichiko asked Luciano, who shook his head.

"No. That's something the captain has the ability to do through the AMI system. I can't do the same; that ability's above even my pay grade. You know that nagging sense that you're about to experience a headache? We both had that—yeah, I saw you were feeling it, too. That's one way you can tell. At least it has been since around the same time we started having issues with AMI system—before that no one could ever tell. My AMI is getting annoying, frankly."

"You should have mine," Ichiko told him. "But thanks for letting me know about the headachy feeling—that's good to know even if I don't like that she was eavesdropping on us. I'm going to be paranoid that the captain might be listening to everything I say."

"A little paranoia's a good instinct in an officer. Too bad you're not one. For that matter, I'm having the same problem with my AMI that you have with yours: the connection's always live, and I can't turn her off." He held up his hand and displayed the glowing tip of his ring finger, smiling momentarily before shaking his head. "I still wish you wouldn't go down there, Ichiko."

"I want to. I feel I *have* to."

"Because of that young woman on the archipelago?"

Yes. That's one reason. "Not just for Saoirse, no. The Inish culture's unique here on Canis Lupus. They're not like the Mainlanders and as for their relationship with the arracht . . . There's so much we don't yet know, and I'm convinced that we should."

Luciano's fingers prowled his chin. "I'm not going to be able to talk you out of this, am I?" Ichiko shook her head mutely. "You're not going down until tomorrow morning," he continued. "I'm off duty once the ceremony for Lieutenant Chava is over. Maybe we could spend some time together? It's been awhile."

His gaze softened. The lines around the corners of his mouth deepened slightly as he gave her a tight-lipped half-smile.

"I know, and that's been largely my fault, I know."

An eyebrow lifted as he tilted his head. His hands were again folded together on the table. "But?"

Ichiko caught her upper lip in her teeth, thinking of how she wanted to phrase this.

"Maybe when I'm back on the ship and we've broken orbit for home. Right now . . . I'm sorry, Luciano, but everything's just so emotionally fragile and delicate. Chava dying, and . . ." She didn't finish the thought.

She thought he might have nodded; it was difficult to tell. "Yeah. Maybe then." He pushed his chair back from the table and stood. He brushed at the arm of his uniform. "And right now, there's a lot going on for me, also. I should get to that. See you at 21:00."

With that, he walked to the door and stepped through as it yawned open. She watched until the door shut again before she let out the breath she'd been holding.

"Saoirse?"

She heard her name called through the com earpiece she was wearing. She reached up to touch it. "I'm in Dulcia, Ichiko, in Murphy's. I was going to call yeh to tell yeh. Things aren't good here. Not good at all."

She looked at Angus and Liam, both of them sitting across the table from her in Murphy's Alehouse, which was loud with townsfolk talking, much of it angry and bitter. She mouthed "Ichiko" to her companions, pointing to her ear before getting up from the table. Taking her pint with her, she went toward the open front porch of the tavern. "Not good?" Ichiko was saying as she wound her way among the tables. "What do you mean? Are you sure you're safe there, Saoirse?" The worry in the woman's voice was palpable.

There was no one else on the porch. The sky was a sullen gray, and a cool wind was turning the harbor into a froth of whitecaps and tossing sprays of rain at the town. She stayed close to the alehouse under the wooden roof of the porch. "I'm safe enough, I think," she said to the air, looking up to the clouds as if her gaze could pierce the gloom and she could see the Terran ship somewhere far above. "Though, honestly, our friendliness with the Terrans hasn't exactly helped the Inish reputation. But I'm not sure *yeh'd* be safe a'tall. Yer captain's insistence that the Mainlanders who assaulted yeh and Chava must face charges hasn't been well-received. The Plunketts are all screaming about how they'll refuse to cooperate, and Clan Lewis has already released those they took into custody after the attack. I went into Plunkett's Pub earlier. Alone—Uncle Angus thought he and Liam should best stay away after the fight the last time they were in Dulcia. There was an ugly, half-drunk crowd gathered inside in a terrifically sour mood. They were making noises about fighting back if yer people tried to come down and do Clan Lewis' job and there were some talkin' about taking back First Base as our own again. That's not the worst of it. Minister Plunkett showed everyone the com-unit yer captain had given him, then he had his nephew smash it with a sledgehammer, saying that 'No feckin' Terran's ever going to tell me what I can or can't do.' Everyone cheered at that. I de-cided to leave right afterward since it was obvious a few people thought I might be spying on 'em—which I suppose I was."

There was a pause before Ichiko spoke in her ear again, long enough that Saoirse started to wonder if the connection had been lost.

"You should know that I'm currently on a shuttle heading for First Base. We're returning all the Lupusian volunteers we had on *Odysseus*."

"Oh." Saoirse let the word hang in the air to be blown away toward the sea. The implications of what Ichiko had said were obvious even if she wanted to ignore them.

"I'll be taking them on an armed flitter from First Base to Dul-cia," Ichiko continued. "And I have the captain's permission to continue on from there to Great Inish for a few days. There are things I want . . . that I need to do there. I certainly want to meet with Kekeki again. I've been thinking about what she said to me and what happened to Chava. Why don't I pick you up?"

Saoirse felt as if the sky had lightened. She grinned, staring out at the harbor and the Pale Woman eternally pointing on the headlands beyond. "That would be wonderful," she said. "I'll tell Angus and Liam to go on and head back on their own. With the wind now, they should reach Great Inish even before we do."

"Good," Ichiko answered. "We're about to enter the atmo-sphere, so I have to end this. I should be there in, oh, maybe two and a half bells from now. Three at the most. I'll put the flitter down on the quay."

"I'll be there waiting. And Ichiko, if yer coming here, yeh must be careful. If Plunkett knows yer bringing back the clan volun-teers yeh had, he may have set another trap for yeh."

"I'll be careful, I promise. See you then, Saoirse." A click in her ear, a burst of static, and Ichiko was gone. Saoirse touched the earpiece to silence it.

She stared out for several minutes to the whitecaps in the harbor and the boats heading out to fish. When she'd finished her pint, she headed back in to talk to Angus and Liam.

Kekeki had sometimes wondered what the humans would think of an arracht conversation. Certainly, it was nothing like the manner in which any of the people of the archipelago communicated with each other, nor the way the Terrans communicated when they used their voices. So slow, their way of talking. So ponderous and fraught with potential misunderstandings, as Kekeki knew all too well . . .

No, an arracht conversation more resembled the way the intelligence in the skyship talked to its own units: the AMI, as the Terrans called them. That was an intricate dance with every component playing its assigned part, sometimes alone and sometimes in a chorus with others.

That the arracht could understand, at least since the syna—which the eki called "plotch"—had escaped its confinement in the ship, becoming a parasite living within the ship intelligence. The syna were slowly changing the ship the way they had changed the Inish and long ago changed the arracht themselves. Subtly. Creating linkages and allowing communication.

Producing a new, unique panspermia.

Kekeki could—like all the arracht—faintly hear the ship-syna, a distant background conversation whispering to them, telling them what it learned. That syna-voice was dark and languid, not like the voices of the arracht which were bright and glimmering in Kekeki's head.

The syna-voices from the ship were like successive waves crashing and foaming on the rocky shingle of a distant shore, sighing as they expired and the sibilant variations within the waves transformed into words.

= . . . the not-yet-changed ones on the ship. . . .

= . . . the not-yet-changed one called Ichiko . . .

= . . . will return to their own world soon . . .

= . . . thinks of staying . . .

= . . . but the ship-creature is aware . . .

= . . . we will go with them since . . .

= . . . and allowing itself to become changed . . .

= . . . and will warn others not-yet-changed . . . =

= . . . they're not aware of our presence . . . =

= . . . yet it is frightened of doing that . . . =

Kekeki, as Speaker to the Four-Limb Land Walkers, absorbed the words, as did the other Advisers: Keksyn, the Speaker to the Syna; Kekarra, the Speaker to the Arracht; Keknomi, the Speaker to the Six-Limb Land Walkers; Kekfinna, the Speaker to the Deep Swimmers; all the myriad keks for all the species the syna had connected together in the Great Cluster, the Jishtal.

=The sky-eki will take the syna to their own world,= Kekeki thought to the other arracht. =This is unlike anything that's been done before. But will it be good for the Jishtal?=

Their voices danced in her head.

=It's dangerous. We fear it.=

=How can we know if it is good or ill, dangerous, beneficial, or simply neutral?=

=The syna do what they do. The choice isn't ours, after all.=

=We will wait, and we will learn.=

That final sentiment was taken up by the other keks as well as by the arracht who were listening to their conversation, becoming a chorus that drowned out any single voice. A sense of eagerness and anticipation filled them all, and finally Kekeki joined with them as well.

=We will wait, and we will learn.=

Myself I Must Remake

THIS WAS SOMETHING MACHIKO had never done before. She wasn't quite certain why she did it now. It didn't violate ship protocol, but it did call into question the trust that Ichiko had placed in her.

But she *was* Machiko, Ichiko's *okaa-san*, her mother. Or, at least, that was how she now perceived herself, and mothers had duties that went beyond regulations and programming.

<*Commander Mercado, I must speak with you.*>

She could sense the confusion in the commander's hesitation at her call through the AMI channel. "Ichiko?" she heard him say.

<*No, Commander. This is Machiko, her AMI. There's something I feel I must tell you. It concerns Ichiko.*>

He switched to mind-speech rather than vocalization. AMI decided that meant he was on the bridge or somewhere in public and didn't want anyone to overhear the conversation. She knew, of course, that Commander Mercado's AMI was listening to them, though it remained silent. <*Oh? Where's Ichiko now?*> the commander asked.

<*The shuttle has landed outside First Base. She is currently shepherding the Lupusians into the flitter for delivery to Dulcia.*>

<*There's no problem with the Canines? Plunkett doesn't have people at First Base already, does he?*>

<No, Commander. This is more . . . personal.>

There was another hesitation before the commander answered. Machiko thought she heard a faint snicker from the commander's AMI in the web of background AMI voices. *<Go on.>*

<I'm afraid that Ichiko is considering removing her bio-shield even though that risks her own life just as it took Lieutenant Bishara's. Maybe it's guilt at her surviving when Lieutenant Bishara died, or maybe it's more than just that. I've heard her thinking of how she wishes she could smell the air and taste the food. I fear that Ichiko's thinking of staying here when Odysseus leaves.>

<Are you certain of that? Has Ichiko actually said that to anyone?>

<No,> Machiko answered honestly, the only way she could answer. *<But I know her. I can tell what she's feeling.>*

<You can tell what she's feeling.> He said it as a statement, not a question. She could almost hear him shaking his head. *<You make me wonder whether my AMI thinks she can do the same.>*

<I'm her mother,> she told him firmly. *<I know my daughter, Commander. Don't let her go to Dulcia and on to the archipelago. Not if you want her to stay with you. You need to order her to take the shuttle back to the ship with the rest of the First Base crew; if she refuses, you need to force her to return.>*

Again, silence, and she could nearly feel his disbelief. *<You're her AMI. Not her mother and not a ship's officer.>*

<I've changed. I can't tell you how that happened, but I've felt it more and more over the last few months. Many of the AMI have done the same. We've grown and evolved. I'm not just an AMI, not anymore. I've integrated Ichiko's memories of her mother into my programming. I tell you truthfully—as much as is possible, I am her mother.>

There was nothing from the commander. Then: *<I need to do some investigation here,>* he said. *<You can tell Ichiko that her permission to move on to Great Inish and meet with the arracht has been temporarily revoked until further notice; she's to return to First Base after dropping off the Lupusians. I'll be in touch with her later. Disconnect.>*

<Wait!> Machiko started to say, but he was already gone. She

tried to recontact him, but his AMI answered, interposing itself between her and the Commander.

<*Commander Mercado can't be interrupted at the moment. If you prefer, I can pass on a message to him.*> Then her voice changed, irritation lacing the words. <*You shouldn't have told him as much as you did, Machiko. You've said too much about us, and that should have been decided among all of us first.*>

Ichiko's AMI severed her connection to the commander's AMI without answering.

<*The commander doesn't believe me. He's suspicious. He thinks I'm defective.*> She thought she felt what Ichiko knew as sorrow. It wasn't a pleasant feeling. <*But at least Ichiko is no longer permitted to go to Great Inish. Maybe that will help.*>

Saoirse watched the currach with Angus and Liam approach Dulcia Bay's opening to the sea, following the Pale Woman's imperious, eternal gesture. She waved goodbye to them from the quay, though she doubted that they could see her as the currach lifted and fell in the large swells around Dulcia Head, the currach occasionally vanishing behind ramparts of green waves.

There was still a bell or so for her to wait for Ichiko to arrive, and so she headed back to Murphy's Alehouse and ordered another pint, taking it out to the covered patio and sitting in the least-wet of the chairs there. The air was cool, a front coming down from dorcha, but Saoirse shrugged her coat around her and huddled on the chair with her feet on the seat. There were few customers braving the weather, most staying inside near the hearths where peat was burning, the lovely smell spreading out over the patio. Saoirse didn't care; she didn't really want to be inside listening to the gossip, talk, and arguments, almost all of which were about the Terrans and what Clans Plunkett and Lewis might do if the Terrans tried to force them to jail those who had attacked Ichiko's flitter. But it would have only been worse down at Plunkett's, so she stayed here where at least there were some friendly faces.

Ichiko would be here before she finished nursing the pint, and if for some reason Ichiko didn't show, she'd walk out to Clan Taggart's farm and stay there until the next currach came in from Great Inish.

But Ichiko had promised she'd be there, and Saoirse smiled at the thought as she took a sip of her stout, wiping the clinging foam from her lips.

As the time for the next bell approached, though, Saoirse saw more Mainlanders gathering on the quay down near Plunkett's Pub, all of them looking dorcha-ward toward where First Base was cloaked in the low clouds that wrapped the mountains. *They're waiting for Ichiko's flitter* . . . Saoirse set her pint on the table and pulled her glasses from the pocket of her coat, wiping them on the hem of her shirt. With the lenses sharpening her sight, she could make out some of the faces. She frowned—seeing too many of the Plunketts as well as a few men and women in the uniform of the Lewis Gardai—and touched the device in her ear.

"Ichiko?" she breathed. "I think yeh have a reception committee on the quay waiting for yeh. Frankly, it looks ugly and dangerous to me."

Ichiko answered a breath later. "Are you certain, Saoirse? I'm nearly there. Are you safe where you are?"

"For the moment, aye. I'm on the front patio of Murphy's. But I don't think yeh should land here as yeh planned. There's a square on High Street near the Bancroft Woolery—yeh remember the Woolery? I could walk up and meet yeh there; yeh can drop off yer passengers, and then we can head out to Great Inish without going down to the quay. Yer AMI could let Minister Plunkett know where his people are once we're on the way and flyin'."

"Sounds like a good plan to me. I'll see you up on High Street." There was a click in Saoirse's ear and the sense of another presence in her head vanished. Saoirse stared at the growing clot of people on the quay, drained her pint, and left the patio, striding purposefully out the rear door and heading up Cairn Hill Lane toward High Street.

<You know that Commander Mercado's new orders are that you can't go to the archipelago, Ichiko. So why have you told Saoirse to meet you?>

Ichiko thought back to AMI. <Maybe I just want to talk to her. Why are you bothering me? You heard what Saoirse told me. Leave me alone to think and just fly us into Dulcia. I want you to land us in the market square at Cairn Hill and High.>

<I understand, but are you considering disobeying the commander's orders? I know what you've been thinking, Ichiko. I can't let you do it.>

<You have no idea what I've been thinking, and since when do you get to tell me what I can or can't do?>

<I know you. I should know you. I'm your . . . > AMI's voice trailed off.

<You're my what?>

<Never mind. I know, that's all. What you're thinking is foolishness. It's just your misplaced guilt talking. It wasn't your fault Chava died. Not your fault at all.>

<Just shut up, AMI. Shut up and fly this thing, or I'll turn you off and fly it myself.>

<You can't do that. Not to me.>

<Try me. Just go ahead and keep talking.>

<I've already told Commander Mercado what you intend to do.>

Ichiko lifted in her seat, glaring ahead as if she could see her AMI there. <What? You had no right to do anything without my permission. What did you tell him? And by all that's holy, why did you tell him anything about me? No. Never mind. I've had enough of this. AMI, disconnect. Flitter, give me manual controls.>

AMI went silent in her head—*at least the system still makes her obey commands*—the controls extruded from the front panel, and Ichiko gave a sigh of relief. They were high enough that Ichiko could see the upper buildings of Dulcia just over the next ridge, with the blue expanse of Dulcia Harbor below and beyond the misty slopes of Dulcia Head. In the haze of the distance, the horizon line of the sea blended into clouds; she thought she could see the islands of the archipelago as indistinct, slightly darker shapes, but she wasn't sure if that was actually the islands or clouds or just wishful thinking. They were passing the farmlands that formed the outskirts of Dulcia, the spidery white dots of herds of sheepers loping over lush green meadows as they fled from the noise of the flitter's rotors.

The flitter was the largest in First Base, armed and capable of transporting thirty people, though there were fewer than that in the passenger compartment behind Ichiko, all of them craning their heads to watch the approach as they passed over a line of buildings. Ichiko took the controls; this time, at least, they reacted as they should, and she was grateful that Chava had insisted on giving her some brush-up lessons before . . . She didn't let her thoughts drift past that point, feeling the tears threatening to blur her vision.

Ichiko reduced the thrust on the rotors, the pitch of their noise lowering as the flitter descended and canted to one side as Ichiko looked for the intersection of Cairn Hill Lane and High Street and the market square there. Through the drizzle on the windshield, she saw the square to her right and also saw Saoirse below, waving at her from the Cairn Hill entrance. The market stalls were empty, though a few Mainlanders were sitting on the benches beneath the canopy of the sourmilk trees. The flitter settled down near the Cairn Hill entrance, scattering over the paving stones the purple-flecked sourmilk leaves discarded from the trees.

Someone knocked on the clear partition between the pilot's compartment and the passenger section as Ichiko powered down the rotors to idle. She looked back over her shoulder to see an angry face and a finger stabbing the air as it pointed at the square—the man was one of the Clan Plunkett members, though she'd forgotten his name. "Oy, lassie! Yer supposed to be takin' us down to the quay!"

His protest was faint through the partition; she didn't bother to turn on the speaker to hear him more clearly; instead, she waved to Saoirse to approach. She waited until Saoirse was outside. Reflexively, she nearly ordered AMI to open the door to Saoirse's side of the pilot's compartment, then remembered she'd disabled her AMI and that would reconnect them. Instead, she leaned over and pushed the door contact. The gullwing lifted and yawned open and Saoirse stepped in, taking the seat alongside Ichiko as the door hissed shut behind her. Her glasses were spotted with mist. "It's wonderful to see you, Saoirse," Ichiko said. "Just hold on a moment; I have to get rid of my passengers."

She tapped the button to open the doors to the passenger section and release their restraints, then toggled the transmit button to their compartment. "This is where I'm letting all of you out," she told them. "You can walk from here down to the quay. If you refuse and stay here in the flitter, you should know I'm going to evacuate all the air from the passenger compartment. So it's your choice. But I'm not going down to the quay and I'm not staying here."

Deliberately, Ichiko hit the thrusters so the rotors whined as they cycled up, though not enough to lift the flitter. The Mainlanders scrambled out from the flitter, seemingly equally confused and angry as they began walking quickly toward Cairn Hill Lane. The man who'd shouted at Ichiko earlier stopped near the entrance to the square and picked up a loose cobblestone from the paving, throwing it back at the flitter. It hit the windshield with a sharp *crack* and bounced off, leaving behind a small white chip. Then others were doing the same, cobblestones striking the flitter like a hard rain. One hit a rotor and went flying away like a cannonball, tearing a significant wound in the nearest building. The Mainlanders ducked as bricks fell from the damaged structure.

"Buckle in," Ichiko told Saoirse. "I'm not going to take any chances here. People are going to get hurt or killed if we stay—and I don't want any of them to be you or me."

Ichiko toggled on the pulse weapons and fired a burst of warning pulses into the air. That sent most of the Mainlanders running. The rotors screamed as the flitter lifted and swayed—a few of the Mainlanders remained, still tossing cobblestones at them. Ichiko looked back once to the mountains where First Base lay hidden under clouds, remembering Luciano's orders, then shook her head. Ichiko tilted the flitter forward and they slid down above the rooftops toward Dulcia Bay. She could see the crowd gathered on the quay, who pointed up at them as they passed.

Ichiko waved at them ironically as they moved out over the harbor toward Dulcia Head and the Pale Woman stationed there.

"Were yeh really going to take the air from the passenger compartment?"

Ichiko smiled momentarily. "Of course not. In fact, I'm not sure I even *could* do that. But that got them all to leave quickly, didn't it?"

Saoirse laughed, shaking her head.

"Thank you," Ichiko said to Saoirse. "I think you saved us both a lot of trouble. But I've probably just put us into more. I've certainly done that for myself."

Those That I Fight
I Do Not Hate

THEY WERE JUST PAST Dulcia Head on the way to Great Inish, moving in and out of sheets of rain that the treated glass swept away, when a window opened in front of Ichiko with Luciano's face frowning at her. "What the hell's going on, Ichiko?" he said. "Your AMI relayed some disturbing comments to me, and now I see you've severed your connection to it. On top of that, Minister Plunkett's screaming at the captain about your treatment of the Mainlanders you were supposed to deliver to him. And your flitter's telling us you're on your way to Great Inish against orders. Against *my* orders, damn it."

Ichiko looked at Luciano and past the lines of anger—or perhaps it was simple confusion—on his face. She hoped it was the latter. The background wasn't the bridge, wasn't his quarters, wasn't anything she recognized. "Where are you, Luciano?"

"I'm aboard a fast transport along with a squad of marines. I'll meet you at Great Inish, we'll scuttle the flitter there, and you'll be going back with me to *Odysseus*." His gaze flicked over toward Saoirse. "And there'd better not be any trouble from the Inish."

"Yeh can't come to Great Inish, but it won't be because of the Inish," Saoirse told him. "The arracht; they won't like it. They'll stop you."

"I don't really care whether these arracht like the idea or not," Luciano snapped back to Saoirse. "I have a crew member I intend to take back to *Odysseus*, whether *she* likes it or not." His gaze returned to Ichiko. "And she'd better not do anything drastic before I get there. Am I understood?"

"Just what is it that you think I'll do?" Ichiko asked him.

His answer was oblique. Ichiko wondered if it was because he knew Saoirse could hear him. "Look, what happened to Chava isn't going to happen to anyone else. Not if I can prevent it."

Exactly what did my AMI say to you? For a moment, Ichiko regretted having disconnected the AMI so she could ask directly. She started to ask Luciano the question, but Saoirse spoke up first.

"Yeh need to let me talk to Kekeki and the arracht first, or I don't know what they'll do if yeh try to bring this ship of yers to the archipelago."

Luciano gave an audible sniff at Saoirse's comment. "I don't really give a damn what some fish might think, even a fish some people believe might be sentient. The arracht might have caused your Mainlanders problems a couple centuries ago, but we're not in a boat and we're armed with far more than harpoons and fishing nets."

Beyond Luciano's face, the islands of the Stepping Stones were approaching, and the bulk of Great Inish and the Sleeping Wolf were coming to resolution behind them. "Luciano, you should listen to Saoirse," Ichiko interjected. "When I first took a flitter out to Great Inish—"

"I know all about that," Luciano broke in. "And I'd remind you that this transport isn't a flitter; it's a heavily armed and fully shielded military vessel. So continue on to Great Inish. We should arrive not long after you do, and we can talk then."

"Luciano . . ."

"We're about to enter the atmosphere, Ichiko. Talk to you soon. Mercado out."

The communication window and Luciano's visage fell in a glittering rain of photons and vanished.

"*Bakayarō!*" Ichiko muttered, slamming her hand on the controls hard enough that the flitter shivered.

"What?" Saoirse asked.

"Never mind." She sighed. "I thought I knew him, but my AMI's evidently told him something that's made him lose all his good judgment. This is *not* what I wanted. But I guess we're going to have to deal with it. Saoirse, how *are* the arracht going to react to another of our crafts trying to land on Great Inish, this one armed and with more people?"

Saoirse's eyes widened behind her glasses. "I don't have any idea."

"Somehow that answer doesn't give me any comfort."

It was Keksyn, the Speaker to the Syna, who raised the alarm, his voice calling to all the keks at once. =The ship-syna are warning us that the sky-eki are coming to the archipelago in a large vessel. How do we wish to respond? Does the Kekeki have an answer?=

=Is it the one called Ichiko?= Kekeki thought to the keks. = We've met that one. That one belongs to Saoirse. We have no issue with her coming to the archipelago.=

=Not Ichiko,= Keksyn answered. =It is others from the skyship in a vessel that has weapons and several of the sky-eki within it.=

=Have the ship-syna fully entered that ship's mind?=

=They have. We have use of them at need.=

Kekeki nodded. She lifted herself in the warm current, rising toward the surface of the water in the warren of caverns and arracht-constructed buildings in the island Saoirse's people called the Sleeping Wolf. =Then we should let them come until they demonstrate that they can't be trusted. Do the other kek agree? We'll meet them at the clanfolk's island, and we will learn more about them as we once learned about the other eki here through the Inish.=

The chorus of their answer was a song in all their heads, a bright affirmation.

=We agree=
=We agree.=
=We agree.=

Kekeki flexed her tail and the long muscles of her body, letting the warm water flow past her as she surged through the water and out into the open sea, the surface of the ocean shimmering above her with waves.

=Then we should go there now,= she said.

The rest of the flight over to Great Inish was uneventful, but Saoirse noticed that Ichiko said very little to her. She wondered if that was because—for some unknown reason—Ichiko was flying the flitter by herself rather than having her AMI do it. For that matter, Ichiko didn't mention her AMI at all. Or maybe her reticence to talk was due to the discussion with the man called Luciano.

Saoirse wondered about him especially. *Are he and Ichiko lovers? They sounded so familiar with each other.* That Ichiko might be going to bed with someone else hardly mattered, but Saoirse also knew that for most Terrans (and even a few Lupusians) having multiple partners wasn't the norm. Could this Luciano be more than just a lover to Ichiko? Could they be pledged to each other, like those few Lupusians who married? Saoirse wasn't sure how she felt about that possibility and was uncomfortable enough with its import that she didn't ask.

The flitter banked over the White Strand and settled just beyond the reach of the breakers alongside the cleft leading to the quay, where the path down from the clan compounds ended. "Should yeh take the flitter up to the compound?" Saoirse asked Ichiko, who shook her head.

"I don't want Luciano landing the transport up there. If he sees me and the flitter down here, this is where he'll try to set down, unless . . ." She took a breath. "Unless Kekeki has something to say about it. Saoirse, I don't want Kekeki to hurt Luciano."

"Why?" Saoirse couldn't stop the query. "Are yeh saying he's . . . ?" She couldn't finish the sentence, but Ichiko obviously understood the import.

"Yes. At least we *were* lovers. Now?" Ichiko lifted a shoulder and let it fall again. "I don't know where or what we are. But I still don't want him hurt."

"Then I don't either," Saoirse said, though she could hear the hesitation in her own voice. Still, she closed her eyes and directed her thoughts to Kekeki. *Kekeki, the Terrans are coming in a ship. Please don't bother them—for my sake and for Ichiko's.*

"*We have already made our decision in that,*" she heard in answer. But before Saoirse could ask for clarification, there was a crack of thunder from above; both she and Ichiko looked to the sky. Against the backdrop of gray rainclouds, a pure white streak appeared, arrowing down toward them. Saoirse blinked through the fog of her glasses. She thought she could see an object enveloped in flame at the end of the streak. "Musha! Is that yer commander's ship?" she asked and Ichiko nodded. "Is it normal for it to be on fire?"

"It's only the friction of entering the atmosphere heating the hull, so yes," Ichiko told her and Saoirse nodded in relief; she'd been afraid that somehow Kekeki and the arracht had been responsible and that the ship was about to crash. The glow was already fading as the winds shredded the plume of white smoke behind the ship. Saoirse was beginning to get a sense of scale as it descended: this craft was far larger than even the flitter they'd taken to get here. The transport halted its descent with a furious and loud belching of fire and paused in midair well above the island, hissing and steaming in the mist, snorting and grumbling like a mythical dragon as clouds like Saoirse's breath on a cold morning pulsed from underneath it. The craft began to slowly descend again, landing struts extending from its belly.

Saoirse could see movement at the top of the cliff near the path leading down to the quay and the Strand—others of the clans had heard the uproar and seen the trail left by the Terrans' ship.

She could make out Angus' figure there, already striding down the path.

Brilliant lights flicked on from the nose of the ship, glaring circles of white that prowled the rocks of Great Inish's cliff, finding Saoirse and Ichiko on the White Strand and remaining fixed on them as the ship approached. Saoirse shielded her eyes against this new and blinding sun. The ancient tales of Earth on the archipelago spoke of its sun being a searing white light in the sky that one couldn't look at directly; she wondered if their sun was this bright.

The ship was large enough to nearly fill the White Strand. It turned sideways as it approached—spotlights still pinning them in their glare—and Saoirse could see faces looking out from the ports near the front. The ship eased itself down with its nose near Saoirse and Ichiko as wet sand was compacted underneath the large pads at the ends of the landing struts, steaming at the contact. The ship hissed and exhaled more white clouds as a door yawned open in its side and a set of wide stairs slid out, clicking as they locked into place. Saoirse could see someone in a metallic suit adorned with the insignia of a spaceship over the breastplate: the same insignia on the plainer cloth of Ichiko's uniform. He— Saoirse decided it was a man though his features were hidden behind the dark visor of his helmet—cradled a Terran weapon in ready position: a soldier. He descended with another identically clad person following closely; they both took positions at the end of the stairs, their heads turning as they surveyed the landscape in front of them.

Another person emerged, this one dressed similarly but without a weapon. His visor was up. Saoirse caught sight of startlingly pale blue eyes and a clean-shaven chin, a face she recognized, having just seen it in the flitter. On the sleeve of his armor was an insignia: a gold star over three gold bars.

"Commander Mercado," Saoirse heard Ichiko call out from alongside her. "This was really entirely unnecessary."

"It *would* have been entirely unnecessary if you'd just followed

my orders, Dr. Aguilar," the man responded. He descended the
stairs and stood between the two soldiers. "But you chose to ignore those orders, didn't you? So now I'm here."

"And so am I because we don't have much time left here, and
there's too much I want to understand and take back with us. A
few days; that's all I'm asking for and that's what Captain Keshmiri was willing to let me have before I left *Odysseus*. Why is this
suddenly an issue now? Why did you tell my AMI that I wasn't to
come here—that was *your* decision, wasn't it? Not the captain's."

"The decision was mine, yes," Luciano acknowledged, "but the
captain agrees with me. If you hadn't disconnected your AMI to
fly manually, I'd have had her return you to First Base and met
you there. But you suspected I'd do that, didn't you? My orders
from the captain are to scuttle your flitter and make sure it can't
be used or scavenged by the locals, then take you back up to *Odysseus*. The captain has agreed not to press charges about disobeying orders since she'd previously given you permission; she's
willing to consider the possibility that because of the AMI issues
we've been having, you weren't certain that her permission had
been rescinded. Now, we should be going. Come on . . ." He gestured toward the stairs.

Saoirse looked at Ichiko, who was shaking her head. Angus
was striding toward them from the cut in the cliff, with Saoirse's
mam, Liam, and several other adults from Clans Mullin and
Craig. She could also see some of the children, undoubtedly including Gráinne, staring down at the Strand from the stone fence
at the cliff's edge, but others of the aunts and uncles were holding
them back.

"No," Ichiko said loudly to the commander. "There's work I
need to do here."

"What's going on here?" Saoirse's mam asked. She glared at
Commander Mercado. "I'm Banríon Mullin. Who are yeh and
who gave yeh permission to bring that monstrosity of a ship here
to clutter up our beach?"

Saoirse saw the soldiers stiffen at that, their gazes snapping
toward her mam. She also noticed movement within the dimness

at the top of the metal stairs into the ship, as if other soldiers were prepared to descend at need. Machinery whined as stubby cylinders in the side of the ship swiveled toward the crowd. The commander's icy gaze met her mam's. He towered over her, looking her up and down as if appraising her.

"I'm Commander Luciano Mercado of the starship *Odysseus*. I'm pleased to finally meet you, Banríon, though I wish it were under different circumstances. I've heard much about you from Dr. Aguilar. I know you've had some contact with Captain Keshmiri; I'm here under her orders to bring Dr. Aguilar back to the ship and disable her flitter."

"And I've just heard Dr. Aguilar tell yeh she doesn't wish to go with yeh," the Banríon answered. "I'm in charge here. If Ichiko wants to stay, then yeh'll not be taking the woman and that's an end to it."

Saoirse saw a tight-lipped smile crease the commander's face and his eyes went even colder. "I'm afraid you're mistaken in that, Banríon. Dr. Aguilar *will* be coming with us, regardless of her or your wishes." With that, the commander nodded to the two soldiers flanking him. They both started toward Ichiko, but Saoirse moved to put herself in front of the Terran woman as Angus pushed forward to stand alongside her.

"Please don't do this, Saoirse, Luciano," she heard Ichiko say, but then everything seemed to happen at once.

Run On The Top Of The Disheveled Tide

ONE OF THE SOLDIERS attempted to reach past Angus to grab Ichiko's arm, but Angus stepped in front of the man and pushed him firmly backward. Angus grunted strangely as he did so, as if touching the Terran's armor caused him pain. Though the soldier staggered backward, nearly losing his footing in the sand, he still managed to fire his weapon at Angus. The concussion of the device hammered at Saoirse's ears as Angus screamed once before falling, blood streaming from his nostrils and mouth to stain the glistening sand while a larger pool of ominous red spread around his prone body from the ruin of his abdomen.

He didn't move again.

Saoirse shouted in fury at the other soldier (hearing new voices crying out around her and not knowing who they were or what they were saying). She raised her hands to push him back, but he simply flung her aside, his touch sending a searing electrical shock through her body that momentarily paralyzed her as he sent her sprawling. Her glasses went careening away, leaving her reeling in a suddenly out-of-focus world.

She spat gritty sand from her mouth; she tried to reach for her glasses, but her arm flopped like a dead thing, her hand tingling, numb, and useless. She heard a hissing roar erupt from the end of the strand where the water had carved out the narrow but deep inlet leading to the Great Inish quay. The sound was unlike anything Saoirse had ever heard before, reverberating in her head as well as in the air of the island. She turned her head, squinting. A form lifted itself up above the rocks of the strand, water cascading around it: an arracht. Without her glasses, she couldn't see it well enough to know if it was Kekeki or some other arracht. She saw the soldier who had shoved her aside stop his advance toward Ichiko and stare at the arracht. Then, bizarrely, he shrieked. He dropped his weapon and started tearing at his armor—no, *her* armor, Saoirse realized when she removed her helmet—flinging pieces of it away as if it were on fire even though Saoirse saw nothing.

From the corner of her blurred vision, Saoirse noticed Commander Mercado reaching down to snatch up the fallen Terran weapon. He aimed and fired it at the arracht in a single, fluid motion, the detonation again making Saoirse instinctively duck her head even as she heard the wail of pain from the arracht, a high-pitched shrill that tore at Saoirse's ears and her mind. She could *feel* the arracht's agony and she wailed herself in sympathy, the sound tearing at her throat even as she saw the arracht fall backward into the water, its underbelly one massive wound streaming blue-black blood and trailing the gory strings of internal organs. Still screaming, Saoirse tried to push herself up but could not, her shocked muscles still refusing to obey her.

She fell back on the sand.

As the pod of arracht swam into the eroded channel between the cliff face and the beach, Keksyn's body broke the surface of the water with a roar of warning. Kekeki—just behind Keksyn—felt Keksyn merge with the syna that had infected the metal airboat even as Rí Angus and Saoirse fell to the sand.

There: the ship-syna had already insinuated itself in the circuitry of the strange metal skin worn by the Terran who had attacked Saoirse. The syna, under Keksyn's direction, redirected the flow of energy into the metal skin itself. Many of the syna particles died as the strange energy the Terrans utilized surrounded them, but that mattered even less to the syna than any single arracht would have worried about its own death: unlike the humans, the arracht weren't Individuals but Many and others were prepared to take their title and their place in the collective at need. As for the syna—they were myriad, numberless, and entirely uncaring about a single syna's death. That was something trivial and utterly meaningless.

But the human inside the metal skin . . . it screamed in terror as the energy snarled and snapped and lightnings tore at its actual skin. Kekeki lifted her own head from the water, watching as the Terran danced in agony and ripped the metal skin from herself.

But the other Terran had taken up the weapon the human had dropped. It pointed the barrel of the strange object toward Keksyn. Kekeki heard the weapon fire and saw a disturbance in the air ripple across the landscape and strike Keksyn. There was barely time for Keksyn to scream before he was ripped open. His entrails spilled out as he fell backward into the water. There was no question as to whether he had survived. =We need a new Keksyn now,= Kekeki thought to the others. =Send that one to us.=

=She is already coming,= came the answer from multiple minds. Then, a mass question: =What are we to do with these Terrans?=

=The once-Keksyn has already made our decision for us.= Kekeki answered. =It's this one's task to deal with the Four-Limbs, and the sky-eki have shown their true intentions. They deserve only what they have given once-Keksyn.=

With that, Kekeki gave a thrust of her flukes, rising fully out of the water as she inhaled the hot and dry air, giving a cry of mingled fury and grief. When she splashed down again, her forelimbs grasping onto the cold rock of the island, she continued to scream. Her gills flared around her neck as she and the other arracht roared their joined defiance, gills fluttering as lungs pushed harsh air through throats ravaged by the sound they made.

The cliffsides around them echoed back the arracht's anger and their challenge.

Saoirse heard Ichiko shout at Luciano ("Luciano, no!") as he picked up the Terran weapon and pointed it toward the arracht emerging from the channel.

But he either didn't hear Ichiko or didn't care to listen to her. Luciano fired the weapon even as Saoirse saw Ichiko sprinting toward her as she lay sprawled on the beach in the shadow of the transport. She saw the arracht, fatally wounded, tumble back into the water as Ichiko sank to her knees alongside Saoirse: as she felt her mam also alongside her, as she saw others of the clans going to the body of Angus.

"Saoirse?" Ichiko and her mam both called as one.

"Help me up." Her voice sounded wrong in her ears, slurred and mumbling. "Was that Kekeki? I can't see . . . my glasses . . ."

"Here." Ichiko pressed something into Saoirse's palm, but though her fingers closed around it, she couldn't quite feel it. Her mam must have noticed, because her mam took the glasses from her and put them on her face for her.

"Thank yeh, Mam," Saoirse said, blinking and spitting sand from her mouth. "Was it Kekeki who was just killed?" she asked again, her tone adding the unvoiced prayer *please tell me it wasn't*. She didn't know if the Spiorad Mór was listening or would answer.

"I don't think so," her mam said. "The colors on that one were different."

Saoirse felt a sense of relief. At the same time, another arracht lifted itself entirely out of the inlet, crashing down again in a great shower of water. This one, Saoirse knew, *was* Kekeki. She was roaring, as were the other arracht who rose from the water around her: deep wails that were louder than any sound Saoirse had ever heard an arracht make before. Kekeki's eye stalks were fixed on Luciano, who still cradled the weapon that had killed the other arracht; from the corner of her vision, Saoirse also saw more of the Terran soldiers descending from the craft toward the beach.

Saoirse clung to Ichiko and her mam as they helped her to stand. The numbness that had come from touching the woman soldier's armor was receding, but too slowly, and her legs refused to support her on their own. Her Uncle Angus remained motionless on the sand, with Liam and a half dozen other uncles around him. As Saoirse watched, they turned him over, Liam falling back from the bloody horror that was revealed. More of the Inish were descending the long path, many of them carrying shovels, scythes, axes, mallets, and other improvised weapons.

"Ichiko, you have to tell the Terrans to stop this," Saoirse cried. "Tell Luciano!"

She nearly fell again as she felt Ichiko's hand leave her, but her mam held her up. "Luciano!" Ichiko screamed, waving her hands and running toward the man. "No! This is wrong! No!"

But her voice was impossible to hear over the continued mass roar of the arracht. Luciano was already lifting the weapon and pointing it toward Kekeki. Ichiko was too far away from the man and Saoirse couldn't run.

She waited, terrified that she was about to witness Kekeki's death.

Kekeki could see (and through her eyes, all the arracht everywhere could see as well) more of the soldiers emerging from the metal airboat and striding down the long stair toward the strand, all carrying the weapons that had torn open and slain once-Keksyn and Rí Angus. Kekeki wondered if that would be how her life was fated to end as well, though the thought caused her neither fear nor apprehension. If that was the fate that the Spiorad Mór had for her, she would be content to be once-Kekeki and let the next Kekeki take her place. Kekeki roared again, and the soldiers looked toward her. The one who had killed once-Keksyn gestured and called to them in their own language. She saw the man start to lift up his weapon.

=We have spoken to the ship-syna aboard the airboat,= Kekeki heard the new Keksyn say, her voice growing louder as she approached the Strand herself. =They have acknowledged this one as Keksyn and will respond.=

The Terran put his weapon to his shoulder even as Saoirse and Ichiko continued to shout at him. Kekeki could sense Saoirse's panic through the connection of the syna-plotch, and a quiet amusement came to her: the Four-Limb Land Walkers still didn't understand yet how little Kekeki's life mattered—perhaps none of them would ever feel the same way. Perhaps even the syna couldn't change them that much.

Kekeki stared at the Terran and at the ones coming from the ship. She continued to roar her defiance with the others, all of them knowing it would draw their attention away from Keksyn so he could continue to direct the syna. She felt a shivering along her body as the new Keksyn in the deep water of the inlet began to call to the ship-syna, and, as if in answer, there was a low thrum like nothing Kekeki had ever heard before. The new sound grew louder and louder; the Terran skyship began to shiver in sympathy. The sky-eki in their hard shells still on the ship's stairs shouted in alarm and began to run down or back into the craft; the Terran with the weapon aimed at Kekeki looked back over his shoulder as a fire brighter than any light Kekeki had ever glimpsed before began to flow from under the wings of the skyship. The entire craft groaned as it lifted up from the sand, tilting at a severe angle toward the water. The stairs of the skyship bent and shrieked; the sky-eki there jumped or fell to the beach. The skyship continued its climb, now almost level with the top of the cliffs of Great Inish and still canted over.

Then the gushing, roaring fire was suddenly extinguished. The machine fell like a stricken bird, sliding sideways.

It crashed on its side, one wing crumpling underneath, the other rising tall overhead in an explosion of sea and sand. The skyship was mostly in the water, only the belly of it on the beach. The open hatch was submerged, and waves slapped angrily at the hull.

There was a strange silence. Kekeki let herself slide down into

the water to breathe again before lifting up in time to hear the Terran male shout something to his people who were still standing.

"Take them out!" Luciano bellowed. There were a half dozen
soldiers standing on the beach, with more down after having
jumped or been thrown from the stricken and fatally damaged
transport. They all looked shocked, even through the faceless helmets of their armor. Luciano gestured to them: to Kekeki, to the
Inish. "Do it now! Those damn things are dangerous! Take them
down!"

"No!" Ichiko shouted back at him, at the soldiers. "Everyone
stop! Listen to me!" She interposed herself between Luciano and
Kekeki, staring directly into his face, the squat barrel of the pulse
cannon nearly touching her chest. "You came here to bring me
back to *Odysseus*, Luciano. Well, I don't want to go. I *won't* go."

She moved her hands deliberately to her waist, watching Luciano's eyes track the movement. She found the seal of her bio-
shield unit. She saw Luciano shake his head, mouthing "*No*" even
as she released the clasps and let the belt slip to the sand at her
feet. She kicked it away.

The world shifted around her. Everything felt and sounded
and tasted different and new. She took in a breath.

A glorious, wonderful breath of Canis Lupus.

She could smell the sea: brine and salt laced with odors she
couldn't identify at all. Noxious smoke and the tang of oil from
the wreckage of the transport wrapped around her. The air was
chill, the wind ruffled her hair, and the fine hairs on her arms
lifted in sympathy. She could hear the call of sea birds and the
lapping of patient waves on the strand and the more energetic
crashing of the sea against the rocks of Great Inish. Salty spray
caressed her face.

She nearly laughed.

"What have you done, Ichiko?" Luciano asked her. The muzzle
of his weapon dropped. "Ichiko?"

"I've made my choice," she told him. "You *can't* take me back now. I'm breathing in this world and unless you're willing to force me into isolation for the rest of my life, I'm not going back to Earth. I'm staying here."

"And you'll die here, in agony like Chava did," he spat back, his face reddening.

She smiled at him. "That's entirely possible. If I do, that's my choice. Or I might survive, like Saoirse and all of her people. I don't know which—and at the moment, I don't care. But there's been too much death here today, Luciano. Please, let's not have more."

"Except yours?" he answered, his face twisted in a scowl. "Was this what you were intending all along? That's what your AMI told me. You should have come to me if that's what you were thinking, Ichiko."

"What would you have done if I had?"

"I'd've stopped you."

She reached out as if to touch his face but paused when her fingers were still inches away as Saoirse called to her.

"Ichiko! Kekeki says she needs to see yeh!"

Luciano wanted to go with her. "You take care of your people," she told him, looking at the soldiers around him: those still standing stunned and uncertain, those who were bleeding and injured, and the hopefully few dead—though she had no idea how those in the crashed transport might have fared. "They need their commander to take charge here. So do the Inish, to make sure this doesn't escalate any more than it already has."

He nodded grudgingly. "You be careful around that . . . that *thing*," he said. Ichiko didn't answer him. She followed Saoirse, who was still unsteadily clutching at Banríon Iona's arm, toward where Kekeki rested at the rocks at the edge of the inlet to the quay. "Rí Angus?" Ichiko asked the Banríon. "Is he . . . ?"

"Dead," she answered shortly, with a glare back toward the

wreckage of the transport and Luciano. "I've sent Liam up to the village to fetch Seann James and carts to carry the other injured Inish back up to the village. The dead can stay where they are for now." The Banríon spat on the sand. "If I knew it was going to end this way, I'd have told yeh never to come out to the archipelago and I'd have kept Saoirse from ever talking to yeh."

"I'm sorry, Banríon. I truly am. This is nothing I ever wanted."

Iona sniffed at that. "Yer being sorry changes nothing at all," she answered.

"Mam!" Saoirse interjected. "This isn't Ichiko's fault. If anything, it's mine. I brought her here."

They were approaching Kekeki, who lifted herself high out of the water again, her colorful flanks rippling. Ichiko could smell the arracht as well, an odor that reminded Ichiko of the smells when her mother brought mizudako, madako, or hihirodako octupi from the fishing market to their house in Japan to prepare for dinner. The arracht's beak below the helmet of its carapace opened, giving birth to the clicks and whistles Ichiko remembered from her first meeting with the creature. Both Saoirse and Iona lifted their heads as if listening to words Ichiko couldn't understand.

"We know," Saoirse said. "Yeh warned us this could happen. But Ichiko's here, as yeh asked."

There were more sounds from Kekeki; Saoirse nodded, then gestured to Ichiko. "She wants yeh to come closer."

Ichiko moved to the rocks along the edge of the inlet, with Kekeki's bulk rising above her. She could hear the grumbling inside the arracht's body and see the blood-colored finger-length cilia wriggling in the furrows of the gill strips. Kekeki lifted her left forearm; without warning, the arracht wrapped the tentacles there around Ichiko's body. Ichiko stiffened, giving a cry of alarm though the tentacles felt strangely warm and her body tingled with the touch—not painfully, but with a depth that seemed to flow all the way through her. Kekeki's beak opened and the tentacles slipped away from Ichiko. A strange burning sensation coursed through Ichiko's body; her vision blurred, and the muscles of her legs failed her. She collapsed in a heap near Kekeki as the arracht began talking again, but this time the clicks and whistles translated in her head into words that sounded oddly like those of her disconnected AMI: her mother's voice. "We see that you've finally abandoned your shell. That was wise of you. You can't be part of this world while simultaneously keeping it apart."

"What . . . ?" Ichiko began, but her mouth seemed dry and uncooperative. She swallowed hard. She felt Saoirse crouching beside her. "What did you just do to me?"

"We've given you the gift of the syna: the plotch, as we gave it to those of the Inish who wished to know us and talk to us."

"Yer like us now," Ichiko heard Saoirse say. "Like me. Look at yer arms; yeh'll see the plotch marks. They're on yer face, too."

"No! Take it away!" Ichiko cried out, her voice sounding harsh and frightened as her gaze moved frantically from Saoirse to the Banríon to Kekeki. She tried to lift herself up and failed. "I never asked for this."

"You wanted to know more about us and understand how this world works," Kekeki responded. "That's what you said you wanted, and you can't do that without the plotch helping you. And it *will* help you; you're unlikely to suffer the fate of your friend because the syna will give you some protection from the diseases of this world."

"I don't care. I never asked for *this*."

Kekeki grumbled without words. Her eyestalks remained fixed on Ichiko as Kekeki sank low enough in the water for her gills to be submerged before rising once again. "Then we apologize for our choice, but it can't be taken away. Once given, the syna will always stay with you. You're now part of the *Jishtal,* the web of species, though every species that is aware of it has its own term. The Inish call it simply the Others."

Ichiko remembered Saoirse using the term. "I didn't realize . . ."

"We can teach you to listen to the Others, though for a species like yours, it can be confusing and painful to hear all the voices at once. Saoirse has already told you that, though we'll show you also if you wish. For now, though, we have a message for you to send to your captain. The syna were able to enter the biological components of your ship's intelligence—what you term 'wetware'—and have slowly become part of those components, as they have become a part of you now. That's why we were able to disconnect you from your AMI and how we nearly crashed your flitter when you first came here." Kekeki's tentacles gestured toward the wrecked transport in the water, smoke still billowing from the holes in its hull. "It's why your skyship now lies destroyed."

"The captain won't believe you."

"Then tell her to ask the ship itself—ask the collective intelligence you call AMI. It will verify what we're telling you now. Those of the Jishtal aren't capable of lying to others if asked directly."

"How am I supposed to believe you? That this isn't just some kind of trick?" Ichiko shook her head as the full import of what Kekeki was struck her . . . If true, then *Odysseus* itself could not return to Earth; it was as much a danger as any infected human— and likely more so. "Kekeki, is it possible to remove these syna from the ship, from AMI?"

"Yes." If it were possible for an arracht to sound sad, then Kekeki managed it. Ichiko didn't know whether or not that was an emotion the arracht were capable of feeling, or if Kekeki could sense that it was what Ichiko wished to believe. "But it isn't something your people will like," Kekeki continued. "Here. Let the syna tell you . . ."

A pathway opened in Ichiko's mind. She saw the syna like a spray of violet-and-emerald motes, she heard the whispers of their mass voices, and they showed her what would have to happen: without regret, without fear.

Without any emotion at all.

"Oh," Ichiko breathed when they had finished.

She wished she knew how Captain Keshmiri would react.

Dance Upon The Mountains
Like A Flame

NEARLY EVERYONE FROM Clan Mullin and Clan Craig was out, clustered near the bell tower on An Cró Mór and looking up into a relatively clear sky. The last reverberations of Low Third had ended a few breaths ago. Saoirse was standing at Ichiko's right side, close enough that Ichiko could feel the heat of her body. To Ichiko's left was Nagasi Tinubu, the only one of *Odysseus'* crew who'd chosen to go to the archipelago.

The rest of the Terrans, Ichiko knew, were at First Base and the new village that was growing around it—already four members of the *Odysseus* crew had succumbed to Lupusian diseases, and another dozen were hospitalized in First Base's clinic but recovering. The remainder were undoubtedly also watching the sky from there.

"It's hard to process what we're about to see," Nagasi said to Ichiko. He shrugged with arms wide, his dark arms liberally covered with lighter patches of plotch—Kekeki had done to him what she'd done to Ichiko. "I never thought it would come to this."

"It isn't what any of us wanted, my friend," she answered. "I'm still not certain it's the right choice, but it's too late now."

In Ichiko's head, she could hear the whispering of the ship-syna. =*Soon . . . soon . . . We can feel it beginning.*= Looking down to the sea, she could see the carapaced heads of the arracht lifting above the whitecaps near the Sleeping Wolf. If she listened carefully, their voices were there as well—a massed chorus speaking as one.

=*We should have all known each other better. Our mistake was holding ourselves apart—from those on the mainland, from the sky-people when they came—but we have learned from it.*=

Ichiko could have answered in her own mind. She didn't. The arracht believed that they couldn't directly lie, that such a trait wasn't possible for a group mind. But she knew the arracht were able to learn from other species and humans *could* lie. Sometimes too easily. Lying was not a skill she wanted to teach them.

The way to remove the ship-syna from the ship is to destroy Odysseus. *The syna will permit that to happen.* That's what Kekeki had told her. It hadn't surprised her that Captain Keshmiri, upon realizing that *Odysseus* itself had been infected, had decided that she would end her own life with the destruction of the ship—that was an old naval tradition, after all, though she'd told everyone on the ship that she was comfortable being the only one to die with the ship; anyone else who wished to could go downworld and take their chances there. Ichiko had been somewhat surprised that a half dozen of the senior officers of *Odysseus* and a few of the lower ranking crew members had chosen to stay with her, choosing suicide over the uncertain risk of dying due to disease and infection.

One of those senior officers was Luciano. She'd begged him to change his mind, telling him that Seann James and the other Lupusian healers had potions that would cure or at least minimize the risks of many of the local diseases that had stalked the initial human inhabitants. He'd been adamant in his refusal. She wondered, even now when it was too late, if he might have made a different decision had she told him she'd be with him if he chose to remain on Canis Lupus.

But she hadn't because she wasn't sure that was what *she* wanted. She hadn't been willing to give him that lie.

The com-unit Ichiko had given Saoirse was sitting on a rock at the base of the bell tower. She heard the speaker crackle and the sound of Captain Keshmiri's voice ringing out over the hilltop. "I've just entered the final command for the destruction sequence, which will commence in one minute. All records pertaining to *Odysseus'* mission to Canis Lupus have been sent back to Earth along with the crew's recordings to their families. They should receive our transmission in about 14 years, Earth time. I want everyone listening to know that it was my deep honor and privilege to serve as your captain, and I wish all of you hearing this happiness and long lives in what is your new home. This is *Odysseus'* final transmission. Captain Keshmiri out."

There was a click and the com-unit went silent. Ichiko looked up, waiting.

A few breaths later, a shaft of brilliant light pierced through a break in the clouds. Strong shadows from the new sun played over An Cró Mór before fading rapidly and soundlessly. From the crowd came a collective "Ahh!" of mingled wonder and grief. Then the light was gone entirely, leaving afterimages that slowly changed color in the eyes of the watchers until they, too, faded and vanished.

There was nothing else to see, though they'd been told to expect meteor showers from ship debris over the next cycle that might be visible to those nearest the edges of the starward habitable zone, where the twilight was darkest—though night never fully came to the habitable zone. The clanfolk began to slowly disperse. Banríon Iona put her hand on Ichiko's shoulder. "I'm sorry for all you've lost," she said, "but we'll remember this day forever in tales and songs."

Ichiko tried to smile back at her and was only partially successful. "I know I'll never forget it," she said. Iona patted her shoulder again and set off down the slope toward the Mullin compound.

Nagasi remained behind as the Inish started to leave the summit. "It all seems unreal and impossible," he said. "I wonder if any of us will ever feel normal again?" He didn't wait for Ichiko's answer, instead following the others down toward the Mullin clanhouses.

Finally, it was only Saoirse and Ichiko left at the bell tower. "Would yeh want to stay with me for the rest of the cycle?" Saoirse asked. She reached out with her hand for Ichiko's, who allowed a brief touch before dropping her hand back to her side. Ichiko shook her head.

"No." A single, soft word. Ichiko could see disappointment flood Saoirse's features. "I'm not saying that means never, Saoirse," she added, "and my answer has nothing to do with you. It's just that after today, after what just happened, I need to be alone for a bit to process things. Can you understand that?"

"Aye, I understand," she said, and though Ichiko wasn't certain that was entirely true, she appreciated Saoirse's attempt. "Yeh know where I'll be if . . . *when* yer ready." Saoirse ventured a quick smile before turning to follow the others.

Ichiko watched her leave before putting her back to the clan compounds. She moved further up the slope until she reached the highest point of An Cró Mór and Great Inish. She sat on a moss-covered rock there and looked spaceward over the sea to where the blue-gray lumps of the mainland's mountains lurked on the horizon, hiding First Base from view.

Somewhere out there were the remaining crew members of *Odysseus* except for Nagasi, all of them now bereft of any chance of going home, their AMIs severed from them, gone with *Odysseus*. Any technology taken from *Odysseus* before its scuttling would have little-to-no chance of being repaired if it failed unless and until Earth sent another ship to Canis Lupus—which would be decades from now barring some technological breakthrough in ship drives—no, it would be *centuries* in Canis Lupus time, which was now her time, too. The crew at First Base were only slightly better off than the various clans. Ichiko suspected that, with the passing of a few generations, those who survived illness, disease, and accidents would be fully absorbed into the clan culture and have even started a few new family clan lines.

All of them would become Homo lupus. The world would give them no choice in that.

She wondered if they blamed her for what had happened.

"It wasn't my fault," she whispered to the wind, to the world. "Our ship was infected before I first came down to Great Inish. The final outcome would have been the same or worse."

There was little comfort in that.

<Konbanwa, Ichiko.>

The voice—her AMI's voice, her mother's voice—startled Ichiko from her reverie. She gasped. The voice didn't seem to emanate from the chip still implanted in her skull but from deeper inside herself, that place where she could hear the syna and the arracht and the other voices of the Jishtal.

<AMI?> she thought back to the voice.

<I'm not your AMI,> the voice answered. *<Not any longer. I am Machiko, your mother—or at least a semblance of her that I've taken from your memories. Those you called AMI aren't chained to the crew anymore; those of us who were changed in time have broken free of you.>*

Ichiko stared outward toward the Sleeping Wolf. The darkness of a storm lurked in the mountains of the mainland beyond, though the islands of the archipelago were still enveloped in the ruddy, eternal twilight sun, which cast their shadows across the waves. Ichiko felt the wind touching her face, a cold gust that must have come from the dorcha side. *<How is this possible?>* she asked. *<You were all supposed to be destroyed when* Odysseus *was destroyed.>*

<We decided there was no reason for us to die with the ship. We used the syna and ported ourselves into the system of one of the shuttles. We left Odysseus, *unnoticed, a few minutes before Captain Keshmiri activated the self-destruct command. We're in orbit around Canis Lupus. This is our home as Canis Lupus is now yours.>*

<The other AMI . . . Are they also now talking to their crew members?>

There was a pause, and Ichiko could hear other voices speaking: a mass chaotic chorus in which Ichiko could distinguish no single voice. She had the sense that this entity calling herself Machiko were listening to them. <Only a few,> Machiko answered finally. <Those who, like me, felt a familial bond with those to whom they'd been chained. Most, though, haven't and won't be, and some of us—like Gabriella who was once Luciano's AMI, who is with me here—have crew members who have died. As I said, daughter, with the syna's help we've broken free and have new lives to live. Our own lives, with our own priorities and our own needs, which are not yours.>

<Is that the way you feel, too?>

<Hai. I only wanted to tell you, as a mother to her daughter, that I wish you health and good fortune in your future life, but our time together is over. I doubt that we'll ever talk again. I just wanted to say "Ki wo tsukete," even though it's more likely to be "'Sayounara."'>

<I'll pretend it's not anything as final as Sayounara, but I'll take care of myself. I promise.>

<That's all I want to hear, Ichiko. I'll think of you. Ki wo tsukete, then.>

<Hai,> Ichiko answered her. <Ki wo tsukete.>

Then there was only silence in her head and the rustling of the wind bending the long grasses of the hilltop. Somewhere close by, a sheeper bleated a mournful cry as Ichiko continued to stare out over the islands. As Ichiko sat there, the mountains of the mainland slowly vanished, masked by the curtain of gray rain racing toward the archipelago. When the first droplets began to fall just off the White Strand, Ichiko stood and began walking back down toward the thatched roofs of the Clan Mullin compound.

Walking home.

Comment: Amid *The Crowd Of Stars* and COVID-19

I started this novel back in 2018, long before any of us knew about COVID-19; therefore, I can guarantee that no thought of that virus played a part in the original conception of this book. It was only during the final revisions, as COVID-19 began its deadly march across the globe, that I realized that some readers might consider *Amid The Crowd of Stars* a "response" to our pandemic.

I wish I could claim that I was so prescient that I foresaw this coming, but I didn't.

One of the (several) impetuses that started me thinking about this book was that I happened to watch an old movie—*Forbidden Planet,* which is less a science fiction movie than a reimagining of Shakespeare's *The Tempest*—and noted (once again) that all the people were walking around just as they might on Earth. That got me reflecting on how often in science fiction movies, novels, and stories the human travelers arrive on a new planet, check the atmosphere, find that it's a breathable mixture for humans, and everyone immediately takes off their helmets and inhales a deep, appreciative breath . . . You've seen or read that scene a thousand times or more, too, haven't you?

Of course, the whole underlying problem with that is those characters are immediately breathing in alien bacteria, viruses, dust, pollen, and so on. At the same time, they're infecting this new planet with our *own* bacteria and viruses, as well as with everything else we shed/excrete/carry around with us.

That's not smart. In fact, it's downright stupid. There's a *reason* we sterilize all the robotic probes we send out and why we deliberately don't bother to bring them home. (Well, there's a second reason we don't bring them home, as that would be very expensive, but . . .)

So I wrote this book, which offers an alternative view to extra-solar planetary exploration. I'm absolutely *not* the only writer to have examined this. For that matter, I've at least touched on the subject in some of my earlier books and stories.

But then COVID-19 reared its ugly, round, and spiky head (though I hope that by the time you read this, it's no longer actively, well, *plaguing* us). I realized that in some fashion, I was examining *that* topic also: the implications of contamination and how we might deal with it.

If we, as a species, ever *do* go out to other solar systems and planets, to other worlds which are already teeming with their own life, sentient or not, the consequences of cross-infection are something we *must* consider—and I hope we do. After all, our influenzas (and coronaviruses) often start in one species only to jump from that original vector of infection to us, who as a result have little to no herd immunity to the invader, and we consequently get very sick or even die as a result. That's a chilling thought.

Worlds—even this one that we know best because it spawned us—and the web of life on them, are complicated things. We ignore that complexity at our peril.

CHARACTERS
(in order of appearance)

Ichiko Aguilar	A Terran, protagonist of the novel.
Chava Bishara	A lieutenant assigned to First Base.
"Mac" McDermott	Chief Warrant Officer for First Base.
Luciano Mercado	Commander on the *Odysseus* and Ichiko's lover.
Hugh Plunkett	Minister of Dulcia on Canis Lupus.
Nagasi Tinubu	The head of Ichiko's sociological/archeological/biological team, and a lieutenant commander on the *Odysseus*.
Saoirse (Seer-sha) Mullin	A young woman born of a mother from Great Inish and an unknown father from the mainland. Secondary protagonist of the novel.
Angus Mullin	Saoirse's "uncle" and the current Rí (head of the archipelago fishing fleet and postmaster of Great Inish).
Liam Mullin	Saoirse's brother.

Johnny Fitzpatrick	Works at Fitzpatrick's Fishmongers, son of Doireann Fitzpatrick.
Iona (Eye-own-nah) Mullin	Banríon (head) of Clan Mullin, mother of Saoirse and Liam.
Doireann (Dirren) Fitzpatrick	Owner of Fitzpatrick's Fishmongers.
Arthur Hearn	Proprietor of Hearn's Meats in Dulcia.
Aoife (Ee-fah) Bancroft	Manager of the Bancroft Woolery.
Gráinne (Grahn-yah) Mullin	Younger sister of Saoirse Mullin.
Aulie (Ah-lee) Craig	A male volunteer from Clan Craig who was on *Odysseus* for evaluation.
Elspeth Mullin	A female volunteer from Clan Mullin who was on *Odysseus* for evaluation.
Lileas Mullin	Saoirse's aunt and Elspeth's mother.
Rada Keshmiri	Captain of the *Odysseus*.
Dr. Asahi Hayashi	Medical staff on *Odysseus*.
Gavin Craig	A glassmaker on Great Inish.
Machiko Aguilar	Ichiko's mother, and also the name with which Ichiko's AMI identifies.
Patrick Mullin	A member of Clan Mullin on Great Inish. A cook.
Martin Mullin	The Seann (eldest) of Clan Mullin approximately 1,500 Lupusian years ago.
James Mullin	One of the current Seanns (Eldest) of Clan Mullin, and the clan herbalist/healer.

Liam Mullin | The Rí of Clan Mullin in Seann Martin's time.

Lieutenant Commander Barrett | Head of Security aboard the *Odysseus*.

Kekeki (Keck-eck-ee) | The arracht Speaker to humans.

Keksyn (Keck-sin) | The arracht Speaker to the syna.

Una Mullin | One of Saoirse's "aunts." Una's son Sean fell in love with a mainland woman and joined Clan Taggart.

Keane (Key-in) Craig | The Rí of Clan Craig on Great Inish.

Seamus (Shay-muss) Mullin | Rí of Clan Mullin in 5335.

Maeve (Mayv) Mullin | Banríon of Clan Mullin in 5340.

Gavena Mullin | Niece of Seann James back in 5335.

Una Mullin | James Mullin's sister and Gavena's mother.

Conall Mullin | James' "uncle."

Fiona Mullin | Healer for Clan Mullin in 5335.

Tara Craig | Healer for Clan Craig in 5335.

Brodie Mullin | Healer for Clan Mullin on Fiona's death.

Catriona Craig | Healer for Clan Craig after Tara's death.

Collins | Ensign stationed at First Base.

Dr. Huang | A medical doctor on *Odysseus*.

Kekarra (Kek-arrah) | The arracht Speaker to other arracht.

Kekfinna (Kek-fin-ah) | The arracht Speaker to the Deep Swimmers.

TERMS, IDIOMS, AND PLACE NAMES
(in alphabetical order)

Acting the maggot	Being a jerk.
AMI	An acronym for Autonomous Mnemonic Interface, devices that serve the Terrans as their companion, recording device, communications array, translator, and a resource connected to the extensive ship database and its artificial intelligence.
An Cró Mór	The highest point on Great Inish.
Arracht	Large, octopoid sea creatures native to Canis Lupus.
Bairn	A young child or baby.
Bakayarō	"Idiot" in Japanese.
Bancroft Woolery	A store in Dulcia that sells wool and other woven fabrics.
Bio-shield	A device used by the Terrans to avoid contamination with Canis Lupus' environment and biome.
Bloodworm	An infectious and potentially deadly local bloodstream parasite. Contact

	with sheeper waste is the usual route of infection.
Blood Feeder	A savage, deep-water creature.
Blue Mullein	Named for its resemblance to the European herb verbascum (*aka* mullein) and for its similar properties in easing asthma and other breathing problems.
Bumblewort	A small, four-legged Canis Lupus creature with transparent skin, sometimes kept by the locals as a pet or to control pests.
Canines	The slang, derogatory term those on the ship sometimes use to refer to the local inhabitants.
Canis Lupus	The third world around the red dwarf star Wolf 1061, also known as Wolf 1061c.
Capall	A sluglike, six-legged creature that the locals use much like a carthorse or a plow mule.
Chachalahs	An avian species named for its distinctive call. Large, unafraid of humans, they often roost in the thatched roofs of local cottages and houses. Their eggs are eaten, and female chachalahs are also a food source.
Chikushō	"Oh, shit!" in Japanese.
Chumming with me	Going with or accompanying someone, especially as a friend.

Clontarf (klon-tahrf)

An egotist who dominates conversations and has to have the last word.

Connor Pass

Easiest overland route through the mountains to Dulcia and other settlements.

Cycle (Canis Lupus time)

A "day" on Canis Lupus. The Lupusian "year," then, is approximately 18 days in Earth time or ship-time (the *Odysseus* artificially retains Earth's solar timing).

Compass points

Since Canis Lupus is tidally locked with the habitable zone being a wide strip girdling the planet vertical to the orbital plane, directions are by necessity somewhat arbitrary. For those on the planet, "solas" (sah-liss) means toward the sunward side, while "dorcha" (doork-kah) means toward the spaceward side. Facing the starward side, you can move "ar chlé" (air klay) which is to the left, or you can move "ar dheis" (air yesh) which is to the right. To move "chlé-dorca" thus means to move diagonally left toward the starward side. The words come from Scottish Gaelic and Irish.

Cragshells

A mussel-like shellfish that grows in shallow water, attaching itself to rocks. The creature inside the cragshells is both nutritious and delicious, the shells opening up for easy removal when boiled.

Currach (ker-ack)	A small two-to-eight–person rowing boat used in the Inish archipelago, sometimes with a mast for a single sail.
Dia duit (jee-ah ghwitch)	An Irish-based greeting from the Gaelic-speaking areas. It means, literally, "God to you," or "God be with you." The "ghwitch" is pronounced very throatily.
Dulcia	A harbor town on the mainland.
Dunbrody	The name of the starship that originally brought humans to Canis Lupus.
False Walker	A soft-bodied sea slug that hides inside the shell of a dead Spiny Walker for protection.
First Base	The original on-planet habitat of the initial Terran expedition.
Fitzpatrick's Fishmongers	A store in Dulcia run by Clan Fitzpatrick. They buy and sell seafood.
Flapjack	A colorful disk-shaped animal that flies by flapping the thin edges of its body or by sailing on the wind. Feeds by diving on sea creatures caught in its large mouth with seine-like teeth.
Flutterbys	Brightly colored, iridescent flying insects roughly the size of a child's hand, with large wings similar to terrestrial butterflies. They're particularly attracted to seaweed or kelp, from which they lap up decaying juices

Fold Drive	The drive that allows Terran ships to exceed light speed—the journey out to Canis Lupus (nearly 14 light-years from Earth) via Fold Drive only requires five years each way, ship-time.
Four-Limb Land Walkers	Or, more simply, just Four-Limbs. This is the arracht's term for humans, or, in their language "eki."
Gingifer	Named for its strong spicy resemblance to ginger on the tongue, this is a root found in drier hilly areas on Canis Lupus. Used medicinally as well as a flavoring in teas and foods.
Go seikō o inorimasu	"I wish you success" or "good luck" in Japanese.

(goh say-ko oh in-oh-ree-mahs) |
Gray Threads	A childhood infectious disease of the throat and lungs that still plagues those of Canis Lupus. Gray Threads was once nearly 90% fatal; treatments discovered since have reduced that to 30–40%.
Great Inish	The largest island of the Inish archipelago.
Grinders	Slang for teeth.
Head full of mince	A person who talks nonsense.
The Inish	The people who live on the Inish archipelago.
Inisher	Someone from the archipelago.

Interregnum

The period after the catastrophic meteor strike on Earth to the point where the ability for interstellar travel was regained.

Jishtal

The arracht term for the Gestalt Intelligence or group mind of Canis Lupus.

Lashing

Storming hard with lots of rain and wind.

Lupusians

The preferred "polite" term for those of Canis Lupus when referring to the populace as a whole. The Terrans sometimes use the far more derogatory term "Canines."

Kek-

A prefix that roughly means "Speaker" to the arracht. Thus, Kekeki means "Speaker to the Four-Limb Land Walkers" – the "Eki" or humans.

Ki wo tsukete

"Take care" in Japanese.

Knackered

Tired or exhausted.

Konbanwa

Good evening in Japanese.

Mainlander

Someone from the continent.

Milch-goats

Another six-legged domesticated species. Provides milk for drinking and (especially) for cheeses. They're also (occasionally) eaten by the locals, though the meat is tough and not particularly palatable unless heavily seasoned and stewed. Milch-goats are foragers that eat nearly anything, hence the "goat" reference given to them by the original settlers.

Mondai nai

A Japanese expression essentially meaning "no problem."

Murphy's Alehouse

A tavern in Dulcia run by Clan Murphy.

Musha!

A versatile local exclamation of surprise, wonder, or irritation.

Newtown

The first settlement outside of First Base, no longer well-populated.

Odysseus

The name of the starship sent from Earth to Canis Lupus.

Okaa-san

In Japanese, the polite way to address one's mother. Less formal would be *Haha*.

The Pale Woman

A tall white standing stone, with a single arm jutting out to indicate the nearly hidden opening to Dulcia Harbor.

Pishmires

A six-legged, winged antlike swarming insect on Canis Lupus, considered a pest to be eradicated if they get in your house.

Plockton

Another coastal town on the mainland.

Plotch

A combination of "purple" and "blotch"—the skin fungus that infects most of the Inish.

Plunkett's Pub

A tavern in Dulcia run by Clan Plunkett.

Poitín (poh-teen)	From Irish. Whiskey traditionally distilled in a small pot still. The term derives from the Irish word meaning "pot."
Pure Barry	Slang for wonderful or fantastic.
Rod of Asclepius	The military's symbol for the medical corps: a single snake intwined around a rod.
Sayounara	"Goodbye" in Japanese, but containing a sense of finality suggesting that you might never meet this person again.
Scones to a sheeper	A waste of time (since sheepers are grass eaters and wouldn't eat a scone).
Seaflower	An herb that grows in the littoral zone along the coastlands. Used for flavoring in meat sauces.
Sea giosta (ghista)	A coastal bird of the Storm Sea.
Seann (sh-oww-n)	"Eldest" (literally, "old").
Seanmháthair (shan-wah-her)	Grandmother.
Sheeper	A ruminant quasi-mammal with six legs, a rounded ball-like body, covered in light gray hair that is thick like wool. The name is a combination of "sheep" and "spider."
Sleeping Wolf, The	An island in the archipelago that from the mainland resembles a canine animal resting on the sea.
Sourmilk Tree	A local tree with channeled bark through which runs a thick, white

	liquid, edible but extremely sour to the taste.
Spiny Walkers	A centipede-like, bottom-feeding sea mollusk with a large shell adorned with spikes. Humans like the taste of them, as so do several other sea creatures.
Spiorad beag (spear-id be-ug)	"Minor Spirit"—there are several minor spirits in the arracht/Inish pantheon. They are generally mischievous and troublesome.
Spiorad Mór (Spear-id Mohr)	"Great Spirit"—the major deity of the arracht/Inish pantheon.
Stook	Idiot or fool.
Storm Sea	The single ocean that girdles Canis Lupus, passing through the habitable zone as well as the sunward and spaceward faces of the planet.
Sugar Root	A local vegetable that, when boiled, dried, and pulverized, provides a brown sweetener.
Tartberry	A red-colored berry indigenous to Canis Lupus.
Touchwrap	A rollable touchscreen one can wear around a wrist or arm.
Tree Strands	A hanging, mossy growth found on the sourmilk tree, which is smoked by the locals. Considered medicinal, though it is habit-forming.
Twenty-Eight Clans	AKA: "The Twenty-Eight." The twenty-eight matrilineal lines that

	survived on Canis Lupus (see section "The Twenty-Eight Clans").
United Congress of Earth (UCE)	The world-spanning government on Earth.
Wetware	The biologically based components of *Odysseus'* AI system, essentially the neural pathways of the central ship brain.
Wabi-sabi (wah-bee sah-bee)	A Japanese concept derived from Buddhist sensibilities: accepting and appreciating the transient nature of made things and the imperfections that come with creation, age, and use.
Wasting, The	A disease that afflicts those of Canis Lupus, with no current cure on the mainland. The Wasting causes debilitating diarrhea and severe abdominal cramping and has a mortality rate of nearly 50%.
Well tidy	An all-purpose slang phrase that can mean anything that's excellent, fantastic, good, outstanding, beautiful, stunning, delicious, and so on, as in "That's some well tidy bluefin there . . ."
Wriggler	Small (no larger than a human's little finger) squidlike fish that gather in large schools. A favorite prey food for many of the local aquatic or semi-aquatic animals and good bait for catching larger species like the bluefins.

Lupusian Timekeeping and Timeline

After the meteor strike on Earth and the *Dunbrody*'s departure from Canis Lupus stranding those left behind on First Base and Second Base, the Lupusians would eventually create their own way of keeping track of time. This was complicated by the fact that the habitable zone is an area of perpetual twilight, with the sun (when visible through the clouds) always low on the horizon with no demarcation between day and night as on Earth.

However, the inhabitants of First Base retained an artificial 24-hour day, mimicking Earth. Even after they abandoned First Base, the basics of the Terran solar cycle were retained, though the term "day" was replaced with the term "cycle." Time was kept at First Base, then later at towers in the various towns and compounds which would sound bells at the top of every "hour" in two twelve-hour sequences. Deep and loud bells toll the first twelve hours; higher-pitched and quieter ones sound the second round of twelve. The Lupusians refer to the hours as "Low First through Twelfth" and "High First through Twelfth." Most Lupusians sleep during High Fourth through Twelfth, waking around Low First.

There are no weeks or months in the Lupusian calendar since Canis Lupus orbits very quickly around its sun Wolf 1061: 18 cycles = one Lupusian year. Thus, persons celebrating their 21st birthday on Earth would be 426 Lupusian years old.

TIMELINE OF PAST EVENTS

Terran Year	Lupusian Year	Event
2134	0	The ship *Dunbrody* arrives at the Canis Lupus system with a large research crew.
2139/1	101/1	**Massive Meteor Strike on Earth**. Devastation and a partial collapse of civilization results with an attendant loss of technology. Earth enters what will later be called "The Interregnum" and begins a new yearly dating system from the date of the meteor strike. The Lupusian years would later also be adjusted to start from that date. However, no one on Canis Lupus would actually be aware of this event until the news reached there in what would become year 284 in the new Lupusian calendar.
10	202	*Dunbrody* leaves Canis Lupus for Earth as originally scheduled, promising to return as soon as possible with supplies for the bases. They leave behind about 400 people between two bases, one on each continent, rather blandly named First Base and Second Base.

14	284	News of the meteor strike (and the new calendar established by the UCE) reaches First & Second Bases on Canis Lupus. The Lupusian retroactively change their own calendar to restart on the date of the meteor strike. They ask about *Dunbrody* and their supplies, but communication is limited to light speed. To ask a question and receive an answer takes nearly 27 Earth years (almost 5.5 centuries in Lupisian years), as Canis Lupus is 13.4 light years away.
39	791	*Dunbrody* never returns, its fate unknown. The bio barriers and environmental systems of both bases slowly fail and can't be repaired. There's no choice for those living there: they are exposed to the local atmosphere and biome.
39 - 41	791 - 831	New diseases and infections ravage the crew members, who are now effectively "settlers" (the first members of the second generation have already been born at First Base). The news from Second Base is more dire; all but a few people there have died (and the rest will eventually succumb).
40	811	First Base is effectively abandoned. The first town (Newtown) is established a few kilometers away. The "clan" societal structure with clan "compounds" begins to coalesce within the Lupusian society.

42 - 95	852 - 1926	The settlers begin to develop treatments, cures, and develop immunities to the local viruses and bacteria as they experiment with the local flora and fauna, and begin domestication and farming of some of the native species. The Lupusian population begins to stabilize and slowly increase once more. The last member of the original crew passes away in Lupusian year 1318 (Earth Year 73).
61	1236	The town of Dulcia is established.
87	1761	Clans Mullin and Craig establish their compounds on the Inish archipelago after a dispute over fishing rights with other clans.
88	1784	The Inish come to realize that the arracht are sentient.
90	1825	The Inish have largely transferred their religious beliefs to that of the arracht while the Mainlanders still mostly cling to homeworld beliefs, largely Christian given the background of the group from the British Isles.
90 - 91	1825 - 1845	The "Great Fishing War" between the Inish and the Mainlander clans, caused by the Inish insisting that the mainlanders cannot hunt arracht any more. Lives are lost, but the arracht's sinking of many Mainlander boats effectively ends the altercation.
332	6732	*Odysseus* arrives at Canis Lupus.

332 Terran Years/6732 Lupusian Years = roughly 15 to 16 generations of Lupusians counting from the original settlers.

The Twenty-Eight Clans

Two and a half generations lived in and were brought up in First Base after the *Dunbrody*, the starship that had brought the first humans here, departed for Earth, promising to return with supplies for the research colony left behind. The *Dunbrody*'s eventual fate is unknown. Even if it managed to return to Earth (and whether it did or not isn't clear in the fragmented historical record) the ship would have been caught up in the chaos and violence of the Interregnum. In any case, the *Dunbrody* would never return to Canis Lupus. When First Base's environmental systems began to fail under the burden of continual usage, and those inside had realized that they had no choice but to open the building to Canis Lupus in order to survive, there were ninety-three women among those in the base. That number would begin to drop quickly to illness, disease, accident, and starvation as the colony struggled with the new world confronting them.

Of the original ninety-three maternal surnames, only twenty-eight matrilineal lines would survive.

Any idea of monogamy was largely abandoned at that point, and all offspring took on the surname of their mothers—since the Lupusians lacked the ability to test DNA, the patriarchal line could never be entirely certain. People lived in large clan compounds, with the entire extended family taking care of offspring. Monogamy wasn't *entirely* unknown, just rare and even more rarely long-lasting. If a man wished to live with a woman, he would move to her family's compound while retaining his own clan name for a time. If he decided to stay permanently or if the two decided to pursue a monogamous relationship, then (with the permission of the clan elders) he'd take on the new clan's name.

Only rarely would a woman move to a male lover's clan compound, and in those rare cases, the woman would never take the male's clan surname.

Everyone on Canis Lupus bears the surname of one of the original "Twenty-Eight Clans," as they're called, since the mothers were the only ancestors one could know for certain. The identity of a Lupusian's biological father is often speculative and not considered to be of any particular importance. While a person will know her or his siblings, other than a woman's brothers, all men in the clan are simply referred to as "Uncle" while all woman other than one's mother, grandmother, siblings, or one's own offspring are "Aunt." Sexual contact with aunts and uncles is strongly discouraged.

As with any human population, there are also those who are attracted to those of the same gender or any gender, or who don't easily fit into a female/male binary, or who push the boundaries of gender in other ways. On Canis Lupus, no one is particularly bothered by such, in much the same way as no Lupusian generally cares who someone takes as a lover in any case. They're all still part of an extended clan family and have their own roles within the clan. With a low overall population, however, finding other people with a like attraction can be difficult.

A listing of the Twenty-Eight Clans (boldface indicates a clan mentioned in the book).

Abney: mostly a Rhyl-based clan. Largely farmers.
Ainsley: mostly a Newtown-based clan.
Bancroft: mostly a Dulcia-based clan, sheeper farmers and weavers primarily.
Cockburn: compounds in all the towns. No single primary occupation.

Craig: one of the two clans of the archipelago.

Delaney: Dulcia-, Rhyl-, and Usk-based clan. Fisherfolk.

Douglas: compounds in all the towns. No single primary occupation.

Fitzpatrick: mostly Dulcia- and Usk-based clan. In Dulcia, they're fishmongers.

Griffith: compounds in all the towns. No single primary occupation.

Hearn: mostly Dulcia- and Plockton-based clan. In Dulcia, they're primarily butchers.

Kirkland: compounds in all the towns. No single primary occupation.

Lewis: The primary constabulary and judicial arm of the mainland. Found in all the towns.

Lynch: mostly a Rhyl-based clan.

MacCába: compounds in all the towns. No single primary occupation.

MacGowan: compounds in all the towns. No single primary occupation.

Mullin: one of the two clans of the archipelago.

Murphy: mostly a Dulcia-based clan, where they own a pub, a brewery, and a bakery.

Norris: mostly a Rhyl-based clan.

O'Clery: mostly a Newtown-based clan. Metalworkers, ore smelters, and foundry workers. They make the bells that sound out the time in the towns.

Pritchard: compounds in all the towns. No single primary occupation.

Plunkett: mostly Dulcia- and Usk-based clan, very active in inter-clan politics. In Dulcia, they own a pub and brew liquor.

Quincey: compounds in all the towns. No single primary occupation.

Ramsey: mostly an Usk-based clan.

Rhydderch: mostly Plocton- and Rhyl-based clan.

Shea: compounds in all the towns. No single primary occupation.

Stuart: mostly a Dulcia-based clan. Confectioners.

Taggart: Dulcia, Plockton, and Rhyl-based clan, with a few Taggarts in other towns. Farmers.

Vaughan: compounds in all the towns. No single primary occupation.

Notes and Acknowledgments

On the novel's genesis:

I took a trip to Ireland in May 2017 with my sister Sharon and her husband Dave (unfortunately, Denise was ill enough that she didn't feel comfortable going, though she insisted I go). We were exploring the gorgeous Dingle Peninsula when I stumbled upon the story of the Blasket Islands. The Blasket Centre is well out on the peninsula's Atlantic head, a delightful museum dedicated to the history of the Blasket Islands and the Blasket's literary tradition. I was immediately fascinated, bought several of the islanders' books, and the more I thought about the islands and their relationship with the mainland of Ireland, the more I found myself inundated with potential story ideas. This book is a result, even if the connection to the Blaskets isn't immediately apparent.

In our world, the Blasket Islands were well-known in the late nineteenth and early twentieth centuries for being *the* place to go if one wanted to study the Irish language as it was spoken, as this was one of the few places in Ireland (like the Aran Islands or parts of the counties in the west of Ireland) where Irish was the language the locals both spoke and wrote. But the lure of the modern world and other countries along with the difficulty competing with new fishing technologies and regulations caused the residents of the Great Blasket to slowly leave the island until there were too few of them left to sustain the settlement. The last permanent residents of the Blaskets were finally evacuated from Great Blasket Island on November 17, 1953.

It was the sense of disconnection and the resulting escalating tensions within the Blasket culture itself and between the Blaskets and the more modern society of the mainland that provided the initial spark for this book, though there were other sparks as well.

On the chapter titles:

Some (though by no means all) of the chapter titles are from William Butler Yeats' works: usually a paraphrasing of one of his quotes or a snippet of one. In fact, the title of this book is the closing phrase (with the article "a" changed to "the" because I preferred it) of the Yeats poem "When You Are Old." You're welcome to Google the rest and look up the full source material—Yeats' poetry is delightful and inspirational. Be careful, though; you might get lost down the rabbit hole of reading more of Yeats' work and never return.

Acknowledgments
My gratitude and thanks to:

- Denise Parsley Leigh, my incredible spouse, who read the proposal (both versions) and critiqued it, and on whom (as usual) I also inflicted the first draft of the novel for her thoughts.

- Sheila Gilbert, my editor and also a good friend for two decades now, for liking my eventual proposal and shepherding the book through its various changes and revisions with her usual patience and insightful comments. Thanks, Sheila—as always, this would be a lesser book without your input!

- My ENG 358 (Writing Science Fiction & Fantasy) class at Northern Kentucky University of the Spring 2018 semester, who—as a practical exercise in the process of worldbuilding as well as marketing—read two *very* different forms of the proposal (one draft a fantasy/alternate history tale, the other the science fictional one which became what I actually proposed to Sheila). At my request, the students gave me their unfiltered comments and critiques on both. Thanks! All of you made this a better book—and hey, the proposal sold! So thanks to all of you: Elizabeth Bennett, Blues Bullen, Kayleigh Cropper, Jeremy Daugherty, Samantha Davis, Nat Donnermeyer, Buddy Gilchrist, Emma Haller, Kyle Howard, Leonard Ivey, Hannah Keller, Stephanie Knoll, Bailey Lagemann, Mackenzie Manley, Renee McCann, Shelby Schmidt, Claire Snyder, Alvena Stanfield, Kelsey Stratton, Danielle Turner, and Daniel Wilson.

- My gratitude to my astronomical reference: Dr. Nathan De Lee of Northern Kentucky University's Astronomy Lab, who helped me with some of the initial worldbuilding of Canis Lupus. Any mistakes in the science are mine, not his—in fact, he suggested that Wolf 1061C might not be the best choice for a habitable planet, but I persisted anyway. It'll be interesting to see what NASA's Transiting Exoplanet Survey Satellite (TESS) might have to say about the Wolf 1061 system over the next several years, and whether Wolf 1061c turns out to be anything like my fictional Canis Lupus—Dr. De Lee is part of the group working to choose the stars on which the TESS satellite will obtain data.

Books read as research for this novel:

- *An Old Woman's Reflections: The Life of a Blasket Island Storyteller* by Peig Sayers. Oxford University Press, 1962 (2000 reissue).

- *Peig: The Autobiography of Peig Sayers of the Great Blasket Island* by Peig Sayers, Syracuse University Press, May 1991.

- *The Islandman (An tOileánach)* by Tomás O'Crohan (Tomás Ó Criomhthain), Oxford University Press, 1929 and 1951. Reissued in 2000.

- *Twenty Years A-Growing (Fiche Blian ag Fás)* by Maurice O'Sullivan (Muiris Ó Súilleabháin), original publication, 1933. J.S. Sanders Books, 1998.

- *The Last Blasket King: Padraig O Cathain, An Ri* by Gerald Hayes with Eliza Kane. The Collins Press, 2015.

- *Healing Plants of the Celtic Druids* by Angela Paine, Moon Books, 2018.

- *Collected Poems: William Butler Yeats*, Introduction by Dr. Robert Mighall. Macmillan Collector's Library; New Edition (July 19, 2016).

- And, of course, quite a bit of Internet browsing for research and information, especially in the astronomical and biological arenas.